Praise for the Alex Craft Novels

Grave Ransom

"Dark urban fantasy fans will delight in Price's fifth Alex Craft, Grave Witch novel. . . . The story is filled with fast-paced action and creepy, immersive worldbuilding."
—*Publishers Weekly*

"Over the course of this transfixing series, Price has built a uniquely compelling world and made sure her characters were truly unforgettable!" —*RT Book Reviews*

"*Grave Ransom* was an exciting, interesting and wild adventure." —*The Reading Café*

Grave Visions

"*Grave Visions* has been a long-waited-for read and it certainly delivers." —*A Great Read*

"If you love urban fantasy, DO NOT miss out on this series." —*Kings River Life Magazine*

Grave Memory

"A truly original and compelling urban fantasy series."
—*RT Book Reviews*

"An incredible urban fantasy. . . . This is a series I love."
—*Nocturne Romance Reads*

D1020398

"An action-packed roller-coaster ride. . . . An absolute must-read!"
— A Book Obsession

Grave Dance

"A dense and vibrant tour de force."
— All Things Urban Fantasy

"An enticing mix of humor and paranormal thrills."
— Fresh Fiction

Grave Witch

"Fascinating magic, a delicious heartthrob, and a fresh, inventive world."
— *New York Times* bestselling author Chloe Neill

"A rare treat, intriguing and original. Don't miss this one."
— #1 *New York Times* bestselling author Patricia Briggs

"Edgy, intense . . . a promising kickoff to a series with potential."
— RT Book Reviews

"This series is more addictive than chocolate."
— Huntress Book Reviews

The Alex Craft Novels

Grave Destiny

AN ALEX CRAFT NOVEL

KALAYNA PRICE

ACE
New York

ACE
Published by Berkley
An imprint of Penguin Random House LLC
1745 Broadway, New York, NY 10019

Copyright © 2019 by Kalayna Smithwick

ISBN: 9780451416599

First Edition: April 2019

Printed in the United States of America
1   3   5   7   9   10   8   6   4   2

Cover art © Aleta Rafton
Cover design by Katie Anderson

To M and T.
I love you.

Grave Destiny

Chapter 1

The first time I'd knowingly woven planes of existence was under the light of the Blood Moon. That was six months ago, and I'd been under the power of a madman at the time, the ability bursting from me in a magical hemorrhage. Since then, I'd shoved reality around a bit and occasionally pushed or pulled things between planes, but I hadn't made many strides in learning to harness my planeweaving. Last month I'd intentionally woven a net of reality for the first time in an effort to save my best friend. My hands now bore the evidence. Dozens of shiny pink scars crossed over my palms and marred my fingers. Thankfully I hadn't lost any function or feeling, but the scars acted as a daily reminder that I was fumbling my way around a magic I knew almost nothing about.

There had to be a better way.

I needed training. And the only two planeweavers anyone had heard about in generations—besides me, of course—resided in the high court. Which no one could tell me how to reach. I was surrounded by fae these days, even lived in my own Faerie castle, but information on the high court was limited.

My housemate, Caleb, had been born an independent fae and knew very little about the inner workings of the courts. The Winter Queen's knight, Falin, was far more connected, but he was young for a fae and had been raised outside Faerie to increase his tolerance for iron and technology. Ms. B, the brownie who'd appointed herself office manager of Tongues for the Dead, had told me she didn't pay much attention to the "overgrown" court fae when I'd asked her. Not even the rather ancient frost fae ghost who haunted my castle could tell me more than rumors. Unfortunately, that left the list of fae I could ask about the high court depressingly short.

I could request an audience with the Winter Queen—she had to know. But the price she would extract might be worse than my fumbling attempt to learn on my own. The other fae I could ask would be easier to approach, but he was a mystery wrapped in a contradiction. He was a fae in hiding who didn't belong to the local court—which shouldn't have been possible—as well as a prominent member in mortal government, in a party called the Humans First Party, which was basically a hate group against fae and witches. Oh yeah, and he was my father.

My name is Alex Craft, and as one might guess, I have a complicated relationship with my family. I'm a private investigator for Tongues for the Dead, a firm I run with my best friend and fellow grave witch, Rianna McBride. We specialize in raising shades of the dead so that they can be questioned, but we'd take about any case from missing persons to discerning curses on knickknacks. Unfortunately, because of a recent PR nightmare in which I was accused of magical mass murder, business was so dead we could barely justify keeping the lights on. It gave me a lot of time to study the scars and dwell on how very badly I needed a teacher. Which was why I was now staring at my father's phone number. I didn't want to call him, but where else could I turn?

I hit the dial button. He picked up on the third ring.

"My errant daughter. To what emergency do I owe this honor?"

Yeah, maybe I didn't call my father often. But I didn't exactly trust him. Plus, he'd kind of hidden the fact that he—and thus I—was fae, and oh yeah, he more or less excommunicated me when my grave magic appeared and couldn't be hidden.

"No emergency. I just need some answers. How would I contact someone in the high court?"

The line was quiet so long that I pulled the phone away from my ear and checked the screen to make sure the call hadn't been dropped.

"That's not the kind of information I can just give away," he finally said.

Great. "But you do know a way?"

"I do."

"So what will it cost me? A favor? A quest?" If he said my firstborn, I was never speaking to him again.

Again the drawn-out silence. Finally he said, "I have a request of you. There is an . . . issue that I believe you will be asked to investigate very soon. Accept. Do what you can. *Please.*" The last word sounded like he'd had to painfully pluck it from his mouth.

I blinked in surprise, realizing what he was offering. Apparently it wasn't that he *wouldn't* tell me how to contact the high court, it was that he *couldn't*. But he'd just offered me a way to put him in my debt and force him to tell me.

"What will this case involve? And who should I expect to bring it to me?"

"You won't be able to miss it."

"Why is that not reassuring," I said, but I was speaking to empty air. He'd hung up.

The bell on the door chimed while I was still staring at my phone. I jumped to my feet. *This can't be the case already.* But we hadn't had a client in weeks, and I couldn't feel Rianna's magic—or any magic—so it wasn't her. I rushed around my desk, shoving the phone in my back pocket as I hurried to my office door. I pulled on my gloves in quick, practiced motions—the scars drew too much attention. Then I forced myself to slow down and smile before I stepped into the lobby. I didn't want to look desperate.

Normally—or at least the more recent normal—Ms. B would have been in the front office to greet potential clients, but while she showed up exactly on time each morning and checked for messages and appointments, she'd started leaving for the bulk of each day. Not that I faulted her. Sitting around an empty office was boring at best, and downright depressing in truth. Rianna wasn't in the office today either, as we'd taken to alternating who got the discouraging task of minding the office each day, so that left only me. Which, if this was the case my father wanted me to work, could be a good situation. Or it could be a very dangerous one.

A man stood just inside the door, his gaze scanning every inch of the room. There was a stiffness to his posture, an attentiveness to the way he efficiently searched the space, that spoke to the fact that he wasn't admiring the furnishings but was looking for threats. I forced my smile to hold and kept my own posture nonthreatening. After all, people were often jumpy when dealing with grave witches. Then the man's attention focused on me, and my smile froze, turning brittle. The greeting that I'd been about to utter caught in my throat, tangled with a knot of fear that lodged at my sternum before melting down into my stomach.

It wasn't that the man looked particularly threatening. In fact, if I was honest, he was rather attractive. Tall, with dark hair pulled back from a well-angled face. The dark suit he wore looked ridiculously expensive and expertly tailored over his obviously muscled body. He carried no overt weapons nor any trace of magic, though one hand was suspiciously close to his waist as if a twitch away from an unseen sword. He smiled as our gazes met, striding across the room without hesitation now that he'd determined there were no hidden threats.

Or perhaps he'd been searching for potential witnesses.

"Prince Dugan," I said, forcing myself to stand my ground and not flee back into my office. My fingers itched to draw the enchanted dagger hidden in my boot, but I didn't. The prince of the shadow court wasn't my enemy—and I didn't want to make him such—but he wasn't exactly a friend either. He definitely had to be the case my father wanted me to work, though I had no idea how he'd gotten here so fast. I'd literally just gotten off the phone when the bell on the door had chimed.

"My lady," Dugan said, inclining his head ever so slightly toward me. His ground-eating stride took him to a spot less than a yard in front of me before he stopped. He smiled again, but there was little warmth to the expression. His lips moved, but his eyes were weary, guarded. Not hostile, though, and he didn't try to close the last bit of space he'd left between us.

The professional smile I'd been clinging to shattered, giving way to a suspicious frown as I studied him. The afternoon sunlight streaming through the front window seemed to shy away from him, or maybe it was that the shadows in the corners of the room reached out toward him. I wasn't sure if that was a passive effect of being a prince of the shadow court, or if he was using glamour to draw in the shadows like a cloak, even in the light, but it was an eerie effect.

"My father mentioned you'd be coming, but he didn't tell me anything about the case you're bringing."

The prince cocked his head to the side, a look of genuine bewilderment crossing his features. "Your father?"

My frown deepened. "He didn't send you?" But I could already read the answer before he shook his head.

"I've not seen nor spoken to him in months."

Right. So then was this not the case he'd mentioned? And if not, what was Dugan doing here? Not just in my lobby, but in Nekros City. "What can I do for you?"

"That is your . . . office?" He said the last word as if it were a foreign concept to him, but he nodded toward the door I'd emerged from when I'd heard the bell chime. "You usually take clients there?"

I nodded, stepping aside as I gestured to the door. He didn't hesitate, but swept past me, the misplaced shadows following him into my small office. I stared after him for a moment, wondering again what the hell he was doing here. Nekros City was winter court territory, and I was fairly certain the Winter Queen would take none too kindly to the presence of any shadow fae in her land, let alone the prince of their court.

As if summoned by my thoughts, the front door burst open and the queen's knight, Falin Andrews, stormed into the lobby. His movements were smooth and lethally efficient as his icy blue eyes made a quick sweep of the room. When his gaze fixed on me, relief softened the hard planes of his handsome face as he assessed that I was safe and seemingly alone.

"Come on, we have to go," he said, holding out a gloved hand toward me. "The prince of the shadow court has entered Nekros."

Aside from being the Winter Queen's knight—her bloody hands she sent to do any dirty work she might have—Falin was also the head of the local Fae Investigation Bureau, my one-time-only lover, a housemate of sorts, and a friend. It was impossible to miss the fact that he'd been worried when he'd entered. Which meant he really wasn't going to like what I was about to say.

"I know. He's here."

Right on cue, Dugan stepped out of my office. Falin's gun was in his hands and aimed at the fae behind me before I even had time to register that he'd drawn the weapon.

"I claim the right to open roads," Dugan said, opening his palms in a gesture clearly meant to show he was not going for a weapon.

Falin didn't lower the gun. "That custom was intended for use by independents, not a *Sleagh Maith* prince."

"Still, all the same, I can claim it."

I frowned between the two of them. "Is someone going to explain what's going on? What is the right to open roads?"

Falin's eyes flickered toward me, but he kept his gun trained on Dugan a moment longer before he apparently decided he wasn't going to shoot the prince and lowered the weapon. But while it wasn't trained on the other fae anymore, he didn't holster it.

"The right to open roads is a very old agreement the courts made that dates back to a time when communication and travel were more difficult. It gives an outside fae the right to pass through the mortal realm territories of a court in which they don't belong as long as the two courts are not at war and the fae is not banished, exiled, or otherwise named an enemy of the court. It can only be invoked once a year and only for twelve hours." He nodded to Dugan. "You have your token?"

Dugan reached into his pocket—causing Falin's hand to visibly flex on his gun. The prince didn't miss the movement. His eyebrows rose, but he kept his motions slow as he pulled a small stone from his pocket and held it up for Falin to examine. A deep blue light pulsed in the center of the stone. I couldn't be sure, but I was guessing the "token" marked that his twelve hours were still in effect.

"Fine." Falin barked out the word, less than happy but bound by the laws of Faerie. "Now shouldn't you be using your open roads to move along?"

"I am also invoking the Sanctuary of Artisans."

If Falin's glare had been frosty before, it now turned subzero and he spared a flicker of it for me.

"Wait, the what of the who? What am I missing here?" I asked, glancing between the two men.

"What did he hire you to do?" Falin asked, studying me.

"Nothing." Yet.

"We haven't gotten that far," Dugan said, and for the first time, true emotion bled into his voice. That emotion happened to be annoyance. Awesome. "I only just arrived, but as you can see, I have come to her place of business with the purpose of commissioning her. So my presence here is justified by the Sanctuary of Artisans."

I crossed my arms over my chest. "Is anyone going to explain that one to the girl that didn't grow up in Faerie?"

The two men stared at each other. Dugan was clearly being purposefully nonthreatening, and it was just as clear that the necessity of the action annoyed him. For his part, Falin had also taken things down a notch, but it definitely irritated him that he couldn't challenge the Shadow Prince over his presence in winter's territory. I was between them, both physically and metaphorically. I'm not a short girl, but both men were taller than me, and broad with muscles, so I felt absolutely petite. Which was rather irritating. I crossed my arms over my chest, standing up straighter, but it didn't make a difference. The Shadow Prince was all darkness with his tailored suit and inky black hair. Falin, in contrast, wore a crisp white oxford, his platinum blond hair pulled back from his well-chiseled face. I felt stuck between yin and yang, but it didn't make me feel balanced. More like a tug toy.

"Well?" I asked, glancing between them.

"The Sanctuary of Artisans allows fae to contact and commission artisans of rare skills and talents who reside in lands ruled by other courts. It also protects those artisans if they must go to the lands of another court from the risk of being held there or enthralled to stay against their will," Dugan said.

"That's remarkably altruistic for Faerie." Because enthralling and capturing talent seemed to be the courts' basic modus operandi.

"It's not for the benefit of the artisan," Falin said, his frown deepening. "It's so the original court doesn't risk losing an asset." He turned back toward Dugan. "I'd hardly call a private detective an artisan."

"Ah, but she makes shades. A very rare talent."

That first part wasn't strictly true, as shades were memories stored in every cell of a dead body. My magic just collected all those tiny traces, joined them together, and projected them into something that could be seen, heard, and questioned. The second part was true enough, though.

"You are twisting the purpose of those ancient agreements to their limits," Falin said, and Dugan grinned, his entire expression changing from the stern warrior of the shadow court to that of puckish amusement.

"We are fae. That is our nature. Now, my time is limited." He lifted the dark, softly glowing stone he carried that held his right to open roads. "There is business to discuss."

Chapter 2

Dugan turned and strode into my office. The movement was efficient, but also grandiose, as if a cape he wasn't wearing should have been flapping behind him. I opened my shields, not far, just enough that I could peer across the planes of reality, and more importantly, see through glamour. Sure enough, the expensive suit vanished, replaced by dark armor and yep, a dark cloak. A sword hung at his waist, and I caught sight of at least three daggers. He might not look armed in mortal reality, but he had plenty of weapons under his thin veneer of glamour. Not that I expected anything else.

I didn't immediately close my shields, but waited until he looked back and I got a clear view of his face. His features didn't change, which was a relief. For a halting heartbeat, I'd been afraid he'd look back and I'd see someone else, someone who didn't want to approach me with their own face—I had my share of enemies in Faerie. But the once again guarded face that frowned when he noticed me studying him was that of the Shadow Prince. I couldn't fault him for wrapping his armor and weapons under a suit of glamour. After all, walking down the sidewalk in the Magic Quarter looking like he stepped off the cover of a romance novel about a medieval dark knight or assassin wouldn't exactly help him keep a low profile.

Falin moved closer as I studied the prince. He leaned toward me, his voice pitched low so that his words were for me alone. "You don't have to treat him any differently than any other potential client who walks through your door. The protections he's claimed do not guarantee him your services, and he cannot compel or threaten you to work for him without violating the very same agreements that he is hiding behind. You may demand he leave at any time, and if he refuses, I will enforce your request."

I nodded my understanding, and I think Falin assumed I'd let him immediately kick Dugan out of my office. I didn't. I was curious about what the Shadow Prince wanted to hire me to do. Also, I hadn't dismissed the idea that this might be the case my father wanted me to take. My father played the long game and had his hand in a lot of pots. Just because Dugan hadn't spoken to him didn't mean my father wasn't aware of whatever situation had sent the prince to me.

Closing my shields, I walked into my office. Falin followed close behind.

"Are your client meetings not typically confidential?" Dugan asked, his disapproving gaze boring into Falin.

"I try to protect clients' privacy," I said, and turned toward Falin. I didn't actually want him to go. While I was confident in my ability to deal with most clients who walked through my door, I wasn't about to turn Falin away when dealing with the Prince of Shadows. I felt safer with him here. The thought must have been clear on my face.

"This is a matter of court security." Falin crossed his arms over his chest, his posture daring the prince to challenge his words. "No law protects a private investigator's meetings, not in the mortal realm or Faerie. The rights you invoked don't specify a private audience either. If you want to talk to a citizen of winter, you will do so within my presence."

Dugan glowered, his dark gaze moving from Falin to me. I gave him a halfhearted shrug, the motion conveying a nonchalant *What can we do about it?* But in truth I was relieved. The—no doubt ancient—agreements Dugan had invoked offered me some protection, and likely had magically binding stipulations, but I knew enough about the fae to guess there were ways around most things. Those ways might start a war between the courts, but the end result for me would still be potentially deadly, or at the very least, bad for my freedom. Caution and keeping my allies close were smarter than arguing for client confidentiality.

I rounded my desk and sat, trying not to look like I was ready to spring to my feet again at the smallest provocation. But, of course, I was. Dugan looked between me and Falin one more time before deciding his business was important enough to tolerate the Winter Knight's presence and sinking gracefully into one of my client chairs. For his part, Falin remained standing, moving to a spot near the door and leaning against the wall with his arms crossed, but at least he wasn't looming. Dugan seemed to be making a point of ignoring him. Which was fine by me.

"So what can I do for you . . ." I trailed off, searching for the right honorific to use. Typically I called clients *mister* or *missus*, but I didn't know Dugan's last name. Hell, I didn't even know if he had a last name. For all I knew he was older than the custom of having surnames. Maybe he was *Dugan, son of* . . . someone. I could have said *Prince Dugan*, but that sounded odd and stuffy, and besides, my pause had been too long now, so I tried to play it off as if I had properly ended my question and forced a smile, hoping he wouldn't note the missing inflection.

"I'm here to secure your services."

I waited, but that was apparently all he planned to say. I pressed my gloved hands together in my lap and tried to maintain my smile. "I assumed as much. I need more details than that."

Dugan's eyes slid to the side, toward Falin, but he didn't turn. "It is a sensitive matter. Suffice to say that there is a body we need questioned."

I nodded, letting the movement hide my relief. I'd been sure I was going to have to explain that my planeweaving services were not up for hire, but a body meant he was interested in my grave magic. "So just a ritual and time spent questioning the shade, then?" I asked as I opened the drawer beside my desk and fished for the standard ritual form Rianna and I had created. I had no doubt it would need a little tweaking, but it would be a good starting point. "Where is the body currently? If it is in the shadow court, it will have to be transported to the mortal realm. There is no land of the dead in Faerie, so I can't raise shades there."

Dugan's frown etched itself across his face. "We need to question the . . . shade, yes. But we can't move the body. Not immediately." Again he hesitated, and this time he twisted in his seat to face Falin. "Winter Knight, must you hover in my blind spot? It is an unbecoming way to treat a fellow warrior. Unless you intend to slide your blade into my back."

He's stalling. Though I had no doubt he was unnerved to have a potential enemy at his back. Falin's lips twitched, and I couldn't tell if he was biting back a smile or a frown. Then he crossed the room and leaned on the wall behind my desk. The movement put him at my back instead, but that was okay. I trusted him—most of the time.

"If the body can't be moved, I'm not sure I can help. I can't raise shades in Faerie." It wasn't possible. I couldn't make it any clearer than that.

Dugan glared over my shoulder, at Falin. The Winter Knight was making him extremely uncomfortable, but even though he'd complained about the other fae's presence at his back, I didn't think fear of a sneak attack was what had him on edge.

He leaned forward. "Would it not be possible to have some privacy?"

"No." Falin's word was hard, clipped.

Dugan glowered at him. "I can offer you whatever assurances you require that I mean no harm to my betrothed."

I cringed at Dugan's final word. Behind me, I could feel the weight of Falin's shocked gaze slam into the back of my head. I considered crawling under my desk, but that wouldn't have helped me escape his scrutiny.

I waved a hand through the air, as if dismissing the sudden tension in the room, but I was still cringing. "It's a long story and not something I have agreed to."

And now both men were staring at me. Great. Falin

stepped to the side of the desk so that he could see my face.

"Moving on . . ." I said.

"No. Not moving on. When exactly did you get betrothed to the *Shadow Prince*?" There was a chilly calmness to Falin's voice that spoke of intense emotion just below the icy surface.

"When I was a baby, I guess?" I said, and glanced at Dugan. He nodded. "So maybe not such a long story. Moving on . . ."

There were so many questions obvious in the turbulence in Falin's eyes, and I thought I caught a small thread of jealousy—his outrage more personal than just protecting an asset of the winter court. Which wasn't fair to either of us, as we weren't together, and had never truly been together. We'd briefly been lovers—and he got no complaints in that department—but he'd been the one to decide we shouldn't be together as long as the Winter Queen kept him bound as her knight. So we were just friends, with the occasional lustful glance here or there. That was pretty much the state of my love life all around.

Falin shot a disgruntled glance at Dugan but remained silent about the betrothal. I would hear about this later, and I had no idea how I would explain it. There were lots of things I hadn't told Falin, and probably shouldn't because while I trusted his intentions, he was bound to his queen's will, and she was not my ally.

"About that privacy?" Dugan asked, and I shot a glare at him. "The case is of a sensitive matter. I do not wish to share it with the winter court."

"You do know I am currently aligned with winter, right?" Not that I had any kind feelings toward the queen, but I was technically an independent in her territory.

Dugan made a dismissive gesture. "A year and a day as an independent is barely an allegiance. That time will pass in the sigh of a dreamer, or the door might move before the agreed time is over and this territory's court will change."

"You are not speaking to Alex alone," Falin said, turning his attention back to Dugan. "If you would like to run out the time you have open roads through this court that is fine, but she is not leaving my sight."

Dugan's glare should have seared Falin's flesh. I sighed.

"What if you could have privacy to say your piece without Falin leaving?"

Dugan's brows knit together. "And how would that be accomplished?"

I glanced down at the charm bracelet on my wrist. "I have a privacy charm." I'd ruined most of my personal charms recently, but that was one I'd recast already. It tended to come in handy.

Dugan looked perplexed, but Falin shook his head. "No."

"It's just a sound bubble. You would be able to see everything and there is no barrier to cross." The only downside was, I was rather terrible when it came to crafting spells, so the size of that bubble was limited. It was slightly larger than the last one I had made, but not by a lot.

Dugan was obviously interested, though not convinced. "And this charm blocks all words? You are certain of it?"

Instead of answering, I pushed away from my desk and stood. I considered walking to the wall, but the amount of space the charm protected was small enough that they were both outside that bubble already. I channeled a small amount of Aetheric energy into the charm. Magic buzzed across my skin as the spell took effect, and since the sound bubble went both ways, silence fell around me.

"Hello," I said, waving.

Both men stared at me blankly. I screamed at the top of my lungs, lifting the charm as I did. In the middle of the scream, I pulled the magic back out of the spell, canceling the effect. The confused look on Dugan's face turned into the smallest cringe as the last part of my scream cut through the air. Stunned silence fell over the room when I finished.

I smiled. "No sound escapes."

"You could have just said that. I would have taken you at your word."

Of course he would have. I was fae. I couldn't lie. The demonstration had been a little more satisfying, though, and it also proved to Falin that he wouldn't have to be far to be outside the privacy bubble. I looked to the Winter Knight. He was still scowling, but he gave a very small nod, indicating he'd be okay with this plan.

I walked around my desk and pulled the other client chair closer to Dugan's. He lifted a dark eyebrow, watching me as I sat on the edge of the seat, my knees all but brushing his. I didn't like the proximity, but my spell covered very little area. I activated the charm and let my senses stretch, feeling for the edge of the bubble. Dugan was right on the edge of the effect. If he stirred or breathed too deeply while he spoke, every few words would escape. I scooted my chair even closer, and I could feel the chill of Falin's stare as I had to angle my hips to keep my legs from touching Dugan's. But he was safely inside the privacy bubble now.

"So, tell me about the case," I said, trying not to squirm

in my seat. I would have liked to sit back, but the bubble
of privacy was centered on me and any comfortable position would have put Dugan too close to the edge.

He gave one sideways glance toward Falin, and then
turned partially away from him—not so that the other
man was at his back, but so that he didn't have a clear
view of his face, and I guessed, his lips. I had no idea if
Falin could read lips, but whatever the prince wanted to
discuss, he certainly was concerned about keeping it secret. Of course, the shadow court was also known as the
court of secrets, so maybe it was just his nature.

"What I and the shadow court need to hire you for is
very delicate. Yes, we need you to raise a shade, but if
possible, we need you to examine the scene. To document any evidence the same way you would for a mortal
court of law."

I held up a hand. "I'm an investigator, but I don't solve
murders. That is a task for the police."

"I believe you have been instrumental in solving several murder cases of late."

That was true, but I hadn't walked into any of those
cases planning to investigate murder. And I definitely
didn't work cases in such a way that they could be presented before a judge and jury. Heck, in most of those
previous cases, once I'd finally tracked down the killer,
they'd ended up as decayed ash and someone with a very
high pay grade had marked the cases classified and re-
dacted any and all mentions of me.

"That's not the kind of investigator I am. If you need
a case built, especially one that would hold up in the
mortal realm, you need to contact an official authority.
Nothing I documented would be considered admissible
or within chain of evidence." My gaze moved to Falin,

because he was one of those authorities. He was the lead agent in charge of the local Fae Investigation Bureau.

Falin caught my look, and I noted the anxiety snagging at the edges of his eyes and lips as he tried to read what my expression might mean. I gave him a weak smile, trying to reassure him, but it must have been pretty poor because it only made him look more worried.

Dugan's lips twisted with thought, not quite a frown, but a very serious expression as he considered my words. "Questioning the deceased is the most important thing. Anything you could document about the scene would be a helpful bonus. Learning the connection between the bodies, and why our fae was where he was when he died, is of the most importance. And who killed him, of course."

"Bodies?" As in more than one. But it sounded like Dugan's interest was focused more heavily on one.

Dugan nodded.

"Why me? Obviously you need a grave witch, but surely there is someone more easily accessible to you. And as far as investigating the scene, I'm sure your court has its own investigators who are better qualified than me. Someone the equivalent of the Fae Investigation Bureau like the seasonal courts use."

"Shadow has no direct doors to the human realm, so we have no organization like the seasonal courts' FIB because we have no direct interaction with mortals. On the occasions crimes have occurred within our court, we've relied on . . . more archaic means of determining guilt," he said, and I could only imagine what he meant. From my experience, the fae who resided in Faerie tended toward a preindustrial society. Pre-Victorian investigations tended to lack any need for scientific evidence or proof. The dismay on my face must have been obvious, because he nodded solemnly before moving on. "As to why you, there are a number of reasons. As you said, the ability to question the deceased is the most obvious. There are other grave witches out there, but you are the only practicing witch who has interacted with our court. You are also familiar with modern methods of investigating murder, even if you are not officially authorized to do so in the mortal realm. But you in particular because while you are not connected to our court, you are someone our court believes we can trust."

Well, wasn't that nice. I had the trust of the court of secrets and shadows. What did that say about me? "Tell me about the case. This is murder, I'm guessing, but what details do you have?"

"We need a binding agreement before I can tell you that."

"No." I didn't hesitate or waver. I wasn't getting into any binding agreements with a fae without all the details up front. If that meant passing on the case, so be it. It was definitely safer not to work for a Faerie court anyway, regardless of how badly Tongues for the Dead needed a case or if it would put my father in my debt. There would be other cases. And I'd find another way to reach the planeweavers in the high court.

I began to stand. Dugan's hand shot out, wrapping around my wrist. His skin was smooth, cool, and his grip solid, but not painful. "Do not dismiss me yet. We can negotiate."

Outside the privacy bubble, Falin had his weapon in hand again—likely in response to Dugan grabbing me. I held up a palm, stalling him, but I looked pointedly at where Dugan's hand was locked around my wrist. He dropped it without comment. I didn't sit back down, but

I also didn't turn off my charm and walk away. It was a dangerous game to negotiate with fae, but at least I had the upper hand in this case—Dugan wanted something from me, but I didn't need anything from him.

"Where is the scene and the bodies?"

Dugan hesitated so long I thought he wasn't going to answer, but finally he said, "Not in the shadow court."

"Then where—?" I started, and his eyes flickered toward where Falin hovered just beyond the privacy bubble. "The winter court?" I asked it in a whisper, despite my confidence in my charm. "You want me to investigate bodies in the winter court?"

His nod was sharp, quick, but definite.

"And do you know who the bodies are, er, were? Members of your court?"

He leaned forward, closer toward me, but as I was still standing, that made for an awkward angle. He obviously came to the same conclusion because a moment later he stood in one effortless movement. That put us too close together, the space between the chairs narrow so that we were nearly touching.

"How far does the spell extend?" he asked, looking as uncomfortable as I felt.

"Not far. Let's just both sit."

He nodded, looking relieved once we both dropped back into our chairs. At least I wasn't the only one that seemed unnerved. He might consider himself my betrothed, but we were virtual strangers.

"The bodies?" I prompted.

"We are uncertain. We believe we know one identity. He was a goblin named Kordon. But we are under the impression there are two bodies. As we have not been able to visit the scene directly—for obvious reasons—we are not certain of the affiliation of the second deceased."

Two bodies. Maybe. In the winter court. I started to shake my head but caught the motion, not wanting Dugan to think I was dismissing the case out of hand. "So, was your court member an intruder or victim?"

His lips twitched, the movement subtle and quickly erased, his expression returning to a guarded neutral so fast I wasn't sure I actually saw it. Surprise? Anger? Annoyance? I wasn't sure, and when he answered his voice held no inflection. "We did not send him to winter."

Which didn't answer the question. Just because he wasn't sent didn't mean he hadn't been there for nefarious reasons. Of course, it also didn't exclude that he might have been kidnapped and held in winter before his death. Those were pretty important differences. It did explain why Dugan was interested in me documenting anything I could at the scene, though, as obviously his people were unlikely to gain access. Not that I had access. What was I supposed to do, walk up to the Winter Queen and say, *Hey, I heard you have some bodies in your halls. I'd like to remove them and have a chat with their shades.* Yeah, that would not go over well.

Movement outside our bubble of privacy caught my attention. Falin pulled his cell phone from his pocket and glanced at the display before answering. He never took his eyes off us as he listened to the person on the other side of the line.

"Do you have a suspect?" I asked, focusing on Dugan again.

The lip twitch made it all the way to a frown before he caught it this time. "Possibly."

"And that would be . . . ?"

He frowned at me, not answering. So much for trust.

"I'm not going to agree to take a case you can't give me a straight answer about. You want the shades raised and questioned *and* you can get them to the mortal realm, then sure, I'm your girl. We can sign a contract right now and set a time for the ritual. But you're talking about investigating deaths in the winter court—which it doesn't sound like you are in any position to even clear a path for me to investigate. That's not the type of case I work. If there is nothing else . . ." I pushed to my feet again.

He studied me. "I'm not going to insult you by telling you we would pay very well for your time—though we will. But perhaps I can appeal to your compassion—" he started, but he didn't get the chance to finish.

I saw Falin pocket his phone from the corner of my eye, and though we couldn't hear what had been said—the privacy bubble went both ways—something must have alerted Dugan because he fell silent. There was a sudden explosion of movement from both men. Dugan jumped to his feet, knocking me back into my chair in the process. The sword that had been hidden under his glamour was in his hands before he finished turning.

My back, just at my shoulder blades, slammed in the back of the chair, and then the entire chair rocked back, sending me crashing to the ground. I yelped as the air escaped my lungs, but the room had gone still again. Falin stood with his gun pointed at Dugan's head, Dugan with his blade pressed against Falin's throat. A twitch from either fae would have been deadly.

"Stop, both of you," I yelled as I tried to detangle myself from the fallen chair.

They didn't so much as glance in my direction. Of course, I hadn't deactivated my spell, so they couldn't actually hear me. Nor could I hear anything they were saying to each other. That was bad.

I pulled the magic out of my charm, canceling it.

"Drop the sword," Falin said, keeping his gun trained right between Dugan's eyes. It didn't matter how fast the prince might be; at that distance, Falin couldn't have missed.

"No," was the shadow fae's only response. If Falin twitched, Dugan would have sliced through his throat.

"Stop," I yelled again, finally extracting myself from the chair.

I might as well have left my privacy spell in place for all the attention they paid me.

I didn't have much in the way of offensive or defensive magic—I possibly could have pulled their weapons through planes of existence and made them inoperable, but I couldn't have done it quickly. So I went for showy shock value instead.

Dropping my shields, I opened myself to the land of the dead. Every inanimate thing around me decayed—at least in my vision. I wasn't merging planes, only looking at them, so that was something only I could see. The frigid wind that whipped out from the land of the dead was real enough, though. It tore across the room, causing the small stack of papers on my desk to shuffle across the surface. My curls whipped around my face, stinging my suddenly icy cheeks. No one I've met enjoys the clammy touch of the grave. Fae, being long-lived enough to be nigh-immortal, tended to react to the wind extra poorly. It hit the two men at the same time. Both were too well trained to jump, but I saw the tension tighten in Dugan's back and Falin's eyes narrow. Both broke their staring match of death to glance at me.

At the edge of my vision, I saw something dark skitter in the corner of the room. Something not in the mortal realm, but one of the others I could touch. I slammed my shields closed again—after all I wasn't protected by a circle, and besides, the shock value I'd been going for had worked. Now to use the momentary distraction.

"Back off, both of you. No one is killing anyone in my office. Ms. B would have a fit over the mess."

Dugan blinked at me. Falin almost smiled.

"Now what the hell is going on?" I asked, leaning down to straighten the toppled chair.

"Bodies were found in the frozen halls," Falin said. He may have glanced at me, but he hadn't lowered his weapon.

Neither had Dugan.

"And one of them is from the shadow court," I said, already knowing the answer.

Falin gave the tightest nod. "Pretty convenient timing for the prince to show up here, in the middle of winter territory, with no one sure how he crossed over from Faerie."

"Believe it or not, I'm actually here trying to prevent war. Not make it," Dugan said, his sword pressed hard enough against Falin's throat that the smallest trail of blood had crept down to the collar of his white shirt.

I frowned. "Threatening my friends with decapitation is not a good way to prevent war. Drop the sword."

"And be dragged before the Winter Queen by this fledgling knight? No."

They stared at each other. I wanted to scream at both of them. Instead I took a deep breath and let it out before saying in as calm a tone as I could force, "Prince Dugan, to your knowledge, did the fae found in winter's territory have orders to be there given by you or the king?"

"No."

"Falin, to your knowledge, did the Winter Queen give orders to have the shadow fae found in her halls brought there and killed?" I didn't actually know the answer to this one, so it was a gamble, but my gut said that even if she had, he wouldn't have that information.

He answered without hesitation, though he ground out the word between clenched teeth. "No."

"So you are trying to kill each other because . . . ?"

"The shadow court has been deemed a potential threat and probable enemy. The prince's conspicuously convenient timing has made him a suspect, so open roads no longer protects him."

Great. "Safe passage can be terminated that quickly? He doesn't even get a chance to get out of a now-hostile territory?"

"Not when suspected of violating the goodwill of the court allowing open roads."

"Do you have direct orders from the queen to bring him in?"

A muscle in Falin's jaw worked. This was a precarious path, but only a direct command from the queen, in her own voice, was binding. As Faerie didn't have cell phones and she didn't leave the court often, I was guessing he'd spoken to some other fae. Which meant there might be a little leeway in this situation.

Falin didn't answer, which was answer enough. No. He had no direct commands.

"Fine. Then you're not arresting anyone in my office. Think of this as neutral ground."

Falin scowled. "This is still winter's territory."

So killing each other in the middle of my office was the solution? I had to defuse this situation.

"Do you want me to try to pull part of the shadow court into this room so he isn't in winter territory?" I asked, holding up my hands.

Falin's gaze darted to my lifted fingers. I wore gloves, but he was familiar with the scars they hid and how they had happened—he'd not only been there when I'd gathered strands of Faerie to create a small net of it in the human realm, but he'd supplied some of the needed strands of Faerie that I'd used. He also knew that "try" was a very key word in my sentence. I probably could use the shadows in the room to make a pocket of Faerie, but as I'd be fumbling blindly, there was no telling how much damage I'd do to myself and reality in the process.

Falin's jaw clenched, and the moment stretched long enough that I was afraid I'd have to follow through with my threat. Then he said, "I suppose I could agree to a mutual truce until we both walk out of this building."

A flash of surprise flickered at the edges of Dugan's face, gone a moment later. He didn't lower his sword. "A binding oath?"

"You obviously knew about the bodies before we did, as that appears to be what you were discussing with Alex. What reassurances can you give me that this is not an attack on the winter court?"

"I could demand the same. It is our courtier who is dead in your halls."

"Damn it, both of you," I said. "Are you seriously too stubborn to accept any alternative but killing each other?"

Dugan glanced at me from the corner of his eye. "It's not that we're too stubborn. It's that we are too proud.

But you do have a point . . ." He lifted his thumb to his blade and opened a small slit across his flesh. "By my blood, I swear I will do you no harm unless I need to defend myself until we both leave this building, as long as you swear the same."

Falin glared at him for several seconds. Then he reached up and swiped some of the blood trickling down from the wound in his throat. "By my blood, I swear I will do you no harm unless I need to defend myself—or defend Alex"—he tilted his head in my direction—"until we both leave this building."

The air seemed to zing as the last words left his mouth. Both men immediately dropped their weapons, the oath preventing them from continuing to threaten each other. Falin stepped back, holstering his gun. Dugan's sword vanished under his glamour again. He smiled at the other man.

"Well, perhaps once we step outside, you'll leave your little gun behind and duel me properly, like a true warrior," the prince said, rolling his shoulders back. They had to be sore after holding that killing pose so long.

Falin scowled. Their oath not to harm each other clearly didn't extend to verbal jabs.

"Prince Dugan, you were going to appeal to my compassion, I believe," I said, forcing myself to sit. My body felt too tense, too flooded with adrenaline, but I tried to at least look calm as I crossed my legs in the chair. "So there is a dead shadow courtier in the halls of the winter court?"

Both men nodded.

"And the second body belongs to . . . ?"

"A winter noble," Falin said, his gaze never leaving Dugan's face, as if searching for signs of guilt. For his part, Dugan gave away nothing at the news, though I knew from what he'd said earlier that he hadn't known the identity of the second fae. "Currently it appears our noble was assassinated, but he fatally wounded his killer before he died."

I cringed. That definitely sounded bad for the shadow courtier.

"The queen requests us both in court immediately," he said, turning to me.

Requested. Right. More like I had no choice. But we couldn't leave yet. The moment both men left my office, their oath would be complete and they would likely attempt to kill each other. At least one would most certainly succeed. While I would be sad if Dugan died, in the same way someone would be sad when anyone was killed, the idea of Falin getting injured hurt something deep inside me. It was the difference between dragging someone out of the way of a bullet, and being willing to take that bullet for them. Which meant I had to find a way to ensure there was a more encompassing truce between the men before we left this building.

"I'm assuming she wouldn't ask for me to be there if it were truly that clear-cut?" Though she might. She had a grave witch in her territory, an independent fae who couldn't ignore her summons—why wouldn't she use my magic when bodies showed up in her hall. I wasn't the most knowledgeable about fae laws—I'd only found out I was fae about half a year ago—but from what I understood, as the ruler of the territory I resided in, the queen could demand my presence, but she couldn't force me to use my magic. Oh, she could find a creative reason to have me tortured, I'm sure, but I was Sleagh Maith, the noble line of Faerie, and that awarded me certain rights.

Dugan had been silently studying us—or perhaps simply digesting the implications of what Falin had said—but now he crossed his arms over his chest and said, "I am already in the middle of negotiations with Alexis. I hold a prior claim to her investigating these deaths."

Falin visibly bristled. "Being granted a *consultation* does not award you any claims on a winter resident."

This was getting us nowhere.

"You want me to investigate this to what end?" I asked, looking at Dugan.

"To the end of preventing a war, as I said earlier." He hesitated, a frown etching itself deep as he studied my face. He seemed to come to some conclusion because he continued by saying, "With the solstice tomorrow, winter is heading into the peak of her power. King Nandin would not appreciate my candor, but the truth is that if war were to start now, it would be very poor timing for our court. I do not wish to risk the wrath of winter in her prime. I honestly did not expect the knight to find me here, and certainly not so quickly. I would not have risked this conversation in this manner had I known it appeared our fae assassinated a noble."

"You didn't know?" Falin sounded skeptical. "And yet you clearly knew about the deaths before we did."

Dugan gave him a half shrug. "Even the icy halls of the winter court have shadows, and shadows will whisper their secrets to those who listen." He lowered himself into the chair across from me, his expression distant, thoughtful. "But I'm not sure if it was luck or design that we heard about the deaths. We heard nothing about how, why, or by whom the fae were killed. We knew only that our fae was dead in your halls, and that one way or another, he shouldn't have been there."

I turned to Falin. "Do you know anything more?"

"Not that I'll share in present company."

No shock there. But not helpful. I also had to wonder how my father tied into all of this. The deaths had to be the case he'd mentioned, though who had he expected would approach me? Had he known Dugan had entered Nekros? Or did he anticipate the Winter Queen's summons? She'd called for me before when a body had turned up in her court. But how had he known about the bodies in the first place?

"If the queen is requesting my presence, it sounds like I'll be raising these shades one way or another. I don't think there is anything we need to negotiate," I said, turning to Dugan. Which kind of sucked. Dugan had mentioned paying me—the queen was unlikely to make such an offer and I would have to negotiate carefully to get any form of compensation for the rituals. Tongues for the Dead really needed the business, especially if I was going to end up doing it regardless.

The prince frowned and shook his head. "If you are not working for the shadow court, you will not report back what you learn. We still wish to hire you."

"No," Falin said.

"Why not?" I asked, looking between them. "Nothing I do can influence the testimony of a shade. It doesn't matter who hires me. Shades are incapable of deception. They have no will. They are just memories."

"Your line of questioning could be biased," Falin said.

Which was the opening I needed. "What if both winter and shadow hired me equally?"

"How could it ever be equal? You are apparently *betrothed* to him." Falin spat the words like they'd rotted between forming and being spoken. Yeah . . . That was going to be a fun conversation later.

"And she is a member of your court, but I can trust her to be impartial." The words were a dig, as if Dugan, who barely knew me, trusted me more than Falin. They were cleverly worded too—he'd said he *could* trust me, not that he *did* trust me to be impartial.

Of course, that trust was unwarranted on a personal level—I had no true connection or loyalty to Dugan or the shadow court, but they were justified professionally. As I'd said, shades couldn't lie, and regardless of whether one or both courts hired me, I'd look for the truth. Falin knew me well enough to know as much.

"If you trust her impartiality, then why insist shadow be the court to hire her?"

Muscles above Dugan's jaw bulged, but when he spoke, his voice was a carefully controlled neutral. "Because we wish to be kept apprised of the situation." Dugan leaned back in his chair. "When I came here, I assumed our fae had been taken against his will, murdered, and dumped in winter territory. I am not yet convinced that is an un-likely scenario. I know the fae in question, and I can think of no reason he would have to enter winter, let alone at-tempt to assassinate a winter noble. But whether he en-tered on his own or was taken against his will, we need to know the players involved. Was this an isolated grudge? Or is a conspiracy at hand? Either way, we need proof that our court was not behind it, and proof of who is if it is a conspiracy."

"You think you are being set up?" I asked.

Dugan cocked his head to the side, and I thought he was considering my words until I realized he was simply trying to parse out my phrasing. Dugan was a very old fae who didn't interact with the human realm often. That was hard to remember when looking at a face that appeared not much older than my own.

"I mean that you think someone might be trying to create tension between shadow and winter," I clarified, and Dugan nodded.

"The king was . . . very displeased to hear of the death. The knowledge added stress he did not need."

I considered that statement. Fae rarely gave an entire answer to a question, and if I read between the lines, I could guess that it wasn't just fear that the Winter Queen would declare war that had Dugan in my office. There was a risk that the Shadow King might have felt forced to take action against winter if his man had been kidnapped and killed.

"When I asked you earlier if you had a suspect, you said possibly. Who were you thinking about?" I asked.

Beside me, Falin huffed under his breath. "How can he have a suspect if he didn't even know the circumstances of the murder? His fae is the suspect."

Dugan scowled at him, but all he said was, "The inner courts have very little reason to quarrel with the seasonal courts."

And that was what I meant by not fully answering a question.

From what I understood of Faerie's hierarchy, the seasonal courts spent the year waxing and waning in power, but light and shadow, having no direct doors to the mortal realm, were outside such struggles. Which would explain why the seasonal courts and the courts of light and shadow rarely found points of contention. The high court would be one of the inner courts as well, but considering I couldn't find easy access to enter the high court, or any members of the high court, it didn't seem like the citizens of the high court interacted with the rest of Faerie, so I guessed he didn't suspect anyone from that court. That left the court of light. I knew only one fae with ties to the light court.

"Do you think Ryese . . . ?" I started, looking at Falin.

He shook his head. "The son of the Queen of Light is banished from these lands. We would know if he entered our territory."

Well, there went that idea. Ryese, who was not only the Light Queen's son, but also the Winter Queen's nephew, had made his play to try to overthrow his aunt recently. He'd very nearly succeeded. All of his known associates were dead or banished, but he might still have sympathizers inside the winter court. As long-lived as fae were, they had a lot of time to create histories, friendships, and feuds.

I clasped my hands, steepling my fingers as I thought. Something occurred to me and I turned to Falin. "How did you find out Dugan entered winter's territory?"

"A call came in to FIB headquarters that the prince was seen passing through the Bloom."

Surprise followed by suspicion crossed Dugan's face. "That is not possible. I have gone nowhere near the Eternal Bloom nor the door to the winter court."

"Then how did you get here?" Falin asked, and it was his turn to sound suspicious.

Dugan's gaze flickered toward me, the glance quick, but I doubted Falin missed it. "Through more neutral territory."

So somewhere I'd merged the planes in the past. Sadly, there were several spots in Nekros that described at this point. The largest was in my father's mansion, but considering the fact that Dugan said he hadn't spoken to my father recently, I was guessing he'd found another spot.

"The Bloom is in the center of the Magic Quarter, only a few blocks from here. Perhaps someone saw you and assumed . . ." I trailed off as he shook his head.

"I am the Prince of Shadows and Secrets. No one saw me come here." He seemed genuinely insulted that I'd suggested it. Then his intense gaze fixed on Falin. "If your informant said I was at the Eternal Bloom, how did you find me here so quickly?"

Falin scowled at him, but I knew the answer. When Falin had burst through my door, he hadn't expected to find Dugan.

"He came to secure me," I said, because it seemed obvious enough. Either as a friend or because I was an asset of the Winter Queen, getting me somewhere safe when a perceived threat from Faerie had crossed into the territory had been one of Falin's priorities. After all, he didn't know I'd had contact with the shadow court—and Dugan in particular—several times in the last few months, but he did know that the king had made a play to secure me as a planeweaver for his court once before in an act that was near equal parts rescue and kidnapping.

"So, we have two bodies in the winter court, who appear to have killed each other, but you"—I nodded to Dugan—"say the shadow fae had no orders to be there, and to your knowledge, no reason to want to kill a noble in winter. Your court heard whispers about the death before the bodies were even found, but with limited details as if the news were designed to inspire a knee-jerk reaction. And someone reported Dugan's entrance into Nekros to you"—this time I nodded at Falin—"except the information passed on to you was clearly false. It was effective in getting you here, though. Did your agent get the identity of the informant?"

Falin ran a thumb along his jaw before shaking his head. "I'll have to check what information was logged, but I don't think so. If you were never near the Bloom, then that would make the message relayed to me a blatant lie."

Which meant the caller had to be human. Fae couldn't lie—bend the truth until the listener was convinced up was down, sure. But they couldn't outright lie.

"A changeling, maybe?" I asked, and Falin looked thoughtful. "Whoever it was, the lie certainly adds some weight to the fact that there might be more going on here than what it appears."

Both men gave grim nods. Of course the queen wasn't known for her patience or levelheadedness—granted, all of my interactions with her had been while she'd been being slowly poisoned into madness. I was told she was saner now, but I could easily imagine her declaring war or demanding recompense for her lost noble based solely on the appearance of the scene. Which meant Falin needed to get to Faerie soon and lead the real investigation, and it sounded like I was going with him, at least for part of it. I glanced at Dugan before turning to face Falin.

"Would the queen allow me to question the shades with Prince Dugan present?"

"He is an untrustworthy element who should not be within winter's territory until this matter is resolved."

I frowned at him. "Dugan in particular or all shadow fae? Because from what he's said, this isn't an attack on the winter court. Not one initiated by him at least. He has very plainly stated that his goal here is to prevent war."

I could almost hear Falin's teeth grinding, but to his credit, he considered it. Finally he said, "There are nefarious ways to prevent war."

I wanted to throw my hands in the air in frustration. "What, do you think he sent his fae into the court so that he could demand to see the body in person and once he was allowed into the icy halls he plans to assassinate the queen?"

Falin didn't answer.

Dugan rubbed his thumb and fingers over his mouth, and I wondered if he was trying to wipe away the desire to smile at my frustration. "If it helps," he said, "as I have already stated, neither the king nor I sent Kordon to the winter halls. He was a quiet fae, and rather peaceful for a goblin. He was a masterful shadow-crafter who rarely left his workshop. I've known him since I was a boy, and I can't imagine any reason he would try to assassinate a winter noble. I'm not sure how he would even know one of your nobles."

Falin frowned at him. "Tonight the longest night of the year begins. All doors in Faerie will open to the winter court so we can join together to celebrate the changing of the seasons. Faerie will enact the ancient truce that binds all her residents during solstices and equinoxes. Will your right of open roads last until sunset?"

Dugan nodded. "And for several hours after."

"Then with your oath that you intend no harm to the winter court, and will attack no member of our court, I will allow you to accompany us."

I blinked at Falin in surprise. "Not that I'm complaining, but how did you just go from planning to try to kill

him when he walked out this door to inviting him to go
to a murder scene?"

"If he hasn't violated the pacts in open roads, then
technically, he can remain in our territory. I'd rather
have him where I can keep an eye on him than let him
wander around alone. Considering he will be invited
into our lands in a few hours, I am only offering to extend the truce a short time."

"And what reassurances will you offer me that this is
a true invitation, and not a trick to let you drag me before
your queen with no resistance?" Dugan asked, studying
the other man.

I turned my exasperated glare on the prince. They
couldn't make this easy, could they? Of course, anytime
I went to court, I feared for my own freedom, so I couldn't
exactly blame Dugan. A prince would make a good cap-
tive if war was imminent.

"I can make no promises on behalf of the queen, but
I can give my oath that, short of a contradictory command from my queen, I will cause you no harm as long
as you do not violate the hospitality of the court." Falin
turned to me. "But before I do, we need to reach an
agreement with you. If we are both to hire you, it must
be equally. Again, I cannot bargain on the behalf of the
queen, but I can hire you for the FIB."

That worked for me. I glanced at Dugan, and when he
didn't protest, I retrieved a client contract from my desk.
The standard form needed quite a bit of augmentation.
We ended up with a contract that included both a ritual
for two shades, as well as hourly rates for investigation
since I was apparently going to the scene whether I
wanted to or not. I tacked on a hefty hazard fee per hour
in Faerie, though I didn't call it that. I tried to keep the

guarantees in the contract as loose as possible—I had to raise the shades, but I didn't have to solve the murders. There was a small financial penalty if I walked away from the case. I would only get paid for half my time if the case went unsolved and I was the one who decided to stop investigating, but I wasn't bound to keep investigating until it was solved. That was an important clause Falin suggested. I'd have to remember it. I didn't want to accidentally lock myself permanently into a case that couldn't be solved. Either man could, of course, decide not to fund any more hours after the initial contracted amount at any time whether I had solved the case or not, but I wouldn't be penalized for the hours I'd already worked as long as I could prove they'd been billable hours.

I read back over what we had. It looked good. I'd be paid more than fairly and didn't see any snags I could get magically tangled in, but there was one more thing I wanted to try to get in the contract.

"On top of monetary compensation, I want answers to three questions, asked at a time of my choosing." Because if this case didn't work out in a way that forced my father to tell me how to reach the high court, it would be helpful to have a way to ask Dugan about it without winding up in his debt.

Dugan frowned. "I would happily pay a higher rate to forgo such a bargain." He reached into his jacket and pulled out a drawstring bag. "I brought this as payment."

I stared at the little bag dubiously, but accepted it when he handed it to me. I let my senses stretch, reaching with my ability to sense magic. Nothing. So probably benign. Opening the bag, I dumped the contents onto my palm. Four gold coins, a ruby the size of my pinky nail, and an iridescent pink pearl.

"Uh . . ." Bartering. Fae negotiate and barter. I had no idea what these treasures were worth, but I was guessing a hell of a lot more than my retainer. If the coins were solid gold, they could always be melted down, but while I didn't recognize the figurehead stamped into them, I was guessing that the coins were even more valuable as they were than their base metal worth. The pearl was perfectly round and nearly glowed it had so much luster. I'd need an appraiser, and to find a buyer, before I could figure out how much of my fees it covered and how much I'd need to return.

And then there was the ruby.

It was flawless, a vibrant red, and expertly faceted, which no doubt made it very valuable to a jeweler. It was even more valuable to a witch. A simple probe with my senses proved that it was capable of storing massive amounts of raw Aetheric energy or just about any spell. Magically speaking, it was more valuable than anything I'd ever owned aside from my enchanted dagger.

I put the coins and pearl back into the bag and held up the ruby. "I would be willing to accept this along with the questions in trade for the price of the retainer and . . ." I scrambled, trying to come up with a reasonable number of hours. If I quoted too few, I'd be offering a very bad deal. Too many, and I'd have to refund him cash if I didn't end up using them all. Considering that I wanted to keep the ruby, so only Falin's portion of my fees would actually go toward the operating expenses of the firm, I definitely couldn't afford to refund him money. "Fifteen hours," I finally said. I would be getting the better end of the deal, but it was probably fair-ish.

Dugan held up a hand. "Keep everything in the purse and no questions or answers."

That would be a really good financial deal for me. Having gone nearly a month without clients, Tongues for the Dead seriously needed some income. But the cash flow issues were hopefully temporary. I needed to find a teacher or I was going to end up maiming myself.

"The ruby and two questions for ten hours," I said, since bargaining required compromise. I couldn't imagine one question would be worth five hours of my rate, but that was for him to decide. Besides, if he went for it, that still gave me an initial and a follow-up question. Not terrible.

Dugan's frown deepened. "Keep the coins and the ruby . . . and one question, for seven hours."

For a stunned second, I didn't respond at all. I had a moment of wondering if I'd misunderstood, but no, he just put a hell of a lot more value on secrets than I did. He didn't even know what the questions were yet—they could be perfectly benign ones he would have answered anyway. But if avoiding being contractually bound to answer questions was more valuable to him than precious gems and metals, that was his prerogative. Of course, it was also possible Dugan had no idea the value of local mortal currency and I was more or less taking advantage, but he seemed fairly knowledgeable about the human world for a fae who wasn't supposed to visit it, and he was a big boy who could have asked about exchange rates or whatever if he needed.

Schooling my face to neutral, I looked to Falin. "That sound acceptable?"

"That bargain is between you two. If that is what you both decide is fair, then fine." He shrugged. "Me, I'm paying with the ever-popular agency credit card."

I almost laughed at that, catching the sound at the last

minute and smothering my smile. We took a few minutes to finalize and sign the contract, and then the two men exchanged another oath that ensured that the truce between them would last beyond my office—thank goodness. With that done, there was nothing else to do but head to Faerie.

Chapter 3

The Eternal Bloom was Nekros City's only fae bar. The public side was a kitschy tourist trap with a limited but overpriced drink selection and an even more pricey short-order food menu. No one would have given the place a second glance—and certainly not much patronage—except that it was one of the few places humans were guaranteed to see unglamoured fae. The fae employed on the public side of the Bloom were paid to allow humans to gawk at them, and that started with the bouncer in the main entrance.

Today the bouncer was one I hadn't seen before, and I couldn't identify what manner of fae he was on sight. He had two rows of small black eyes and a mouth that ended with a pointed beak. He was so tall that, even sitting on the provided stool, he had to hunch down to avoid brushing his head on the ceiling. But while he was long, he was thin, like someone had put him in a taffy puller and stretched him. He reminded me of some sort of stick bug. Not that I'd tell him as much.

His small beady eyes scanned over our group as we stepped through the door. He nodded at us and lifted an arm, pointing to a small lectern in the corner of the room, and beside it, the VIP door. The ledger was one of the most important things in the room, and I headed straight for it as Falin checked his gun with the bouncer. I meticulously signed us all in, writing as clearly as possible, and putting the exact time in the arrival box. While the public portion of the Eternal Bloom might be a tourist trap, the VIP room was a pocket of Faerie. An in-between space that led to the door to the winter court. The bouncer was there in part to prevent humans from wandering into Faerie unknowingly, but more than that, to ensure that everyone who did enter signed the ledger. The door was easy enough to walk through, but time sometimes did funny things if you didn't document your arrival and departure properly.

It had been a while since I'd visited the Bloom. Since my castle had dug itself out its own little pocket of blended mortal and Faerie reality a couple months ago, there hadn't been much reason for me to visit the bar and its unpredictable door. Not much had changed in that time. Masterfully carved tables and chairs were scattered through a room larger than should have been able to be contained within the building as it existed in the mortal realm. A motley gathering of fae sat at those tables, some played dice in the corner, and a few had even joined the endless dance in the most distant corner of the room. In the center of the room was the amaranthine tree, its varied ever-blooming flowers giving the bar its name. And above it all, the impossible stretch of

Faerie's sky. Normally the sky had little correlation to the sky in the mortal realm, but today the sun hung at nearly the same spot as when we'd been outside, but this sun looked larger, closer than the one in mortal reality. Also, despite a lack of clouds in the soft blue sky, it was snowing, though that snow never seemed to reach the ground.

A hush fell over the bar as we wove through the tables, the vacuum of noise rushing out in front of us and then filling back in with quiet whispers in our wake. I knew why. The silence stemmed from the fact that Falin was the queen's knight, her bloody hands. The whispers were likely because we were accompanied by the Shadow Prince. Knowing why the fae reacted so strongly didn't make it any less unnerving.

While I might not have visited recently, I had gotten more familiar with the place when I had been dining here regularly. I didn't know most of these fae by name, but I recognized many of the faces that were now tilted toward their neighbors, voices pitched low. A *glaistig* and a water nymph eating a companionable lunch looked up as the sweeping hush flowed over them. They took one glance our way, dropped their food, and fled to the door of the Bloom without a backward glance.

Falin watched them go, a grim frown etching itself across his face. He didn't like being the bogeyman of the winter court, but as any cop would tell you, running at the sight of authority was a good way to look guilty. He'd remember those two and likely look into their recent activity.

We reached the base of the tree, which acted as the door to Faerie, and I hesitated. Falin gave me a moment—he was used to my reluctance to cross into the court—but Dugan openly studied me.

"You're afraid to enter?" The question was curious, not holding a hint of ridicule, and yet I still felt heat rise to my cheeks.

"It's not the entering that's the problem. It's the fear that I won't be able to leave again."

Dugan nodded. "A reasonable fear given your . . . uniqueness. I admit, I'm hesitant for much the same reason. Even with the knight's vow, walking into the winter court is a treacherous proposition."

"Then why do it? I've been summoned and as I like living in Nekros, I kind of have to respond. You could go back to the shadow court and wait for me to let you know what I learn. We have a contract; I'll keep you updated."

"While that sounds safer, I have reached the stage of needing to make a calculated gamble. Our court looks like the guilty party. If I leave now, I look as suspicious as those two independents who fled at the sight of the Winter Knight. Mitigating damage and preventing war is my main mission. If I fail, it really doesn't matter if I am captured now or stand with a desperate cause later in the shadow court."

Put that way, he was rather between a rock and a hard place. "I guess it's time to put on our brave faces then," I said, taking a deep breath.

Dugan gave me one of those looks again, like he was trying to puzzle me out. I shot him a weak smile and walked toward the tree. Falin fell in step beside me. After the barest hesitation, Dugan took up a position on my other side, so that we all circled the tree at the same time.

The world around us blurred, colors smearing as the warm lights and deep wood tones of the bar were washed away. They were replaced by the glimmering whites and icy blues of the frozen halls of the winter court. The amaranthine tree was gone; in its place stood an enormous pillar of ice, carved with intricate scenes of fae in snowy landscapes. The hall around us was solid ice, the walls lined with what appeared to be statues carved from glistening ice but I knew from experience were guards that could awaken and attack at the queen's whim.

Not that there was a shortage of living guards.

Six stepped out to block our path as soon as the hall solidified around us. I'd never seen more than two guarding the doorway before. The murder clearly had the queen on edge.

"Knight," the guard in front said, dipping her head.

I guessed at her gender based solely on the pitch of her voice. The blue ice armor she wore was identical to that of her companions and showed little of her shape beneath. The hoods the guards wore covered their faces, so all I could see was the triangle of her jaw and chin; the rest of her features were lost in shadows too deep to be natural. Despite that, I could feel the moment her frigid gaze swept over me, assessing, before moving on and leaving my skin prickled with gooseflesh. When her gaze reached Dugan, her hand fluttered to the sword strapped at her waist.

"Stand down," Falin said, stepping between the guards and Dugan. "He is here as a guest."

There was a moment of uncertain shuffling in which the guards kept their hands on their swords, their hoods twitching slightly as if they were catching each other's eyes from behind those shadows. But Falin was the Winter Knight, and when it came to security in the court, his word was second only to that of the queen. I held my breath, my heartbeat thudding in my ears, but it was only a small hesitation, and then the guards dropped their hands from their weapons. But they didn't relax.

"Where is the queen?" Falin asked, his posture straight, demanding.

"The library, awaiting word from you," the same guard who had spoken earlier said. She was clearly the leader of this band of guards.

Falin nodded. "Then we will assess the scene first."

"As you wish." She made a hand motion to one of the other guards, who nodded and broke formation, turning to lead us deeper into the court.

Falin followed without another word or backward glance, trusting Dugan and me to keep up. The rest of the guards didn't move, forcing me to pass so close to one of them that I could feel the chill coming off his armor— which had to be an intentional magical effect. The ice making up the walls and floor didn't radiate cold, and the temperature in the hallway was pleasant, so the armor likely only chilled those close enough to be in combat with the wearer.

As we followed the guard through the seemingly endless halls of the winter court, I noticed that Dugan had released his glamour. Gone was the suit he'd appeared to wear in my office. In its place was his dark armor, his black cloak flowing behind him like a living shadow. He cut a terrifying figure stalking down the frozen halls, and I hurried to catch up with Falin. Not that Falin looked any less dangerous. He didn't need creepy armor for the killing grace of his every movement to shine through. Of course, I'd also seen that particular strength and grace aimed at far more enjoyable activities, so I appreciated it in a different way.

The guard finally stopped in front of an icy archway and gestured. I didn't bother trying to look into the room—whatever I saw wouldn't be whatever was actually there when we stepped through the passage. Doorways in Faerie were weird. Two other winter guards stood to either side of the archway. They nodded to Falin, but their swords were drawn.

"A shadow trails you, Knight," the one on the left side of the door said, as if we'd missed the fact that Dugan was behind us this whole time.

"He is here as a guest, currently. He will observe the investigation. You will let him pass." Falin delivered the commands with authority. The guards didn't lower their weapons, but the one who had spoken gave a small, tight nod. Falin half turned and glanced from me to Dugan. "Let's go." He stepped through the archway and vanished, leaving Dugan and me alone in the hallway with three nervous-looking guards.

I hated doors in Faerie.

I hurried after Falin, and the world lurched as I passed through the archway, the door taking me somewhere else in Faerie. Then the world settled and I stepped into what was obviously a bedroom. Falin had stopped just inside the door, blocking most of my view of the room, but it wasn't a large area and around his broad shoulders I could see the posts and canopy of a bed carved from pale wood. Gauzy blue curtains hung from the canopy like dangling icicles. A spray of reddish-brown marred the curtains near the head of the bed and I looked away before I saw more than I wanted.

A guard stood to one side of the doorway. He nodded to Falin, but I was too close to see if Falin returned the gesture. He hadn't traveled more than one large step into the room. Which was going to make it very uncomfortable when Dugan joined us.

As if summoned by the thought, Dugan stepped into the room behind me, crowding the doorway where we lingered. To our side, the guard jolted in shock at the sight of the Shadow Prince. Then he sprang into a flurry of action. An icy blade zipped through the air, leaving a trail of frost in its wake. Just as quickly, Falin was there, his two long daggers crossed, catching the blade before it completed its path toward Dugan's head. Not that the prince looked caught unawares. His own sword was out, bleeding shadows into the air around it.

"Stand down," Falin commanded.

The guard drew back but didn't sheathe his sword. His cloak hid everything but his mouth and chin, which revealed only that his lips were curled back, exposing gritted teeth that were far sharper-looking than a human's, but he obeyed his knight.

"The Shadow Prince is a guest here to observe," Falin said, and then glanced over his shoulder, not at me, but at someone beyond me.

I hadn't noticed the sentry on the left-hand side of the doorway when I'd entered. She was the complete opposite of the hooded and ice-armored guard. She wore a very modern black pantsuit that was fitted to her wasp-thin body. Her short black hair was slicked back on her head, except for two small antennae that hung forward just above her forehead. I couldn't actually see the dragonfly wings that kept her lifted a foot off the ground—they were only a blur of movement as she had to keep them in continuous movement to hover in one spot the way she was—but I was familiar with them because I recognized her. Agent Nori, one of Falin's FIB agents.

"Sir," she said, tilting her head toward her boss and studying him with multifaceted eyes.

I scanned the room, wondering if there was anyone else I'd missed. If one FIB agent was here, preserving the scene, shouldn't more have been here working it? Or at least waiting for Falin so they could start working the scene? But no one else was present. No one living, at least.

Now that Falin was no longer directly in front of me, I could more or less see the entire room. My gaze skittered over the prone figure on the bed and the copious amounts of blood surrounding it. Another figure lay sprawled on the floor only a few feet ahead of me, as if he'd been running for the door and almost made it. I'd known before walking in that there would be two bodies, but it was slightly unnerving to realize that I'd been standing so close to one and hadn't sensed it. With no land of the dead in Faerie, grave essence didn't reach for me. I couldn't *feel* bodies. I wasn't used to that.

As a general rule of thumb, I didn't like blood. Hell, I didn't really like dead bodies either, though they were often unavoidable in my line of work. But the small body only feet in front of me didn't trigger an immediate need to look away, no rising nausea or panic. Perhaps it was because I couldn't feel him, so my mind could dismiss him as something other than a body. Without contact with the land of the dead, there were no obvious signs of decomposition, so he looked like he could be sleeping—if anyone would sleep facedown on a floor made of ice. There was also remarkably little blood—though the sword sticking out of his back was a pretty clear sign of the violence that had killed him. Or maybe it was easier to look at him because he was so visibly inhuman.

The fae were a diverse people. Some looked nearly human, but many more were wildly different. He was on the humanoid-shaped-but-obviously-not-remotely-

human side of the scale. He was the size of a child; I'd
guess no more than three feet tall. His skin was green
and rough-looking, like an alligator's. He had no hair, at
least none I could see from this distance, not even on his
eyebrows. But the most unusual thing was the fact that
he had three arms: one on his left side and two on his
right. Make that the second most unusual thing. The
most unusual was how pristine the floor around him was
despite the sword jutting out of his back.

"Do goblins bleed?" I asked, scanning the floor between the small body and the bed. There was a *lot* of
blood close to the bed and I didn't look at it too hard, but
only a smudge or two of blood was near the goblin's body.

"Yes," Falin said, his eyes making the same journey
mine had. "Their blood is a little darker than a human's,
but it flows as freely as any when they are cut."

"Then this scene is wrong," I said.

Falin nodded. "Very." He turned to Nori. "You've
checked the goblin?"

"He doesn't appear to be glamoured or spelled."

I glanced at where Agent Nori still hovered beside the
doorway. She had no forensic kit with her, no bags for
evidence, nor a camera. I knew Falin didn't have anything, as I'd arrived with him.

"Do you have a team coming to process the scene?"
I asked.

Falin half turned toward me and opened his mouth
like he was going to answer, but then his head snapped
back around. While I'd been rather analytically observ-
ing the scene, Dugan had sunk to his knees next to the
goblin's body. Dugan had mentioned he'd known the
shadow fae since childhood. By the obvious grief on his
face, it was clear he'd known him well.

"Don't touch the body," Falin said, and the emotion flowed off Dugan's face as if he'd only just realized we'd been witnessing his moment of grief.

"Kordon," Dugan said, the word barely a whisper and nearly lost even in such a small room.

"What?"

"The goblin, his name was Kordon." Dugan stared at the small figure. "You checked to see if he was fake, but did you make any effort to revive him?"

I shot a skeptical glance at the giant sword protruding from the goblin's back. "I'm fairly certain it is safe to assume he is beyond resuscitation."

Dugan frowned at me from where he knelt by the body, but it was Falin who whispered, "Death is not always a permanent condition in Faerie."

I blinked at him in surprise. "Fae can heal mortal injuries?" I mean, I'd seen Falin heal some pretty bad wounds, and quickly at that. But they were more in the category of *could prove fatal* as opposed to the *he was dead this morning* type of injury.

Falin lifted one hand and twisted it in a *sort of* movement. "Some fae can naturally heal anything that doesn't outright kill them. Goblins are a race that tend to heal nearly anything. But death, true death, cannot be self-healed. That said, if the body remains in Faerie, it is not uncommon for life to be magically restored by a healer."

"Can they ever leave Faerie after that?" I asked, suspecting I already knew the answer.

Falin shook his head. "Not without great risk. Some pass through the mortal world unscathed. Others drop dead unexpectedly with no apparent cause. A fae may visit the mortal realm multiple times without incident before suddenly falling dead with no warning while there."

I could guess why. I couldn't prove it, not without seeing a fae who had been revived, but I would guess once the body died, even if it was later healed, the connection between the soul and body was damaged. Here in Faerie, without a land of the dead, that likely didn't matter. But in the mortal realm . . . A restored body might not mean a truly living body. Soul collectors would likely take the soul if they saw one walking around.

"Has a healer been summoned?" Dugan asked, still kneeling beside the goblin.

Falin looked to Nori. She nodded. "Stiofan is beyond healing. His heart is missing."

A frown tugged at the edges of Falin's lips, but he nodded.

"And Kordon?" Dugan asked. There had been mostly sorrow in his voice before, but now his tone sharpened in anger. Nori turned her large, insectlike eyes on him. A thin membrane passed over her eyes as she regarded him, but she didn't answer. He scoffed, shaking his head. "Of course, your healer didn't even check. He wasn't your court."

"He's also our suspect," Nori said.

Dugan glared at her before returning his attention to the small goblin. He cocked his head to the side, a quizzical expression crossing his face. He reached out for something hidden from my view by the sprawled body.

"I said not to touch anything," Falin barked as Dugan lifted a dagger from where it had been half hidden under Kordon's third arm.

The Shadow Prince frowned at Falin, his hand stalling, the dagger only halfway lifted. "You said not to touch the body."

"You're really going to argue semantics. This is a

crime scene. Don't touch anything." I could almost hear Falin's teeth grinding as he spoke. "Now your prints will be on that dagger."

Dugan resumed his motion, lifting the dagger and examining it. "It would already have my prints," he said. "It's my dagger."

That stopped whatever Falin was about to say—which I'm sure would have been to kick Dugan out of the scene. He lifted an eyebrow, regarding the prince.

"Yours? How long has it been missing?"

Dugan frowned. "I didn't realize it was until I saw it here, but it is definitely mine. It's a handsome blade, commissioned for me as a gift. Unfortunately, its beauty is all it has going for it. It has never held an edge well and it is poorly weighted. I keep it on display."

"Somewhere public?" Falin asked.

Dugan's frown deepened. "No."

Agent Nori's wings released a shrill keening of alarm as they rubbed together. "So, your fae. Your dagger. *And* you compromised the scene? The queen could demand your head for less."

"Nori," Falin said, her name a warning, but he didn't look like he disagreed with her. He turned to Dugan. "Put the dagger down, back up, and don't touch anything else or you'll be held accountable for interfering with the investigation." He gave the other fae an appraising look as if he could find guilt physically on his person. "We will discuss the dagger after I finish with the scene."

Dugan set down the dagger and backed away from Kordon's body, but while he made a point of lifting his hands as if in surrender, his movements as he rejoined me in the doorway were too casual. He seemed to be making a point of moving slowly, his steps easy as if he were trying to convince everyone present that moving away from the body was his own idea. Falin scowled but didn't say anything more to him.

After studying the scene from the doorway a moment longer, Falin walked a careful circle around the goblin's body. He studied the floor, the blade Dugan had replaced, and the sword in Kordon's back, never touching any of it. Finally he turned to the other body. He couldn't get too close to the bed and the body on it without tracking through the blood and contaminating the scene, but he walked up to the edge of the blood pool. I didn't follow, but Nori did.

She hovered a foot off the ground, her wings buzzing as they kept her above the blood pool. "As you can see," she said, hovering near the head of the bed and gesturing to the body, "the goblin must have been in a rage. I haven't counted all of the knife wounds, but there are at least two dozen."

Falin looked away from the body and studied his agent. "And how did this go down? What do you guess were the series of events?"

Nori blinked, an iridescent membrane sliding over her large insectlike eyes, and then she glanced between the dead goblin and the dead Sleagh Maith. Her lips pressed into a thin line as she studied the scene.

From his post beside the door, the guard cleared his throat. "Isn't it obvious? Stiofan was surprised and overwhelmed, as he must have been asleep when the attack began. The goblin was vicious and rabid, but Stiofan was able to reach his sword. He plunged it into the goblin, driving it away, but he succumbed to his wounds. The cowardly goblin tried to run away, but the blow Stiofan delivered proved fatal."

"That's certainly how it is meant to appear," Falin said.

"But you are not convinced?" Dugan asked.

Falin glanced at him. "What do you see?"

The Shadow Prince grimaced. "It does appear as he said."

Falin grunted, and then he met my eyes. "What is wrong with this scene?"

"Besides the lack of Kordon's blood?" I let my gaze drift over the prone figure on the bed. There was no lack of blood there, and the murdered fae definitely didn't look like he was sleeping. One leg hung unceremoniously off the bed and his face was contorted with pain; both arms were flung over his head as if he'd been trying to ward off blows or maybe like his wrists had been pinned over his head. And blood. There was so much blood. And his torso—I couldn't even look at the mess that should have been his chest. I let my gaze move on quickly.

I focused on the goblin again—he was much easier to study. I walked the same circle around him Falin had. I didn't want to look at the sword protruding from his back, but I forced myself to study it, simultaneously trying to trick my brain into accepting that I was looking at something else, something less gruesome.

There was a small amount of shiny dark liquid on the back of Kordon's tunic where the sword had entered, but not nearly enough. I'd shed more blood from skinned knees before. There was no blood on his hands or arms, not dark goblin blood nor bright Sleagh Maith blood. The blade of the dagger was slick with shiny red blood that looked as if it might have been spilled only a moment beforehand, but there wasn't a drop on the hilt. The goblin was barefoot, but there was no blood on the soles of his feet. I frowned and glanced back toward the bed without actually looking at the body lying on it.

"There are a few scuffed footprints leading from the bed in this direction, but he has no trace of blood on his feet. Neither his blood nor the noble's," I said. "Is the sword pinning him to the ground enchanted? Could it have frozen his blood on contact? Could that be why there is none of his blood around him?"

"Possible, and we will have to test the blade for enchantments, but Stiofan was not known to own any enchanted weapons." Falin continued to watch me. "What else?"

This felt rather like a test, but it was in my contract that I'd be helping with the investigation, so I scanned the scene again. "If Kordon was vigorously stabbing the winter noble, how did he end up with a sword in his back?"

"He was obviously running away," the guard insisted.

I let my eyes dart to the figure on the bed once more. "No. Stiofan has a dozen or more wounds and was clearly overpowered. Why would the goblin have suddenly decided to turn and run? Also, the noble's arms aren't extended like he'd delivered a blow or fumbled for a weapon—they are up, over his head. Which means driving a sword through the goblin wasn't the last thing he did."

"Don't judge fae based on mortal fragility—many can take much more damage than a human," Falin said, but despite the correction, he had an odd note of pride in his voice, as if my deductions had impressed him. "But in this case, I have to agree with you. Goblins, while they heal well, aren't particularly durable, and unless his individual anatomy is unusual, that sword pierced his heart. It would be instantly fatal. He wouldn't have been able to continue an attack, let alone flee across the room."

I nodded. "And you said Stiofan couldn't be healed because his heart is missing?"

"Magic can heal and mend mortal wounds, but it can't regrow missing body parts," Dugan said. He was watching me with curiosity.

"That's not what I'm getting at. Where is the heart?"

"The goblin must have eaten it," the guard said, sounding sure in his conviction.

I shot him a frown. "So you're assuming the goblin was in a battle frenzy that resulted in two dozen stab wounds and eating an organ. Then he cleaned his hands and the hilt of his dagger—but not the blade. And *then* Stiofan rammed a sword through his back, at which point the goblin turned and fled but paused at the edge of the blood pool to wash his feet?"

"Perhaps he was betrayed by an accomplice?" Nori suggested. "Look at the voids in the blood splatter." She gestured toward the blood on the curtains and then to the bloody sheets on the bed.

Falin leaned closer, but I made no attempt to approach the bed or look for any pattern in the blood. I might be assisting in the investigation, but I had my limits. I'd let them tackle that one.

Falin made a sound and then pulled back, scanning the room again. "It does appear that either something was removed—and I see no evidence of that—or there was at least one other person here at the time of the murder, likely helping to hold Stiofan down."

I frowned at Kordon's body. "Then one way or another, we are missing a killer."

Chapter 4

Nori and Falin continued to study the blood splatter and Stiofan's body, but I retreated back to the doorway. I'd seen more than I wanted already, and I was starting to feel a buzz in the back of my brain from the panic I'd been suppressing for too long now. At least my stomach hadn't joined the game yet—getting sick at a crime scene was never good. The fact that the air held the same sweet scent the winter court always seemed to smell of instead of decay helped. I'd spent time trying to identify the scent of the court before, but I couldn't quite place it all. It was part evergreen and part clean snow, but there were also floral scents that I couldn't identify. Not that any of that information helped with this case, but it did provide a momentary distraction.

I expected more FIB agents to arrive. This scene should have had people flagging evidence and taking pictures so that everything could be bagged and taken elsewhere for processing. But no one had walked through the doorway. We'd been here a while now. Someone should have arrived by this point.

I tried to wait patiently, but after ten minutes I found myself shuffling my feet and tapping my toes. By the time Falin finally walked back to the doorway, I'd given in and begun pacing. Dugan had spent most of the time watching Falin and Nori as they discussed and analyzed the scene, but more than once I'd caught him watching me, his gaze assessing. I doubted I measured up to whatever scale was in his eyes.

"Can you sense anything about the bodies?" Falin asked, looking at me.

"Magically?" I shook my head. "No land of the dead here, remember? They could be constructs and I wouldn't be able to feel the difference until we get them back to mortal reality." Though, while it wasn't widely known, my planeweaving ability allowed me to see through glamour as long as Faerie hadn't accepted the glamour as real, so maybe that was what he meant. Or maybe he was being very literal and he actually meant sense as in my ability to sense magic. I was more closely attuned to witch magic, though I'd started sensing more fae magic in the months since the Blood Moon. The Aetheric plane was thin in Faerie, and the energy tended not to like the fae, so it wasn't common to find witch magic in Faerie. That didn't mean it couldn't be here, though. I just hadn't thought to look for it.

I cracked my mental shields, tentatively at first, and then letting the opening widen slowly. I didn't have to worry about grave essence assaulting my psyche as soon as I opened my mind here; in fact, most of the planes I normally interacted with simply didn't exist here or were too thin to make much impact. No rot or decay touched anything in my vision, and no wind or chill whipped out to surround me. The Aetheric plane technically existed here, but only the thinnest, horribly faded wisps of raw magic trailed sporadically through the air. Whatever plane souls existed on when still tied inside a body existed in Faerie, but the collectors' plane didn't, leaving the souls trapped in bodies that never decayed. With my shields fully open I could see the soft glow of silver emanating from deep within all of my companions as well as the butchered body on the bed. The goblin held no shimmering glow.

I frowned, narrowing my focus. Different souls looked different to my mental sight. Human souls emitted a happy golden-yellow light. Every full-blooded fae I'd met thus far emitted silver-ish light. Feykin, those of mixed blood but who favored their mortal heritage, tended toward blue colors, though their colors were a bit more amorphous, sometimes seeming more silver and other times gold enough that if I wasn't paying attention, I could mistake a feykin for human. I'd never specifically looked at a goblin soul before, but I should have sensed something inside the body. Even the creatures from the land of the dead who had no soul in the way a living creature understood it, I could sense as darkness. But the goblin was empty.

I opened my shields wider, stretching my senses. The body looked real and it didn't change in my vision as if coated with glamour. I didn't sense any spells on the body either, though the dagger by his third hand had some sort of enchantment worked into it. The dagger's magic was fae in nature and while I could feel something was there, I couldn't begin to guess what it might be. There was no trace of magic on the body, though, no runes or glyphs either.

I must have been staring at the body too long, because Falin stepped closer to me. "Alex?"

"So, a few possibilities. One, goblins don't have souls—unlikely. Two, that's not a body—possible. Three, something that eats souls, or at least that can pull them out of bodies, is loose in the Winter Halls and took Kordon's soul but not Stiofan's—possible, and I wouldn't dismiss it, but I'm leaning against it because why take one and not the other? Or possibility four, Kordon didn't die here and at some point his body was outside Faerie long enough for a collector to find him and remove his soul."

Falin stared at the body. "And you think that last possibility is the most likely?"

"It would be the easiest to explain. Souls don't come out of bodies easily." I hesitated. "Though we have run across a few methods that didn't leave much evidence," I said, thinking about the soul bottles the necromancer had been using last month. "So we definitely can't dismiss that possibility."

"Anything else?"

I forced my gaze to sweep over the room and even skitter over the body on the bed. Nothing else looked or felt strange to my senses. Any glamour in the room had been fully embraced by Faerie because nothing changed in my vision. Well, except the guard. With my shields open, I could see most of his face through the shadows, which answered that question about the shadows being magical, but it shed no light on the scene. When I closed my shields and shook my head, Falin turned to Nori.

"Take the sword and dagger to the lab for further examination. On the way, tell the guards we need someone to transport these bodies to the entrance—we will be taking them to the mortal realm."

Nori nodded, but Dugan cleared his throat.

"My fae should be seen by a healer and an attempt to revive him must be made before his body is taken to the mortal realm."

"He's not in there," I said, because even if his body could be healed, there was no soul left to bring back.

"As you say," Dugan said, giving me a curt but polite nod. "But I still insist healing be attempted before the possibility is lost by taking his body to the mortal realm."

Falin regarded him a moment before saying, "You do realize that if he is revived, he will have to be questioned. Under the circumstances, the queen will likely do it herself." What he left unsaid was that she'd likely do that questioning in Rath, her torture chamber. Whether the goblin was guilty or not, he might not walk out again.

"Did you not determine he could not have done this?"

"We only determined that he couldn't have done it *alone*," Falin said, emphasizing the last word.

Dugan frowned. "He is my citizen and I still insist."

"Fine." Falin turned to Nori. "Secure the weapons and then send for a healer."

She nodded and flew to the corner of the room where a small black messenger bag was stashed. She pulled a couple types of evidence bags and a pair of surgical gloves from the bag before heading toward Kordon's body. She slid the dagger into a manila evidence envelope. Then she bagged the hilt of the sword. When she tried to pull the sword from Kordon's back, she fluttered into an odd upside-down U shape, her wings pulling her up but her arms not moving when the sword refused to budge. She tried again, with about as much success.

"Sir," she said, panting from her efforts.

Falin stepped forward and gave the sword a good tug.

It lifted a few inches but didn't pull free of the goblin's body. Falin frowned. Kneeling, he lifted Kordon slightly, peering under him.

"The sword has been driven not only straight through him, but several inches into the floor as well," Falin said.

"So he was already prone on the ground when the blow was struck," Dugan said, his scowl not aimed at anyone present, but turned inward, likely with murderous thoughts directed at whoever had pinned his friend to the floor.

"Anyone else getting the feeling that wasn't the blow that killed him? Or like he wasn't even alive when Stiofan was murdered?" I asked as Falin pulled the sword free. He handed it to Nori. I frowned. "Shouldn't you take photos or something before moving the bodies and removing evidence?"

Falin only shook his head as he leaned over the body, examining it. "Faerie doesn't like technology. Digital cameras won't turn on. Older mechanical cameras will at least function, but while I've tried various types of film, I've yet to find anything that reliably can be developed. At best they show ghosts of images, blurred and blown out, but most of the time nothing at all appears on the film." He rolled the goblin over. The small form moved as a solid unit, stiff, arms and legs remaining exactly in the same position as when he was on his belly. "We must examine everything we can here, immediately, and note it as well as we can. Now that the occupant of this room is dead, Faerie may preserve this room as it is forever, or once we leave, Faerie may take this room and we may never find it again. Same with any physical evidence—Faerie could at any point move it or give it to a new owner."

Well, that did complicate things. And I had no doubt it was true. On one of my first visits to Faerie, I'd lost my dagger in the winter court and it had reappeared later in the shadow court. Faerie wasn't exactly sentient, but it definitely had a will of some sort.

While Kordon had very little blood on his back, and no puddle of blood around where he'd been pinned to the floor, now that he was flipped over, we could see that dark blood soaked the front of his pale tunic. Unlike the blood near the bed, this blood was dry and crusted, flaking in places. None of the blood had transferred to the floor where he'd been lying. *He definitely didn't die here.*

I avoided the hole in his chest where the sword had protruded, though that wasn't even where the darkest concentrations of blood were gathered. Falin touched the green skin at Kordon's neck and it shifted, revealing the deep gash nearly bisecting his throat. I looked away.

Falin tried to lift one of Kordon's hands, but the goblin's joints were locked, his hands stuck in position, slightly elevated from the floor now that he was on his back. Falin tried to turn his head with the same result.

"He's in full rigor mortis?" I asked, trying to only watch from the corner of my eye.

"Seems that way," Falin said, moving to examine the goblin's hands instead of trying to break the rigor.

"Is that important?" Dugan asked.

I glanced back at him. "Have you ever seen a body in rigor before?"

He looked thoughtful before shaking his head. "I do not believe so. I'm only familiar with the term from having read it in a human novel once. Honestly, at the time I assumed it was something fanciful the author invented." I must have looked surprised, because he gave me a small half smile. "Very few tangible things make it from the mortal realm to such a deep place in Faerie as the shadow court, but novels are one I go out of my way to acquire. Fantasy novels from before the Magical Awakening are a personal favorite, but I've acquired a few mystery novels over the years."

The Prince of Shadows and Secrets was a reader. *You learn something every day.*

"It's not fictional," I said. "You haven't seen it because bodies don't decay here. But for Kordon to be in full rigor, he had to have been in a realm that touches the land of the dead for at least six hours, probably closer to twelve—if goblin physiology passes through the same predictable patterns humans do, that is."

"Then . . ." he said, a truly mournful expression on his face. "It truly is already too late to revive him."

It seemed like I should try to console or comfort him, but I wasn't good at that. Instead I turned to Falin. "Does the FIB have a medical examiner?" I knew they didn't have their own morgue. He'd had me raise a shade in the Nekros City Precinct morgue once, but human authorities weren't allowed to autopsy fae and any fae body found had to be turned over to the FIB. It was part of the agreements and peace treaties the fae had forged with the human government back in the early years of the Magical Awakening. I assumed the fear was that humans might murder fae for the sole purpose of dissecting them for science. So surely he had someone with a forensics background.

Falin shook his head. "The fall court has a *bean sidhe* who has gone through a human university and internships, but while I have discussed it with the queen, no progress has been made on that front."

Sounds like the queen didn't prioritize it. I wondered if Falin would agree to letting Tamara look over the bodies. She was Nekros City's lead medical examiner as well as one of my best friends. I'd trust her completely with the task, but I doubted the court would feel the same way. Of course, depending on how my ritual went, it might be a moot point.

After looking over Kordon, Falin moved on to Stiofan. I was curious to learn more about Stiofan's condition after discovering Kordon was in rigor and soulless—he *must* have been in the human realm at some point—but I couldn't get past the blood. It was everywhere. Splatters were on the curtains and the inside of the canopy top. Pools of it had soaked into the sheets and the pillow, as well as trailing down to puddle on the floor. I shivered and looked away.

If Kordon had been planted in the court to throw suspicion on the shadow fae, the true murderers did a crappy job. Not only was Kordon suspiciously bloodless from his own wound, but there was no way he could have stabbed Stiofan so many times—let alone rip his rib cage open and remove his heart—without getting absolutely covered in the other fae's blood as well. *Who would believe such a sloppy frame job?*

I glanced at the ice guard. He'd believed it. Dugan had taken it at face value as well. The killer likely hadn't considered that anyone would look deeper. A plausible enough story had been told with the bodies, if the viewer was only looking to confirm the preconceived conclusion of what was presented. It was the small details that made that story impossible. So whoever staged this probably had little knowledge of crime scene investigation.

*Which narrows our suspect pool down to almost
every fae residing inside Faerie. Maybe most of the older
changelings as well. Awesome.*

Falin made a sound and I looked his way before my
brain caught up with the motion. He held a pillow splat-
tered with blood and was studying it intently as if it held
some new secret he hadn't noted before.

"Isn't everything over there covered in blood?" I asked.
My stomach begged me to turn away, but I forced myself
to look, to try to see what had drawn Falin's attention.

"Yes, but this was beside him, bloodied-side down.
That means it was flipped over at some point." Falin examined both sides of the pillow, and then he leaned forward, studying Stiofan's head. "I think it's possible his
face was covered with it."

"So the shade might not have seen who attacked
him." That would suck. I frowned. "That also means we
are up to multiple killers. Someone to stab. Someone to
hold the pillow and pin his arms." Or someone with
more than two arms. I glanced at the three-armed goblin. But no. Everything indicated he'd been dead before
the attack.

Falin had walked in the blood pool to get close enough
to examine the body. Nori's messenger bag had provided
covers for his shoes, and he stripped off the now-bloody
covers carefully and bagged them before heading back
toward us. I frowned. His first two steps, before he removed the covers, now had bloody, vaguely shoe-shaped
prints. They were the only recognizable footprints in the
room. There were a couple other smudges, but they
weren't large enough or consistent enough to be footprints. So could the killer—or killers—fly like Nori? Or

had they cleaned up the scene? I knew there was a technique the cops used to detect residual blood, but I had no idea what it was, only that it involved sprays and maybe special lights. I was guessing if Faerie didn't like cameras, it would tolerate such techniques even less.

I needed to raise the shades. My head was starting to hurt from all the speculation, so I was glad when Falin rejoined us and said, "I think we've learned all we can from the scene." But then he had to spoil my relief by adding, "It's time to see the queen."

The guard who had escorted us to the scene earlier had returned to his post, and the two that had been guarding the outside of the door were now collecting the bodies, so we were on our own to find the queen. Not that it looked like Falin needed any help.

He set a quick pace down the seemingly endless halls. My pace was considerably less quick, Dugan getting ahead of me as I dawdled. I didn't want to get left behind, though—getting lost in these icy halls was not how I wanted to spend my afternoon.

Falin stopped at an archway that looked no different from dozens of others we'd passed. He waited for me to catch up and shot me a thin smile I could only guess was supposed to be encouraging, or perhaps a show of camaraderie, but it came off as worried. We did not have good news for the queen. It wasn't bad news either. It was just rather . . . uncertain news, and from everything I knew about the queen, she would not be pleased by the ambiguity of the scene.

"Wait here," he said, shooting a glance at Dugan. The

prince gave him an incredulous look, clearly assuming Falin intended to leave him behind, but when Falin grabbed my wrist and motioned me to the side, not through the door, Dugan simply crossed his arms over his chest, watching and waiting.

"What?" I asked, arching an eyebrow.

Falin shot a conspicuous glance at my wrist, or, more accurately, the charm bracelet around it. "Do you still have that privacy charm?"

I frowned but nodded, drawing the raw magic in my ring and pushing it into the small, lock-shaped charm dangling from my wrist. I hadn't paid much attention to the persistent soft sounds of music that seemed to drift through all of Faerie until they all fell silent as the bubble of privacy snapped into place around us.

Falin noted the change and began speaking immediately, though he kept his voice to barely a whisper. "The queen is likely to react badly to the Shadow Prince's presence, even if the guards have already reported that he is with us."

"Shouldn't you be telling him that, not me?"

Falin ignored my interruption. "Do not get between the two of them. Do not come to my defense either, no matter what happens."

My eyes widened. "How bad are you expecting this to get?"

Falin's gaze went distant, considering the question, and he shook his head. "I'm not sure. The queen is still . . . not herself."

That surprised me. "I thought she was sane again now that she is no longer being poisoned."

His wince was small, only visible at the very edges of his eyes and mouth, but I caught it, and for a moment I thought he'd decided he'd said too much and wouldn't answer. Then he whispered, "She is better, and she is not. The fact that her powers are nearing their peak with the approach of winter helps, but when it begins waning during spring . . ." He grimaced. "I'm not sure she will be able to hold her court, or even that Faerie will allow her to."

Which was bad news. I'd witnessed what had happened when she'd been poisoned and began losing control of her court. These halls had been a mix of blizzards and slushy ice melt. Faerie itself, at least in the winter court, had been a miserable and discordant place. And Falin had lost a lot of blood fighting duels as nobles noticed the faltering queen and tried to take her throne. When spring came, if Falin was correct, the duels would begin again, and as the Winter Knight, Falin would have to fight them. How long could he continue to win?

"Do we have a plan I should know about?"

He gave a half shrug. "Go in; I'll report our current findings and that you intend to raise the shades. Hope to get out without bloodshed."

"Great. I'm guessing that since she summoned me, I can't skip this?"

The look he gave me was answer enough. "Keep your head down. And whatever you do, don't mention that you're *betrothed*."

My turn to wince. Yeah. That wasn't high on my to-do list.

He turned when I nodded my agreement. I followed, dropping the privacy bubble as I walked. Dugan watched us both, his dark eyebrow raised speculatively, but he didn't say anything as we returned to the doorway.

Falin walked in first, Dugan following close behind. I

stepped into the doorway barely a heartbeat later, and
emerged into an enormous room lined with shelves upon
shelves of books. I'd never seen so many books in all my
life, and I'd seen some pretty impressive libraries in my
lifetime. The shelves were at least twenty feet high, and
every last visible piece of wall space sported books in the
enormous room. I was so busy gawking at the sheer vol-
ume of books that I didn't immediately spot the people.

The queen sat at a large table near the center of the
room with a dozen scrolls spread across the icy surface
before her. Two other tall figures leaned over the scrolls
on either side of the queen, deep in discussion about
something I couldn't hear from the doorway. As I followed Falin closer, I could see that some of the scrolls
appeared to be maps, while others boasted strings of text
that were written not only in a language I didn't know but
also an alphabet I couldn't identify.

The woman beside the queen looked over first,
straightening when she saw us, and I nearly stumbled. All
thoughts of maps or scrolls fled from my mind as I registered her familiar features. I'd only met Maeve a handful
of times before, but the last time I'd seen her, she'd been
dead on the floor of the queen's throne room.

*Apparently Falin wasn't exaggerating about death be-
ing less permanent in Faerie.*

Lyell, another member of the queen's council, was
still saying something, gesticulating to the map, so the
queen hadn't looked up yet. I took a moment to dart a
glance around the room. I half expected to see Blayne,
the final member of the queen's council. He'd also died
last I heard, but judging by his absence, his condition
must have been more lasting.

We were only a few yards from the table when the queen finally turned. Falin immediately dropped to one knee, bowing deep before his queen. When I didn't follow suit, he shot me a look and I obediently dropped into a curtsy, dipping my head but keeping my gaze up and locked on the queen. I didn't want to be caught unaware because I was staring respectfully at the ground. Dugan remained standing.

The queen gave us a grim smile and then her gaze landed on Dugan. Her eyes widened slightly, her smile failing, but that was the only overt sign of surprise she revealed. Pretty much everyone else we'd encountered so far had moved to attack Dugan on sight. The queen only raked her cold gaze over him before turning to Falin. Either she'd been forewarned so her surprise was only that he was still in the winter court, or she was biding her time.

"Did you bring me a snake, Knight?"

Falin shook his head, still bowing. "The Shadow Prince is here as a guest to help us in our investigation."

"I was unaware we needed help." She smiled at Dugan, but it was a cruel thing, cold and menacing. "Though I imagine it would be of great help if an enemy of war were to walk right into my torture chamber. I have not spent much time in Rath recently."

"Hello to you as well, Cousin," Dugan said, inclining his head fractionally to the queen.

It was my turn to gape at him. *Cousins?* I had been told before that the nobility of Faerie were rather interconnected, and now that I looked at them, I could see some family resemblance. They had the same ebony hair with light eyes. The same sharp features, though those were common on most Sleagh Maith. I had to wonder if the Shadow King had sent the prince on this particular mission hoping the queen would show some leniency to her own cousin if he was caught in her territory. It certainly didn't sound like the family tie was helping him much.

"Declaring war prematurely would be unwise, my lady. And of the many traits I've heard attributed to you, 'unwise' has never been one of them," Dugan said. His own smile was equal parts dazzling and menacing, and I wasn't sure exactly how he accomplished that one, but it made me want to take a step away from him.

"And why would it be unwise to attack an adversary, little prince?"

And all pretense of familial friendship dropped.

"Because it appears we have a mutual enemy who would like to see us at each other's throats. If you waste your resources and energy on attacking shadow for perceived crimes, you will leave yourself weakened and an easy target for whoever it was who actually killed our fae."

"You say that as if you do not know who killed my noble. Was your courtier not found at the scene?"

Dugan inclined his head. "He was. But your knight and Alexis have found evidence that he died before your fae was killed."

"Lexi?" The queen turned the nickname she'd given me into a purred question.

Crap. I'd really been hoping I would not come under her scrutiny. I started to straighten from my curtsy, but her eyebrow shot up. Behind her, Lyell shook his head ever so minutely. Right, she hadn't released me to rise yet. I held back my sigh and hoped my legs wouldn't shake from holding the awkward position as I considered her implied question.

What Dugan had said wasn't strictly true. It wasn't a lie either, but we didn't know when Stiofan had died. Without the land of the dead, his body could have been lying in Faerie for hours or for centuries unchanged. All we really knew was that Kordon's body had been outside Faerie for a period between when he'd died and when he'd been pinned to the floor of Stiofan's room. It seemed unlikely, but it was conceivable that the goblin had been complicit in the murder, left, been killed, and then his body returned to the scene of the crime. I couldn't know for certain until we had more answers. The scene didn't add up, but that didn't exclude shadow from being behind the deaths.

"Talking to the shades will hopefully shed some light on what really happened," I finally said, committing to little.

The queen considered me, her blue eyes narrowed and her full red lips compressed in a thoughtful line. "And I suppose you wish to bargain for a payment for raising these shades?"

There was censure evident on Maeve's face at the idea, and Lyell, whom the queen couldn't see, looked worried at the queen's tone. I wasn't sure if his worry was on my behalf or simply because his day didn't go well when she was unhappy, but it didn't matter. I shook my head.

"Not necessary. Your knight has already retained my services." I didn't mention that he was splitting them with Dugan.

The queen's dark eyebrow lifted in a perfect arch.

"Has he now? How very . . . industrious of him." She turned to Falin. "Were you not the one who told me one should approach a crime scene with an open mind? And yet it sounds like you walked into the scene of our butchered noble already expecting it to be something other than it appeared."

"The message I received indicated you desired Alex's presence," Falin said, and I could almost feel the effort it took him to not look at me or Dugan. "Hiring her expedited the process and best utilized your available assets."

"Hmmm. Perhaps." The queen turned back to the papers spread over the table, her dark curls falling forward as she leaned to roll the scrolls closed. When she finished, she turned back around. Her appraising gaze cut at me, and from her expression, I came up lacking. "Lexi, my dear, we really must work on your wardrobe. Your outfit choices are always so unbecoming of a lady of your station."

She lifted her hand and my cringe made me sink deeper into my curtsy—she'd changed my street clothes to ball gowns in the past, and they didn't tend to change back.

"My clothes are very functional for my job," I stammered, hoping she'd leave them untransformed. I was rather fond of the silver sweater and leather pants. They were comfortable but dressy enough for meeting clients, in my opinion at least.

The queen tsked under her breath. "Females in the mortal realm act like pants are the only practical option." She motioned to her own gown. It was admittedly the simplest dress I'd ever seen on her. Usually the gowns she wore featured full skirts, lots of layers, corsets, silk and lace. Her current dress was of an exquisite and no-doubt-magic-made material garnished with sparkling snowflakes—real ones, not embroidered—but the material looked more substantial than her typical fare, and the dress itself was a simple sheath with splits in the skirt so her legs were unconstrained; a small silver cinch accented her waist. A scabbard hung at her side, an enormous sword sheathed there. "I could ride a horse in this. Or I could"—she lunged forward and the sword was suddenly in her hands, the tip at Dugan's neck—"slit a throat."

She hadn't drawn the sword; it had simply materialized in her hand, the move shockingly fast. Dugan stared at her, seemingly unruffled. He didn't step back or lift his own sword to deflect the blow. The moment stretched, and I realized I was holding my breath. Falin looked unconcerned, but I could see the slight tightening of the skin around his eyes and the way his shoulders stiffened despite the fact that he didn't rise from his kneeling position. He was definitely *not* relaxed.

Falin had told me not to get involved. Not to defend Dugan no matter what. But I really didn't want to watch the queen murder him in front of me. It wasn't my fault he was here—*he'd* hired *me* and insisted he wanted to observe the investigation, but he was still my client. As if reading the intent in my posture, Falin's gaze slammed into me, and he shook his head ever so slightly, a single finger lifting in a motion to wait. I hesitated, the muscles in my legs twitching either in the need to move or simply from holding the curtsy too long.

The queen and the prince stared at each other, and then a ghastly smile spread across the queen's face. She opened her hand, releasing the sword. It fell less than an inch before dissolving into a fine sprinkling of snow. The sword reappeared in her scabbard a moment later and the breath I'd been holding rushed out in a hiss of relief.

"Are you very brave or very foolish, I wonder, Cousin," the queen said, leaning back against the table. "Why are you here?"

"To prevent war," Dugan said without hesitation.

The queen considered him. She tapped her long nails on the tabletop, the quick, staccato beat the only sound in the room.

"War with shadow gains me little," she finally said, but her eyes narrowed, her cold gaze slicing into Dugan. "That does not mean I will not take this war to your doorstep if need be." She turned to me. "Lexi, question the shades. Find out who is at fault for my noble's death."

I nodded because I was still in the same damn curtsy I'd been in since we walked in, and my legs were on fire so I wasn't going to attempt to dip any deeper. I'd been hired to raise the shades; it was what I planned to do anyway, but it was good to have permission.

The queen turned back to the scrolls on her table, dismissing us. Lyell and Maeve turned toward the table as well, instantly focusing again on whatever they had been discussing before we entered. *Well, that went better than I'd feared.* Falin stood in one graceful motion. He made the movement look effortless. I, on the other hand, didn't land on my butt as I tried to straighten, but that was about the best that could be said for my effort as I tried to get my trembling legs under me. My muscles were stiff, seeming stuck from my overdrawn curtsy, and I wobbled, taking too wide a step sideways. Dugan caught my elbow, supporting me. I gave him a polite nod and stepped away from him as soon as I got my feet under me. The muscles in my legs felt like rubber bands that had been pulled too tight too long and now were the wrong size.

"Oh, Cousin," the queen called from behind us.

Crap. We'd almost been out.

We turned. The queen hadn't moved, her attention seemingly fixed on the scroll she'd unfurled across the table. She didn't look up, but her voice reached us across the room as if she were right beside us.

"If you compromise or attempt to steal my plane-weaver, Cousin, next time I will not stop my blade from tasting your spine."

Chapter 5

The bodies were waiting for us by the pillar of ice that marked the exit to the Bloom. They had been placed in black body bags and dumped unceremoniously on the floor. Nori hovered nearby, the bagged weapons in her arms, but no one else was in the hall. No one living, at least. The guards must have carried the bodies this far, but they'd vanished back to wherever they waited to ambush anyone who entered the court.

"The healer said that while the damage was not great, she could do nothing," Nori said, and while she might have still considered Kordon—or at least the shadow court he came from—a possible suspect in Stiofan's murder, there was sadness in her voice as she delivered this news. Fae didn't die often, and they didn't like death.

Dugan nodded, but he looked like he'd already been resigned to that outcome.

I frowned. There was no sign of any kind of stretcher or gurney to carry the bodies out on.

"How do we—" I started, but the answer became apparent when Falin leaned down and scooped the closest bag off the ground.

"Time to make yourself useful, Shadow Prince," he said, nodding to the second bag.

For his part, Dugan didn't protest, he just leaned down and scooped up the second bag—which totally would have not been my response if I'd been asked to carry a dead body. He had the smaller of the two bags, which I guessed must contain the goblin—it was rather jarring to not sense the whispers from the grave and know for certain. He slung the small body up, over his shoulder, and I cringed. This was totally not the proper way to handle evidence, let alone a person, but it was admittedly better than the last time we'd removed a corpse from Faerie. That time we'd walked out with a duffle bag crammed to bursting with disassembled bones.

Falin turned, heading for the pillar, Nori and Dugan following.

"Uh, are we seriously going to walk down the streets of the Magic Quarter with bodies slung over your shoulders?" I asked, not following. "We'll have SWAT after us before we reach the parking garage."

"I would assume the plan is to not be seen by mortals?" Dugan looked to Falin for confirmation. The other fae nodded and stepped forward, vanishing around the edge of the pillar. The other followed and I trudged behind.

I emerged into the Bloom last. A complete hush had fallen over the crowd, the only sound in the room the distant strands of fiddle music from the eternal dance, which I tried to ignore. There were fewer fae than when we'd passed through the first time, but there was still a big enough crowd that the silence was eerie. I could only imagine how it looked, the queen's bloody hands and the Prince of Shadows and Secrets emerging from Faerie with bodies slung over their shoulders. Every eye was on us as we wove around the tables. I stared straight ahead, but I could feel the stares, the skin between my shoulder blades tightening until I was sure it would crawl off if we didn't reach the door soon.

The sense of relief I felt once we reached the street was palpable. And bonus, less than fifteen minutes had passed in the mortal realm while we'd been inside Faerie. I couldn't sense the glamour that covered us as we walked toward the car, but no one stared at the two fae carrying body bags, so clearly it was in place.

When we reached the garage, Nori split off from us, carrying the weapons to her own car to be taken back to FIB headquarters for processing. Since they'd obviously been planted at the scene, that likely wouldn't turn up anything useful. But then again, old fae versus modern forensics might just work in our favor. Especially if they'd assumed that awful staging job would fool everyone.

After a brief debate, we loaded the bodies into the trunk and headed back to Tongues for the Dead. Did I want two dead bodies in my office? No. I wanted them in the morgue—*where dead bodies belonged.* But there would be jurisdictional red tape and official records if we took them to the city morgue. I briefly considered performing the ritual in the parking garage. I'd raised a shade for the winter court there in the past, but my office offered a permanent circle and privacy. The latter we likely could have achieved with glamour, but the former was the real tipping point. My circles weren't terribly strong, especially circles drawn in a public place with a little wax chalk. Considering one of the bodies still contained a soul, so I'd have to evict the ghost, I wanted the strongest circle I could cast. The permanent circle carved into my office floor offered me that.

"How secure are the doors into the winter court?" I asked as we drove. "Or the shadow court, for that matter?"

Falin glanced away from the road only long enough to frown at me. "The true doors of the court are very secure. Some of the borders, though . . . They are like their equivalents in the mortal realm. We try to monitor who passes through checkpoints, but sometimes people slip through."

"So assuming Kordon was the killer," I said, and when Dugan began to protest in the backseat, I held up a hand. "Yes, it looks like his body was brought to the scene, but hypothetically, if it had been him, where would he have been able to slip into winter?"

"One of the private holdings, most likely. Some land that connects to something in a neutral territory." Falin gave me a look that indicated there was something more he wanted to say but wouldn't in present company. Most likely something about the castle I currently called home. It wasn't common knowledge inside Faerie that I owned it, and he clearly didn't want to discuss it in front of Dugan. After a moment he said, "As a whole, the more important the fae, the harder it is for them to travel through different parts of Faerie. A goblin isn't terribly important, but they are rather unliked, so I wouldn't guess he'd have an easy time entering."

"But regardless, someone inside winter would have to help, right? Someone would have had to let the killer in through their own private lands?"

Falin's expression turned grim, but he nodded. It wasn't good news, and he'd likely already reached the same conclusion. Winter had a traitor in its ranks. How else would outsiders have passed through without notice?

We reached the alley in front of Tongues for the Dead before anything more could be discussed. Normally I insisted on cars being parked on the main street, but considering the guys were carrying bodies, I let it slide. I locked the door behind us and left the sign in the window that stated the investigators were currently in the field, the words followed by a phone number where potential clients could leave a voice message. While questioning a couple dead people wasn't at all unusual for me, doing it in my office was. My luck was that if I left the door open, my first real—human—client in weeks would walk in while I was midritual and subsequently flee in terror.

"Where should we put them?" Falin asked, glancing around. His gaze moved toward the love seat in the lobby, and I quickly pointed toward my office door.

"There is a circle in the far corner of the room." Not that I'd drawn it intending to raise shades in it, so it was small, meant to be a place just big enough for me to comfortably sit with maybe a few supplies to craft or recharge my charms. But it was a permanent, reinforced circle, so I'd make it work.

Dugan and Falin placed the bagged bodies in the circle. Kordon fit without issue, but Stiofan's form inside the bag was longer than the widest part of my circle, the head and foot of the bag hanging over the carefully etched line in the floor. I stared at the dark bag. I could feel the fact that the material of the bag included the pretty standard body bag spells that helped keep smells as well as all liquids inside and blocked the contents from outside magic.

Well, most witch magic, at least. I'd yet to find one that warded against grave magic. But the spells on the bag meant that the material couldn't be allowed to touch my circle—let alone cross it—or it would interfere with the barrier.

I'm going to have to touch the body.

Well, the bag at the very least. Stiofan was tall, and the large lump comprising his head rested on the edge of my circle, but there was excess bag on either side of his form. Now that we were back in the mortal realm, the grave essence reached for me, clawing at my senses, and there was no denying the lumps were anything but dead bodies. I could *feel* the weight of their deaths. Could tell without even thinking that both bags contained males and that they were old. Older than my magic knew how to calculate. With humans I could usually guess the deceased's age to within a few years, but I couldn't narrow it down to decades or even centuries for either dead fae. The grave essence coming off a murder victim or someone who died far too young always seemed to feel slightly colder, sharper, than when I encountered a body that died of natural causes, but that biting chill felt even more exaggerated with fae corpses, as if the abrupt loss of potential centuries of continued existence gave the grave essence teeth.

Falin must have seen me staring and realized why I hadn't moved or made any attempt to start the ritual. He squatted beside the foot of the bag and gently rolled the contents, moving Stiofan until the body formed a C contained inside my small circle. I shot him a relieved smile by way of thanks—I really hadn't wanted to touch the body, even through a bag.

One major problem still remained: Stiofan's soul was

inside his body. Ejecting it would be easy enough, but then it would be stuck inside my circle. Shades were harmless collections of memories, but souls transitioned to ghosts as soon as they left a body, and ghosts had wills and personalities, just like the living. While ghosts were usually fairly harmless—it took an enormous amount of energy for a ghost to interact with anything on the mortal plane— the fact that I was a convergence point between planes meant ghosts had no trouble interacting with *me*. I hadn't known this fae in life and he hadn't died peacefully. There was a good chance he'd come out angry and I would be an easy target. I did have some defenses against ghosts, but it involved draining them, causing them to cease to exist. I was hesitant to use it.

You're getting ahead of yourself. After all, maybe Stiofan would come out grateful for not being stuck in a dead body inside Faerie forever. Not likely, but possible.

I'd raise Kordon's shade first.

Activating my circle, I dropped my mental walls and removed my charm bracelet holding my additional shields. The bitingly cold wind of the land of the dead ripped through me, rustling the body bags and sending my curls flying, but my circle contained it, leaving the rest of the room untouched. Around me, the world seemed to decay. I didn't pay too much attention to the moth-eaten body bags or the rotting hardwood below them. I had a thin, bubblelike shield still encircling my psyche, and it helped prevent me from merging planes unintentionally, but if I paid too much attention to what my psyche saw in the other planes, gave it too much credence, sometimes my magic pulled it through into reality. Ms. B would be furious if I ruined the floors.

Reaching out with my magic, I channeled it into the smaller body. My magic flowed toward it quickly, greedily—it had been almost too long since I'd last raised a shade—but as soon as my magic sank below the flesh of the corpse, sharp pain zinged through me.

I yelped, stumbling backward.

"What happened?" Falin asked. He stood just outside the edge of the circle, but thankfully he hadn't touched it.

I rubbed my hand, as if the pain had been a physical thing, a prick of the finger or a slice of the palm, but it hadn't been. It was like something had hurt my grave magic. That had never happened before. I reached out with my magic again, more tentative this time. I let it trickle into the little goblin's body, waiting for the stab of pain again. The pressure of the grave pushed under my flesh and the chill warred against my living heat, but there was no unexpected pain so I released my own living heat, let it travel the path my magic had carved, sending it into the body.

A small form sat up from the bag. I hadn't known the goblin in life, but I'd seen his body. Being only memory and magic, his green leathery skin looked pale and washed-out on the shade but still had the lightest cast of green. His tunic was the same as the one we'd found him in, blood staining the front. My dislike of blood extended to ghostly projections, but my curiosity won out and I looked at his chest where the sword had emerged from his physical body. As I suspected, there was no sign of it now.

Dugan made a sound—surprise? alarm?—I wasn't sure. He'd never seen me raise a shade before. Maybe, despite his long life, he'd never seen a shade at all. I shot him a wan smile, checking to ensure that he hadn't crept any closer to the edge of my circle. Assured he wasn't about to charge my barrier, I turned back toward the little collection of memories that was Kordon's shade.

"What's your name?" I asked the shade, more from habit than need.

"Kordon the shadow-sculptor," the small shade answered, his voice much deeper than I would have expected for a fae so small. Just because he was the size of a child didn't mean I should expect him to be childlike.

I shot a glance at Falin. "You guys can hear him okay?" I asked. At his nod, I focused on the shade again. "How did you die?"

"I was in my workshop, sculpting a particularly intricate shadow. I didn't hear anyone enter, but I felt the hand land on my shoulder a second before the pain cut across my throat. I struggled, choking on blood. Darkness closed in on me." The shade said all of this without a hint of emotion touching his voice or the horror he must have experienced changing his placid expression. "Everything went still and silent. I couldn't move. Nothing sounded right. Nothing felt right. And then . . ." The shade trailed off as the memories ran their course to the end.

Dugan's brow furrowed. "And then what?"

"Normally this is where I say 'and then he died.' But in this case, I think he died a while before the 'and then' because the memories I use to create shades record until the soul leaves the body. His body was dead, so time and sensation would have been harder for his trapped soul to process." I gave a half shrug and then frowned at Dugan. "It sounds like he was murdered in the shadow court. You knew which of your fae was dead in winter before you walked into my office. Did you search your court for signs of foul play?"

Dugan's lips twisted, not quite a frown, but an expression that said either he was trying not to scowl or he was thinking about something that almost provoked a scowl. After a moment he said, "When rumors reached us that he was dead in the winter halls, I went to Kordon's home and let myself in. Nothing looked out of place. I searched for his workshop but could not locate it."

"I'm assuming you don't mean that you got lost?"

Now he did frown. "Faerie taking his workshop was enough for me to believe he was indeed missing and that the whispers of his death were true."

So as Falin had warned when we'd been in Stiofan's room, Faerie had begun reclaiming the deceased's properties. That meant we might never find the crime scene, so we needed to get as much information as we could from Kordon.

Dugan stepped up to the edge of my circle. "Kordon, you saw nothing of who attacked you?"

The shade didn't answer. Shades couldn't hear anyone but the grave witch who raised them. I rephrased the question before I repeated it.

"Did you see who attacked you?"

"No."

"Do you know who attacked you?" I asked before Dugan could form his next question because shades, having no will or personality, tended to be very literal. He could know something but not tell us because I phrased the question wrong.

"No," the shade said again.

So much for that theory.

"Did you have any unusual commissions or clients recently?" Dugan asked, and I repeated the question.

"No."

"Has anyone been displeased with your shadows?"

"No."

Well, we weren't making much progress.

Dugan asked several more questions relating to Kordon's shadow-sculpting, but there was no indication his death was related to his work. When Dugan finally ran out of questions, I interjected my own.

"Did you know Stiofan of the winter court?"

"No."

I frowned at the shade. Aside from learning the location of the first crime scene, he hadn't been helpful and I was already starting to tremble from the grave chill seeping through me. I didn't want to hold his shade much longer if he couldn't tell us more. Stiofan's body was going to be trickier and I didn't want to be exhausted if his ghost emerged enraged.

Falin stepped forward. "Goblins have exceptional noses—though you might not guess it from their poor hygiene. Ask him if he smelled anything out of place before the attack."

It was the first thing Falin had said since I began the ritual, and I repeated the question for the shade.

"Honeysuckle," the shade said. "I noticed it right before I felt the hand on my shoulder and noted that it was odd because honeysuckles don't grow in the darkness of the shadow court."

I shot a glance at Falin as the shade spoke. He looked contemplative, but he didn't offer any more questions. I didn't think honeysuckles were any more likely to grow in the frost of the winter court than they were to grow in

shadow. That definitely seemed to point to someone outside either court wanting winter and shadow at each other's
throats, but how had they moved so freely through both
courts?

"Any more questions?" I asked, glancing first at Falin
and then Dugan. Both men shook their heads. "Rest
now," I told the shade, drawing back my living heat and
magic with the words. The shade melted back into the
body bag and then it was gone.

I turned toward the other bag. With my shields open,
the bag appeared tattered and worn, the body—and the
silver glow of the soul—visible underneath. I reached outward with my magic, letting it sink into the body. The soul
inside was warm and vibrant and didn't like the frigid
touch of the grave my magic carried. It fled from me but
had nowhere to go, as the body around it was dead and
just as cold.

I shoved with my magic, and the tethers holding it to
the flesh, which were already weakened by death, snapped.
The soul rushed out of the corpse. It shimmered, almost
too bright to look at for a moment. Then the brilliance
faded and the soul transitioned to the land of the dead.
The glow dimmed, the form solidifying into a ghost. Stiofan's ghost's arms flew up and he ducked, cowering as if
hiding from a blow—which was likely the last thing he'd
done before his body had died around him.

I reached for the ghost with my magic, let my psyche's
invisible fingers tangle around him, ready to drain off
energy if he charged me. At the same time, with the same
invisible net of power, I exerted just enough magic to
make the ghost visible to Falin and Dugan.

"Stiofan?" I said, keeping my voice calm, level.

The ghost jumped at his name, cringing back from me.

He didn't have many places to go. The circle was small and most of the space was filled with body bags.

"Stiofan, you're safe. No one here wants to hurt you." Which was true enough. He'd already suffered pretty much the worst thing that could happen to him. I could pull the very energy from his soul, but I wouldn't as long as he didn't threaten me. So, aside from the already-being-dead part, he was in pretty good shape.

Stiofan lowered his arms, peeking over his clenched fists, but he remained crouched. His nearly translucent eyes were wide, flickering quickly as if he was trying to look at everything, but likely seeing nothing in his panic. I didn't hold that against him. He'd been murdered recently. If there was ever a reason to panic, that topped the list.

Unlike Kordon's shade, who'd manifested looking like the very last memory his body recalled before the soul vacated, Stiofan's ghost showed no sign of the trauma he'd suffered before death. His clothes were clean of blood and were some sort of dated court ensemble I could only summon the world "frippery" to describe. The ghost sported no visible wounds and, aside from the cowering, looked like he'd been through nothing worse than the strong wind still whipping through the circle. While shades were a corpse's memories given shape by my magic, a ghost was a soul's energy given shape by their own willpower. Ghosts tended to be how a person saw themselves instead of a true representation of how they looked. They had all the knowledge and personality of the person they had been—were the essence of the person they had been, sans body. And just as with a living person, my magic had absolutely no control over them.

"Stiofan," I said again, crouching down to his level.

The bag holding Kordon's body was between us, and I had no intention of stepping over it. One, I didn't like the idea of crawling over a dead body, and two, I might need that extra space if Stiofan switched from flight to fight in his panic. I could have touched Stiofan, offered that very human reassurance of a sympathetic hand on his shoulder. But neither of us was human, and just because I was a grave witch and he was dead didn't mean I had any more ability to comfort this stranger than if he had been alive. "Stiofan, can you hear me? No one here is your enemy."

His frantic gaze landed on me and caught long enough that he actually saw me. He jumped, scrambling back until his ass hit the edge of my circle, stopping him. Being stopped by what likely seemed to him to be nothing more than thin air jolted him again, and he fell back against it, his shoulders and head slamming into the barrier.

A permanently etched and frequently used circle was stronger than a temporary one, even with my weak mastery of witchy magic, so while I could feel the feedback in the barrier, it didn't so much as shudder. That didn't mean I wanted the ghost to stay plastered against the edge of the circle. Stiofan would eventually overload the circle, and probably get a lot of his energy sapped in the process.

"I'm Alex Craft. I mean you no harm."

The ghost blinked at me. The panic was still written in every tense line of his face and jerky movement of his hands, but a spark of recognition lit in his eyes. He stilled, wrapping his arms across his chest, and thankfully leaned away from the edge of my circle. "You, you're the queen's planeweaver."

I opened my mouth to dispute the Winter Queen's

claim to me, but then I squashed the urge. The distinction wasn't important for this interview. I forced what I hoped was a reassuring smile.

The ghost's gaze moved past me, and I saw the small cringe, the slight hitch of his shoulders, and the compression of his lips when he spotted Falin. If he'd reacted to almost anyone else that way I would have been suspicious that they might be involved with his death, but I'd seen the court fae around Falin before. While the independent fae feared him because he enforced the queen's will, the court fae despised him because he carried the entire court's shed blood. Every death from every duel or execution throughout the court's history had been passed to the queen's knight and then from knight to knight, leaving the courtiers spotless. It granted Falin, as the current knight, some magical benefits in everything from endurance and healing to strength, speed, and skill. But it made him the pariah of the court. He was a reminder of the fact that while the fae may be extremely long-lived, they were not immortal. That unfair stigma and disdain was what I saw in Stiofan's face when he looked at Falin, a prejudice he'd likely held for centuries and long before Falin was born or became the current Winter Knight.

Little late to fear mortality now. But some habits were too entrenched to let a little thing like his own death interfere or change.

His gaze moved on, and as soon as it landed on the Shadow Prince, his shoulders slammed into my circle again as he tried to backpedal.

"Stiofan, this is Prince Dugan of shadow. I am helping him and the winter court get to the bottom of what happened to you."

Stiofan glanced at me, and for a moment, incomprehension animated his features. Then he straightened and stood. The movement was graceful with no sign of the jerky panic that had flooded him the moment before. His hands moved to the frilly ruffles peeking out from the cuffs of his coat, straightening and fluffing them. As he did, I could all but see the layers of arrogant confidence close around him like a type of armor. By the time he looked up again, it was to scan the room and its occupants with the aloof disdain I was quite familiar with seeing on the faces of court fae.

"What manner of horrible little hovel have you brought me to? I demand to know the reason I am here."

"This is my office. You're here so we can ask you some questions."

Stiofan sneered and flicked—almost certainly imaginary—dust from his fine jacket. "I have no interest in answering questions and I demand you return me to the court at once. Either way I will be taking this up with the queen, but perhaps my language will be kinder if you release me quickly."

Good luck with that one. Not only would the queen not be able to see or hear him without me, but without a land of the dead, he couldn't exist in Faerie. I glanced at Falin and Dugan. The former scowled at Stiofan, not aggressively but as if he considered the dead fae's disdain a waste of time. Dugan, on the other hand, looked so carefully blank and unconcerned that his expressionless mask betrayed that he was hiding his reaction. Shock? As he'd never seen a ghost before. Anger? As this particular ghost was an ass. I wasn't sure.

Technically, I didn't need Stiofan's ghost to answer any questions. I just needed it out of the way so I could get to his shade. Raising his shade in front of his ghost seemed a little callous, but if he was going to be an obstinate jerk, I might not have many options. Shades had to answer me. Ghosts could do whatever the hell they wanted.

"What is the last thing you remember?" I asked, giving the ghost one last chance to cooperate.

He tilted his chin so that he appeared to look down on me despite being nearly the same height. "I recall being assaulted in my bedchambers. I assume I have you three miscreants to thank for that." He sneered at me. "I don't care how special the queen thinks you are; when she hears that you've captured one of her nobles and used some sort of magic to hold me against my will . . . Well, let's just say I wouldn't want to be you. I doubt you'll see the outside of Rath this century. Kidnapping a noble—"

I attempted to interrupt him. "One, that isn't what is happening here," I said, lifting first one finger and then following it with a second. "And two, we have the queen's—"

He wasn't about to allow me to cut him off, but spoke louder. "—is a near unforgivable offense, which you might know if you weren't a glorified feykin pretending to be a true-blooded Sleagh Maith. Now release me from your ridiculous spell before I grow truly angry and make you wish you hadn't hesitated. In fact—"

My teeth snapped shut, the irritation clawing at me as cutting as the wind whipping around the circle. Apparently I wasn't the only one sick of listening to Stiofan insult and threaten me.

"You're dead, you pompous prick," Falin said. The words were soft, but clear. Spoken much quieter than Stiofan's haughty threats. And yet they shut the ghost up immediately, his sentence left incomplete.

"Is that a threat, Knight?" Stiofan still had his chin raised, his expression frozen in disdainful irritation, but there was a slight quiver in his hands, and his Adam's apple wobbled when he swallowed.

"The Winter Knight is being quite literal," Dugan said. "You died, thus you are dead. No threat. Just a statement."

Stiofan's ghost shot a skeptical glance from Dugan to Falin before shaking his head. "What manner of vicious prank is this? And how are you managing to tell such falsehoods? Am I victim to some spell you've concocted to allow lies past your lips? I'm not dead. That is easily evident. I'm . . ." He lifted his hands, looking at them. "Fine." He frowned, flipping his hands over and then back again. "I'm fine?" The second time he said it, there was clear uncertainty in his voice. His gaze moved down until it landed on the body bag near his feet.

The body bag containing his own body.

He stared at it for one drawn-out moment while I tried to figure out what to say. With him having gone from panicked and cowering to imperiously disdainful, I was less inclined to try to make any attempt to comfort the ghost. At the same time, his realization that he'd been killed was unfolding in front of me, and it was painful to watch.

Stiofan knelt and reached for the body bag. His hand wavered a moment, and then it thrust forward all at once, reaching for the zipper as though if he didn't grab it right at that moment, he would lose his nerve and never be able to touch it at all.

His hand passed through the zipper, disappearing into the sealed bag. He yelped and jerked his hand back as if stung. I doubted it had actually hurt him—though it was his own body in the bag, so maybe that changed the rules of interaction—but most likely it was surprise that the world around him wasn't tangible that had caused his reaction.

"What deceit is this?" he asked, his angry, disbelieving gaze slamming into me.

"It's true. You died, tonight presumably." My words came out kinder than I felt, which I was rather proud of. "You were attacked in your bed. We are investigating your murder."

Chapter 6

Being a ghost, Stiofan couldn't actually blanch—he lacked the blood supply—but he wobbled as if he might faint. "I'm dead?" He looked smaller now, the self-importance he'd been holding himself up with deflated. "How . . . ?"

"You mentioned being attacked," I prompted. "Can you tell us what you remember?"

His gaze took a long time to focus on me, as if he was gazing through all the could-have-beens that had been lost with his death. "Pain."

"What?" Dugan asked.

"Pain. It was what woke me." Stiofan's lower lip trembled with the words, and he caught it between his teeth, stilling it. "Someone held my arms above my head, pinning them down. A pillow was over my face. And the pain, lancing through me, over and over. It was like a nightmare that wouldn't end."

Shades, being only magic and memory with no soul,

might have been unaffected by reciting the events of their deaths, but ghosts had no such buffer. They were souls, the very essence of the person they had been. And the horror of his death played over Stiofan's face as he spoke. His arms wrapped across his chest, and he seemed to shrink with each word and each remembered stab.

By the time he fell silent, it wasn't just his snobbish attitude that had vanished, but the court finery was gone as well. He now wore bloody nightclothes, the slashes wet and seeping. His death had become his reality, warping him until he was stuck in the terror of those moments, at least temporarily. I'd never seen it happen before, but then ghosts weren't exactly common.

"Could you tell how many people were present?" Falin asked, and thankfully his voice was soft. I'd heard him use the tone with victims before. Stiofan was an entitled ass, but he was also a victim, and he was vulnerable right now.

The ghost frowned, wrapping his arms tighter around himself. Half-transparent blood streamed down the front of his nightclothes and dripped on the floor below. "Two at least. Maybe three. Maybe more?"

"Could you identify anyone?" Falin asked.

Stiofan shook his head.

"Was there a goblin with three arms?" This question from Dugan. I frowned at him. Hadn't we already determined Kordon had been dropped in Stiofan's room postmortem?

Stiofan's head shot up and he glared at Dugan. "I don't know. I had a pillow over my head! Is that who did this to me? One of your dirty goblins?"

I answered before Dugan got a chance. "Your murderers wanted us to think so. A goblin was found a few feet from your body with your sword driven through his back. Considering you said your arms were pinned, I'm assuming . . . ?"

He gave a mournful shake of his head. "I wish I could say I struck down one of my attackers, but I struggled, never freeing myself before I . . ." He hesitated. ". . . Died." He sank to the ground, a dejected, nihilistic figure abjectly accepting the idea of nonexistence.

"Is there anything you can tell us about your attackers?" Falin asked, clearly trying to get the ghost talking again before he sank so far into despondency that he ceased to hear us.

The ghost sneered, his face torn between melancholy and rage. "They are cowardly scum and I hope you kill them as surely as I was killed."

Not exactly a helpful clue we can use to find them.

"Did any of your attackers say anything?" Falin asked.

Stiofan closed his eyes, as if concentrating hard. New wounds appeared on the ghost, translucent blood pooling at his feet. His eyes sprang open, wide, haunted, and he hugged himself.

"I . . . I don't think so." His words came out hoarse, tinged with panic.

Falin continued to press him for useful clues. "Could you smell anything out of place? Hear anything odd?"

The ghost rocked back on his heels as his shoulders rolled inward, like he could curl into himself for protection. A wound opened near his collarbone, ghostly blood spraying outward and missing me by mere inches. "I don't think so. I don't want to think about it anymore."

Dugan stepped close to the edge of my circle. "I'm not sure he is our best witness," he said, his voice low— though, as small as my circle was, Stiofan could surely hear. Dugan shot a meaningful glance to the body bag near the ghost's feet.

I had to give the Shadow Prince credit; for someone who had—presumably—seen his first shade only today, he understood the principles of the magic pretty well. Stiofan was caught in the trauma of his death, and it was clouding the details of the event. His shade wouldn't suffer the same issue. Of course, raising his shade in front of him might very well expand on his trauma.

"Stiofan, I think you've done enough. I'm going to open my circle and let you leave, okay?"

The ghost's head snapped up. "Leave? Where am I supposed to go? I'm dead! You deal with ghosts. I demand you find a place for me where I will be comfortable and happy. And certainly somewhere less run-down than this hovel you call an office."

Now that he was temporarily distracted from the details of his murder, the wounds vanished from the ghost, his court frippery appearing once again, and he sneered at me, seeming to look down his nose even from his lower vantage of the floor. I frowned at him. My office was actually fairly nice now that Ms. B had decorated it. Of course, he was viewing it in the land of the dead, which was pretty much a disintegrating purgatory landscape, so it probably did look pretty shabby, especially when compared to the grandeur of Faerie. But he wasn't going to escape the land of the dead. Not until his soul moved on, and he needed to find a soul collector for that to happen.

I knew a few collectors. I had even dated one of them. Unfortunately, I had no idea how to locate Death—which wasn't actually his name, but I had to call him something. Too many secrets. That was one reason my relationship with Death hadn't worked. Even the passing thought of him still stung and I pushed it away.

There was one collector whom I could typically find if I tried.

"There is a nightclub I can direct you to. A soul collector hangs out there when she isn't busy. Might be a little early in the day for her, but I'm sure she'll be around eventually. Or you can hang out at a hospice care center. A collector will almost certainly be around there from time to time."

The ghost's lip curled, the look contemptuous. "Soul collectors? I don't want to be collected, you twit. If I cannot return to Faerie, you need to find me a place to live, as it were."

Yeah. No. There was no estate for the mortality-challenged that I had secret access to. My castle hosted quite a mixed group of occupants these days, two of them ghosts that had more or less followed me home during cases, but I was not about to adopt Stiofan. With his attitude, I'd end up having to kill him a second time.

"Not in my job description," I said as I pulled the energy out of my circle. The barrier collapsed and the grave wind that had been contained ripped across my office, ruffling papers and tousling Falin's and Dugan's hair. The ghost stared at me, and I gave him a smile that I didn't even waste energy trying to make look friendly. "I'm going to continue my investigation into your murder. You might find this next bit rather disturbing. If you don't want to witness it, I suggest you leave."

He looked from me to the body bag at his feet. "Are you going to do something to my body? How dare you."

The ghost took a step forward, and Falin was suddenly there, standing between the ghost and me, his silver daggers drawn. It was a sweet gesture—not necessarily practical, as Stiofan would only become tangible if I expended magic, or, I guess, if he touched me. But the thought was nice.

From the corner of my eye, something dark moved in the shadows. I snapped my head around, searching.

Nothing.

I glanced at Dugan, but he was watching the ghost. If he'd had anything to do with the thing in the shadows, it didn't show. Whatever it was, I needed to recast my circle pronto.

"Get out, or stay. I don't care. You have five seconds to choose." I only half looked at the ghost as I spoke, most of my attention directed toward where I'd thought I'd seen movement.

"Five."

The ghost didn't move, but stared at me, his chin jutting up and out.

"Four."

Falin still stood between the ghost and me, but the ghost ignored him, his incredulous expression daring me to try to kick him out. But I didn't need him gone. Dismissing him was for his own benefit.

"Three."

The shadows shifted again, this time closer. I reacted immediately, throwing magic into my circle. The barrier flashed into existence; a low sizzle and a few sparks shot across the edge closest to the corner of the room.

"Hey! You didn't make it all the way to one," Stiofan yelled, taking a step forward.

I didn't even look at him. "Shut up."

Something moved at the edge of the circle, drawing

back. The magical barrier calmed, the sparks fading. I'd thwarted it, thrown the circle up in time, but what the hell was it? Something not quite on the mortal plane, but I couldn't see it any clearer with my shields open, so not something from the land of the dead or the Aetheric plane either.

Falin's gaze followed mine, and he gestured with his blade from the edge of the circle to Dugan. "Is that your shadow spy?"

"Why would I spy on myself?" Dugan asked, but he peered into the dark recesses of the room.

The Prince of Shadows lifted his hands, and the predictable shadows cast by my file cabinet, the dog bed, and other items in the corner of the room quivered. Then the shadows pulled away from the corner. Well, most of the shadows. One small blob of darkness remained frozen in the farthest corner. A shadow not cast by any object in the room.

It had no features, but the shape was vaguely humanoid, though small. Seven inches at most and thin, as if cast by something much smaller in late-afternoon sun when the shadows stretched long. It hunched down as it realized the shadows it had been hiding in had vanished. Its spindly neck seemed to turn, the stretched head swiveling back and forth.

Dugan twisted his hands, his fingers straightening and reaching toward each other. The room's shadows rushed back into the corner. They wrapped around the stretched shadow, twisting into dark vises that caught it and pinned it in place. The strange shadow quivered and thrashed, but it was stuck.

"What a repulsive creature." Stiofan spat the words,

and I frowned at him. Unless he could see something I couldn't, it was just a shadow, hardly repulsive at all. Though that didn't mean it wasn't dangerous.

Dugan stalked across the room, shadows twisting around him as he moved. If I'd been the small shadow staring at the approaching prince, I would have been terrified. When he reached the corner, he snatched the thrashing shadow as if it were more than just an absence of light but had true substance and mass.

"Who are you? And who sent you?"

The shadow trembled in his hand. Dugan lifted the shadow closer to his face. The natural Sleagh Maith glow of his skin brightened with his magic, but his dark hair and armor seemed to drink down the light and become a living shadow of their own. It was an eerie and fascinating juxtaposition.

I strained to hear if the shadow answered, but the only sound in the room was the unarticulated grumbling from Stiofan. Beside me, Falin was still, silent, and just as intent on the shadow as I was.

The small shadow convulsed, and then it folded in half, draping over the back of Dugan's hand. I frowned because that didn't look natural. Then the little shadow dissolved, growing thinner until we could see Dugan's fingers through its body, and then it vanished into nothing.

"You killed it?" Falin asked, his voice guarded, suspicious.

Dugan shook his head as he turned to stare at each shadow in the room. They wavered under his scrutiny, but the movement was from his searching magic, not from an another intruder. "No. It was nothing I did. And I'm not sure if it self-destructed or if whoever sent it had a fail-safe spell in place in case it got caught."

"Was it an imp or a crafted shadow?" Falin asked. His daggers were still out and bared as he watched Dugan's survey of the room.

"That was a shadow master's handiwork—an imp would have left a body."

"So . . . someone from your court?" I asked.

Dugan shot me a frown. "Not necessarily." He waved his hand in the air and every shadow—except those inside my circle—scurried up the walls to meet in a giant ball on the ceiling.

It was disorienting, and I swayed, wishing there were something to grab hold of inside my circle. Falin offered his arm, but the dizzying effect had already passed, so I shook my head. I glanced around at a room now absent of darkness. Not a single disembodied shadow remained, so I assumed that meant there were no more spies hiding in my office.

Dugan's hands twitched, and the shadows streamed back where they belonged. This time I did grab Falin's arm. He made no comment about it, but both Dugan and Stiofan frowned at me. I ignored them.

"If it wasn't 'necessarily' someone from the shadow court, who could have created it? And what was it doing here?" I asked, dropping my hand as soon as the shadows stilled and the disorientation passed.

"It appeared to be attempting to join either your or the knight's shadow, likely so it could follow you around and report back to its controller," Dugan said, his frown deepening. "As to who could have been controlling it . . . the list isn't exactly short right now."

"Right now in particular?" I asked, shivering, but not because something could jump into my shadow and spy on me. Not entirely at least. My shields were still open, the grave clawing deep into me with icy fingers. If I was going to raise that second shade, I needed to get on with it.

Stiofan scoffed. "'Right now' because his courtiers are fleeing that cesspool of a court like rats from a sinking ship."

Dugan shot the ghost a look that might have been able to do serious damage if Stiofan hadn't already been dead. Beside me, Falin discreetly lifted one shoulder, cocking his head ever so slightly in what I could only interpret as a *sort of* expression. Apparently he didn't disagree with Stiofan's assessment.

Maybe Falin's motions were not quite as discreet as I'd thought, because Dugan all but growled out the words, "There has been *some* turnover of late. And I will look into who might have constructed our interloping shadow, but in the meantime, perhaps we should wrap up your interview?"

He wasn't wrong about that.

I glanced at Stiofan and Falin, both trapped in my circle with me. I didn't really want to drop my barrier again. Not because I thought another shadow would attempt to ambush me but because I didn't want to expend the energy. I'd given Stiofan a chance to leave already; he'd missed it. He was going to have to deal with the consequences.

Reaching with my grave magic, I let it slide into the corpse at the ghost's feet. The shade sat up, bloody and disheveled. Stiofan screamed.

"What is this? Is that me? This is dark magic." He scrambled to the edge of my circle, but he could get no farther.

I ignored him.

"What is your name?" I asked the shade.

"Stiofan Greenmeadows."

I lifted an eyebrow. Last names were rather rare in Faerie, but more than that, "Greenmeadows" didn't exactly sound like it should belong to a winter courtier.

"You weren't born to the winter court?" I asked.

"How is that relevant?" the ghost of Stiofan snapped, but his shade merely answered, "no."

"How did you die?"

Ghost Stiofan glared at me. "Didn't we cover that already? I—you don't have to answer that."

His shade didn't notice the protests of the soul that had once resided in his body. "I was sleeping when pain woke me. I was pinned and stabbed repeatedly. I heard things breaking. Hands reached inside me and I lost consciousness."

The shade said it with no emotion, no fear or hesitation. Stiofan clearly felt the horror at the words, though, based on the way wounds opened on the ghost once again. He swayed, the front of his nightshirt filling with blood.

"Stop it," he whispered. But I wasn't sure if he was talking to me or his shade.

"Did you see any of your attackers?"

"No."

"Could you tell how many attackers were present?"

"No," the shade said, and I grimaced. He had answered the question I'd asked, just not the one I'd meant to ask.

"Can you guess how many attackers there were?" Falin asked, and I repeated the question, even though I knew it was unlikely to be answered.

The shade remained silent. He wasn't cognizant. He couldn't guess anything, couldn't draw any conclusions Stiofan hadn't considered or concluded before his death.

For his part, the ghost shook, blood pooling around him as he watched his shade.

"Did you hear or smell anything out of place? Did any of your attackers speak?"

"Yes. A female. She said, 'Don't make it too fast. He should suffer.'"

The ghost stared at his shade. "That . . . I do remember that. It sounded like . . ." He trailed off, sliding down the edge of my circle until he was sitting in the ephemeral pool of blood spreading around him.

"Who did it sound like?" I asked.

"Lunabella Blossommist," both the shade and ghost said at the same time. Without looking up, Stiofan added, "My onetime wife."

Well, that was a start. It wasn't a definite ID, or the shade would have identified her as an attacker, but it was a name.

Chapter 7

∗⊸——◦ ◦——⊸∗

The shade didn't have much more information. Dugan and Falin both pelted me with questions to ask, but Stiofan hadn't seen, heard, or in any other way sensed anything else about his attackers. Stiofan's ghost hadn't said anything after identifying Lunabella. He had simply curled in on himself at the edge of my circle and stared at some point of nothingness.

He still hadn't moved by the time I wrapped up the ritual, put the shade back into his body, and released my circle. Ghostly blood dripped from the many wounds covering his spectral body, so I guessed he was still caught in the details of his own death. I wondered if he would make it out again or if this experience had broken him completely.

For my part, the ritual had cost me some sight and warmth, but while I'd kept my shields open for an extended period, the time I'd actually raised the shades wasn't long, so I still had some of my vision. I wouldn't want to drive a car right now, or have to run for my life, but I could cross the room without running into anything or anyone, so that was something.

I shrugged into my coat and sent a small spiral of magic into the enchantment Rianna had recently placed on the fabric. It immediately warmed, pouring gentle heat into me. The chill of the grave had sunk all the way to my bones, so it only helped a little, but it was better than nothing. Slightly warmer and with at least partial vision, I glanced at Falin.

"So we have the smell of honeysuckle in the shadow court, and possibly a fae named Lunabella in the winter court. Is she a winter fae?"

Falin shook his head. "I've never heard of her."

"Lunabella Blossommist," Dugan said, tapping one long finger against his lips, his gaze distant as if digging through very old memories. "Summer court is the court most enamored with having several names, so she was probably born to that court. I would guess that was where your Stiofan originated as well, but as he has since left, it is possible she has moved on as well."

It was a place to start, at least.

"Summer, huh. Think she smells of honeysuckle?" I asked, pulling my coat tighter around me.

Falin lifted one shoulder in a slight shrug. "It seems more plausible than shadow or winter, certainly."

"So then, how do we go about questioning a courtier from summer?"

"Now that," Dugan said, giving me a small nod, "is a very good question."

"I'm guessing walking into the summer court and asking to question Lunabella would not go over well?" I said as

I stared at the coffeemaker in my office, willing it to brew faster. I was tempted to swap the pot for my coffee mug, but Falin and Dugan were present so it wouldn't exactly be polite. "What is the normal protocol when you suspect someone from another court of murder? And please don't say 'war.' That would be too big an overreaction for even me to believe."

One edge of Falin's lips tilted up at my last sentence, but it was a rueful amusement. It didn't give me a whole lot of hope. "No, war is not the typical first response," he said.

"Fae are long-lived and generally avoid anything that could endanger that longevity." Dugan lifted his hands, his long fingers sliding gracefully through the air as he spoke, accenting his words. "Wars involve casualties. While there are several ancient battlegrounds from wars nearly forgotten in Faerie, the courts haven't been in a conflict that involved a true war for as long as anyone can remember. War, true war, has been forbidden by the high king. The costs are too great."

"He's not wrong," Falin said. "Even I have seen the ancient battlefields littered with the bodies of the dead."

Yeah, and that was definitely a downside to no land of the dead. Entire areas of Faerie where the blood and bodies were forever fresh on the soil. And all the souls stuck forever in those sightless, motionless, undecaying shells. I shivered before fixing my gaze on Dugan again. "And yet you state that your reason for being here is to prevent war?"

"The shadows of Faerie have been whispering of war for some time. It is coming. All of Faerie may well be caught in it. I want to make sure my court survives."

"Are the whispers prophecy?" The stream of coffee slowed, and I snatched the pot before pouring a tall mug for myself and two paper cups for the guys. "Or are they overheard discussions?"

Dugan accepted his cup and shrugged. "A little of both. Most prophecies make their way to our halls. Secrets too."

"If it's forbidden, how could it happen? Doesn't Faerie more or less enforce rules and taboos on its denizens?"

"Yes, but the high king hasn't been seen or heard from since shortly after the Magical Awakening. Some say he is losing his hold on Faerie, and if that is the case, his laws will no longer bind us." Dugan lifted his coffee and sniffed the contents of his paper cup. His expression didn't change, but he didn't drink any either. "Had shadow's courtier ended up in any other season, I would not worry so strongly that these deaths might be the tipping point that starts a war, but winter has . . . not been herself recently. Her rule—and ability to rule—might be in question, so she out of all the courts seems the most likely to act unpredictably."

Dugan said all of this casually, as if discussing the weather or some inconsequential matter, but I noticed that he never looked at Falin as he spoke. For his part, Falin's icy glare cut at Dugan, but he didn't correct him or jump to defend his court or queen. I supposed he couldn't have, as he'd said much the same to me about the queen only a couple hours earlier.

"At the rate at which the whispers of war are buzzing in the shadows, the high king's law will not hold back war much longer," Dugan said, still looking only at me. "I do not believe it is a question of 'if' it is coming. Only when and where."

"Well, that is ominous." And bad. I wasn't truly part of any court, and I didn't know how war in Faerie would affect me as an independent, but war anywhere was never good. Innocents would die.

And Falin would most certainly be caught in the middle of any war involving winter. The very idea made things in my stomach twist uncomfortably.

I took a long sip of my coffee. It was almost too hot for comfort, but I barely noticed. "So then back to my first question: How do we question a member of the summer court? There has to be some precedent for this."

Falin nodded. "We can ask the Summer King's permission to question his subject. And if that isn't granted, a duel is the best avenue available."

I nearly choked on the coffee. "Six months ago, a duel wouldn't have even entered a conversation as a likely possibility, let alone be described as a 'best avenue' for anything."

"Then you had a charmed childhood," Dugan said. There was no malice or sarcasm in the words. He meant them.

I'd never thought of my childhood as particularly good. My father claimed that sending me away, disowning me, and the spell he'd locked my true nature away with had all been done to protect me. I'd thought he'd been full of shit and just didn't want the hassle, but maybe he really was shielding me from the darker sides of Faerie. I tucked that line of thought away for another time and focused on the problem at hand.

"So how would that work? We would duel her for the right to question her as a suspect?"

"No, one of us would have to challenge her for answers. Three, traditionally," Falin said, and I frowned. "It wouldn't be ideal, but there are few resources for crossing court lines without the monarch's permission."

"We could question her at the solstice celebration that starts tonight," I suggested.

"*If* she attends," Dugan said, setting his untouched coffee on the edge of my desk. "And that's a big 'if,' as she might not if she has committed crimes against winter. If she attends and we question her, even if she confessed to the murder, there would be nothing we could do but wish her to be merry because of the truces enacted around the celebration."

"And you can bet she would be impossible to reach after the celebration in that case," Falin added. "Better to pin her down when we are in a position that the queen could demand recompense of the Summer King."

I wasn't sure exactly what "recompense" would be when it came to a murdered courtier, but clearly stalling until tonight wasn't an option. "Wouldn't she be dead if you dueled?"

Falin shook his head. "Very few duels are to the death. Most are only until third blood or until one party yields. A duel for secrets would probably only be until first blood."

"So a duel to question a suspect." I shook my head, scoffing, and then said under my breath, "You better have three damn good questions. Who knew you could duel for answers?"

Dugan frowned at me. "You can duel for anything. Love, land, position, or yes, secrets."

I blinked at him. "So how do you stop the strongest from taking everything?"

He stared at me, his expression torn between surprise at the question and disbelief that I could be so naive.

Right. Nothing.

Nothing at all prevented the strongest from taking everything from the weak.

That realization must have been written across my face, because Falin inclined his head slightly before saying, "The weak attach themselves to the strong for protection. Even then, for most it is safest to own nothing made of anything more valuable than glamour. And if one does have something of value, to hide it away so that no one else decides it is worth fighting for."

"That's barbaric."

"That is the way it has always been." Dugan shrugged away the unfairness of it all. "But before we resign ourselves to dueling, we should ask the Summer King for permission to question Lunabella. Luck might favor us."

Falin glanced at Dugan. "I don't suppose you can contact the summer court?"

The Shadow Prince frowned and looked around. Not seeing what he sought, he turned to me. "Do you have a mirror?"

"In the bathroom." I pointed vaguely in the direction of the small restroom attached to the Tongues for the Dead lobby. Dugan turned, heading in the direction I had pointed. I frowned after him. Despite his run-in with the Winter Queen and his brief exposure to the grave wind blowing off the land of the dead, he didn't have so much as a single dark hair out of place. He certainly didn't look like he needed to gussy up for his conversation with the Summer King. Then again, he was a prince calling on another monarch. Appearances likely did matter.

He paused when he reached the door to my office and glanced back. "Are you coming?"

"To the bathroom with you? No," I said, finishing my

coffee. I glanced at the cooling cup he'd abandoned on my desk. Dugan hadn't actually drunk any. It would probably be fine for me to liberate it.

"Not the bathroom. To the *mirror*." Dugan emphasized the last word.

Yeah . . . I got the feeling he wasn't suggesting I fix my hair. Abandoning the coffee, I led everyone to the small bathroom. The tiny room was all but claustrophobic for one long-legged person, whose knees would inevitably hit the sink while sitting on the commode. It definitely wasn't made for three.

Dugan shot the small space a dubious look from the doorway. "There's no other mirror?"

"Maybe a hand mirror somewhere." Rianna likely had one in her spell kit, but I didn't want to dig through it without permission.

"That would be too small. This is barely large enough as it is." He indicated the oval-shaped mirror. It was slightly larger than a dinner plate and some of the reflective material had flaked off the back, leaving dark spots. "We will make do."

He stepped into the small bathroom, and then seemed unsure where to go to make room for the rest of us. Ultimately he stepped over the toilet, squeezing into the far corner beside the mirror. Falin gestured for me to go next, but there wasn't really anywhere to go. Once Falin joined us, even though he pressed himself against the wall, I had to lean forward with one foot balanced on the toilet seat so that I could see the mirror around him. I could have sat on the back of the commode, but then I would have been brushing up against both men. If I was going to share personal bubbles with anyone, I'd prefer to keep it to just Falin.

Dugan pressed his hand to the mirror, and shadows crawled over the surface, swirling and slithering until nothing of the room was reflected in the darkness coating the glass. Once the mirror was nothing more than inky blackness, Dugan called out, "We seek an audience with the Summer King."

Nothing happened.

I waited, watching the twisting shadows. Still nothing happened. I glanced at Falin, but he was staring at the mirror. I waited what felt like ten minutes, until my leg was cramping and I was considering sitting on the commode anyway.

"Is something supposed to happen?" I finally asked.

"It is happening," Dugan said, not lifting his hand from the mirror or glancing away.

We waited a few more minutes and I fidgeted with my coat sleeve. The charm in it had already powered down. It wasn't completely exhausted, but it would take some time to recharge before I could use it again. I didn't need it right now anyway. I was very aware of the heat from Falin's body pressed against my side.

"Are you sure this is working?" I asked, as I tried to figure out if I could switch which leg I had propped up without falling down. Not that I had room to fall.

"While it is almost incomprehensible in the mortal world of cell phones, instant communication isn't exactly popular in Faerie." Falin breathed the words into my hair. And I knew that was true enough. In the past when I'd needed to get a message to someone in Faerie, I'd scrawled a letter on a leaf. A mirror did seem slightly better. If it worked.

"Also, he is a king," Dugan whispered. "Taking his time is his prerogative."

"And wasting it is a foolish and dangerous endeavor," a booming voice said from inside the inky darkness covering the mirror.

The glass cleared, but instead of reflecting the three of us crammed in the small bathroom, it filled with what I thought at first was just an image of the sky. Near the bottom of the mirror was a picturesque scene of fae in wildflowers surrounded by several trees lazily blowing in a gentle wind. A faun played a set of pipes near the very edge of the mirror's view; a woman with green skin and brilliant purple flowers growing in her hair played a harp beside him. A group of women who had bark for skin danced to the music, dragging with them a young man with shaggy dark hair who looked suspiciously human. Near the bottom of the mirror was a man lounging among the flowers. He was shirtless, his skin a tanned gold and his chestnut brown curls glowing with gold and red highlights in the afternoon sunshine. A small crown of twisting green vines was almost lost among the curls. A delicate-looking fae lay with her head in his lap, her eyes closed and peaceful, her shimmering butterfly wings fluttering softly in her slumber. Another fae sat behind him, weaving small forget-me-not flowers into his curls.

"A prince, a knight, and . . ." The king leaned forward, peering hard at me through the glass of the mirror. "What might you be?"

"An investigator," I said at the same time Dugan said, "The planeweaver."

I tried to hide a cringe, but the king's chestnut eyebrow rose. He waved off the fae decorating his hair and leaned even closer to the mirror, filling most of it so that we could only see slips of a cloudless sky around him.

"Now, that does make this call more interesting." His

gaze swept around the small room. "Where are you calling me from? That is surely neither the shadow nor winter court."

"We are in a less-than-ideal spot in the mortal realm," Dugan said.

"And your monarchs know you are contacting me?"

I didn't shoot a nervous glance at Falin, but it was a near thing.

Dugan, however, didn't miss a beat. "We are acting within the instructions we were given."

And *that* was why getting an honest answer out of fae was damn difficult. Not being able to lie didn't mean the truth you got out of them wouldn't imply a lie. Dugan was instructed to stop a war by the Shadow King, and we were charged with finding Stiofan's killer by the Winter Queen, so we were, in fact, following the tasks we'd been given. But neither monarch had sanctioned—or even knew we were—contacting the summer court. And I was pretty sure the Winter Queen wouldn't approve.

"I see," the Summer King said, measuring Dugan's words.

The image in the mirror rippled. Then the image swirled, breaking apart into a mesh of colors with no distinction. I glanced at Falin, afraid we'd offended the king before we'd even gotten a chance to ask about Lunabella.

Falin held up a hand, silencing the questions on the tip of my tongue. He gestured toward the mirror. The shapes were becoming more distinct again, the most obvious of which was a very feminine, and very naked, ass and pair of legs. The woman's skin was silvery and covered in scales. She took a step forward, and a water droplet fell from her ankle. The image in the mirror rippled.

"Are we talking to the king from inside a pool?" I asked.

"A pond, more likely," Falin answered in a low whisper.

Dugan shrugged. "Anything reflective works for this spell."

The scaled woman, who must have been a water fae of some sort, set a bowl down in front of the Summer King. He smiled at her and nodded slightly, acknowledging her action. It surprised me. He seemed warm, even kind, interacting with his fae. It was no huge gesture, but I couldn't imagine the Winter Queen doing the same.

The king waited until the scaled fae had vanished from our view before turning back to us. The pleasantness he'd shown his own fae hardened as he studied us again. It wasn't that he looked particularly unfriendly, but certainly less jovial, less open.

"Winter is no friend of summer. I do not take it as a great thing to be called upon by her bloody hands. But, last I had heard, shadow was no friend of winter either. So what brings these two very different men together?" The king looked at me as he spoke.

I opened my mouth to say it wasn't me, but that wasn't completely true. Finally I said, "A request."

"Really? And what might that be?"

"We are—" Falin began, but the king cut him off.

"I do not wish to speak to you, Knight." He turned to Dugan before the other man could speak. "Or you, Prince. You are both insignificant and uninteresting." He fixed me with his brilliant green eyes and flashed me a dazzling smile. "Planeweaver, you interest me. You may speak."

A muscle in Dugan's jaw bunched, but he said nothing. Falin turned toward me, fixing me with a look that spoke volumes of caution. I didn't need the warning.

The Summer King might seem warmer than the Winter Queen, but he was still a king of a Faerie court, and he couldn't hold that position without being both cunning and ruthless.

"We are looking to speak to a fae named Lunabella, who we believe is a member of your court," I said, making sure my phrasing was neither a question nor a request.

"And for what purpose would you like to speak to her?" the king asked.

I shot an imploring glance at Falin, wishing we'd discussed what needed to be said before we started this damn call.

"Don't look at him, look at me," the king said, leaning in closer.

His green eyes were so bright, so close, it looked like I could have reached right through the mirror and touched his face. He looked friendly again. Approachable. It wasn't until I felt my hand moving that I realized my reaction was caused by magic. I balled my hand into a fist to keep it still and cracked my shields, letting my vision slip across the planes. That didn't work out well for me in this instance, as the spelled mirror was shattered in my grave vision and the spell itself was a swirling mist of shadows among the broken shards. I could see pieces of the king's face, but the effect was too distracting. I closed my shields again.

The king studied me. He likely hadn't missed the glimmer of light that escaped my irises when I'd opened my shields, but he didn't mention it. He just continued to smile, the pressure of the magic he was exuding heavy against my skin, but now that I knew what he was doing, it was easier to ignore. Falin's gloved hand slid over mine, his fingers squeezing mine lightly, offering me support.

The king didn't miss that either. His eyes narrowed, the smile losing some of its strength.

"Visit my court. Let me dazzle you, and I will let you talk to whomever you wish," he said, amping up the radiance of his smile again.

I could feel myself wanting to trust him. To think the best of him. I shoved the feelings down hard. If his personal glamour was this beguiling through a reflection, how much worse would he be in person? Then I considered what he'd actually said.

"Whomever I wish? You guarantee it, my lord?" I asked, and Falin's hand tightened around mine. Warning? Or encouragement? I wasn't sure, and he wasn't looking at me. Lunabella might have been one of Stiofan's killers, but if she was, she hadn't been working alone. If she named accomplices in the summer court, it would be good if we had access to them as well.

"Visit my court. Let us woo you. And yes, you may have an audience with anyone you want. Except, perhaps, the queen. I cannot compel her to speak to you if she does not wish to."

I blinked. Not every court had both king and queen, but apparently summer did. I could no longer see any of the females who'd been fawning over the king when this conversation began, but I certainly hadn't noticed a crown on any of them. None had been Sleagh Maith either. While that didn't exclude the possibility of them being queen, not being of the noble line of Faerie did seem to greatly lower the odds.

Those details weren't terribly important right now. They were just something for my brain to focus on other than the possibility of willingly walking into Faerie again. This time into a different court. One that might be part of a conspiracy to pit the winter court against the shadow court. I fought to keep the frown from my face, but I must not have succeeded.

"What is troubling you about my proposal, plane-weaver?" the king asked, that dazzling smile pressing down at me through the mirror.

I opened my mouth twice before words came out. "Your offer to let me speak to anyone I wish in your court is generous. But you have mentioned nothing about guarantees of my safety in your court. Nor of my freedom to leave again after I enter."

"Clever girl. And they say you've only known your heritage a few moons, so either you're a quick study or you've had an interesting few months. Okay, come to my court and I will grant you safe passage for"—he paused, considering—"three days and nights. If you wish to leave, I will let you, but after the cold halls of winter, I think you will find summer quite refreshing."

Three days was much more than I needed. Especially since time in Faerie would climb closer and closer to parallel with the mortal realm as the longest night and solstice approached. We only had a few more hours before the festivities would begin, and that would complicate everything.

It was a good offer. The king was being generous with both protection and safe passage. He really was quite different from the Winter Queen. Far kinder, fairer.

I opened my mouth to agree, but a wave of cold magic shot up my hand, so frosty it seemed to burn my fingers where Falin's gloved hand touched mine. I yelped, whirling on him as much as I could in the confined space. He just stared at me, his features carefully blank. I narrowed my eyes and then realized what I'd been about to agree to. The king's glamour was affecting me more than I'd realized. There was no way I was walking into the summer court alone.

I turned back to the king, my smile carefully in place. I was going to have to examine everything I felt around this fae. He could manipulate me far too easily.

"I would require Prince Dugan and the Winter Knight to accompany me."

"No."

No negotiation, just a no. Behind the dazzling smile that kept trying to bespell me, the king's expression was hard. I fought to keep my own expression friendly. We needed to speak to Lunabella. The king wasn't our only avenue, but he was the only one that didn't involve bloodshed.

"I would be happy to meet with Lunabella on neutral ground," I said, and then added, "She should be at the revelry tonight, won't she?" I smiled more brightly. The king didn't need to know that our business with Lunabella would be complicated by waiting for tonight. Of course this could simply result in him forbidding her from attending the solstice celebration, but it was a calculated gamble.

To my surprise, the king laughed. A full-bellied laugh that caused his head to tilt back. I glanced at Falin and Dugan, but they both looked as perplexed as I felt.

"Your mortal upbringing is showing, little planeweaver," the king said, and his green eyes crinkled with mirth. "You ask for something and want instant gratification. The revelry is in mere hours. I could hardly plan an adequate visit for you before that time."

"A room to speak in would be sufficient."

"Then how would I entice you to my court? No, you must see us in all our splendor."

Well, crap.

"Then I would be willing to visit your court twice. I can come now to speak to Lunabella and in the process see what the true nature of your court is. Kind of like popping over to a friend's unannounced and learning if she only scrubs her toilet when she knows guests are coming," I said, with a vague gesture to the toilet under my foot. It was spotless, but that had more to do with having a brownie for an office manager than anything to do with my own personal habits. "And I would visit again at a later date, for the three days you have requested. At that time you can try to impress me to your heart's content. But both times, I require an escort of my choosing."

The king sobered, the mirth bleeding from his features. "You have flipped the tables. You have taken my offer of hospitality and twisted it until you are gracing us with your presence. Do you think yourself so valuable?"

Falin's grip tightened to the point of pain and Dugan watched me from the corner of his eye. I considered the king. His face was open, inviting, but waiting. Would he fall on the side of taking offense? Should I backtrack and claim that wasn't what I meant? Or did I want to push on down this road? Making an enemy of a king was a bad idea, but he'd seemed amused by my rougher edges so far. Hopefully that would hold true.

"You are welcome to wine and dine some other planeweaver." I delivered the words with a smile, because the only other planeweavers were a pair of changelings in the high court. Currently, I was the only fae plane-weaver.

The moment stretched, my words loud in the tense silence in the small bathroom. Falin's grip was a vise around my fingers, and if I hadn't been trying to act as confident as my words, I would have jerked my hand from his. After a dozen of my thundering heartbeats boomed in my ears, and I was sure I'd made the wrong choice, the king laughed.

"You *are* interesting. It would be my pleasure to host the fine lady planeweaver and her escorts, once we establish an agreement," he said. "You may even come immediately and speak to any of my people whom you like. But in exchange, I want your vow that you will visit again on a yet-to-be-determined date of my request, and you will stay no less than three days."

I swallowed the knot of apprehension lodged in my throat. Three days in the summer court. I could do that, as long as we negotiated for safe passage. I didn't want to, but it would grant us entry into summer and give us access to our only lead.

Chapter 8

It took nearly half an hour of negotiating before we agreed on the terms of our visit. By that point my legs were cramping and I was feeling rather claustrophobic. I was ready to cheer by the time the king's face vanished and the shadows parted to show our reflection in the mirror again. Except that meant we now had to go to Faerie again. *And I'm contracted to take an even longer visit later.*

Stiofan was still sitting in the middle of my inactive circle when we emerged. He wore his tattered and bloody nightclothes, but at least he was no longer bleeding ghostly blood all over the floor. I knelt beside him and called his name a few times, but he didn't so much as blink. I didn't know what to do about a catatonic ghost, so I left him there. It wasn't like I could take him to Faerie with me. I'd have to talk to Roy later. He was the oldest ghost I knew. Maybe he could make some suggestions.

"So how do we reach the summer court?" I asked as

we headed for Falin's car. If we had to drive to another door to Faerie, that would eat a lot of our time, and the afternoon was already growing long. Dusk would arrive soon, and with it, the start of the revelry. Which meant all doors to Faerie would open to the winter court and the longest night of the year.

Falin's gaze flickered toward me, but all he said was, "Quietly."

Dugan didn't seem interested in expounding on that statement. In fact, he was eerily silent. I twisted in my seat to study him where he sat scrunched in the back of Falin's sporty car. He looked out the far window when he noticed me watching him, not saying anything or meeting my eyes. *What is that about?*

Falin parked outside the Bloom and I raised an eyebrow. Apparently we were reaching the summer court through winter's door.

The Eternal Bloom was even emptier than when we'd visited a couple hours earlier. We passed through the hush that fell around us quickly. I even managed not to hesitate at the door to Faerie. I almost expected to emerge in a sunny field when the bar melted around us, as if the desire to reach the summer court would be enough to direct the door—hey, it worked with other doors in Faerie—but the halls of ice materialized around us.

A squadron of guards blocked our path before we could take more than three steps past the pillar of carved ice that marked the door between the mortal realm and the winter court. At least they didn't draw weapons on Dugan this time.

"The queen is still in her library," the leader of the guards said.

Falin acknowledged her words with a nod, but all he

said was, "We are continuing our investigation. I will not disturb the queen until we have more information."

It was a dismissal, and the guards took it as such. They didn't ask about our investigation, or even where we were going. They stepped aside, allowing us to pass. Falin said nothing more as he took off down the seemingly unending halls of ice. I stuck close to him, biting my tongue to resist asking more details on how we were getting to the summer court. Getting there "quietly" clearly meant he didn't want the queen forewarned. I had no doubt she would know soon enough. Her ice golems lined the halls, waiting for her command to come to life. I had no idea if they could actually see when not activated, but I could feel eyes on my back as we hurried down the halls, so I had no doubt we were being watched.

We walked for what felt like a very long time. The archways and golems we passed all looked identical, as if we were walking in a large circle, except the hall rarely turned and never curved. It was just an endless corridor. When we turned a corner and the hall ended in a large double door, I almost stumbled in shock.

The doors were solid ice and carved with the same kind of intricate scenes as the pillar that tied the winter court to the amaranthine tree at the Eternal Bloom. A large oak tree made up the door's frame on the right, and an equally large ash tree made up the frame on the left. The frozen branches met over the door, twisting and tangling together with large icicles dangling from their frozen bark. Guards stood on either side of the doors. They shuffled as if nervous as we approached, but they did not stop us. Their job was not to prevent fae from leaving the winter court, but to stop intruders.

So if Lunabella was present at Stiofan's murder, how

did she get inside? And for that matter, how was Kordon's body brought into the court?

Falin nodded to the guards as he hauled open the large ice doors. Swirling white mist filled the doorway, snowflakes dancing between the arching trees, obscuring what was on the other side. Falin turned toward me and held out a hand. As doors were odd in Faerie, and didn't always lead to the same place or time, and as I didn't know where we were going beyond a vague "to the summer court," I didn't hesitate to take his offered hand. When he stepped forward, I matched him step for step, walking into the mist.

We emerged in a small clearing inside what appeared to be a dense grove of trees. I glanced back over my shoulder. The intricate ice door was still there, identical to what it had looked like on the other side, the oak and the ash supporting it. But now those trees were free-standing, surrounded by similarly snow-laden trees. But with each tree farther from the door, the trees began to change.

On one side, the frost thinned, brown leaves still clinging to some of the branches instead of icicles. And farther in, leaves in the brilliant golds, reds, and oranges of fall. As these trees reached their pinnacle, oak and ash once again met, with dark wood doors between them. I wasn't close enough to clearly make out the scenes carved into them, but I guessed they depicted fae gathering harvests, falling leaves, and other autumnal scenes. The door to the fall court, no doubt.

Heading in the opposite direction from winter's doors, the frost thinned, and buds appeared on the trees, followed by flowers and fresh green shoots. Where the oak and ash met on this side, the door was covered in blooms, a mosaic of flowers that depicted fae waking trees and tending freshly sprouting plants. Spring's door.

I turned. Directly across and opposing winter's door was summer's door. The trees surrounding it had deep, strong green leaves. The doors the oak and ash surrounded didn't appear to be doors at all, but grass, heather, and mushrooms on a hillside. If there were carvings in the door, I couldn't see them from where I was.

Dugan stepped through the winter doorway, and the doors closed, blocking the mist and snowflakes of winter. I dropped Falin's hand and stepped to the center of the small clearing, turning to take in the entire scene and the seasons that transitioned seamlessly from winter to spring to summer to fall and back to winter again. This was where all the seasons mingled, and it was beautiful. As I looked around, I realized that there was a warm brightness that seemed to emanate from between some of the trees, while others had an endless darkness. There was no rhyme or reason for these spots. No source for the light or shadows.

"Are those paths to the light and shadow courts?" I asked, gesturing toward the two different patches that would have touched each other if not for a single thin birch tree separating them.

Dugan nodded. "The court of light and the court of shadows both touch all the seasons, but are part of none of them."

I looked around. That seemed accurate, as the light and darkness appeared in every season's part of the grove.

"There are more paths of light than shadow," I observed idly, and Dugan grimaced. Then he turned to glare at the light in the grove, as if he could will the shadows to overtake some of the paths.

"I meant no offense," I said when his glare took on a ferocity I hadn't previously seen in him. It wasn't aimed at me, but it was startling to see on the typically stoic fae, and I was reminded once again he was a prince of Faerie and not actually an ally.

Dugan waved a dismissive hand, but I wasn't sure if he was waving away my words or using the motion to rid himself of his own thoughts. Whichever was the case, his dark features returned to a brooding neutral.

"Faerie is out of balance," was all he said as he swept past me, heading toward the summer door. His dark cloak whirled behind him, the shadows crawling outward around him, but they avoided the streams of light.

I gave Falin a questioning look, but he only shook his head and motioned toward the door. I looked around the clearing one more time. The seasonal courts might ebb and flow in power throughout the year, but they looked perfectly in balance here. Light definitely dominated shadows, though.

I started toward the summer door and then stopped short, looking back. "Where is the door to the high court?"

Was I just missing it? Like I had the paths to shadow and light at first? If I could return to this clearing after the case, take a door to the high court, and petition to study with their mortal planeweavers . . .

Falin shook his head. "It's not here."

"So where—?" I started, but he only shrugged.

"I don't know," he said, and we both turned to look at Dugan.

The prince frowned. "Only Faerie monarchs are privy to knowledge about reaching the high court."

"And Faerie princes?" I asked, trying not to sound

too imploring. If Dugan couldn't help me even if we solved these murders, I was back to placing all my hope on the favor my father had dangled in front of me.

Dugan's frown only deepened, and he didn't answer. Instead he leaned forward, placing his palm against the plot of hill that served as the summer door. This close, I could see that the grass and heather tumbled in an unfelt wind, and as it moved, the twisting flora created shapes. I caught images of fae swimming and dancing, and then I saw an elaborate scene of a very large orgy and decided to stop looking. I was far from a prude, but little twisting blades of grass shaking and shivering to form tiny people getting it on was just weird.

The hillside opened under Dugan's hand, swinging in like it actually was a door. Bright sunlight and the swirling notes of a panpipe escaped through the opening. We hadn't even stepped through yet, and I could feel the warm sunshine on my face.

"All together?" Dugan asked, holding out his hand.

Was he nervous about entering yet another court? I couldn't blame him if he was. I definitely was, despite the fact that we'd negotiated our passage already.

I took his offered hand. It was cool and dry against my gloved fingers, despite the blood he didn't hide on his palms. It occurred to me I'd never actually touched him before. He might be an ancient Faerie prince, but his hand was just a hand, seeking as much support as it gave. With my other hand, I reached out and locked my fingers with Falin's gloved hand.

"Don't let the king bespell me," I whispered.

Then we stepped through the hillside doorway and into the streaming sunlight.

*   *   *

"I do'na think ye belong in the summer court," a deep voice said before my eyes had time to adjust to the bright sunlight.

I blinked. Normally my eyes liked Faerie, but I couldn't step into bright sunlight and not expect some time for adjustment. I hoped Falin and Dugan were adjusting faster than my damaged vision because I felt rather vulnerable, promises of safe passage or not. Falin clearly agreed. His fingers tightened around mine and then jerked me lightly sideways. He released me and I felt more than saw him step in front of me. In the shuffle I lost contact with Dugan as well, so I was suddenly alone and blind. That was not cool.

The voice that had spoken hadn't sounded particularly threatening, but it also hadn't sounded very welcoming and it definitely hadn't sounded like the Summer King. Not that I actually expected the Summer King to be hanging out at the door to his court waiting for us. There were surely guards on his door like winter had stationed at hers. Had the king informed his people we were coming? He hadn't seemed particularly concerned with expediency. For all I knew he was still lounging in the clearing where we'd spoken to him through the mirror.

A few more blinks, and my vision finally cleared. I'd expected with the amount of sunlight that we were in a field or maybe on top of a hill of heather. Instead there were earthen walls around us, flowering vines growing down them in thick curtains of green with bright flashes of color. Above us, the ceiling—if there was one—was lost to the bright sunlight. The floor under us was all greenery, but we were definitely in some sort of hall, the structure not that dissimilar from the winter halls, if completely different in decorating choices.

A small cluster of what could only be guards stood in front of us. In the winter court, the queen's guards were nearly indistinguishable from each other, their features hidden in magical cloaks and ice armor, but these summer guards could not be more different. A small pixie with armor stitched out of leaves and reinforced with acorns held a doll-sized blowgun in her small hands and hovered just out of reach at the height of Falin's nose. A fae who appeared to be more boulder than flesh and stood no taller than my knees carried a stone club that he held in two thick hands. A pale, wispy fae with dried leaves in her hair and a paper-thin tunic that reminded me of birch bark brandished no weapons at all, but I had the distinct impression that she could kill with a single touch of her spindly fingers. A satyr with a bow and some form of draconic beast that I wasn't certain if it was more pet or person rounded out the group of guards.

Yeah . . . I definitely wasn't feeling particularly welcomed.

"We've been invited by the Summer King," I said, since neither of my companions had said it.

"Have ye now, lass?" the boulder fae said, and his deep gravelly voice was the same as the one that'd spoken when we'd first stepped through the door. "You'd think we'd be informed of something like that."

"I believe we are about to be," the pale, wispy fae said. Her voice was thin and raspy and had the same quality of the wind-through-the-reeds sound very faded ghosts sometimes displayed. It was extra eerie coming from a living throat. She turned, lifting a hand, and a brilliantly colored bird landed on one of her long fingers. It chirped softly, and her head nodded, making the dried leaves in her hair rustle. "They are, in fact, invited guests."

The tiny pixie chittered, diving toward the bird. It ruffled its feathers, hopping from one foot to another. It responded with a few short chirps, and the pixie chittered again, gesticulating toward us with her small hands.

The birch woman, who could clearly understand the language of both the bird and pixie, shook her head. "It is the word of the king." She looked at us. "Come, I will escort you."

She flicked her long fingers and the bird took flight. Then she turned and took a long but unhurried step forward. She made no sound aside from the rustling as she moved, but as I watched her sluggish progress, I realized that every time she put down a bare, slender foot, roots shot down into the ground and broke away when she lifted her foot again.

The progress we made was slow, and the halls of the summer court seemed as endless as winter's, only perhaps worse, because there didn't appear to be any doors in these never-ending halls. More than once I found myself wishing I could urge the birch woman to move faster. Lunabella, while our best lead, was not likely to be the end of our case and time was short. But I doubted she could move any faster, and all the other guards had remained behind aside from the pixie, who flittered in irritated circles around Falin, Dugan, and me. I didn't think the diminutive fae was inclined to help.

After what felt like a mile of walking, the birch fae stopped. I frowned. There was nothing around us but more vines and flowers. She reached out one pale hand, and the vines slithered away from her. It wasn't so much that they revealed a door—I'd been able to see the earthen wall behind them in places before they had started moving—as that they formed a doorway that had not previously been there.

And this was why I would never be able to navigate around Faerie on my own.

Falin gave the birch woman the smallest nod before reaching back to offer me his hand. I took it, trying hard to ignore the pixie as she dive-bombed my fingers. I didn't want to wait around to see what the pixie would do next. She clearly didn't like me. Or maybe it was my escorts. Either way, her skin had changed from the softly glowing green it had been when she'd been with the other guards, to first yellow, then orange, and now she simmered an angry red.

I lifted my eyebrow at Falin, tossed a glance backward at Dugan, and when both men nodded, we stepped through the doorway.

Chapter 9

❦

I expected the doorway to take us to the wildflowers and pond where the king had been lounging during our conversation.

It didn't.

For a moment I thought we'd somehow stepped back into the Eternal Bloom based on all the tables spread around us, each laden with food and surrounded by fae eating and making merry. Music played gleefully, and I could see dancers off to my left. But unlike the Bloom, which still attempted to resemble a room despite the Faerie sky and living amaranthine tree that functioned as its ceiling, the "room" we'd been led to appeared to have no walls, at least not before the tree line I could see on the edges of the field. There was also no floor, the tables and chairs spread haphazardly in the grass.

The birch woman hadn't followed us in, but the pixie had. She chittered at me once more, hovering right before my face. Then she kicked me in the nose.

"Hey," I yelped, jerking my hand up to bat her away. I didn't even come close to touching her as she zipped out of reach, and I rubbed the tip of my nose. She hadn't done any damage, but the kick had stung.

She stuck her tongue out at me, and her color changed to a deep crimson. Then she turned and flew away, vanishing among the tables.

"What was that about?" I asked, resisting the urge to rub my nose a second time.

"I have no idea," Falin said, his eyes scanning the tables of fae. "And both of our guides have now left us, so I guess we are on our own."

"I suggest we look for the largest table, if we are looking for the king," Dugan said, scanning the scene.

"And if we just want to look for Lunabella?" I had the feeling I already knew the answer. I asked anyway.

Dugan turned away from the festivities in front of us to shoot me a frown. "I don't suggest we do that."

Right. Well then, I guess we had a king to find.

Without a guide, we made our way through the field slowly. The revelry for the longest night would start tonight, but it looked like the summer fae were pregaming their celebration quite hard. Or maybe this was common for the court. I had little to base it on. Despite the sun blazing overhead, bonfires had been lit in the field, and fae of all manner danced around them.

I hadn't been around many large gatherings of fae. I visited the Bloom occasionally, but most of those fae were independents who lived near mortals. I'd been to the Fall Equinox revelry, but I'd been a little overwhelmed that night and hadn't been able to pick out who belonged to which court after their initial procession. Looking around, I realized I probably wouldn't have been able to

group the summer fae together anyway. The winter
court boasted a wide range of fae, but from what I'd seen,
they all dressed very formally in attire that fit some Renaissance or maybe Victorian-era ballroom. There was
no unifying element to the wardrobes of the summer fae,
except perhaps that there was a considerable amount of
flesh on display. Some wore clothes crafted out of leaves
and bark. Others appeared to be wearing nothing more
than smoke or water vapor. A few wore handspun frocks
and simple tunics. Leather and fur also made an appearance on many. And then there were some who were completely naked. It was far more chaotic than the winter
court, but the fae also looked happier than at the winter
ball I'd been compelled to attend.

As we wove around the tables and avoided the dancers,
our presence, if noted at all, was met with mixed reactions.
Some fae smiled widely, lifting goblets or beckoning us to
join their dances. Others scowled, sneered, or even fingered weapons. None stopped us, though.

As Dugan predicted, it was the largest table we needed
to find. We spotted it in the center of the field. I expected
the king's table to be set apart somehow. Perhaps on a hill
or a throne on a platform. Instead his enormous table was
in the very center of the most activity in the field. Dozens
of fae sat at the table—more than could possibly be his
inner circle of advisors—and more mingled around the
edges. Many of the fae at the table were Sleagh Maith, but
there were just as many or more who were not. Nymphs
and dryads, satyrs and trolls, and many others I couldn't
name off the top of my head gathered at the table.

The king had added a deerskin vest to his wardrobe
since we'd talked to him, but it left as much of his tanned
chest bare as it covered. It was nice view, and I might

have enjoyed it—after all, it's always nice to look at a gorgeous body—except a green-skinned nymph balanced on one of his knees, her hands casually caressing the muscular abs visible above the king's brown trousers. Another fae had her arms around his shoulders, her brilliantly pink hair falling down over one of his arms. Yet another fae was joyfully feeding him grapes, and either she wore only a rainbow-colored cloak and nothing else or she had rainbow wings folded down her back and was naked as the day she was born. The whole scene looked a little too much like the start to a very well-costumed pornographic movie. If this turned into an orgy, I was out of here.

The king looked at us and smiled broadly in welcome.

"Planeweaver, make merry with us," he called out, picking up an enormous leather flagon that spilled over with amber liquid. He lifted it as if in a toast to me, and several other fae at the table lifted their cups as well. Then he drank an enormous gulp from the flagon. His eyes sparkled as he set the drink back on the table. "Unless, of course, you wish to examine the toilets first."

Heat rushed to my cheeks as several fae shot curious glances in my direction.

"I'll pass," I muttered.

The king's smile spread. "Sit."

It was a command, regardless of how friendly it was delivered. Three seats were suddenly vacated in front of the king, and I found myself herded into one. Food was set in front of us, followed quickly by an array of drinks in goblets, flutes, and flagons. A few months ago, the feast that was spread in front of us would have astounded and terrified me. The first because there was just so much food. And the second because it was Faerie food.

That time was past, and I had become rather accustomed to Faerie feasts. And I didn't fear them. There was some mortal blood in my heritage, but I had "blooded true" as they said, and was in all discernible aspects fae. I opened my shields enough to scan for any spells on the food, and not finding any, selected a leg of something large and savory. It was delicious, and my acceptance of the food seemed to please the king. I'd skipped lunch, and I wasn't sure where this investigation would lead us, so I gave myself a moment to eat.

"So what do you think of my court?" the king asked, watching me eat.

I had to swallow a rather large bite of food before I could answer. "It is very . . . sunny."

"Is that a bad thing?"

"Not at all," I said, glancing at the fae gathered around the table. Was Lunabella here? I cut my gaze toward Falin. He was eating as well, though a little more gracefully than I had been. Dugan was not eating. I turned back toward the Summer King. "I thought you said you couldn't pull together festivities on such short notice."

He smiled, his green eyes glittering. "Who said this is in any way out of the ordinary for my court?"

I looked around and shrugged. "They're having too much fun. If this was your daily dinner routine, it would be more subdued."

"We could be that fun-loving."

I shook my head. "Even the best party eventually gets tiresome."

The king lifted a chestnut-colored eyebrow but finally conceded with a shrug. "We are celebrating the last hours of sunlight before the beginning of the longest night and the official start of winter."

"But fall is the dominant season right now. Will it make that big a difference when winter arrives?"

Beside me, I could all but feel the two men go still, but the king only laughed.

"We are opposite the wheel of winter. When she is strongest, we are weakest. It is a long season for us. So we make merry in these last few hours of light." He leaned forward. "But you did not seek my court for a lesson on Faerie."

That was true. I glanced at the drinks in front of me, hoping for something to wash down the meal I'd been eating. Of course, nearly half a dozen cups and not one looked like it contained water and all looked alcoholic. Usually that wouldn't bother me, especially since my fae nature asserted itself and the amount of alcohol it took for me to so much as feel a buzz had significantly increased. But I was in the middle of a case and I was visiting a Faerie court, so I needed all my wits about me. Also, I had to be careful. While mortal alcohol had little effect on me these days, Faerie liquors tended to be much more potent. I grabbed a wooden mug that looked like it contained a pale ale, judging that it would be the least impairing. I took a small sip, found it to be malty but good, and took a slightly larger sip before I looked up at the Summer King again.

"Where would we find Lunabella?"

The king flashed me a dazzling smile. "First, you must dance with me."

It was not a request. It was a command. I didn't like it.

"I don't dance."

"I'm fairly certain I noticed you dancing with the Winter Knight at the Fall Equinox," the king said. He stood, the movement sending the fae fawning over him scurrying away. "I won't accept no for an answer. One dance, and then you may speak to anyone you like."

"You've already promised me that." Wasn't that the point of all the bargaining we'd done before we left my office?

"Of course. My subjects are yours to discourse with." He leapt over the table. He didn't vault it. No part of him touched the tabletop and not even a single flute of wine stirred as he cleared the table. He simply jumped as easily as a human might hop a puddle and he soared over the table, the feast, and those of us seated. He landed nimbly behind me, all unnatural grace and strength. Then he held out a hand. "But I am a king, and I would be most displeased if you denied me the simple request of a single dance."

He didn't look like a king. In his deerskin vest, disheveled hair strewn with flowers, and easy smile, he looked like some mischievous youth who was planning pranks. He also looked spoiled and used to getting whatever—and whomever—he wanted. But his people were certainly more comfortable around him than the Winter Queen's subjects. He was among them, interacting with them. Not set apart and untouchable on an icy throne. That did say something for him and his court. That didn't mean I wanted to dance with him, though.

Falin touched my elbow and gave me the barest nod, a warning in his eyes. Apparently, there would be no talking my way out of a dance. I twisted around and rose to my feet, not taking the king's proffered hand. Not yet, at least.

"Promise him nothing," Dugan whispered as I stood. I glanced back at him. His expression was that of bored apathy as he observed the festivities around him, but his whispered words had sounded anything but apathetic. I got the feeling he didn't like this any more than I did.

"One dance," I said, finally taking the king's hand.

The skin on his fingers was hot. Too hot for comfort, even through the material of my gloves. A moment of shock registered on his face, and he dropped my hand, his brows furrowing.

"Typically it takes years inside a court for its magic to begin reshaping a fae, but you are quite icy," he said.

I said nothing. I knew it wasn't winter that chilled my skin, but my contact with other planes, the ones dealing with souls and the dead in particular.

"This should be better," the king said, holding out his hand again. This time, when I took it, his skin was only pleasantly warm, not burning.

He beamed at me, his smile radiant, enchanting. As he took me in his arms and we began moving to the music, it was like I could smell the sunshine, taste the flowers, and feel the music. I felt warmer, as if the summer was seeping into me, chasing away the chill of the grave that clung to me far too often. *It's a glamour.* Even knowing it wasn't real, I felt myself relaxing into it, effortlessly following the king in his dance as the music filled the field around us.

He lifted me in the air, spinning us both, and the sound of merriment grew distant. By the time my boots hit the grass again, it was to silence. I blinked, pushing a step back from the king. I could still see the field of revelers, but I couldn't hear them anymore. In the distance, I could see the long table where I'd been sitting, and by the way Falin and Dugan both shot to their feet, alarm evident on their features, something was wrong.

I rushed forward, intending to head back to the table,

but several hurried steps took me no closer. I whirled around. The king was still one step behind me, exactly where I'd left him when I stepped out of his arms. He watched me, his posture casual, approachable.

I glared at him. "What's going on?"

"A little privacy, for a conversation."

I glanced around. In the grass in front of me grew a line of toadstools. No, not a line, a curve, and following it with my eyes, I realized it formed a large circle. I was in a mushroom ring.

"Let me out. You promised me safe passage while in your court."

The king continued to smile. "And you are perfectly safe. As I said, this is just a little privacy. I have a delicate matter I wish to discuss."

Falin and Dugan were moving now, their eyes scanning the field. Dugan's hand rested on his sword hilt. Falin's hands were at his sides, but I had no doubt he would have a weapon in a heartbeat if he needed it. I could see them clearly, but by the way they were systematically searching, I knew they could not see me.

"You are distressing my escorts." I didn't mention that I wasn't feeling so calm myself.

"They will be fine. I just want a short conversation." He held out a hand to me, beckoning me to follow him. There was what looked like a tent crafted from an enormous upside-down flower in the center of the mushroom ring.

I crossed my arms over my chest, not moving. "I thought you just wanted a single dance?"

"I am a man of many desires."

I snorted.

"Hear me out. That is all I'm asking for." He stepped

over to the tent, peeling back one large petal to reveal a small room beyond.

"And after the conversation? What will you be asking for then?"

He pressed a hand over his chest. "Your suspicion wounds me."

I glared at him. He stepped inside the flower tent. I could see a small table just past the petal-flap, two fluted glasses filled with pink pixie brandy set on it. He lifted one between two fingers and held it out toward me.

"Have a drink with me."

"So now it is a conversation and a drink?"

He frowned. "You are making this difficult."

I resisted the urge to tell him that his difficulties weren't my issue, but that might push him too far. He was the king and I was in his court. I opened my shields, looking at the mushroom ring through the planes. I couldn't see the magic in it—I rarely saw Faerie magic—but I could feel it. I could probably break whatever enchantment was keeping me inside. Of course, I might do a considerable amount of damage to myself and Faerie in the process, so breaking the mushroom ring should probably be reserved for absolute necessity. Which left me with either stubbornly standing there or going inside the damn flower hut and granting the king his conversation.

I sighed but chose the higher road. I walked over to the tent and stepped inside.

As with most things in Faerie, there was more to it than it appeared from the outside. The small round table where the king sat should have taken up most of the space if the inside had matched the dimensions of the exterior. Instead, the table sat in the entry. Beyond it was a small pond that held the most enormous lily pad I'd ever seen and that I suspected was actually a floating bed. I shot a scowl at the king, but he only held out the glass to me again.

The king had lost the deerskin vest at some point, leaving his tanned and muscled chest bare. It was a nice chest, maybe even one of the better I'd seen, and I looked because he obviously wanted me to, but it really wasn't doing anything for me. Nor was the come-hither smoldering look he was watching me with. Not so long ago, a casual romp with a handsome stranger would have been greatly welcomed. After all, he was attractive and clearly interested. Plus he was warm and smelled like sunshine, so it should have been easy to give in. But while his beguiling magics made my thoughts feel a little slow, a little trusting, they didn't inspire lust.

If he'd kept using his enchanting glamour to make me think he was a great and kind king, he might have gotten somewhere—he'd already caught me up in it a few times. But the amorous vibe he was emitting now? It wasn't working. He was a fucking Faerie king. I did *not* want to get tangled in that. My love life was already a trainwreck. There were two very attractive men I had genuine feelings for but whom I couldn't have. Then there was my apparent and unwanted betrothal to the Shadow Prince. Nope. My dance card was full. Besides, I was realistic enough to know that while I was an attractive woman, I couldn't hold a candle to some of the women I'd seen fawning over him earlier, especially not after a long day that had already involved raising two shades.

I took the glass he offered, but I did not sit and I did not drink. "Talk."

The king frowned. I was pleased to see he looked far less charming when he wasn't smiling.

"You are surely aware that a fae planeweaver has not been seen inside Faerie since the time of legends," he said, after it became clear that I wasn't going to throw myself at him.

"I have heard as much."

"I am the oldest seasonal monarch, and they were long gone before my birth."

I just blinked at him, waiting. I doubted he was risking the winter and shadow courts assuming he'd kidnapped me to talk about legends.

The king shifted in his seat, and for the first time, he actually looked uncertain. "After the courts discovered you, I asked our lore keepers about the planeweavers. The planeweavers of legend were rumored to have been capable of many amazing and horrible things. They were said to have been able to reshape the very structure of Faerie."

"It sounds like you know more about them than I do." It was probably true, and why I was looking for a teacher. Talking to some of these lore keepers might be a good idea as well.

"It is said," the king said slowly, drawing out the words, and I got the feeling we were finally reaching the point of this history lesson, "that as well as weaving magics together, planeweavers could unravel magics that were otherwise unbreakable. Even magical bindings."

I waited. Saying nothing. Committing to nothing.

The king watched me for several heartbeats. Then he lifted his glass and drained the pixie brandy in one long sip.

He set it down and stared at the now-empty glass. Then he took the one I'd abandoned and drained it as well. When he was done, he looked back at me. "I would take you into my confidence, but I would need your oath of silence in the matter."

"You separated me from my escorts, you are holding me in an enchanted mushroom ring, and now you would like an oath of silence from me?"

"You do make things sound so negative," the king said. "I had such a sweet encounter planned. This all could have been pillow talk with you satiated and more than happy to consider what I have to say."

He sounded sulky. I said nothing. Maybe his people liked him. Maybe he had a soft—or lustful—touch with them. But I *really* didn't like him.

"Fine, I require no oath from you," he said. "But if you speak of what I am about to say, I will curse you so that whenever you open your mouth, only toads will fall out and no words."

Magic closed around me as he spoke, and I felt the unsprung curse sink into my skin. I glared at him.

"Is this what safe passage looks like in your court? A curse?"

He waved a hand. "It only causes you harm if you choose it to by your own actions. I have in no way broken my oath of safe passage. Really, you are very young and not half as clever as you think."

I broke off my glare to glance back over my shoulder at the edge of the mushroom ring. Maybe it was worth the risk of tearing through the enchantment.

"I was young once too," the king said, leaning back in his seat. "That is the crux of my problem, I suppose. I too thought I was far more clever than I truly was. I made some oaths and accepted some bonds that I foolishly thought were a good idea at the time. And now I cannot be free of them."

I frowned at him. He'd mentioned that planeweavers could unravel magical bonds. I guessed he was back on topic with whatever it was he had orchestrated this conversation to discuss. Did he not stop to think that I would be in a less-than-agreeable mood at this point?

"It's my queen, you see," he said, going on as if I were participating in his conversation. "I am bound to her until death, and the agreement has made us both miserable for centuries."

"In other words, it is cramping your style and impeding your seduction of nymphs," I said sarcastically.

The king only laughed. "It hardly impedes me."

He gave me a sly wink and even his glamour couldn't make me see him as charming. I recoiled, stepping back toward the opening of the tent.

"Don't say no too hastily. I'm willing to offer you anything you desire. Unravel this bond for me, and I would offer you position, power . . ." He looked at me, really looked at me. "Or perhaps what you desire is freedom. I can offer you that, and protect that freedom from the other courts as well."

And that was the first tempting thing he'd said. Not that it mattered. "Let's say I'm capable of what you say—and I'm not saying I am—I have no training and limited control of my planeweaving. I could accidentally cause more harm than help. But if I had a teacher . . . Help me acquire training, and I'll consider your request."

He scoffed and flicked the rim of his glass. It refilled with more pink liquid. "If I knew someone with enough talent to be able to train you, why would I need you?"

"I've heard that there are mortal—" I started, but the firm but delicate sound of a throat clearing behind me forced me to stop.

I whirled around to see a woman entering the tent behind me. She had hair the color of spun gold that fell in soft waves around an oval face. Her eyes were deep green and shone like emeralds, and her mouth was a perfect Cupid's bow. When poets described ancient Faerie queens as being so beautiful that mortal men, having glimpsed one, would then waste away spending endless hours on hills and paths looking for another, those poets could have been describing this Sleagh Maith. And maybe they had been. A golden diadem sat on her brow. She was, without a doubt, the Summer Queen.

While the king and most of those I'd seen in his court seemed to favor revealing to downright bawdy garments—if any clothes at all, nude was definitely an option in his court—the queen's dress was far more conservative. The neckline was high, the billowy sleeves long, and the lines of the dress flattering but far from revealing, ending at the queen's ankles. The green gown was sewn through with golden threads and trimmed with more gold. A belt of beaten gold plates hung at her waist, a small golden dagger attached to it. Green-and-gold slippers completed the outfit. The entire ensemble made her look both elegant and timeless.

She was flanked on either side by what I could only guess were handmaidens. They both wore dresses that were simpler versions of their queen's. Beyond them, outside the tent, were more fae, these wearing armor crafted of bark and leaves and standing at attention in orderly formation. They were so very different from the frolicking fae in the field, I could only guess that they'd arrived with the queen and hadn't been at the festivities when I'd been searching for the king.

The Summer Queen's piercing eyes regarded me only

a moment, assessing. Then they dismissed me as inconsequential.

"Go away," she said to me, and I had the urge to do just that.

I dropped my gaze, unable to look at her face any longer. A small figure hovered behind her, near her shoulder. I hadn't noticed her at first, but she was no doubt the same leaf-and-acorn-armored pixie who had so violently protested my entrance to the court. I guess I knew where she'd flown off to after kicking my nose. *She'd fetched her queen.*

"Husband, mine," the queen said, pointedly ignoring me. "Are you aware that the Prince of Shadows and the Winter Knight are prowling around our court, upsetting our citizens? But of course you are. What strange alliances are you making? Is this girl the offering they brought you to tempt your lecherous appetites?" She gave me another unimpressed once-over.

"Uh. No," I said, although I knew I should probably keep my mouth shut. I don't follow my own advice often enough. The queen's angry gaze slammed into me again, and I felt about as big as an ant. Rolling my shoulders back, I trudged on by saying, "Dugan and Falin are escorting me, yes, but because we need to talk to Lunabella. We negotiated entrance to your court for that purpose alone." I almost added that I wanted nothing to do with her husband, but I didn't understand their complicated relationship and didn't want to make the situation worse.

A perplexed look crossed the queen's beautiful face, as if she were shocked to learn that something she had found on the bottom of her shoe could speak. Then her golden brows knit together and a small arrow formed over her sharp nose.

"Lunabella is not here."

"Come again?" I said, which caused her to give me an even more puzzled look. This time because of the slang. Damn it, it was hard to talk to people who were centuries old and didn't have many concerns for the modern world. "Why isn't Lunabella here? Where is she?"

"Not that I have to answer to you," the queen said, staring down her nose at me. "But she left our court, so if you came here to speak to her, you are wasting everyone's time."

I had the distinct feeling that by "everyone," she meant hers in particular.

I whirled to face the king. He was leaning back in his chair, hands tucked behind his head as if he was enjoying the show.

"She left your court?"

He shrugged. "Apparently."

My mouth moved in several silent but unarticulated words ranging from unspoken curses to unfinished "whats" and "whens." By the time I finally formed complete words it was to splutter, "You said if we came here we could question her."

"Technically, you said you thought she was part of my court, and I promised you could speak to any of my fae. I never said you could speak to her in particular."

I blinked, thinking back to how the conversation through the mirror had played out. He was right. I *hated* fae and their tendency to twist truths and words so deceitfully.

"So where did she go?"

"She left our court," the queen said, still staring at me like she didn't know what to make of me. Whatever conclusions she was reaching didn't seem positive. "After that she was no concern of ours."

Right. Of course. Great.

I wanted to scream, but I restrained myself. Throwing a tantrum in the middle of the summer court wouldn't do me any good.

Giving a tight-lipped smile to the queen, I performed a brusque curtsy and said, "If you'll excuse me, Your Majesties." Then I stormed out of the flower tent without a backward glance at the king.

"So you'll consider what we discussed?" he called after me, his voice nothing if not amused.

Like hell I would. Did he seriously think I would help him now? I had half a mind to tell his queen what he wanted, but I could feel the curse he'd set and I didn't want toads falling from my tongue. That sounded . . . slimy and distinctly unpleasant.

The mushroom ring didn't stop me now. Either the king or perhaps the queen had removed the enchantment in it that had kept me inside, so when I stepped over it, I stepped back into the noise of the fae celebrating in the field.

I made it less than a yard into the field before Falin spotted me. Dugan, who had split from Falin at some point, saw me a moment later. Both men reached me at the same time.

"Are you all right?" Falin asked, his eyes searching for damage.

"Angry, but unharmed. Lunabella isn't here."

Both men frowned, but it was Dugan who said, "I don't suppose you were told where she is?"

The look I shot him was probably enough of an answer.

I could all but feel the venom in my gaze. Of course, that wasn't fair to Dugan. It wasn't his fault Lunabella had left the summer court. And while I would have liked to say that he, being the oldest and the Faerie prince among us, should have caught the duplicity in the king's phrasing, I knew he was on a limited timeline and doubted he would have intentionally let us waste time in the investigation.

"Now what?" I asked, looking around. I didn't even know which way the door out of this field was located, let alone where we should go next.

"We still have permission to speak to any of the summer fae we like, as decreed by the king, correct?" Dugan motioned toward the long table where we'd been earlier. Now that the king had left, many of the minglers had as well, but there were still knots of fae left. "Perhaps she has friends who know which court or region she went to after leaving summer."

"If she has friends, they will surely tell her we are looking for her," Falin said.

"I'm sure she will find out soon enough. But if we don't know where to look for her, our only other option is to call upon fall, spring, and light and fish for information on whether she is in their courts or lands."

He had a point, and the afternoon was dwindling away quickly. We didn't have any other leads and it was unlikely we would get anything else done before dusk and the start of the longest night festival in the winter court.

"I guess it is time to start questioning random fae," I said with a sigh. I just hoped it went better than my conversation with their king had.

Chapter 10

Just because the king had guaranteed we could speak to his fae, that didn't mean he'd promised they would answer us, as I quickly learned. Many of them wouldn't even commit to whether they had known Lunabella when she'd been part of the summer court, requesting promises or favors for so much as acknowledging that she'd once been here. As I wasn't about to start offering up boons to likely not learn more than that she'd left, I moved on. Not everyone wanted to bargain; the nobles in particular seemed fond of informing me that while their king might have agreed that I could speak to them, they were under no obligation to listen. It was *not* going well.

I walked away from a cluster of fae to the tinkling sound of their giggles. This group of dancers appeared to be as much flower as person, and all I'd gotten for my efforts to talk to them was a purple flower tucked behind my ear and lots of giggles. Falin met me after I'd walked a few yards, his features tight and a frown peeking out of the corner of his lips.

"You look like you've had about as much success as I have," I said, shoving my hands in my back pockets.

"No one here wants to get near me, let alone talk." Apparently his reputation preceded him. He glanced at the slanting angle of the sun. "We need to head back to the winter court. The queen requires me to be at these events. She will likely want to show you off as well."

Great. Just what I wanted.

I glanced around. The Summer King was back at his table, surrounded by no less than four adoring women. The Summer Queen and her prim entourage were nowhere to be seen. I had the distinct impression that the court was divided between those courtiers devoted to the king and those devoted to the queen. Likely she had her own celebration somewhere else in the court with far less general debauchery and many more rules. How those two had held a court together astounded me. Of course, the king had said he was older than any of the other seasonal rulers and that he'd made oaths that bound his queen to him when he'd still been young and foolish, so perhaps once they had held more common ground.

I spotted Dugan standing with a cluster of Sleagh Maith. They all looked riveted on whatever he was saying, and for his part, he was smiling. I hadn't seen him often, and I had to admit, he had a nice smile, though I wasn't convinced this particular smile was real. Something about it was off, fake. He saw me looking his way and met my gaze. He tilted his head back slightly, in an upward nod, and then focused on the small crowd around him again. I could tell by his body language that he was wrapping up the conversation and making his good-byes, and the fae around him were disappointed he was leaving. Being a Faerie prince clearly opened some doors that Falin and I just couldn't walk through.

"Tell me you learned something," I said as he joined us.

Dugan's smile spread. "I did. Not exactly what we were looking for, but something."

I waited, and the moment stretched. Falin grumbled something under his breath, and the prince frowned at him.

"Are you planning to make us bargain for it, or are you planning to share?" I asked.

Dugan looked slightly startled, and then his brows furrowed. "I am . . . unaccustomed to freely sharing information. It does not come naturally to me."

Gee, who would have guessed that of the Prince of Shadows and Secrets, but his tone made it clear that this was an unspoken apology. Falin crossed his arms over his chest, but I tried to keep my body language open and encouraging.

"Lunabella left only a fortnight ago, though no one I spoke to knew where it is she went, or perhaps they were unwilling to share. She did visit a friend in the court last week, and at that time she seemed well so it does not seem she fell victim to foul play."

"Who did she visit?" Falin asked. "Do they not know where she went?"

"One of the queen's handmaidens."

"Who would not be in attendance here," I said, and Dugan nodded.

"There appears to be a rather deep schism in this court," he said.

And wasn't that the truth.

"So you didn't actually learn anything useful. I hope

you didn't trade anything important," Falin said, making Dugan's frown deepen.

"I have more." He pulled something from under his cloak and held it out toward me, clasped in his hand.

I hesitated. I couldn't see what it was as his fingers covered it completely, but I could feel magic. It wasn't witch magic, so I couldn't tell what it did and with the day I was having, I was leery of accepting anything. I already had a curse on me for my time in this court. I didn't want to accept an enchanted object. Dugan lifted his eyebrow, and I couldn't tell if he was questioning why I hadn't accepted whatever it was, or if he was daring me to accept it. Falin reached out, but Dugan shook his head.

"I did trade for this. Alexis?"

Damn it. I opened my palm and Dugan dropped into it what appeared to be a golden locket on a chain. Narrowing my senses on it I could feel a warm magic worked deep into the metal, but I still couldn't guess what it did.

"Uh . . . ?" Was this a gift? What was this?

"Open it."

I was skeptical, but I released the clasp and the locket popped open. A woman, no larger than my thumb, appeared in the air above the locket. She had long brown hair and soft dark eyes and she laughed, waving someone unseen away playfully. Then she paused and smiled, clearly posing, before blowing a kiss. Her image blurred, and then she laughed again, the image looping back to what we'd seen when I first opened the locket. I stared. I'd never seen a spell like this. It was like someone had used magic to create something out of a science fiction movie. Except the magic in the locket felt old. Very old. So maybe it was the opposite way—the idea for recorded holograms came from glamour and magic.

"Now we know what she looks like," Dugan said, and there was a smug note to his voice.

I had to admit, that would probably come in handy. There was a chance Lunabella might attend the revelry, and we would have walked right by her without knowing it if someone who knew her didn't point her out. We might even be able to use this image in a tracing spell. Though considering the image was magic, maybe not.

I studied the woman as she smiled at me in miniature size. She was pretty, her features a little rounder and less severe than seemed to be common among the Sleagh Maith. She blew her kiss before blurring and looping back to laugh again. I couldn't imagine her being capable of the kind of brutal murder that had befallen Stiofan, but appearances were often deceiving, especially in Faerie.

"Do I want to know what you had to trade for this?" I said as I closed the locket, sealing the magical image away.

Dugan shrugged. "Nothing pressing. We are only borrowing the locket. I must return it before we leave."

"Oh." Well, there went the possibility of using it as a focus. It probably wouldn't have worked anyway—fae magic and witch magic didn't tend to play well together.

I opened the locket again and the miniature image of Lunabella appeared. I studied it, trying to commit her features to memory. Then I held it out to Falin, allowing him to study it as well.

The small gaggle of fae Dugan had been speaking to waltzed up to us, smiling and all but pushing the red-haired fae in the front of the group forward with their merriment.

"Did you see what you wanted?" she asked, rolling her

shoulders back so that her breasts, which were only covered by the necklaces of flowers she wore, were prominently displayed.

Dugan smiled and held out his hand for Falin to return the locket to him. Falin frowned, but closed it, making the image vanish.

"I believe it was what we needed," he said, unclasping the golden chain. "Your locket, my lady."

He didn't hand it to her, but waited, one side of the chain in each hand. She lifted her flame-colored hair and stepped forward. Dugan bent, fixing the chain around her neck. Once it was secured, she fingered the locket, fidgeting with it where it dangled just above her cleavage.

"You will consider my proposal?" she simpered. I'm not sure I'd ever actually used that word before, but there was no other way to describe the coy way she gazed up at him.

Dugan gave her a small bow. "I promised I would consider it. But now we must go."

She pouted but didn't stop us as we walked away. The smile melted from Dugan's face as soon as his back was to her.

"What exactly did she propose?" I asked, keeping my voice low.

Dugan frowned at me. "She proposed."

I blinked. "Marriage?"

"A contract for one, yes," he said, and his voice was completely flat, as if the topic was boring. Then he looked at me and gave me a smile very similar to the one he'd adorned her with when he'd returned her necklace. Both smiles were completely fake. "I will, of course, not accept any proposals that complicate our betrothal."

Beside me, Falin missed a step. He covered it almost instantly, but I saw it.

"Don't say no on my account," I muttered under my breath. So far most of Faerie didn't seem to know that my father had promised me to the Shadow Prince, and I planned to keep it that way. The Winter Queen was far too likely to consider that complication as "compromising her planeweaver," and that wouldn't turn out good for anybody.

We approached the table where the Summer King lounged with several members of his court. He looked up as we approached, but made no other acknowledgment.

"We will take our leave now. Would you like us to have a guide?" Falin asked, inclining his head more or less a respectful degree toward the king.

For a moment, I thought the king wouldn't provide one and we would have to wander around searching for the door. But letting powerfully placed members of other courts roam his halls apparently didn't seem like a good idea to him—not that we wanted to do anything more than leave. Or at least that was all I wanted. I had no idea what secondary agendas Dugan and Falin might have. The king waved a hand in the air and a faun trotted over.

"Take them to the exit," the king said, and the faun bowed, a movement that looked very awkward with his thin hoofed legs. As we turned to follow our guide, the king called after us, "I will see you at the revelry tonight, and, planeweaver, I shall contact you soon about your extended visit."

An angry flush burned the tips of my ears, but I didn't turn back or make any other indication that I'd heard him. I'd agreed to the visit, so I would have to do it. Even though he'd tricked me and we'd gotten little from this trip, I couldn't go back on our bargain. He was right about one thing: I had to learn to be much more clever.

We parted ways with Dugan in the grove that connected the seasons. As he would be attending the revelry with his own fae, he needed to return to the shadow court before all the doors moved to winter. He walked into one of the shadowy patches between trees and vanished.

"Well, that was . . . different," I said after he was gone.

"Sometime soon, in a very brightly lit room with no shadows and maybe your little privacy spell, you are going to tell me all about this *betrothal*," Falin said, his voice sounding very dangerous, though the venom in it was aimed at Dugan. Not me.

"Are you jealous?" I teased.

He glared at me, and while those ice-blue eyes did hold perhaps a touch of jealousy, it was nearly buried under worry. He was concerned for me.

I dropped my teasing leer and shrugged. "I'm not marrying anyone. Pretty sure I was born under a bad star or something because relationships just don't work out for me."

He reached out as if to take my hand, but I stepped away. We'd had our moment once. Well, maybe a few moments. One rather memorable one being at the last revelry, when he'd told me he loved me and in the same breath pulled daggers on me and told me never to trust him as long as he was the queen's knight. Yeah, our relationship was complicated. But that was par for the course with me and relationships these days. A cursed bad star at my birth seemed pretty damn likely, if such a thing could happen. I was a witch, not an astronomer, so I wasn't sure.

We reached the door to winter and Falin paused. "She isn't going to be happy. Let me do the talking unless you can't avoid answering."

Neither one of us had to clarify who "she" was. In the winter court, there was only ever one "she." The queen.

Falin pushed open the door and stepped into the frozen halls to learn what misery our ill-begotten trip to summer had earned us.

Chapter 11

⟶⟴ ⟴⟵

"She wants to see you," a gravelly voice said from behind an icy cowl as soon as we entered the halls of winter. There were twice as many guards in the entry as when we'd left, so clearly the queen had noticed.

Falin only nodded. "Lead the way."

As I expected, a full half of the guards that had greeted us broke off to escort us to the queen. I stuck close to Falin and watched our escorts from the corner of my eye. I'd long ago given up trying to memorize halls or count doors in the winter court. There must have been a secret to how to navigate the court, but I didn't know it.

After the sunshine and thriving plants in the summer court, the icy halls of the winter court seemed sterile and cold. Not temperature cold; even the flurries that fell from the cavernous ceiling and vanished before reaching our heads or the walls that appeared to be carved from pure ice didn't lower the temperature to uncomfortable. Faerie tended toward pleasant, never too hot nor too cold. No, the frigidity of winter was in the decor, which, while beautifully carved, seemed too controlled and monochromatic when compared to the chaotic explosion of life in summer.

The lead guard stopped in front of a large archway and stepped aside, gesturing for us to enter. Without a word, Falin stepped through the threshold and I followed on his heels.

A folding screen blocked our view of most of the room. Thick sheets of frosted ice composed the panels of the screen, obscuring the room beyond, but not completely obstructing it. I could see shapes moving on the other side, but I could only discern their general size with no details that betrayed which was the queen and who was attending her.

"My queen, may we enter?" Falin asked, not moving beyond the entry.

"Come, Knight," the queen's voice said from beyond the screen.

Falin turned toward me and tapped a single finger over his lips, as if I needed a reminder to keep my mouth shut. Then he walked around the screen. He knelt as soon as he reached the main part of the room, head bowed and down on one knee. I considered curtsying, but I didn't want to get stuck in a curtsy again. I took a knee as well.

Peeking up through my lashes, I took in the room. It was small and appeared to be some sort of dressing room. The queen sat primly on a backless chair, the skirt of her very full ball gown billowing around her. Three fae deftly worked her dark curls into an elaborate updo on the top of her head with shimmering silver pins and combs. It struck me as odd. Couldn't she save a lot of

time and annoyance by using glamour? Though she was
the regent supreme at the revelry tonight, so maybe that
warranted something more real.

The queen, whose back was to us, regarded us in the
reflection of an enormous ornate mirror that took up
nearly one entire wall of the room. Her rosebud lips
compressed into a thin line as her gaze fell on me.

"Lexi, really. That is so very unladylike. Get up," she
said, and I counted that as a win as I climbed to my feet.
Her gaze swung in the glass toward Falin. "I see you've
lost your princely tagalong. I don't suppose you found a
good reason to kill him?"

"No, my lady." Falin hadn't been given permission to
rise yet, so he remained kneeling.

"More's the pity. And your trip outside our lands, I
trust it had to do with the case?" There was a frosty edge
to the question, an unspoken expectation and a warning
if it hadn't been.

"We were following a potential lead."

"And?" One of the queen's dark eyebrows arched daintily where it was reflected in the mirror.

"We are still early in the investigation," Falin said, his
voice even and matter-of-fact. I was glad he was the one
answering the questions. If it had been me, I likely would
have sounded defensive or apologetic. Incurring the
queen's wrath for visiting the summer lands would have
added insult to injury after how badly deceived I'd been
by the Summer King.

The queen waved a hand and the attendants working
on her hair stepped back. She turned so she could look
at us directly. She made the move look effortless, though
I had no idea how she managed it under all the layers of
her gown. Maybe it was just centuries of practice.

"That isn't good enough," she said, rising to her feet. "I must welcome all the courts in less than an hour's time, and I have no idea if one or more is plotting against us."

"Don't you always assume they are scheming against you?" I asked, and then cringed as her gaze moved from Falin to me. Why couldn't I keep my big mouth shut?

The queen regarded me, assessing. "Yes. For the most part, I assume every fae in Faerie is watching to take advantage if I so much as stumble. Which was proven justified when every monarch but my dear sister sent challengers for my throne during my recent . . . illness." And by illness, she meant when she'd been being poisoned by her nephew, but I was smart enough not to point that out. "But an opportunistic challenge is far different from colluding to instigate a war between my court and another. I must know if this was isolated or if someone thinks they can manipulate me."

"We do not have enough information to say, yet."

"What do you know?" she asked, gliding across the room, her skirts making soft shushing sounds as she moved.

Falin still knelt on one knee, head bowed, and the queen laid a hand on the crown of his head as if he were a dog. I had to wonder if she tended to leave him kneeling because it helped her demonstrate her dominance. He was her bloody hands; she wielded him like a tool against both her own fae and the other courts, but if the bond that made him obedient to her were removed, would she actually be able to intimidate him? She'd won her throne centuries ago, so she was a force to be reckoned with, but she'd made him one as well.

"The goblin Kordon was killed inside the shadow court, not here. He smelled honeysuckle moments before

his throat was cut. After his death, he was taken somewhere outside Faerie—most likely the mortal realm—
before he ended up in our court." Falin delivered the
words without inflection or acknowledgment of the slender hand on his head. The queen patted his head idly,
making a small, uninterested sound, and Falin continued,
"Stiofan was murdered in his bed by at least two people
but possibly more. He did not see any of his attackers, nor
could he confirm their identities, but he heard a voice he
thought might have belonged to a former wife. We tried
to interview her, but discovered she'd left the summer
court a fortnight ago and we are not sure yet to which
court she now belongs."

She slipped her fingers into his hair and grabbed a
fistful, using his hair to steer his face up to look at her. I
clenched my own fists, fighting my urge to tell her to let
go of him. He wouldn't have thanked me for my inter-
vention, and it probably would have made the situation
worse.

"So you have a lot of nothing?" she asked, leaning
down to loom over his still-kneeling form.

"We know someone went through a lot of trouble to
try to blame the goblin," I said, stepping forward. I
might not be able to stop her from mistreating Falin, but
I could perhaps deflect some of the abuse. "But we are
still investigating whether the goblin was simply an easy
fall guy to disguise the true identities of the killers, or if
he was a plant to cause a deeper ripple of trouble."

The queen glared at me for a moment. Then she released Falin's hair, stepping away from him.

"Then I will have to assume the worst while hoping
for the best," she said with a sigh that made her entire
body droop. "My power peaks with the solstice. Perhaps

I will simply declare war on all the other seasons and shadow. My dear sister will surely side with me. We could dominate all of Faerie and be done with this foolishness."

I gaped at her and Falin's head snapped up, focusing on her. Her eyes were bright, full of power, but her gaze wasn't focused on anything in the room.

"My queen?" Falin said softly.

The queen blinked and looked around the room as if she'd forgotten for a moment that her attendants were hovering, just out of the way, waiting to finish their work on her hair. She frowned and the glow of magic that had been leaking from her skin dimmed. She returned to her stool and motioned her attendants forward. The three female fae didn't dawdle—that could have been hazardous for their well-being—but they didn't exactly rush back to the queen, considering her current mood. For her part, the queen returned to regarding us in her ornate mirror.

"Knight, I'll want you by my side tonight. If there are designs against our court, I should show my strongest front and remind them that the ice of winter kills all their precious greenery."

I fought the frown trying to claim my lips and bit my tongue, because while winter could kill, definitely, life had a way of reasserting itself, like daffodils poking up through a late-spring snow.

The queen's gaze moved to me, and for one long moment, I was afraid she somehow knew what I was thinking, but what she said was, "Planeweaver, independent status or not, you are a part of my court. You cannot be allowed to represent me in those reprehensible clothes."

I took a step back, sure she was about to enchant my

clothes into some sort of impractical ball gown. The fear must have been clear on my face because the queen laughed.

"Do not fret, little Lexi. My knight has explained to me that your mortal realm wardrobe is deplorably limited and does not have any room for reduction—even if my changes would be vast improvements. My seamstresses have prepared something appropriate for you." She cut her gaze to one of her handmaids. "Go and make sure she is properly attired for the evening. And store that shamble of an outfit somewhere she can collect it later."

"Yes, my lady," the little fae said, handing her combs and pins to another of the handmaids. Then she turned and unfurled large wings that resembled an intricate snowflake. She flitted silently toward me—defying physics with lazy beats of wings that should have been too small to lift her, to say nothing of the lacelike holes in the thin membranes. Yet she moved smoothly and hovered in front of me, two and a half feet off the ground, putting her at eye level. "If you will follow me, lady plane-weaver."

She fluttered toward the door. I shot one last look where Falin still knelt on the ground, but it wasn't like I had a choice but to follow the ice fae.

The dress could have been worse. I kept reminding myself of that fact. The top was a shimmery pale blue corset with silver piping. The skirt was silver with soft blue snowflake embroidery and at least a dozen layers of petticoats. It was sleeveless, which seemed completely impractical for an outdoor celebration on the Winter Solstice, regardless that Faerie was always comfortably warm, even in the snow. The corset also had hard boning that, once tightened, prevented me from taking a deep breath, to say nothing of anything practical like bending. Oh, and the gown had a train.

A train.

I was going to fall over myself all night.

My boots had been confiscated, replaced by a pair of pale heels, and my simple white gloves had been traded for long blue satin ones that reached the middle of my biceps. I felt like I was auditioning for Cinderella. Except if the queen was a fairy godmother, she was a demented one who wanted me to stand around like a doll, not meet a prince.

The worst part of the entire ensemble wasn't that I was going to sprain my ankle, or that I wouldn't be able to breathe. It was that there was no good way to carry my dagger. The enchanted blade used to unnerve me with its bloodlust, but it had gotten me out of quite a few tight spots in the past. Most of my magic was useless in Faerie. I was not about to walk around unarmed as well.

"There is a truce that lasts for the entire revelry," the frost fae said, disapproval threaded thickly through her words. "You don't need a weapon." Her tone implied a lady never needed a weapon, but particularly at this occasion.

I didn't care. The skirt was completely unmanageable. Even if I cut a slit in it, I wouldn't be able to dig through all the layers to reach a thigh holster. I couldn't bend to reach my calf, and without boots or anything to support the holster, it wouldn't have been secure. I tried wedging it into the top of the dress, but there was barely room for *me* in the corset. The dagger and sheath definitely couldn't fit. I briefly entertained trying to use the dagger as a hair ornament, but while my hair drove me nuts sometimes, I liked it too much to let the dagger slice half of it off by accident. The frost fae insisted that it would be an insult if the dagger was visible—or even hidden with glamour, not that I could have hidden it myself. When I refused to leave it behind, she finally relented and found a clutch purse. It was small and the same frosty blue as my dress with a chain of sparkling ice. It wasn't perfect, but the dagger fit, so it worked.

The frost fae was now attempting to tame my dirty-blond curls into something fashionable. She kept muttering very pretty-sounding words in the musical language of the fae that I suspected were none too kind. Her large, pupil-less eyes narrowed as a clump of curl escaped, but she caught it deftly, spinning it to join the rest. She must have had a lot of practice, because her own hair wasn't exactly organic-looking but resembled icicles protruding from her scalp.

"Did you know Icelynne?" I asked, because she looked similar enough to have been the cousin of the ghost fae who haunted my castle.

Her hands went still. A few months ago I wouldn't have been able to identify the emotions that flashed over her not-completely-humanoid features, but I'd been around Icelynne quite a bit, and this fae's reflection in the mirror showed first shock and then sorrow before landing on anger. She pulled my hair hard, giving it one more twist before ramming a silver comb into it roughly enough to send a stabbing pain down my scalp.

"You're done," she declared, fluttering backward.

I turned toward her. "I didn't mean to offend you."

She frowned at me. She had no eyebrows, but judging

by the way she cocked her head, she was considering my not-quite apology and it puzzled her.

"You spend your time with the queen's bloody hands, so perhaps you do not know, but we do not speak of those who are no longer with us."

I blinked at her. "Ever?"

"Once we take our mourning black off, never. They are gone. We live." Her wings folded and she sank to the ground. She was only about two feet shorter than me, but she seemed even smaller as she wrapped her thin arms around herself. "But if I spoke of her, I would tell you she was my sister," she said, her voice very small, and I wished I'd never brought it up.

I considered telling her that while Icelynne was dead, her soul had not moved on yet. But I'd already put my foot in my mouth pretty hard. I'd met Icelynne after she'd already been murdered, and she'd been dead for our entire acquaintance. I'd talked to her just this morning, so I hadn't thought about how hurtful it might be to mention her. Considering this fae's stance on not speaking of the dead, I wasn't sure if learning her sister was still around would be comforting to her or devastating, so I remained silent as she led me back to the queen and what was sure to be the longest night of the year in more ways than one.

Chapter 12

I sucked at being scenery.

Not that I felt bad about that fact. I was bored and fidgety and it hadn't even been half an hour since Maeve had told me to stand in my spot and look pretty. She'd used those words: *Stand there and look pretty*.

Yeah. No. That wasn't in my repertoire. But as I didn't want to piss off the queen, I was trying.

The passages to Faerie would switch over soon, and every door would open to the winter court. Fae from all over Faerie and the mortal realm alike would pour into the clearing and a night and day of merriment would commence. The snow-covered field where we were standing currently looked rather small, but the more fae who arrived to fill it, the bigger it would get. Faerie magic was amazing and weird.

There was a sense of excitement stirring in the fae around me. Anticipation. Joy. Already I was hearing soft whispers of "be merry" as well as wistfully mentioned

remarks about hoping particular singers or dancers from
other courts would be attending, or even speculations
about the food. I listened only because it was a good distraction, but in truth all I was looking forward to finding
right now was a chair. I was tired, and the damned heels
I'd been provided pinched my feet. Enchanted for comfort they were not.

Maeve was in charge of the court's first-impression
appearance. The court gentry were to look casual and yet
undeniably elegant where they congregated just off to the
left of the enormous carved ice dais supporting the
queen's throne. The handmaids were arranged to be frozen flowers waiting on their queen. The two remaining
members of the queen's council were the closest group to
her throne, standing on the dais itself, and Maeve described their role as being dignified attendants. I was
part of none of these groups, placed alone near the foot
of the dais. Maeve hadn't described what my role was in
this living picture she was creating, but I could guess. I
was the queen's prized pet. Her rare planeweaver that no
other court could boast. Goody.

"Stand up straight, planeweaver," Maeve hissed under
her breath as she swept one last glance over the people
she had so carefully arranged. "It will do. She's coming."
And with that, she hurried to her own place on the dais.

The throne and dais faced an opening in the dense
wood line that was framed by frost-covered hawthorns.
The queen emerged from the shadows under the hawthorns, her arm casually draped through Falin's. They
made a striking pair: she petite and dark-haired, wearing all silver and white, and he tall and fair, wearing a
blue so dark it was nearly black with just a touch of silver
throughout. Something constricted deep in my chest,

sending painful stabs down to my stomach, as I watched
them walk up the path to the dais.

Falin, for his part, stared straight ahead. I had no
doubt he was aware of everything around him; he was
the queen's knight, after all, and would be expected to
spot and react to any threats against her, but he never
seemed to look anywhere but straight ahead. Or maybe
he simply didn't look at me.

I'm not sure what expression I wore, but when the
queen saw me, she smiled. It was a private smile, beautiful and terrifying. Then she moved her hand slightly,
laying it more firmly possessive on Falin's arm as they
walked. The stabs in my gut turned hot, angry, though I
couldn't have said if I was more angry at her for being a
royal bitch, or myself for reacting. I tore my gaze away,
not giving her the satisfaction of watching me watch her.

She daintily lifted the edge of her skirts and mounted
the dais, Falin still at her side. The glimmering cloak of
snow she wore glowed in the last few rays of sunset. That
was no metaphor; the cloak was all magic and freshly
fallen snow. As she had walked up to the dais, it had
immediately obscured her and Falin's footprints with a
blanket of snow as it trailed behind her. Now that she'd
mounted the carved ice, it seemed content to cease leaving snow in its wake.

Magic. So very much magic filled the air. Like the
large snowflakes that fell all around, keeping the blanket
of snow covering the field looking untouched, and yet
not a single flake had landed on me, and I would have
noticed as my shoulders were completely bare.

"Knight, you will be on my right tonight," the queen
said, gesturing. Then she half turned, opening her mouth

as if she would address someone else. Someone who wasn't there.

Ryese. The queen's nephew had traditionally been on her left, but now that his treachery had been revealed, the spot was vacant. Had he been more patient, Ryese likely would have been the Winter Prince one day. Now he was exiled, and judging by the condition he'd been in when I'd last seen him, quite possibly dead.

The queen snapped her mouth closed, her lips thinning in her forced smile. It was only a momentary hesitation, but if I'd caught it, I knew others had as well. I didn't like the queen. Fear her? Yeah. But actually respect her? Not so much. But this small slip would be viewed as a potential weakness by those who wished to seize more power for themselves. I cared only because anyone who wanted to challenge the queen had to go through Falin first. He was good, but how many duels could he fight without eventually losing?

The queen climbed to her throne and sat, gazing out over her gathered courtiers. I fidgeted with the purse holding my dagger. Everyone seemed riveted to the last few rays of light sinking over the tree line. The anticipation in the air was almost tangible.

As the glow of light dimmed in the horizon, something in the air changed. A new type of energy filled the field and a collective gasp rushed through the courtiers present. The frost fae who'd helped me dress held out her arms, as if embracing some unseen force, and a pale fox-eared woman tilted her head back, breathing in deeply.

"What's going on?" I mouthed to the frost fae closest to me.

"The doors have shifted," she said with a smile, fluttering her wings to lift herself higher in the air. "All mortal belief in the world is now rushing into winter. Can't you feel it?"

I frowned. I supposed I felt *something*. Definitely an energy shift. But the fae around me were acting like the change was a form of nourishment, or maybe ecstasy. I definitely wasn't feeling anything like that. Even the queen seemed to relax into her throne, at least as much as her corset would allow, and take a moment to relish whatever it was she felt pouring into her court. Falin still stood alert and wary behind her, but there was a certain softness to the edge of his eyes, a small tilt to his lips, that told me he was experiencing what everyone else was. Apparently I was the only one left out. I wasn't sure if that was because everyone else was a courtier and I was only an independent, or if I was less fae than people thought. This certainly wasn't the first time I'd not felt Faerie the way others did.

A gong resounded across the field, and the fae gathered themselves, though some seemed a little more lost in euphoria than others. The queen sat upright, shooting a glance across those of us placed around her throne before turning toward where the very last glow was fading. It winked out, and the queen pushed out of her chair.

"The longest night is upon us," she proclaimed in a voice that resounded through the clearing, as she threw up a hand in emphasis.

A loud cheer rose, louder than I would have thought possible, and I turned back around to discover that the clearing was now much larger than it had been. Thousands of fae were gathered in the newly enlarged space. Some I recognized as independents from Nekros, but far more were complete strangers. More trickled into the clearing from between the archway of hawthorn trees, some alone, others in groups as large as a dozen. All were independents. The courts would arrive with more fanfare.

The queen waved her hand, and long banquet tables laden with food appeared along the edge of the tree line. More cheers erupted. She made another wave, and two large bonfires appeared at opposite ends of the clearing. Blue and green fire danced a dozen feet in the air, but it didn't melt any of the snow around it.

I tried to scan faces, but most of the independents didn't come close to the throne or attempt to present themselves. By and large these fae were those who avoided the courts. They might come here, enjoy Faerie on these rare nights, but they didn't belong to Faerie the same way as the courtiers did. I spotted Caleb, one of my housemates, when he entered. He was a greenman, though he rarely released his glamour. For a long time, he'd been the only fae I'd known. Or at least that I'd known I knew. He escorted Holly, another of my housemates, on his arm. She was fully mortal, but since she was addicted to Faerie food already, the revelry was safe enough for her as long as she had a guardian to protect her and keep her out of trouble.

Fae of all shapes and sizes poured in. Most had dropped the glamours they wrapped themselves in while in the mortal world, but a few remained tightly glamoured, or perhaps were of so little fae blood that their features were completely human. Some approached the queen's dais, bowing deeply, though not nearly as many as I'd seen approach the Harvest King during the Fall Equinox. This time I was close enough to hear their requests.

"I would like to move territories," a fae said, his briar hair cut short like a twisting helmet of razor-sharp thorns around his head.

"And do you seek to join my court or to be independent in my land?"

"Remain independent, my lady." His dark eyes looked up at her hopefully.

She debated only a moment. "No. You will have to wait for the doors to shift if you wish to migrate."

His shoulders sagged as he trudged away. A female fae waited for him a few yards away, a pensive look on her face. When she saw his body language, she deflated as well, even her long tangle of briars seeming to wilt. I couldn't hear what he said as he wrapped his arms around her, but she nodded sadly, wiping a tear from her cheek. I didn't think they'd entered together, and it didn't look like they would be leaving together either. This would be a far less merry longest night for them than it could have been. She must have been in winter's territory. I wondered if they could approach any of the other monarchs, or if the rules of the revelry allowed them to only approach the ruling season.

More petitioners came. Most were about land. The Winter Queen sent away all those who wanted to move into her territory as independents, but she allowed three independents to join the winter court. A few of her own people approached about marriage contracts. She granted a frost fae and a little rowen man a fifty-year contract together, but the two of her Sleagh Maith courtiers who asked for a century she granted only fifteen years. The courtier who asked for the queen's hand was quickly turned away.

I only half listened to these exchanges, most of my

attention focused on searching the faces of the fae for Lunabella. That, and wondering if I could take my heels off without anyone noticing.

The trickle of fae entering the clearing slowed, a last few stragglers scooting in, and then they stopped. Theoretically, if the doors were working properly, all the independents attending were inside. I hadn't spotted Lunabella, and she should have stood out among the other independents—almost no Sleagh Maith lived outside the courts. I glanced to Falin. He met my gaze only for a moment, giving the very slightest shake of his head. So he hadn't spotted her either. That meant one of two possibilities: Either she wasn't planning to attend or she hadn't become an independent when she left the summer court.

A few last petitioners came through, including two who asked to fill the open seat on the queen's council. The queen gave them quests to complete, which made me blink in surprise. One quest sounded far more impossible than the other, so I guessed that she favored one candidate more.

A chime sounded through the clearing, and everyone turned their attention to the break in the tree line ringed with hawthorns. A soft glow emanated from under the icicle-strewn branches, and then a pair of fae crowned in flowers stepped into the clearing. *The spring monarchs.* They were followed by an entourage of fae as colorful and varied as the blossoms their season was known for. I scanned the courtiers as they approached. One brown-haired fae in a flowing pastel purple gown caught my attention and at first I thought I'd spotted Lunabella, but when the fae turned toward me, I saw that her features were much sharper than the image in the locket.

"Hail, queen of the long slumber," the spring monarchs said in unison as they reached the foot of the dais.

"Hail, king and queen of awakening life," the queen said, smiling benevolently down from her throne at the other two monarchs. "The oak is sleeping, its sap sluggish, and its boughs weighted with snow. It is not yet time for you to wake it."

The two monarchs inclined their flowered heads. "The time will come for the snows to melt, the sap to quicken, and life to reemerge from your frozen touch, but for now we are content to wait."

"Then for this night and day, join our revelry. Be welcome in our court and make merry with us as we celebrate the longest night and shortest day."

It was a variation on the ritual greeting I'd heard during the Fall Equinox, following almost an identical pattern with different players. Another cheer spread through the clearing as the queen finished welcoming the spring fae into winter. Fae rushed up to greet the newcomers, and the spring fae scattered, joining different groups who had already started celebrating the solstice. Some of the spring fae had brought instruments and spread out to begin playing, others joining to dance or sing. Those of us who were representing the winter court with the queen had not been released yet, and I saw a lot of anxious and envious glances from the winter handmaidens.

Another chime sounded, and the summer court entered next. Now that I knew to look for the division in their court, it was plainly obvious. The queen stood straight and tall, her gown more elaborate than the one she'd worn earlier, but still not as frilly as the Winter Queen's. The courtiers who walked behind her held themselves stiffly, their clothing fine but conservative.

The Summer King entered beside his queen, but there was more space between them than had been between the spring monarchs. The king had a much finer vest, complete with gold piping and embroidery, but he still wasn't wearing a shirt. The fae on his side of the procession were lined up less orderly and their clothing choices were both more varied and often more risqué.

They repeated a very similar greeting ritual as spring had, only they spoke of long summer days. I scanned the courtiers during the exchange. I knew I was unlikely to find Lunabella among them, as it had been only hours since we'd been told she left the court, but I couldn't help looking. Then the greeting was over and fall entered. Lunabella was not among their courtiers either. That left only two courts—besides the high court, who I'd been told never attended—and we knew she wasn't in shadow or Dugan would have recognized her name.

As if summoned by my thoughts, the shadow court emerged from the hawthorns. The king was a dark and deadly figure in oiled black armor as he stalked toward the dais, not even leaving tracks in the snow as he passed over it. Dugan was an equally dangerous-looking figure two steps behind him. They both wore long cloaks that whipped behind them unnaturally, spreading shadows. The longest night might have belonged to winter and her solstice, but the darkness of the night liked the shadow court. I could feel that in the magic buzzing in the air.

I was so busy watching the king and prince that at first I didn't notice the rest of the court. Or really, notice how little of a rest of a court there was. Perhaps many members of the court had decided not to attend the revelry, but I was reminded of what Stiofan had said about fae leaving the shadow court. Less than two hundred shadow courtiers

made up the procession, and only one aside from the king
and prince was Sleagh Maith. She had hair as dark as
Dugan's, and narrowed dark eyes that scanned over the
clearing. She, I noted, hadn't been required to hide her
weapons. Multiple daggers as well as a sword were
strapped to her, and judging by the stiffness of her dark
gown, I suspected it was some sort of oiled leather armor.
Like her royals, she wore the blood on her hands unob-
scured.

The rest of the court were largely what I often heard
the nobles refer to as the more monstrous fae. Goblins,
harpies, and lamias were the more humanoid of the fae I
could name. Many more I had no single word to describe.
The Shadow King had once ruled the realm of dreams,
and many of his people looked like they might have been
born among nightmares. But while many weren't particularly humanoid, many of his people were hauntingly
fascinating. A sphinx looked around regally as she walked
up the path, and a creature who seemed to be made of
nothing but shadow and glowing moonlight floated along
as if carried by an unfelt breeze. Near the end of the procession, a giant wyrm emerged from the hawthorns,
though only magic could explain how the enormous creature had fit under the overhanging branches. Its gleaming
red scales looked like each carried a small flame inside,
and perhaps they did as the snow melted all around it as
it slithered after the Shadow King.

As the king and prince approached the dais, Dugan
met my eyes. He placed one clenched fist over his heart
and inclined his head ever so slightly toward me. It was a
subtle show of affection, or perhaps simply an acknowledgment of the betrothal I had not agreed to. Either way,
it was unwelcome, and I frowned at him. Behind me, I

could feel a glare searing into my back. I glanced over my shoulder, expecting to see that Falin had seen the exchange.

It was the queen. The air around me dropped several degrees, and I cringed.

"Hail, queen of the long slumber," the Shadow King said, his deep voice booming through the clearing.

The queen regarded him a long moment, looking out over his procession, which, while small in number, still took up a considerable space because of the larger fae attending. The moment dragged on, and tension rippled through the clearing. Dancers slowed, musicians played more quietly, and revelers of all kinds turned to watch a greeting that should have just been a formality.

Shadow and light were not seasonal courts. They did not contend for spots on the wheel of the year or have ritual sayings about the oak. Typically both were welcomed without preamble.

"Hail, King of Shadows and Secrets," the queen finally said. "And if you bring goodwill to my court, be welcomed to our celebration of this longest night and shortest day. But if you bring ill will, begone and do not darken our doorstep."

The clearing fell silent.

No fae moved as all eyes turned to the Winter Queen and Shadow King. This was not a ritualistic greeting. It was not part of the ceremony to start the solstice.

Several of the shadow fae bristled, taking the queen's words as insult. The wyrm's large eyes narrowed, its serpentine head swinging around to examine the much smaller humanoid fae in the clearing. I hoped it didn't eat fae.

The king seemed too stunned to speak for a moment,

but he recovered quickly. Smiling broadly, he said, "Then we will be welcomed!"

No cheer went up this time, but some of the tension broke. My lungs gave an ache in protest, and I realized I'd been holding my breath. I let it out in a rush as the shadow fae left the procession to join the revelry. Unlike the other courts, though, who had scattered and quickly intermixed with the fae already gathered, the shadow fae largely stayed to themselves, remaining on the outskirts of any group they joined.

Music and the general sound of frivolity began again, slowly, but it had not yet reached the level at which it had been before shadow's arrival when the chime sounded, announcing the final court. I turned to the hawthorns, anxious for this last greeting to be over so I could leave my spot beside the damn dais. I'd been too shocked by the queen's words to think about scanning the crowd for anyone who looked too pleased by the apparent animosity between winter and shadow. I hoped Falin had been more observant. Maybe it had even been planned, as both regents knew we suspected they were being played against each other. But it hadn't felt staged.

I fidgeted, waiting as the soft glow formed between the hawthorns. It grew brighter than it had with any of the other courts, and the Queen of Light stepped into the clearing. My breath caught in my throat once again. Not from fear this time, but from wonder.

I'd seen the Queen of Light once before, but I'd forgotten how unearthly beautiful she was. Earlier today I would have said the Summer Queen was the most beautiful person I'd ever seen, but the Queen of Light made the other seem only a pale reflection of beauty. It was no particular feature; in fact, as I studied her face, I realized that she looked very similar to the Winter Queen. They were sisters, so perhaps that wasn't surprising, but I hadn't realized how much of a resemblance they shared. They had the same sharp cheekbones, the same rosebud lips and icy blue eyes. The Winter Queen was dark where her sister was fair, but otherwise, they were nearly identical. Except for the aura surrounding the Queen of Light.

All Sleagh Maith glowed slightly, but the Queen of Light was positively radiant. It lit everything around her, making the night softer, brighter, and I felt an unintentional smile spread across my face. The glow gave her an unreal quality, like something fleeting that needed to be treasured. Glamour? Or just the natural condition of her court? The ethereal light was surely where the breathtaking beauty originated. Which meant it wasn't real. And yet I couldn't seem to look away from her.

"Hail, Sister, Queen of the Long Slumber." Her voice was musical, and just quiet enough that I felt myself straining to hear her, hoping she's speak again.

"Hail, Queen of Light and Daydreams," the Winter Queen said, and the most genuine smile I'd ever seen on her spread over her face. "Well met and be welcomed, Sister."

A cheer roared through the clearing, fae rushing forward to greet the shimmering court of light. I realized I'd been so caught up in studying the queen, I'd never glanced at her courtiers. She had more Sleagh Maith—and more courtiers in general—than any other court present tonight. The glowing throng was huge and already breaking apart to join the festivities. But there, near the back of the gentry, I spotted Lunabella.

Chapter 13

❧═══◦ ◦═══❧

"Let all make merry on this longest night," the Winter Queen said from her throne behind me.

I hoped that meant I was dismissed to join the revelry because I was already moving, trying to keep sight of Lunabella. Most of the light court had the same ethereal glow as their queen, though to a much milder degree, but Lunabella glowed with little more than the typical Sleagh Maith of any court. I guessed she hadn't been in the court long enough for the magic to change her. She wasn't the only one. The light court was the largest attending court, but its numbers seemed bloated with members who didn't glow like the rest. Had they all defected? How long did it take for Faerie to begin changing courtiers after they changed courts?

As if to make up for her lack of light court ambiance, Lunabella wore a gown of cheery yellow, trimmed with gold. A pair of yellow gloves with gold embellishments complemented the dress perfectly. *Could she be hiding blood on her hands?* Not that it was an immediate sign of guilt to have blood on your hands. Hell, I did. I'd earned mine in self-defense. Some earned theirs in duels. Some courts, like the shadow court, refused to hide their blood, while others passed all the blood to one member, like the winter court. *And then they ostracized him.* Of course, it was also possible the gloves were a fashion choice. Many of those in formal attire wore gloves.

Lunabella scanned the crowds of fae. She might have been searching for friends as her head turned first one way and then another, but to me she looked nervous. Guilty conscience, maybe? She finally took off alone, seemingly wandering.

I followed, keeping enough distance that I hoped I wasn't obvious. A group of summer nobles called her name, waving and motioning her over. She'd scanned that area of the clearing a moment ago, her gaze sliding right over the small group, so I didn't think they were who she was looking for, but she smiled and sauntered over to chat.

I glanced around. A musician was playing a few yards from where she was now talking animatedly with the group of summer nobles. I made my way toward the crowd gathering around him, thrilled to discover there were chairs. I sank gratefully into one that provided a clear line of sight of Lunabella where she chatted in front of a banquet table.

The chair put me very close to a group of dancers frolicking in a small space clearly meant for such frivolity. This particular singer's voice was far stronger than his lute, giving his song a bardic feel. The gathered fae clapped in time to the music, and I lifted my hands, trying to keep the beat while watching Lunabella from the corner of my eye. Fae shouted the words in the chorus along with the singer, raising mugs and goblets into the air. Even if I'd been trying to follow what the song was about, I wouldn't have been able to as it was in that strange musical language so many of the fae spoke. I didn't understand a word. Not that I was actually listening. Even as Lunabella laughed at something one of her companions said, she glanced around, alert for something or someone. If she was involved with Stiofan's murder, she hadn't done it alone. I could only hope she'd lead me to her accomplices, and I doubted these nobles fit that bill. She was too distracted as she spoke to them, too anxious to find someone else.

She smiled, taking a step back as she said something. The conversation was drawing to an end. I pushed to my feet, prepared to trail her again.

I was gazing out across the dancers, not really paying attention to them, but I must have looked like I was waiting for a dance partner. A fae with a bestial face and hands tipped in claws bounded up to me. He wrapped his hands around my wrist, the claws carefully held away from my satin gloves. He dragged me forward a step.

"Come dance," he said, trying to lead me closer to the singer and the other dancers.

"I don't—"

He wasn't listening. The music started again and he pulled me along with him as he began to dance. He was strong, and graceful, but with joints that didn't move at all like mine. And no respect at all for the fact that I didn't want to dance. I considered screaming, or struggling out of his grip, but I could see Lunabella every time he spun me and she was scanning the crowds again. If I made a scene, I'd draw far too much attention to myself.

The beastly fae led me on a leaping, twirling dance, and my already blistering feet protested every step. Still the fae wouldn't release me. I twisted, trying to keep Lunabella in sight. She glanced back and forth until her gaze finally locked on who she must have been looking for. She scurried over to a fae wearing a golden cloak. No smiles and laughing this time. The two ducked their heads, Lunabella nodding slowly. I guessed the figure was a "he" only because of height and the width of his shoulders, but in fae, who came in so many shapes and sizes, that might be an assumption I couldn't count on. The beastly fae spun me again, and one of my heels caught in the long train of my gown. I pitched forward, saved from falling on my ass only because he caught me by the waist. He gave me a shy smile full of fangs. I didn't return the smile as I peered over his shoulder.

I'd lost sight of Lunabella in my near fall, and I whipped my head around, searching for her and the golden-cloaked figure. I spotted him first, the gold of his cloak reflecting the blue firelight in an ominous display. Lunabella wasn't with him. My dance partner lifted me in a twirl that had my shoes two feet off the ground. I spotted Lunabella in the middle of the lift, headed toward the back of the clearing, the opposite way from the cloaked figure.

"Lovely dance. Really. But I need to—" I gestured as I spoke, pointing to the edge of the dance.

The beastly fae only smiled. He spun me again, the layers of fabric in the gown swirling around my legs. But I thought he was at least spinning me toward the seats and my escape. Until he handed me to another dance partner.

This one was far less skillful. He wrapped his arms around my waist and tried to pull me along as he leapt in uneven spinning circles. Now I did trip, falling to my knees only to be hauled back up by a third partner.

"I should sit down," I yelled over the music, though what I really wanted to do was escape this dance and kick off my awful heels before tracking down Lunabella. My feet were throbbing.

The fae who had his arms around me, lifting me into the air as he spun us, only cocked his head to the side. He had roughly humanoid features, but he was covered in what looked like bright blue fur. I only realized it was actually feathers when I recognized the magnificent plumage of peacock feathers he had in place of hair.

He said something in a language I didn't know. It didn't have the musical qualities of the fae language and I had the feeling it was a foreign but human language— independent fae lived in every country of the world. The problem was, he couldn't understand I wanted to stop dancing.

I tried to motion to where I thought the chairs were, and got my legs tangled in my skirt's twisted train again. I would have fallen—again—if not for a pair of strong arms that caught me, spinning me away from the peacock fae.

"You look like you could use a rescue," a blessedly familiar voice said, and I looked up into Falin's face.

"Yes. Get me away from here," I muttered, trying not to whimper. I very nearly added a "please" to the request, I wanted out of the dance so badly, but neither one of us would want him to hold a debt over me that the queen could use.

He moved us deftly to the edge of the dance. Someone tried to cut in, but a single glare from Falin sent them scurrying for an easier-to-acquire partner. We

stopped even a pretense of dancing once we broke free
of the group, but didn't stop moving until we were past
the chairs I'd sat in earlier. I limped along, struggling to
keep pace with Falin. Once we were far enough away
that we weren't at risk of getting dragged back into the
dance, he turned toward me.

"Are you hurt?"

"Not really, and far more important, I found Lunabella. She was with the court of light. I followed her but
lost her during the dance."

"I know. I saw you hurry after her," Falin said, and I
almost sighed in relief.

"So you know where she went?"

"Dugan is following her."

I raised one eyebrow, surprised he'd passed following
our only lead off to Dugan. Falin shrugged.

"It was rescue you from that dance or trail Lunabella.
I wasn't sending the Shadow Prince after you. Now,
where are you hurt?"

"It's nothing really," I said, but I lifted my skirt, trying
to get a look at my feet under all the material—not that I
could bend to reach my feet in the restricting corset.

Falin knelt in front of me, and when I lifted my foot,
he slipped off the shoe. I immediately felt better with the
heels off, but then I was left with my bare foot dangling
in the air. I set it down tentatively. The snow crunched
under my toes, and it felt cool, but not cold. It would
suck to walk around barefoot all night, but I probably
wouldn't lose any toes to hypothermia.

Falin glanced at the heeled slipper in his hand. Rusty
red blood coated the blue and silver material where the
shoes had bitten blisters into my foot. Falin shook his
head.

"Only you could get injured by dress shoes."

"Not true—heels are totally unnecessary torture devices."

"Says the woman who normally walks around in thigh-high platform boots," he said, his tone friendly and teasing. Then he looked at the shoe in his hand again and frowned. "But you can't walk around barefoot, especially not with bleeding feet. Let me see if I can fix this. I'll have to put it back on first."

I grimaced, but lifted my foot so he could get the shoe back on. It felt like my foot must have swollen to the next size up in the short period the heeled shoe had been off because it felt even tighter and more painful now. Then Falin wrapped his hands around my foot, and his glamour changed the shoe. It grew softer and more pliable, the heel shrinking to nothing. I held my foot out and examined my new pale-blue-and-silver ballet flat.

"Much better," I said as way of thanks. I lifted the other foot and let him glamour it as well. My feet still hurt—the glamour didn't heal them—but at least they were out of the heels. He fussed with the dress next, and it became a little less full, a little more manageable, and the train shortened, shrinking until the trim of the dress hung just above the snow.

I gave an experimental twirl as Falin stood. The glamour held perfectly, the dress moving around me but no longer a major tripping hazard.

"I could kiss you." I breathed the words as much as said them, a happy sigh tumbling out of me, and wished I had some way of thanking him better.

The edge of Falin's lips lifted slightly, a small, secret smile just for me. Warmth fluttered in my stomach, a mix of awareness of how close we were standing, anticipation that he might take me up on the offer, and embarrassment because I hadn't thought before I'd spoken. Not being able to say "thank you" was hard.

He stared at me, and the warmth spread, an unexpected eagerness with it. Months ago, at the last revelry, had been the last time we'd kissed. That had been . . . complicated. Mix a love confession with a threat at dagger point and maybe "complicated" was an understatement.

Falin lifted a hand like he was going to place it on my cheek, but then he stopped, his fingers hovering just out of reach.

"Taboos are lifted for tonight," he whispered.

The warmth of his fingers heated the air between his hand and my face. He wanted to touch me, I could see it in the way his lips parted, the heat in his eyes. Hell, I often saw it when he thought I wasn't looking. He was forbidden to become further romantically involved with me. I knew that. But for tonight, those rules didn't apply. All of Faerie was entreated to make merry.

I slid my hand over the back of his, giving it the slightest nudge so that his palm cradled my cheek. Even through his gloves, his touch made my skin tingle with anticipation. He gazed at me, intent, intense, and my breath caught. That made him look at my lips, and I knew he would throw caution to the wind.

He leaned down, his lips brushing mine, the kiss chaste. Then his hand slipped from my cheek to the back of my neck and he deepened the kiss. I lifted up onto my toes, balancing a hand on his chest as I relished the kiss. My tongue slid into his mouth, tasting, testing, and he met me perfectly.

It was far from our first kiss, and yet it held the same uncertainty as one. The kiss was exploration, heat but hesitation. We broke off, both breathing hard.

He stared at me, his gaze full of wonder and desire. I had been cherished before. Loved. But when Falin looked at me, and let me see his feelings in his eyes, he looked at me like I was air itself. It was intense. And it was frightening, because in his gaze, I could see that he really saw me. Not just the me dressed up like a doll at the queen's command. Not just the planeweaver. Not even just the grave witch. But all of me. The me that stumbled around searching for coffee when I first woke. The me who'd thought he was an arrogant asshole when we first met. The me that tended to hide from difficult emotions and relationships. And the me that often felt like I didn't know what I was doing half the time. He saw it all, and he still looked at me like I was everything.

I couldn't hold his intense gaze. It was too much. Too real. I glanced away, and the moment broke.

Falin took a step back. "We should . . ." He stopped. His voice was still thick with desire. He cleared his throat, his gaze moving over my shoulder. "That was not a good idea. The queen is in a foul mood. We shouldn't tempt her ire."

I gave a jerk of my head that I hoped came off as a nod as I fumbled to put my hands in pockets, which the dress didn't have. I was still breathing a little too hard, and the corset wasn't helping. My chest heaved with each breath, my breasts threatening to spill out with each lungful of air. *Stupid gown.*

"I guess we should go find Lunabella," I said, stepping back so I wasn't quite as close to Falin and the possibilities that still seemed to hang in the air between us.

Falin shrugged. "Dugan is watching her. Besides, we can't confront her here. If she was involved, we could do nothing as all grudges, crimes, and bans are temporarily forgotten during the revelry. If she wasn't involved, discussing a death during a revelry would be . . . more than just frowned upon." He sighed. "It might complicate things that she is in the light court, or that might simplify getting an interview with her after the revelry. I'm not sure. Either way, we know where to find her. For now that has to be good enough."

"Then why send Dugan to watch her?"

"So I could be the one to escort you, of course." He held out his arm for me to take. "Come on. Let's enjoy the revelry."

I yawned, stretching my arms over my head and breathing in as much as the constraining corset allowed. Dawn was starting to light the horizon, which meant the longest night was coming to an end, and the shortest day was beginning. It also meant I'd been awake over twenty-four hours.

"Don't fae ever sleep?" I grumbled, dropping my arms and slumping in the ice-carved seat I was perched on.

Falin glanced over from his own chair. "During a revelry? Some already are." He nodded toward the edges of the clearing.

Some fae slumped at the great banquet tables, snoring off an overindulgence of pixie wine. Others had bedded down in the snow under the trees, but many of those in the tree line weren't necessarily sleeping.

The idea of taking a nap in the snow—even enchanted snow that wasn't particularly cold—didn't appeal to me.

Still, I wasn't going to be good for much soon. Leaving
was always an option, but even if I stepped out now, at
dawn, it would be sunset when I emerged. I hated losing
an entire day to Faerie. Especially since I'd go directly
to bed when I got home. Losing a day and then sleeping
all night was like adding insult to injury.

"I have to walk around, or I'm going to fall asleep in
this chair," I said, pushing to my feet.

Falin laughed, but he stood in one smooth motion
and extended his arm to escort me.

We wandered. So far we'd dined very well, watched
several plays about Faerie history, listened to more different kinds of musicians than I could name, and even
danced some more, though not for long because even in
the ballet flats, my blistered feet ached. Neither of us had
mentioned the kiss we'd shared.

We were passing close to one of the buffet tables when
one of the revelers caught my attention. I stopped. I wasn't
sure what it was about the man, but something about the
way he stood, or maybe his voice, was horribly familiar to
me. His face didn't look like anyone I knew. His skin was
slightly ruddy and his features a little too round to be full-
blooded fae, so I was guessing he was a changeling or
possibly feykin. And yet there was something that struck
me about his face as well, though I couldn't place it.

When he saw me looking at him, he looked away, turning to a group of revelers beside him that I got a feeling
he wasn't quite a part of. I took a step closer to him and
Falin frowned at me.

"What is it?"

"I'm not sure. There is something about that man . . ."
I opened my shields enough that I could peer across the

planes. I wasn't expecting anything to change, as the man appeared to be at least mostly human.

Appearances can be deceiving.

The glamour he wore vanished under my gaze, revealing a very different face beneath. A face with sharp features that were not that dissimilar to my own. A face belonging to my father.

I strolled up to him, Falin at my side.

"I had heard it was customary to drop glamours for a revelry," I said, as I stepped up beside him.

For a moment he looked like he was going to play innocent or try to deny who he was. Then he sighed, and while the glamoured face didn't change, the expression became one I knew only too well.

"What is it you want, Alexis?"

Yup, that tone that managed to sound both uninterested and disappointed at the same time definitely belonged to my father.

"I'm surprised to see you here." After all, from my understanding, he didn't enter Faerie pretty much ever and no one knew he was fae. "But since you are here, I thought I'd talk to you about what we were discussing during our phone call the other day." I left my words intentionally vague. There were a lot of fae from every court around us. I didn't know what was known about the deaths in the winter court, but I definitely did not want to be the source of any rumors.

My father considered me. The glamour made his eyes look watery and slightly unfocused, and his expression vapid, like he'd had a little too much to drink. His actual eyes were clear and evaluating. His gaze slid to Falin, whose expression was empty, but I could almost feel the cautious curiosity vibrating through our locked arms. Falin did not know who the man in front of us was. Which was fine. I had the sinking suspicion it would cause issues if he found out that an unknown fae that didn't belong to the winter court resided in—hell, was governor of—Nekros. Falin knew many of my secrets, but definitely not all of them.

"You will have to lose your unfortunate choice of a chaperone," my father said, tossing a disparaging glance at Falin.

"I'll be right back," I told Falin before he had time to react to my father's chosen description. For a moment I thought he'd try to stop me, but he only pressed his lips into a thin line, shooting a distrustful glance in my father's direction.

"Don't go far," he said. "With this many fae, it'll be hard to find each other again if we get separated. I'll try to keep you in sight."

I nodded my agreement and then turned to hustle after my father, who was headed toward a scattering of small tables. He picked an empty frost-covered table closest to the tree line and slid into one of the seats. I sat across from him, the icy table between us.

"What kind of privacy spells do you have?" he asked.

I didn't wince—it would have been a sign of weakness he would have jumped all over. "I have a small privacy bubble spell, but it's not big enough to cover both of us when we are this far apart."

He frowned.

"If I sat beside you—" I began.

He waved my words away with a dismissive twitch of his hand. "I've got it."

I didn't feel his magic, but the sounds of the revelry

around us grew distant. The noises didn't go completely silent like they would have had I used my spell, they just became less distinct and softer. That done, he propped his elbows on the table and folded his fingers into a steeple before his face, staring over his fingers at me.

"I didn't think you traveled into Faerie," I said.

He frowned at me. "Normally? No. But all fae are invited to the revelries. It is nice to visit sometimes. I do not believe that is what we are here to discuss, though."

True.

"I accepted the case you wanted." He'd never actually said I had to solve it. "How do I reach the high court?"

He evaluated me so long I thought he wasn't going to answer. Then he asked, "Why is it you want to go to the high court?"

I almost didn't tell him. He'd asked me a favor, and I'd fulfilled what he'd asked. I could feel the debt between us hanging in the air. But he'd intentionally indebted himself, so that did make me feel a little more amicable.

"I need a teacher before I hurt myself. The high court is said to have two changeling planeweavers."

His frown deepened. "You can't reach them. No one can."

I gave him an incredulous look, and he sighed.

"I know you've probably heard rumors of golden halls and grand balls or some other such nonsense, but they are, for lack of a better word, fairy tales. There is no court, per se. There is only the king. A very old king. The very last *seelie* king."

"The what?"

My father sank back in his chair and ran a hand over his face. He looked tired, and his youthful fae face looked older, ragged. "Tonight you've been watching plays on Faerie history and listening to ancient songs depicting legends and events of times long past, correct?"

I gave a small nod, not sure where he was going with this.

"Then let me tell you a story mostly forgotten by time. Once Faerie was not as it is now with its seven courts. Once it was only two courts: *seelie* and *unseelie*. The seelie court was bright and beautiful and full of fae whose glamour was fueled by the adoration and fascination of mortals. The unseelie court was sometimes beautiful but often monstrous. The unseelie reveled in fueling their glamour with the fear of mortals. The wars between the two courts were of epic proportions. They shook both Faerie and the mortal world alike."

He lifted his hands, and a small scene appeared beneath them, conjured from glamour. Under one hand, the landscape was bright and full of gardens. Under the other, the landscape was dark and things seemed to move in the darkness that I couldn't focus on. A small doll or maybe a stringless puppet appeared on each side. They were crude, featureless, but it was clear that the puppet on the bright side was male and the one on the dark side female. I watched, fascinated.

"The final seelie king was cunning and ambitious. After winning his throne, he proposed a century-long truce between the courts through a union with the unseelie queen. They both went into it planning to use the time and marriage to the advantage of their own court, but over the course of the truce, the unseelie queen fell in love with her husband. He dazzled her and her court with the wonders of his court, while continuing to propagate loathing of her court among his people. When the century ended, the queen requested an extended union, but the king refused. He rallied his troops and attacked on the same night the truce dissolved. Some say the queen died of a broken heart. Others say she remained in their marriage bed that last night and at the stroke of midnight, when the truce broke, the king murdered her in her sleep. The war that followed was swift but brutal. The unseelie court was decimated, and the seelie king claimed rulership of both courts, declaring himself the high king of all Faerie."

The little seelie king puppet swung out with a small sword. The queen puppet stumbled back, doubling over, before falling face forward. I watched in morbid fascination as the little king puppet placed his foot on her unmoving back and lifted his sword aloft in victory. The light side of the scene poured over the dark side, driving the shadows to the far corners.

"But Faerie is never only one thing," he said, and the scene began to tremble. The little seelie king puppet stumbled. "The seelie court's total victory upset the balance and Faerie shattered. The new pieces became the courts as you know them now. The seasons balance each other and light balances shadow. The high king sits in the center, ruler of all but connected to none. Faerie keeps him at her heart, allowing his law to bend her, but he has no court, no courtiers; he has only his throne and he cannot step down from it. In the beginning he exerted his will heavily on the courts, made his own house the nobles throughout all courts, enforced truces and created laws, but over the millennia he has become more distant and withdrawn, slumbering away whole centuries."

The scene changed. A wheel appeared under my father's hands. The outside was the seasonal courts, depicted much in the same way as in the clearing that held the doors to all the courts. Inside them, light and shadow made up the next ring. In the very center, as the spoke of the wheel, the little seelie king puppet sat on a throne. Chains bound him to the throne, and his head drooped forward, shoulders bent. Though the puppet still had no features, it looked tired, defeated. The high king bound to his throne. I stared at Faerie laid out in this way, and then my father dropped his hands, and the scene vanished.

"Why has no one ever mentioned any of this before?" I asked, and frowned. "And if the high king has no court, then what about the planeweavers? There are supposed to be two changeling planeweavers in the high court."

He grimaced. "There were. When the king learned that anyone with the gift of planeweaving was being systematically exterminated, he searched for those remaining with the talent. He found only two, both among the mortals, so he secreted them away and put them in a deep slumber, waking them only when needed."

"That's horrific."

My father shrugged. "It is what it is."

"Well, then where are they now?"

"Dead." He looked past me, his gazing roaming over the multitude of revelers gathered for the festivities. He sighed. "You would think, in his overlong lifetime, he would have outlived some of his worst traits, but hubris and prejudice still plague him. When the fae were fading, Faerie dying, and the high king decided that the fae had to reveal themselves to this modern world to survive, he didn't think the humans would accept us if they knew that some of the fae fed off nightmares. And, perhaps, if he were honest, he hated to see how well shadow had thrived even during the drought of belief that had caused most courts to weaken and fade. Shadow's denizens reminded him most of the unseelie. So, before the magical awakening, he ordered the realm of dreams severed from the rest of Faerie. The changeling planeweavers were awoken, and they unraveled the threads binding dreams to shadows. But the task was too great for two mortals. Dreams are part of the human condition. Nightmares naturally conjured in shadows. Small threads proved difficult to fully sever, and the strain killed both planeweavers."

I blinked as shock rolled over me. Then the reality that the only other two planeweavers were dead sank in. The realization hit me like stones, and I collapsed backward into my chair under the weight of them. That meant there was no one to learn from. No one to go to for help or guidance so I didn't accidentally kill myself.

"It was tragic what happened to them, but it was also good they didn't fully succeed. Those small strands still connecting dream to shadow have at least slowed the tragedy that came next. Though with them dead, it left no one to repair the damage."

I just stared at him, still numb from the loss of my own hope.

"What do you see?" My father waved a hand toward the clearing behind me.

I turned, trying to spot what he saw. There were fae everywhere. They laughed and danced, ate and toasted, sang and cheered. There was merriment from corner to corner in the enormous clearing. A dozen or so yards away I spotted Falin, hanging back but keeping an eye on me. My father wasn't looking in his direction, so I didn't think that was what he meant.

"I see fae," I finally said, turning back to him.

He nodded. "Yes, but there are too many solitary in-dependents. There have never been so many unaligned fae before. There are too many fae in the light court and far too few in shadow. The balance is off, and I fear for Faerie if it continues. If Faerie becomes too unbalanced, will it shatter again?"

I studied the man across from me. With my shields closed, the glamoured face he wore was that of a stranger. But in truth, the face under the glamour was nearly as unfamiliar. I'd always known him to be calculating. To be scheming. But never to morosely ruminate.

"If it did, it would become something new again, right? Like in your story when it went from two courts to seven? Would that really be such a bad thing? From what I've seen, the courts could use an overhaul."

His gaze snapped away from the crowd, sharpening as it landed on me. "I let you grow up mortal in a world full of change and with a short memory. This is not that world. Faerie does not deal with change well."

Probably true. Then something he'd said earlier reg-istered. "What tragedy came next? After the planeweav-ers died?"

He waved a hand at the clearing. "You are watching it." And with that unhelpful bit of information, he pushed out of his seat. "I should go. The day is starting and I have a meeting with a senator this morning."

"You're going to miss it. The door will spit you out at sunset." How did he not know that?

My father glanced back for only a moment. Long enough to give me a small, mischievous smile. "The doors can be rather fickle."

Then he walked away, leaving me blinking at his back

as he headed for the hawthorn-lined path. Once he'd disappeared, I made my way back to Falin.

"What was that about?" Falin asked.

I shook my head. "It wasn't related to the case." Not directly at least. "Just someone who owed me some information." Which I hadn't actually gotten. He'd told me a lot of things I hadn't known, but he hadn't actually given me the answer I'd asked for. Of course, if he was right about the changeling planeweavers being dead, it didn't matter. It wasn't like I wanted to go talk to the high king.

"You're the planeweaver," a female voice said behind us.

I winced, but turned. I couldn't exactly deny who I was.

The Summer Queen stood with a handmaiden to either side of her. I blinked in surprise for a moment, then dipped into a small curtsy.

"Your Majesty," I said.

"You are the planeweaver, are you not?"

"Yes."

"And you are also the girl who was with my husband yesterday afternoon?"

I winced again, and I was aware how still Falin had gone by my side. Theoretically, at a revelry the Summer Queen couldn't punish any grudges she might have against me, but I wasn't sure if that was an unbreakable rule that Faerie enforced or just a tradition.

"Nothing happened," I said, realizing how guilty and stupid that sounded as soon as it was out of my mouth.

"Of that I have no doubt. You were still dressed when I arrived." Her perfect lips turned downward. "You must be very much in love to have resisted his glamours. Considering what I know of winter and how she treats her knights, I'm not sure if I should congratulate you or mourn the tragedy of it all."

I spluttered, dropping Falin's arm. I wanted to say we were only friends. But while it was true that we were friends, saying we were only friends wasn't the full truth, and I knew it. Most of the time I had no reason to examine the feelings I had for him because he was, as the Summer Queen implied, off-limits.

Falin, for his part, said nothing, his face cold and blank, like a carved ice sculpture.

"Regardless," the queen said, ignoring my reaction, "I think I would be happier right now had I caught you in flagrante delicto with my husband. Discovering he was in negotiation with a planeweaver is far more concerning. What did he want from you?"

I considered her, this beautiful but rigid queen with her severe handmaidens. Her subjects were not the roisterous and exuberant collective the king surrounded himself with, but her people didn't seem unhappy. Assuming they had the choice, the fae who followed her preferred her more restrained ways. The king had implied he wanted me to dissolve the marriage bond between them. Reading between the lines, that meant one of them would no longer be Faerie royalty. I doubted the king intended to vacate his throne. Did this stern queen deserve to know her lecherous husband's plans? And was it my place to tell her?

Well, I sure as hell would want to know. But there was one little problem . . .

"I think that I would tell you if I could, but it is more complicated than that."

"You took an oath?" She furrowed her brow. Then her green eyes widened. "No, he laid a curse on you. I can see it hanging about you, ready to spring. What are the conditions?"

I just stared at her, unsure if I could speak about the curse without setting it off. Beside me, Falin twisted around, studying me as if he'd be able to spot the nebulous magic stilling my tongue.

"Ah, you can't speak of it, can you? My husband is not horribly original. I suppose you'll start spitting spiders or snails if you do?"

"Toads."

She gave a rueful laugh. "Of course."

Crossing her arms over her chest, she raked her gaze over me, taking my measure once again. This time I came out slightly better than I had in the flower tent. Then I'd felt like an ant; this time, more of a mouse. Not that much of an improvement.

"I'm told you've promised my husband that you will spend three days in our court," she said, looking thoughtful. "I can't imagine you are well pleased with him considering his deception in getting you to court and now this curse business." She waved her hand vaguely as if she could trace the shape of the magical trap the king had set. "No doubt when he made the bargain he assumed he'd charm you, bed you, and have you begging to help him simply for the favor of his smile. That didn't work out well for him."

She certainly had a way of summing up the obvious. I only smiled at her, waiting for her to get to the point.

"Visit me instead. I will show you my gardens and we can have tea," she said, and graced me with her own beatific smile.

She was without a doubt a powerful Faerie queen, terrible in her beauty, and yet I felt no pull of glamour while looking at her. If I ranked the Queen of Light as a ten on the "using entrancing glamour to fuck with people's brains" scale, the Summer King would be a seven or eight. Even the Winter Queen had caught me briefly a time or two when I wasn't guarding myself. But the Summer Queen was simply what she was. I had to admire that. Of course, the cynical part of me had to wonder if she was simply subtler than the other royals I'd encountered.

"I think that would be an agreeable arrangement," I said cautiously, committing to nothing.

"Good. You can tell me about what my husband requested then." She held up a hand to ward off my protest. "A curse laid by a royal can only be removed by another royal, and only after it has been triggered. I will be happy to remove it for you in my garden."

"A generous offer," I said, again not committing to anything. After all, I didn't actually need the curse removed as long as I never attempted to divulge what the king had said.

She laughed. "I do hope you were this reticent with my husband. I will await your visit. Be merry."

It was a dismissal, and I took it as such. I made a small curtsy, Falin bowed his head, and then we hurried away from the queen and her small entourage.

"I'd ask why you didn't tell me you were cursed, but I guess I know the answer," Falin hissed in my ear as we made our way around a boisterous group of revelers.

I shrugged. "I did mention I was pissed off. I just didn't elaborate on *all* of the reasons."

Falin grunted, and I knew he was thinking about what else the queen had said. And what she'd implied.

We'd just swerved to avoid getting caught in a dance

that had spontaneously erupted not far in front of us, when Falin stopped. Half asleep on my feet, I didn't notice he wasn't walking anymore until the arm I had laced through his tugged me back, my own momentum making me stumble.

"What—?" I started, but he turned toward me and pulled me closer to him.

He leaned toward me, and for a moment I thought he was going to kiss me again. Butterflies erupted unbidden in my stomach, but he pressed his lips just beside my ear instead.

"Twelve o'clock, headed straight for us," he whispered. "Smile as if I've said something clever as you look."

I did as instructed. Lunabella and two companions were maybe twelve feet away, coming from the opposite direction, and also avoiding the dance. There was no time to duck out of sight and we were right in their path. Falin's actions made sense; at their angle, and with the way he was pressed against me, his face wasn't visible. Though I'd been displayed with the Winter Queen's court, I was far less recognizable than her knight. We were just another fae couple, caught up in the merriment of the revelry. With Falin's breath trailing softly down the back of my neck, it wasn't hard to play my role. I let my hands crawl up over his shoulders as I watched the trio through slitted eyes.

Lunabella and her two companions—an auburn-haired male Sleagh Maith and a pale, drawn fae woman whose hair writhed like it was alive—were in deep conversation as they passed us, and they didn't so much as glance up. I strained to hear what was being said, but the conversation must have been hidden by magic, because while they passed close enough that I could have reached out and touched the fabric of the auburn-haired fae's topcoat, I couldn't hear a word.

I remained tucked against Falin after they rounded a group of revelers and moved out of sight, not because I was afraid they would suddenly turn and spot us, but because it was warm in his arms, comfortable. I was considering the fact that it might well be worth the Winter Queen's ire for one more kiss when a flash of gold caught my attention. The hooded and cloaked figure I'd seen Lunabella talking to earlier rounded the corner. I couldn't tell exactly where he was looking as no part of his face showed under the deep hood, but it seemed like he was following Lunabella and the other two fae. He hesitated as he drew nearer, and I swore I felt his gaze on me. It felt . . . hostile. He pulled the cloak closed tighter as he passed us, and the skin on his exposed hand was a sickly gray shade, but it glowed as if he were Sleagh Maith. Or maybe I was wrong and the glow signified he was light court? Had he entered with them? I'd been focused on Lunabella, and I couldn't remember noticing him with any court.

The gray hand vanished inside his cloak, emerging a moment later with a fist-sized yellow stone. Topaz? Or maybe a yellow citrine? It was large and uncut, and yet it glowed with golden light. He bent his cowled head over it, muttering something. I caught a syllable or two, but it sounded like he was speaking in that lyrical fae language I probably needed to learn. A deep red light flashed from the jewel, seeming to blot out the entire clearing for a moment, and I jolted. Falin's arms tightened around me.

"What's wrong?" He breathed the question into my hair.

"What was that light?"

We were pressed too close for him to turn to look at me without pulling away, but I could all but feel his puzzlement. He hadn't seen the nearly blinding flash of red light. A glance around the other nearby fae revealed that no one else had been startled either. As if no one else had seen what I had.

I focused on the golden-cloaked figure again. He was still bent over the large stone clutched in his thin hand. The bloodred light was gone now, the unpolished stone glowing a gentle honey yellow again, but at the center of the stone, I caught sight of a swirling cloud of darkness before the fae tucked the gem into his cloak once more.

I cracked open my shields, hoping to catch a look at the fae. Nothing changed. The cloak was real, not glamour. Without another glance in my direction, he shuffled by, moving with a distinct limp.

I shivered after he had passed. He was involved with all of this. I was sure of it.

"Are you quite finished?" a deep voice asked beside me after the cloaked figure had vanished among the crowd.

I turned to see Dugan watching us. He didn't sound jealous that his theoretical fiancée was in another man's arms, just disappointed.

"No, far from finished," Falin answered, looking up to give the prince a meaningful smile, but I was already stepping back.

"Did you follow her all night?" I asked, stifling a yawn. I'd thought I was exhausted before, but now I felt close to falling asleep on my feet.

"Yes, and it's been a waste of a revelry."

"The shortest day has barely started. You can still go . . . revel." Was that a word? I rolled my head on my neck and eased back my stiff shoulders. I couldn't catch my yawn this time.

"I could," Dugan said slowly. "If someone else is going to note her contacts. She's horribly boring, but rather well connected. She appears to be friendly with nobles from nearly every court."

"Winter?" Falin asked.

Dugan shook his head. "Aside from my own, the only other court she hasn't stopped at to converse with some courtier or another."

Considering the only noble present in shadow besides himself and the king was one militaristic Sleagh Maith, I wasn't surprised she hadn't met with any shadow fae. I was more than slightly disappointed she hadn't scuttled off to converse with any winter fae. Discovering her contacts inside the court would have been helpful in narrowing down how she'd gotten inside—if she was involved with the murders. We still didn't have any proof of her guilt. Just a possible identification of her voice by one of the victims.

"Also, if we hoped to surprise her, that has certainly passed," Dugan said. "The fact that we traveled to the summer court looking for her has been frequent gossip."

Both Falin and I nodded. We'd overheard some of those whispers as well.

I yawned again. My head felt too heavy, and a deep ache was forming in my body. "Would it be horrible if I yell 'not me' on the whole spying thing at this point? I think I'm going home. I'm exhausted."

Dugan raised an eyebrow. "You'll lose not only the day but also the hours you then sleep that could otherwise be useful. Would it not be smarter to rest here?"

I shook my head. "Yeah, you see, I'm not really into bedding down in snow forts."

"You could use one of the tents."

I'd been looking around, trying to find the hawthorn path that would lead me to the door, but I stopped at his words. "Wait, what?" I turned toward Falin. "There are tents?" And he hadn't thought to mention that before?

Falin scowled Dugan. "Yes, but they are for the monarchs."

"Technically, they are for all royalty," he said. And as a prince, he apparently counted. It was good to be a prince. He bowed to me. "I would be honored to allow my lady betrothed use of my tent. Rest, and if Lunabella does not leave the revelry early, perhaps we will have time to corner her after sunset when the truce ends."

That sounded like a good plan to me. Falin's scowl could have frozen the sun, but I wasn't about to look a gift fae in the mouth. I turned to indicate that Dugan should lead the way. Then everything seemed to tilt. I thought I caught an echo of the red flash of magic I'd seen in the yellow stone. Then darkness swooped over the world, taking me with it.

Chapter 14

I woke in a bed filled with satin-covered pillows. Had Ms. B acquired new bedding? The castle didn't typically have satin, and certainly not black satin.

I blinked.

It also didn't have dark fabric walls.

I sat up, and immediately regretted it as my brain ricocheted in my aching skull. I lifted a hand to my head, trying to make the room stop spinning. There were faces in the spinning kaleidoscope that whirled in my vision, but I couldn't focus on them.

Everything went red and then black. Again.

I woke for the second time, still on the black satin sheets.

I didn't try to sit up this time. My head was pounding, but at least the room wasn't spinning. Yet. Magic hummed around me, pressing into my skin. I opened my senses to decipher it, and a wave of dizziness washed over me. I snapped my shields back in place and was glad I was already lying down.

Somewhere I could hear voices talking in a low murmur. I turned slightly, and my vision didn't cloud over. That was a good sign. What the hell was going on?

"Hello?" My voice cracked, coming out barely louder than a whisper, as if I hadn't spoken in a long time. I needed water. And to figure out what was going on.

The hushed voices fell silent. Snow crunched under feet. A lot more feet than I expected. I had a moment of uncertainty, wondering if I shouldn't have called out, and then the tent flap opened, revealing a cluster of worried, but welcome, faces.

"Al! How do you feel?" Rianna asked as she hurried into the tent.

"You had us scared," Caleb said, a few steps behind her. Holly rushed in at his side and crossed quickly to the edge of the bed, taking my hand.

Falin said nothing as he entered and crossed to the foot of the bed. There was tension in his shoulders, in the way he stood so still, watching me with eyes that betrayed worry.

Dugan entered last, but he remained by the tent flap, his arms crossed over his chest. That was fine; the better part of my inner circle of friends was around the bed already, and he didn't actually fit into that category. I'd question why he was here at all, except this was probably his tent, so he got a free pass.

"What happened?" Holly asked, placing a palm over my forehead as if to check for a fever. To me her hand was scaldingly hot, but I didn't stop her. Holly was a hugger type and the physical contact seemed to reassure her, even if it told her nothing.

"I was going to ask the same thing." My words came out a croak, and I grimaced.

Rianna turned to a table beside the bed and poured a crystal-clear glass of water from a pitcher. I pushed up to my elbows. The world didn't lurch or gray away, but the movement did cause several objects balanced on my chest to slide down. I glanced at the odd necklace of twigs, pinecones, and rocks. I hadn't had those earlier. They hummed with magic, much of it familiar enough that I didn't have to reach to recognize Holly, Caleb, and Rianna's work. I couldn't tell what the spells did without examining them closer. That could wait. I didn't want to get hit with vertigo again like when I'd opened my shields a few minutes earlier. I could guess they were healing charms. They had that type of feel to them. I frowned. That was *a lot* of healing charms, and clearly cobbled together from whatever they could find quickly in the festival clearing.

Rianna handed me the water and I accepted it gratefully, draining half the cup in two large gulps. I could all but feel the water branching out, filling my parched body, which meant I was much more dehydrated than I should have been. I'd had almost no alcohol during the revelry and had stopped for water several times throughout the night. So why did I feel hungover?

And what happened? Had I passed out? It seemed that way. But why? My mind circled to the flash of red light that only I seemed to have seen. It was magic. It had to be. Had it caused this? There had been several minutes between seeing it and when I'd blacked out, but it was the only suspicious thing to which I could attribute this sudden sickness. I felt like I'd been hit by a bus, not a little flash of light.

As partially sitting up had gone well, I struggled all the way up. The corset made it harder than it should have been, and Caleb grabbed my elbows, helping to pull me up. He cut his gaze over to Holly, who was biting her lower lip. She looked to Rianna.

I frowned at them.

"Anyone know what spell I was hit with?" I asked, but they looked away as I tried to meet their eyes. I looked up at Falin. He didn't look away, but with the way his hands silently worked the empty air at his sides and the way his jaw clenched tight, I had the feeling he was barely resisting the urge to walk out of the tent and start killing things he could blame for whatever had happened. "What?"

It was Rianna who finally answered. "You're . . . unwell, Al."

"Injured?" I seemed to have all my normal limbs. My head was throbbing, and I was disoriented and exhausted. A concussion, maybe?

She shook her head. "Ill."

I frowned. "What, like a Faerie flu?"

"Not a flu," Caleb said, looking down at his hands.

It was the sorrow in his voice that scared me most.

I glanced around. My friends weren't meeting my eyes again. Except for Falin, who still hadn't said anything. So I turned to Dugan. He watched me with an expression I couldn't read. There was some emotion in his face, just nothing deep enough to betray itself.

"Your magic is infected," he said, and he sounded sorry for me. Not devastated like my friends, but the sad you feel for an acquaintance that is terminally ill. I was a political investment for him, not an emotional one.

"A magical infection? So like a curse? Or something

that can be dispelled?" I asked, looking around. Why was everyone acting like they were already attending my funeral?

"Not a magical infection. It's your own magic. It's infected," Rianna said, as if that clarified everything.

"Considering we are in a strange tent, I'm guessing the solstice festival is still happening. Almost every court is represented outside that door. Surely there is a healer who can—" I started, but everyone was shaking their heads.

"Every court sent their best healer," Caleb said.

"None could do anything?" My voice sounded small in my ears, but all in all, considering what I'd just been told, I was proud I wasn't screaming. If the fae healers could bring fae back from the dead, surely they could heal infected magic.

"They. Wouldn't. Try." Falin ground each word out, as if each threatened to break the self-control that was holding him together.

My eyes flew wide and I looked to Caleb.

"This infection, it's been seen before," he said. "It is called the *basmoarte*. It's contagious, spreading from magic to magic. And it is fatal."

Fatal. The word slammed down on me, knocking the air from my body.

"How long?" I asked, my gaze lost, not seeing anything.

No one answered. I blinked and looked around. "How long do I have?"

Again. No answer.

I turned my gaze on Dugan. He was the least emotionally affected, and the most likely to answer. He stared back at me, blank, unexpressive. Then he sighed and shrugged.

"Nightfall, maybe? It is consuming you extremely quickly. I'm surprised they got you conscious again at all."

Nightfall.

No.

No, that couldn't be right. I swung my feet around, aiming for the side of the bed—and was promptly hit by a dizzying press of blackness.

"Shhh. Be still, Al," Rianna whispered, her hands moving to my shoulders, holding me up when the darkness in my vision would have knocked me back again.

"I have to go." My voice didn't sound right. Too high. Too thin. I didn't care.

"Shhh. Slow. Calm. Deep breath." It was Holly who spoke this time, her voice light. Sad but soothing.

I shook my aching head. "You don't understand. I can't die here. Souls don't leave here. They are stuck. I have to go home." Because if I was going to die, it wasn't going to be in Faerie where I'd be just another soul stuck in an undecaying body. Death and I hadn't left on the best terms, but he'd promised he would always come for me. He wouldn't leave my soul to waste away. But he couldn't reach me in Faerie.

Hell, maybe he could even help me. He had before. Of course, that was a huge reason why we weren't together anymore—too many rules and too much rule bending. But even if he couldn't, he would at least help my soul transition. That was his job. I couldn't die in Faerie.

I struggled against the hands that were both helping me and trying to hold me down. I managed to get my feet under me, but my head spun, my balance fading, and I found myself crashing back onto my ass. Still I struggled. I had to get out of Faerie.

"We won't leave you here," someone said, but I was beyond listening.

Something cool and round pressed into my forehead. Magic pulsed over my skin, soothing and feeling of Rianna's energy. A calmness spread through me, making my limbs heavy. I took a deep breath and blinked. The panic was still there, buzzing at the edges of my thoughts, but my head felt clearer. I looked around at the worried faces of my friends and took another breath, forcing myself to stop struggling.

"We won't leave you in Faerie," Caleb said again.

I nodded slowly, trying to let his words reassure me. They helped, though the charm Rianna pressed into my forehead helped more, the spell spreading the artificial calm through my entire body like a magical Xanax. I took another deep breath. It hurt. Not just because of the corset either. My whole body ached.

Infected magic. A contagious infection that would have spread to the healers if they'd tried to purge it. I glanced at the odd necklace of cobbled-together healing charms I wore. They made much more sense now. A charm was safe. Once completed, it no longer tied back to the witch who created it. But a healing charm could only do so much.

"They're sure it is this 'basmoarte' thing? I mean, shouldn't tests be run or something?"

"No." Falin spat the word, his hands clenching. I wasn't sure which question he was answering.

I looked to Caleb. He sighed. "They aren't sure. There hasn't been a basmoarte outbreak in hundreds of years. But the symptoms are well documented. You have them."

"I lived through the last outbreak. There is little doubt," Dugan added from the door.

"What, fainting at a revelry?" I barked out the question, hearing the anger in my sarcasm. My friends didn't deserve that, but now that the initial panic after being told I had some disease I'd never heard of had been silenced, all I could find underneath was anger.

Caleb shook his head, and Rianna turned to look at Holly. She nodded and opened her purse. After digging around for a moment, she pulled out a compact mirror and handed it to me.

I accepted it, but then stared at the small compact for a moment without opening it. I didn't want to know. Maybe if I didn't look, whatever I was supposed to see wouldn't be true. But even I couldn't make that logic work. I opened the mirror.

Then I almost dropped it, shrinking back from my reflection in shock.

Purple lines snaked across one side of my face, reaching up all the way to my temple and crawling down over my jaw to my neck. Around the purple lines, my face looked pale, drawn. Deep blue half circles ringed the underside of my eyes, as if I'd been sick for a long time. Except I'd looked fine when I'd dressed for the revelry.

I moved the mirror, following the purple lines where they traveled over my throat, down my collarbone, and into the front of my corset. More, thicker and darker lines webbed over my shoulder, and I cringed. Months ago, before I'd even known I was fae, I'd gotten infected with a soul-eating spell when I'd been injured by an infected shade. The spell had been stopped, the skin had healed, but the damage to my soul was healing more slowly. The basmoarte had found that weak spot and dug in deep. The scars that had faded to thin white lines were now black, bubbling slightly. The skin around them was gray, dying. More thick purple lines of infected magic ran down my arm, disappearing into the cuff of my long glove.

I closed the compact, ignoring the fact that my fingers were trembling. With very deliberate motions, I placed it carefully on the bed beside me, saying nothing. Everyone watched me, not seeming to breathe, and yet there didn't seem to be enough air. I ignored that feeling; it was my panic trying to overcome the calming spell Rianna had put on me. I couldn't afford to surrender to the panic again.

I had seen all of these symptoms before.

Peeling off my gloves, I held my hands up in front of my face. My palms were coated in blood, but that was no surprise and it wasn't mine but Faerie's very literal interpretation of the term "blood on her hands." It was the rest of my hands I was interested in. One was fine. The other . . . The web of purple lines ran all the way down my arm, growing thicker and darker. The thin scars where I'd shredded my hands while weaving reality were bluish. Not yet black like my shoulder, but definitely changed. The beds of my fingernails were deep bruises, and the tips of my fingers were black, the skin nearly necrotic. While my shoulder looked bad, this was the true infection point. The place the fouled magic began. I stared at my dark fingertips.

Basmoarte was a wasting disease. I'd never known its name, but I'd seen it before. A long time ago.

It had killed my mother.

Chapter 15

"**G**et back." I whispered the words, not trusting myself to speak any louder. The panic gnawing at the edges of Rianna's spell was very close to taking over again. Half of me wanted to let it. If I gave in to the panic, I wouldn't have to think anymore. But that would be giving up, and damn it, I didn't want to die. Not now. Not this way.

"It's only contagious through magical contact. And only among the fae," Holly said, reaching out like she would take my hand again.

I pulled my arms closer to my chest, out of her reach.

"I'm about to use magic, so step back. Just in case."

No one moved.

"Al, it is spreading really fast. Faster than it should. The healers weren't sure why," Caleb said.

"I have some theories on that," Rianna said. "According to the healers, the more magic an infected fae uses, the faster they succumb. Stop using all magic, and it can be managed for a short while. But, Al, your magic never turns off. You are constantly touching multiple planes, which is why you see ghosts and collectors and stuff."

Caleb nodded. "You use magic to not use more magic."

Which meant my magic would literally eat me alive, and fast. But did it also increase the risk to those around me, if the planes were converging through me? I had to actively use magic to make a ghost visible to others, but if I was touching the ghost and a chair, the ghost could touch the chair with no extra magical expenditure on my part.

"Step back," I said again.

"Alex—" Holly started, but I shot her a glare.

I didn't have a lot of time. I was exhausted, dizzy, and very close to freaking out again. If I didn't try to fight this thing now, I wouldn't get another chance.

"Go."

Holly stared at me for half a heartbeat more. Then she pushed to her feet, dragging Caleb with her. Rianna hesitated a moment longer but finally stood as well, retreating to the far end of the tent. I turned to Falin. He hadn't budged. When I looked at him, he only lifted an eyebrow, as if daring me to try to make him move. He was at the foot of the bed, and considering the size of the tent, he wasn't that much closer than anyone else in the small space. He was no more at risk than the others, but would I put them all at risk if I reached for my magic? Another look at him told me he wasn't moving, and he sure as hell wouldn't leave the tent if I asked.

Now, or never.

I closed my eyes and focused on my shields. The pain in my head doubled, and I swayed where I sat. I paused, breathing deep, trying to get my equilibrium back. When the dizziness passed, I peeled open my shields another inch, aware of every crack, of the cost of touching my magic. The hole was a sliver only large enough to let the smallest fingers of magic through. My head throbbed, darkness pressing on me, and I panted with the strain. I pried my shields open a sliver more, and nearly collapsed. Was it enough? It had to be enough, I couldn't manage much more. I opened my eyes.

It was enough.

I could see the spells tied into the charms my friends had made, the thin Aetheric energy in colors each preferred, but more than that, I could see the deeper pattern of the magic under my skin. While the purplish network of magic was visible on my skin, so much more was visible with my shields open. The magic was dark, a network of poison and sickness deep under my flesh. But I could see it.

And what I could see, I could touch.

I held up one hand and poked at one of the trails of sickly magic in my littlest finger. It moved slow as molasses, the effort making my stomach clench painfully.

I gasped, doubling over in pain, but the magic moved, peeling up, out of my skin.

Lifting the string of makeshift charms around my neck, I selected a flat rock the size of my palm and attempted to push the tainted magic into the stone. The black tendril obeyed, but when I released it, the magic wiggled back out of the stone, remaining firmly affixed to my finger. I selected a pinecone next. The fouled tendril of magic seemed more accepting of the pinecone, but try as I might, it wouldn't stick to it. I frowned.

"I need a receptacle."

Falin stepped forward. "What kind?"

I stared at where the magic dangled from the tip of my pinky. It undulated, trying to get back under my skin. It wasn't going into anything inanimate. It was a wasting magic that wanted to sap life.

"Something alive," I whispered, hating it even as I said it. "Something that it will be okay if it dies. A tree?"

No one said anything. Herbs were picked and used in magic all the time. Wood was a common charm component, and a tree or at least a branch was obviously killed for that. But using something still living, knowing the magic would kill it? That definitely fell into the category of gray magic, if not black. And yet no one protested.

Falin gave one sharp nod, turning toward the tent flap.

"I'll come with you," Caleb said, following him out.

That was good. Caleb was a greenman. He'd make sure whatever living tree Falin brought back was only a tree, not a sleeping ent or the home of a nymph at the festival.

After they left, I peeled off the spelled disk Rianna had pressed into my forehead to calm me. I didn't need it anymore. Now that I had a plan, I was in control of my own panic. I focused on the sickly magic. My shoulder was by far the worst part of the infection, the magic festering deep inside me, far too close to my heart. The only other place it had taken deep hold was my hand, in particular my fingertips. The tendrils in my face and the ones trying to grow down my chest were the most loosely connected. Those pulled free slowly, but without much digging with my magic. I was able to peel the fouled magic down, over my jaw and down my neck one agonizing inch at a time.

When I reached my shoulder, the process became much more difficult. I pushed, tugged, and pulled, gaining millimeters before having to stop to let the room stop

spinning. I passed out twice, waking to find Holly dab-
bing my face with a wet cloth. I switched gears and focused on my hand instead, leaving the shoulder for last.

My fingers were nearly as bad. It was slow work. I kept
having to stop to rest. More than once my stomach
clenched so hard I thought I was going to lose all the festival food I'd eaten the night before. I'd managed to free
my hand up to my wrist by the time Falin and Caleb returned, a four-foot sapling, roots and all, carried in a
blanket between them.

They set the baby tree down in front of me without a
word. Caleb backed away, but Falin moved toward the
bed.

"Don't," I said, throwing out my clean arm to halt
him. I didn't know what everyone else could see, but in
my vision, the sickly magic was dangling from my wrist
like a sleeve of writhing, poisonous snakes. It kept trying
to crawl back under my skin, and I was afraid it would do
the same to any fae who got close enough for the magic
to touch.

I scooted to the edge of the bed and looked at the little
sapling. I didn't know enough about trees to tell more
than that it was an evergreen. "I'm sorry," I whispered to
it, reaching out and wrapping the fingers of my bad arm
around the trunk. It wasn't a thinking being, so no debt
opened between us. That didn't mean I didn't regret what
I was about to do.

I grabbed a handful of the dangling magic and pushed
it against the trunk. The magic didn't want to leave me,
but I shoved it under the bark of the tree, and unlike
with the stone and pinecone I'd attempted earlier, this
time it found something to latch onto. It didn't pour into
the tree, but it didn't slide back out either and I was able

to detach a fistful of tainted tendrils at a time. The more of the sickly magic the tree absorbed, the stronger I felt and the easier it became to rip it out of me.

Not that it was easy.

Sweat dripped down every inch of me by the time I had cleansed the fouled magic from the tips of my fingers to my elbow. I had to stop to let the room stop spinning several times as I purged the magic as far as my shoulder. And then there was the shoulder itself. The infection had tunneled into the weak parts in my soul and it did not want to let go. Trying to cleanse the infection was a demented dance of one step back every time I took two forward because I had to exert magic to excise the infection, but the more magic I used, the more the fouled magic spread.

I wasn't sure how much time I spent pulling and pushing the dark magic from me into the tree. It felt like an eternity, but finally I collapsed onto the bed. I was sweating, shaking, and exhausted, but feeling better than when I'd woken. The headache was gone, and having my shields cracked no longer made the room spin. That had to be a good sign.

From where I lay on the bed, I glanced at the sapling. The branches were twisted, the bark blackened, and most of the needles had fallen to the ground. It was, without a doubt, dead.

"Is it done?" Rianna asked.

I pushed up to a sitting position. After wiping sweaty curls from my forehead, I nodded. It was done. For now. I looked around for the pitcher Rianna had poured from earlier. I needed water.

"So . . . you're cured?" Holly asked.

She sounded so very hopeful. I glanced at my hands.

I'd gotten all of the magic that had already fouled and turned against my body, but that was the symptom, not the cause. The poisoned magic would spread again.

"What she did," Dugan said, his voice expressionless, "was the equivalent of eating her own hand to avoid starving to death."

Oh, what a lovely euphemism.

"I'd equate it more to lancing a wound to drain the infection," I said, and Dugan frowned at me.

"You stopped the immediate emergency, but you only bought time. Considering how much magic you used to do it, I doubt you bought yourself much before it tries to consume you again."

"You think I shouldn't have tried it?"

"I think it was brilliant and saved your life," he said, which didn't actually answer the question, but yay for being brilliant. "If you're vigilant at purging yourself like that, you might be the first fae who doesn't waste away in a mere matter of weeks. Then again, the last time I saw basmoarte in Faerie, it was not near so aggressive."

Lucky me. I'd prolonged my death sentence. But at a cost. I glanced at the twisted and dead sapling. "I'd deforest Faerie."

If I killed that many living things with dark magic, what would I become? Would I still really be living, or me?

"If the symptoms can be managed . . . can she heal?" Holly asked. She was ever an optimist. Of course, it was her never-give-up attitude that had gotten her to being an assistant district attorney, and keeping that insane schedule despite getting exposed and addicted to Faerie food. "I mean, Alex, you equated it to draining a wound. You do that so that the wound can heal, right?"

"I don't know." It had been pure desperation that I'd

even tried to remove the magic poisoning me. I knew almost nothing about basmoarte. My mother had faded quickly, or at least it had seemed so to me. I'd been five at the time. She ended up in a human hospital with the doctors bewildered by her disease. That had been the first time I'd met Death. I'd begged him to leave her. I was so sure she'd get better. She just kept wasting away without dying until I'd let her go. She had never started to recover, not even with extra time. Of course, she also hadn't had the magic poisoning her removed. If I could keep draining the poison, could I recover?

I looked to Falin first. He looked less ready to kill something now, but there was still a raw edge to him that told me he had no answers. I looked to Dugan next.

"I don't know," he admitted. "I've never heard of anyone surviving basmoarte, but then, I've never heard of anyone doing quite what you just did. At the rate it was spreading, I would have given you hours. Now?" He shrugged. "Healers have tried to repair the damage in the past, but they can't rip out the poisoned magic. Maybe, given time, your magic will stop warping."

We were all silent for a moment, considering that. A vague "maybe" wasn't exactly hopeful, but it also wasn't a definite "no."

"If basmoarte hasn't been seen in centuries, how did Alex get infected?" Rianna asked, her hands twisting awkwardly in front of her. For the first time I realized her ever-present barghest wasn't at her side—neither in his typical big black dog form, nor in the man form I'd only seen twice.

"I've seen it," I said, and you could have heard a snowflake hit the ground in the tent. "My mother died of it."

Caleb cocked his head to the side. "You're sure?"

I nodded. The black lesions. The purple veining. It was seared into my childhood memories.

"So, I'm guessing no one else saw a flash of red light right before I passed out?" I asked, glancing around. I was met with confusion and curiosity. "I think I know how I was exposed."

I explained how the golden-cloaked fae had pulled out his chunk of rock, and the flash of light I'd seen, followed by twisting darkness. Falin's daggers materialized in his hands, but Dugan only shook his head at my explanation.

"I saw him, and the stone you mentioned. I was watching him because he'd clearly been following Lunabella. I never saw the stone change from its yellow color." Dugan tapped a finger against his sharp cheekbone in thought before shaking his head again. "And that could not be the source of the basmoarte. While highly contagious, it is very specific in how it spreads. When a fae's magic touches an infected fae's magic, a wound in the magic opens. It is said to be painful. Noticeable. And that spot in the magic is where the infection will spread from."

I lifted my hands. The smallest blot of blue was blooming on the tip of my pointer finger. It was barely the size of a pinhead. It looked like I'd touched something.

Like Sleeping Beauty pricking her finger on a spinning wheel.

That thought stopped me. Not the Sleeping Beauty part—I was no princess. The pricked finger part.

"Oh," I said, my head snapping up. "Then, maybe I know. When I reach out with my grave magic, I imagine it as an extension of my hand, reaching down into the corpse. When I tried to raise Kordon, I received what I can only describe as a magical prick to the finger." I held out the hand with the small dark spot of poisoned magic.

There was a stunned moment, and then Falin moved. He had a dagger out and at Dugan's throat before anyone could react. Rianna yelped, ducking out of the tent. Caleb pulled Holly behind him, backing away with her until they reached the tent flap as well. His gaze met mine before he disappeared, and I saw the brief moment of hesitation, the torn loyalty wishing he could get me out of the tent as well, and then he was guiding her out and ducking out behind her.

"It was your fae. Was this your doing?" Falin asked between clenched teeth, his dagger not moving.

"Peace, Knight," Dugan said, lifting his own hands, palms out and empty. "The sun hasn't set on the shortest day yet. The truce still holds all of Faerie."

"Technically your court was only welcomed if you meant no harm," Falin said, and the heat of anger I'd seen in him had turned cold. It was by far his more deadly condition.

Dugan laughed, but one of his hands dropped, inching toward his own sword. "What is your plan, Knight? If you can slice my throat and Faerie allows it, you will assume that means I meant harm? Isn't that rather like when humans tossed suspected witches in lakes? If they floated, they fished them out and burned them. If they drowned, they deemed them innocent."

"I'm willing to take that chance," Falin replied, but he didn't move, keeping the blade right at Dugan's throat. I wasn't sure if he was hesitating, or if Faerie wouldn't let him finish the movement.

"Stop, both of you," I said, pushing up off the bed. I was more pleased than I should have been when my legs held. "Falin, why are you threatening Dugan?"

"Because it all ties back to him. His fae. His dagger.

A shadow minion watching the ritual. He keeps insisting he wishes to prevent war, but maybe it was never about war. It was all a setup to ensure you would use your magic on a corpse infected with basmoarte. He approached you to raise the shade before we even knew about the deaths. The scene made no sense so that even if you hadn't agreed to his request, the queen would have made you raise the shades. The ultimate result was that you would be infected."

"I think that we have all been nicely played in someone else's game," Dugan said, frowning. "I swear on the very essence of Faerie that I mean Alexis no harm. In fact, her continued survival can only benefit me."

The two men stared at each other, but after a moment, Falin lowered his dagger and stepped back.

"I think," Dugan said slowly, as if afraid his words might trigger another reaction, "that we might have been approaching the scene incorrectly. We assumed the murders were committed to start a war between our courts, or perhaps the staging was to cover a personal grudge, but I have to agree with you that it appears to have been a trap for Alexis. Possibly it served as more than one of those scenarios, but surely the last because Kordon did not have basmoarte before his disappearance."

"I have heard rumors," Falin said, his voice low, dangerous. "That basmoarte had been resurrected and weaponized." He looked at Dugan. It wasn't accusatory, not entirely at least; it was more of an inquiry. If anyone had information on such rumors, the Prince of Shadows and Secrets should.

"There have always been rumors. They have never been substantiated." He frowned. "Until, perhaps, now. But if someone has weaponized it, and if it is being selectively delivered, then whoever controls it might also have a cure."

I knew it was only an outside chance, but I couldn't help seizing on the idea. "So then the question is, who would know that I would question Kordon's shade? That is a fairly specific skill set and not utilized in Faerie. And from what I've seen, the courtiers try to distance themselves as quickly as possible from even the mention of death. How many know I'm a grave witch? Hell, how many know what a shade is?"

Falin tapped a finger against his chin. "In the winter court? The council knows, of course. They have seen you raise shades. Of winter's citizens? The courtiers are most likely ignorant. It would be less difficult to believe that some of the independents are aware of your grave magic, as some function in the human world in which you work. In the other courts . . . ?" He paused, considering. "Your wyrd abilities are likely completely unknown aside from perhaps in the shadow court." He glared at Dugan. "And we are back to your court again."

"It does seem someone did their work quite well," he said, and sighed. "Even among my people, it is unlikely to be common knowledge, but it would not be hard information to discover."

There was another player as well. One I hadn't told either man about. My father had asked me to investigate before Dugan had even stepped into my office. But did I really think my own father would try to kill me? I didn't, but if the last few months had taught me anything, it was that I understood him less than I thought.

"What if it wasn't a trap for me?" I asked, a new thought occurring to me. "I mean, I obviously blundered right into it, but I might not be the only one. Do we know if the healer who checked Kordon contracted basmoarte?"

Falin's eyes widened. "I'll have to inform the queen and the healer will have to be quarantined."

"Wouldn't the healer already know if she has it?" I mean, I'd been in horrible shape.

"Your infection, if you only contracted it yesterday, progressed exceedingly quickly," Dugan said. "The largest recorded outbreak of basmoarte was due to healers contracting it and spreading it from patient to patient before symptoms ever started."

I wrapped my arms over my chest. The random assortment of healing charms got in the way of the movement, and I lifted the cobbled-together necklace over my head. The charms in it were exhausted already anyway. "So, if this was targeted at a healer and not me, then it was a calculated attack to cause an outbreak in the winter court."

Falin shook his head. "If this was an attack against the winter court, it would have been Stiofan who'd been infected. Not Kordon. Had Dugan not been so insistent that we try to restore Kordon, we would have sent the body back to the shadow court without a healer ever touching him." His gaze bore into Dugan, and I knew he was thinking this was yet another guilty-looking strike against shadow.

A trumpet sounded somewhere outside the tent, making me jump.

"The sun is setting," the queen's voice said, and the magic of the revelry made it sound like she could have been in the tent with us. I found myself looking around, even though I knew she was likely speaking from her ice throne on the dais in the center of the clearing. "Our merriment comes to an end. May the roads rise up to meet us all."

As the last word left her mouth, the very air around us changed. It was more than just the sound of the revelry, but the feel of it as well. The magic changed, the doors shifted, and the truce holding all of Faerie broke.

"We are out of time," Dugan said, moving toward the tent flap. "We should attempt to approach Lunabella now that the revelry is over."

"We will never locate her before the light court leaves," Falin said, frowning.

Dugan only smiled and grabbed the edge of his cloak, spreading it to his side. A shadow unfolded from the darkness, jumping free of the other shadows. It landed prettily on four small paws, tail high. For a moment, I thought it was a black cat, but then I realized it was a shadow of a cat.

Dugan crouched beside the shadow cat and rubbed between her ears, not with his physical hand, but with the shadow of his hand. I watched, fascinated, and I swore the shadow purred.

"Take us to them," he whispered, and the shadow streaked out of the tent. Dugan stood, glancing back at Falin and me. "Come on. You didn't think I left her unmonitored, did you?"

Dugan followed the shadow cat, and we followed him. We weren't exactly running, but we were definitely moving much faster and more determinedly than most of the fae around us. It was clear that many of the revelers had trickled out of the festival throughout the day, but those who were left seemed in no hurry to leave just because the sun had set and the revelry was technically over. They prolonged their good-byes in small clumps, or moved leisurely toward the hawthorns at the far side of the clearing. That could work in our favor if Lunabella was as reluctant to leave, but it was also slowing us down as we had to weave through fae who were not moving anywhere fast.

The shadow streaked ahead, vanishing into a thick throng of fae. We more or less had to shoulder our way through the first two or three fae, until the fae noticed that it was the Winter Knight and Shadow Prince making their way through the crowd. The sounds of merriment broke around us, fae hurrying to open a path. That hadn't happened during the revelry, but the truce was broken now. Our progress quickened, but the part of me that never fully forgot what it was like being an outsider most of my life hurt for Falin. I hated the way smiles dropped off fae faces as soon as they saw him. The way fae looked away, seemingly preoccupied with something else. Or how some fled, getting as far away as possible.

The shadow cat led us to the tree line and then paused, its back arching.

"Something is wrong," Dugan hissed under his breath.

"What is it saying?" I whispered.

He turned to frown at me. "She's a cat."

Which I guess meant it didn't say anything. How was I supposed to know? Weirder things than cats spoke in Faerie.

The cat took off at a run and we sprinted after her. I'd never been deep into the woods that surrounded the revelries. It was a magical clearing, so in all honesty, I wasn't sure the woods around it were fully real, or if we'd hit some sort of barricade or find ourselves in a magical loop that just led back to the clearing. The latter was my best guess, and maybe if we traveled far enough would prove to be the case, but there was clearly at least a little bit of forest that was real, because we were dodging low-hanging branches and stepping over raised roots. The dark didn't help in that, but at least the snow reflected some of the moonlight.

The glamoured alterations Falin had made to my dress had made all the difference at the festivities of the solstice, but it was still a damn ball gown with a full-length skirt. Not so great for running through the woods. I hiked it up to my knees, gathering as much fabric as I could in my hands, but still ended up snagging sticks and branches, which slowed me down. The fact that the corset allowed my diaphragm only half its normal movement—and let's face it, the fact that I'd been deathly ill for most of the day—didn't help matters either. I lagged behind.

Falin hesitated, waiting for me. I waved him on. He and Dugan were moving all but soundlessly through the underbrush. Me? Not so much. A rendezvous this far out in the woods meant Lunabella didn't want to be seen or overheard with whomever she was meeting. My stomping around would give us away, and my attempts to move silently were far too slow.

Falin seemed uncertain if he should leave me. I motioned again for him to go. *Leave me a trail.* I mouthed the words, unwilling to call out in case we were close.

He looked down, seeming only now to realize that neither he nor Dugan was leaving tracks in the snow. Yup, only my blundering footsteps were visible behind us. I watched him purposefully dig in his heel. Then he turned and sprinted after the Shadow Prince.

I paused. Leaning against a tree to catch my breath, I channeled magic into the privacy bubble charm on my bracelet. The noise-canceling spell sprang up around me, instantly blocking out all the ambient forest noises. I pushed off the tree and hurried in the direction Falin had gone, watching for the path he'd laid for me. Now it didn't matter how much noise I made since the spell hid it, so I didn't worry about trying to move quietly, just quickly.

Of course, the main benefit of the privacy bubble was also its main downfall. No sound passed through the bubble, whether I wanted it to or not.

I focused on following the almost invisible trail Falin had left, studying the spot just before my feet as I ran along, glancing up only occasionally to see if I could spot the guys ahead of me. I'd just rounded an enormous redwood tree when a hand closed around my biceps, pulling me to a stop before tugging me back behind the wide tree.

I yelped. Panic spilled through my brain. I scrambled to pull magic back out of my charm, aware no one would hear me scream inside the bubble. Then more than just the lizard part of my brain caught up. The hand that had stopped me wasn't hurting me. It had just stopped me, and moved me back, but it wasn't trying to drag me away. I spun as Falin pressed a finger over his mouth, obviously not realizing that my scream was contained. From the expression on his face, he must have tried to call to me before he grabbed me. But . . . privacy bubble.

Maybe not my best plan.

I pulled the magic out of the charm, releasing the spell, and the sounds of the forest rushed around me again. I expected to hear murmuring, some secret conversation happening just ahead, but aside from my own thundering heartbeat pounding in my ears, I heard nothing that indicated anything bigger than some forest creatures were close by. I glanced at Falin. His eyes were narrow, his lips pressed thin, and one of his daggers was in the hand not gripping my arm.

"Did we lose her?"

He frowned. "You could say that." He jerked his chin, gesturing forward.

I stepped to the edge of the tree, peeking around the side. My brain perceived the colors first. Cheery yellow. Brown. Bright red. White snow.

It took a second longer for my brain to start categorizing what I saw. That was a foot sticking out from under the yellow and gold trim of a dress. There was a torso in a gray brocade jacket. That was a gloved hand just below a pool of slushy red snow. A few yards away, that brown spot was long hair, the ends dark where they were coated in blood from the neck stump of a severed head.

I squeezed my eyes shut and spun back around, flattening myself against the bark of the tree. It was rough against my bare shoulders, and that was good because it was something solid I could focus on.

"Was she already . . . ?" I started, but then faltered. Two. Had I seen that right? There were two bodies? I sucked down a breath and realized someone was missing. "Where is Dugan?"

"Hunting with his shadows for a trail." Falin's gaze searched the woods around us, alert, his muscles coiled and ready to move if a threat appeared. "And to answer the question you weren't quite asking, yes, they were like that when we arrived. And yes, I arrived at the same time Dugan did. He didn't kill anyone. I'm guessing the rumors that we were looking for Lunabella reached the wrong person and they didn't want us questioning her."

"And the other one?"

Falin didn't look at me as he shrugged. "As they say, three can keep a secret, if two are dead."

Right. So then our visit to the summer court had spurred both deaths. My stomach clenched at the idea. *We* were indirectly responsible. Of course, she wouldn't have needed to be silenced unless she was complicit with the murders, so that fact did mitigate some of the guilt.

"Who is the second body?" I asked, because I didn't want to turn around and try to find the second head.

"Jurin. He was winter court."

"And you're thinking conspirator, not another victim?" *That might explain how the killers had gotten into the court.*

Falin didn't answer, his body still tense, watching the woods. My own hand moved to my purse and the dagger stashed within. Nothing in the moonlight moved beyond the soft swaying of trees.

We hadn't been in the woods long. Assuming Lunabella and Jurin had been attacked at the moment Dugan's shadow cat freaked at the edge of the woods, we had missed the murderer by mere minutes. Which meant the killer could still be close.

Thirty seconds passed. A minute. Nothing moved in the darkness of the woods. Unlike Falin, I couldn't remain on full alert when it appeared nothing was out there. Which didn't mean I put my dagger away, but I did relax slightly, my thoughts circling back as I considered the scene beyond the huge redwood.

"If this was about silencing conspirators, killing them

would be a horribly stupid way to prevent a grave witch from questioning someone," I whispered, chewing at my bottom lip. "I mean, if you guys are right about the scene at the winter court being a trap for me, then the killer or killers still at large know I can question a corpse."

"Look at the bodies again." His voice barely carried, and I doubted anyone lurking could have heard. He still had both of his long daggers drawn, watching, waiting.

Looking at the bodies again was something I *really* didn't want to do. I'd seen enough. Lunabella was headless. I'd seen that. Jurin, well, I hadn't technically seen whether his head was attached or not. Maybe they both had other wounds too that I hadn't spotted with my first quick peek, but that wouldn't matter.

"Science and capability of speech at death really have little to do with a shade's ability to answer questions." Which he knew; he'd seen me raise shades from bodies in far worse condition.

He didn't answer as his head swung around, eyes narrowed. He took two steps forward, blades bared.

"Only me, Knight," Dugan said, seeming to melt from the shadow of the tree. Two shadow cats bounded out beside his legs.

"Anything?" Falin asked, lowering the blades but not sheathing them.

Dugan shook his head. "Whoever did this is long gone and left no trail to follow."

"I don't suppose your cats can identify who killed Lunabella and Jurin?" I asked, looking at the two shadows.

I thought at first they were identical, but then I noticed that one had more substance. It was shadow and it was more at the same time. The way the second mirrored the one with substance, I realized it was the shadow's shadow—however that was possible. So maybe not cats, but cat. The cat sat, and the shadows on its face writhed until big green eyes opened in the featureless darkness.

It blinked at me.

If it grinned, I was leaving.

Dugan glanced at the cat, and then at me. "She might be able to. But cats aren't bloodhounds, and there is no discernible trail to follow to narrow down in which court to look. Basically our suspect pool is the entire population of Faerie. They won't all gather in one place again until the next revelry."

True.

"Now, once we have a suspect . . ." He shrugged.

"Why didn't you attach a shadow to Lunabella that could speak?" Falin shot a disparaging glance at the shadow cat. The shadow in question narrowed her eyes at him. "That would have been far more useful."

"Because it would have violated the truce? We are fortunate I had Ciara follow her or these bodies wouldn't have been found until the Spring Equinox, at the earliest. Considering how far we are in the woods, maybe they wouldn't have been found for centuries."

And likely they weren't meant to be. It didn't matter if I could question the dead if the bodies were sealed in an inaccessible part of Faerie. But now our suspect was dead. Well, there was definitely one other unusual character.

"I have a suspect," I said, pushing off the tree.

"The golden-cloaked fae?" Falin asked, but when I nodded, he frowned. "The problem with that is that we have no idea who he—or she—is, or in what court we might be able to find them. So our suspect pool is still all of Faerie. Unless you know?" He glanced at Dugan.

The prince shook his head. "I noticed that he was watching Lunabella, so I kept an eye on the gold-cloaked figure, but I never saw more than a hand. Certainly not enough to identify or even narrow down a court."

Great.

"Now what?" I asked, because the festival site had to be clearing out by now, and once a fae left, they couldn't return. Which meant we might very well be alone with the dead bodies, and no help was coming.

Or the killer could still be lurking.

The thought made my hand tighten around my dagger again. Of course, I had the Winter Knight and the Prince of Shadows at my side. If the killer was lingering, he—or she—would need a small army to stand a chance. Though he had apparently managed to dispatch two fae extremely quickly and vanish without a trace, so maybe I wasn't giving the killer enough credit.

"The queen will have to be informed, but per tradition she would have left as soon as she announced the revelry complete," Falin said, his eyes sweeping the woods around us one last time before he released his daggers. He didn't sheathe them, they just weren't in his hands anymore. Neat trick. "Lunabella's body will need to be returned to the court of light."

Which meant we had to move the bodies.

Falin stepped around the tree, heading toward the bodies. Dugan followed close behind.

How do I get myself into these situations? Crime scenes were not supposed to be my place. I much preferred the morgue or a nice cemetery.

I stepped around the tree.

There was *so* much blood. Maybe the fact that it had mixed with the snow made it spread. Or maybe I just wasn't used to seeing two bodies completely bled out. I mean, who *would* get used to something like that?

"Should I question the shades before we return the bodies?" I asked as Falin knelt beside Lunabella, examining the snow around her.

"You shouldn't raise either shade," Falin said. "In fact, you shouldn't be using any magic." He turned and nodded to the hand still gripped around my dagger.

I glanced down. The entire tip of my index finger was slightly blue, and a thin trail of discoloration ran from the darkened tip to the first joint. It was only a small area, but it hadn't been that long since I'd purged all the fouled magic. All I'd done magically since was use one charm, and it was one I'd already crafted and only had to activate.

"We need to get these bodies out of here," Dugan said, glancing deeper into the woods. "I have no idea what happens to this space after a revelry ends, but I'm fairly certain there were trees over there a few moments ago." He pointed.

Several yards past where the bodies were lying, a thick gray wall of mist had formed. As I watched, another tree disappeared. Something told me this wasn't a normal fog rolling in.

Our location had an expiration date.

"Right. I vote we get out of here. Fast." Of course, that left one huge problem. "How do we get the bodies out?"

Dugan and Falin exchanged glances. Without a word, they abandoned any precautions about disturbing the scene and ran to the bodies. Falin lifted Jurin's body, slinging it over his shoulder in a fireman's carry. Blood oozed from the stump of neck, running down the front of Falin's dark shirt. Dugan grabbed Lunabella, mirroring Falin.

The heads.

The bodies didn't necessarily *need* their heads, but considering we couldn't come back and claim them later, someone should probably grab them.

And I was the only someone left.

My stomach roiled at the idea, but I didn't give it a chance to protest. Darting forward, I dodged around Lunabella's heeled feet where they dangled over Dugan's shoulder and ran for where I'd seen her head. It lay near the base of a tree. Jurin's wasn't far from it. The encroaching gray mist was only a yard beyond, moving in fast. If it reached the heads, we would lose them.

I grabbed a fistful of hair close to the scalp and lifted. The head was heavier than I would have thought just a head would be. I tried not to think about it. Then I turned and grabbed Jurin's head.

Trails of mist reached out, encircling the tree directly in front of me. With a decapitated head in each hand, I turned and ran.

Chapter 16

The only good thing about my earlier passage through the woods was that I'd left a very easy path to follow on the way out. We ran as fast as we could, Dugan and Falin with corpses slung over their shoulders, and me with a head in each fist. Lunabella's long hair tangled in a fallen branch. I jerked it free without slowing, leaving a clump of hair behind. *This is so not the proper way to treat a corpse.* But I couldn't afford to stop.

I tripped on a raised root and fell hard, my teeth chinking with the impact. What little air I had rushed out, and I gasped. I managed not to lose the heads in the fall but lost precious time scrambling back to my feet. Dugan and Falin stopped, and Falin urged me ahead of them. Apparently if I was going to get sucked into the mist, they planned to go with me. I put on as much speed as I could, knowing I was slowing them down. Maybe I needed to take up running regularly, because I was in no shape for this.

We emerged into the festival clearing with the gray mist on our heels.

The clearing was empty, no trace of the throngs of fae who had been there less than an hour earlier. I didn't waste time looking around but ran right for the hawthorns and the door out. My chest burned, my throat was raw, and my head was pounding from the running. I tried not to think about what I was carrying, but how do you carry severed heads and not think about that? I could feel them bumping into my aching legs as I pushed for more speed. I just wanted to go home. To not have severed body parts be something I had to entertain thoughts about.

Every part of me trembled. My body throbbed, begging me to stop and at least catch my breath. I was almost to the hawthorns. I pushed harder, driving myself under the overhanging branches. Into the door.

"Alex. Where—" Whatever Falin wanted to ask me cut off as I dove into the magical doorway. His hand landed on my arm just before the colors of the world swirled.

I emerged from the door on a grassy hillside. A warm wind blew through the grass, and rows of moonflowers created a glowing path starting at the door and winding lazily down the hill.

Falin, with his hand on my arm, emerged directly after me. Dugan, his fingers clutching the back of Falin's shirt, followed him out. Doors in Faerie were odd. The revelry door, because it opened to absolutely everywhere, was even stranger than most. It was supposed to put fae back where they belonged, sending each to their own court or territory. I was independent. Falin was winter. Dugan was shadow. We hadn't discussed where we were going—

we'd been in too much of a panicked hurry. So had we not been touching, we likely would have all ended up in different places.

I should have ended up outside the Eternal Bloom. That was the revelry door for independents in Nekros. Maybe I could have ended up in winter. But I'd been thinking about home.

So the door took me home.

I hadn't even known it could do that.

I dropped to my knees in the grass, releasing the heads as I fell. They rolled several feet in opposite directions. Even if they'd been murderers, dead bodies deserved more respect, but I couldn't take one more step.

I doubled over, dragging in air. I couldn't get enough. My body was shaking. My lungs burned. My throat ached.

I was breathing too fast. I knew that. It wouldn't help anything if I hyperventilated. I tried to hold the air I sucked in. Couldn't. It burst back and I scrambled for more, not getting enough.

"Alex?" Falin let the body he was carrying slide to the ground before moving closer to me. "Breathe, Alex."

I was trying.

Damn it, I was going to pass out at this rate. The world grew fuzzy. It was more than just panic and adrenaline — though I sure as hell had more than enough of both buzzing through my body. I physically couldn't get enough air.

"Get this" — gasp — "damn" — gasp — "corset off me!"

Falin didn't ask any questions. His dagger materialized in his hand and he cut the laces. The thick, boned material sprang apart, and I sucked in a deep breath. My diaphragm expanded for the first time in over twenty-four hours and I swear I could feel my ribs moving back where they belonged. I sucked in another deep breath.

Held it. Did it again. Released and drew in more air. Deeper. Slower.

Ever so slowly, the world began to firm up again, and my body stopped shaking. I focused on my breathing until it was under my control—not calm exactly, but better.

I pushed back from my knees to sit on the hillside on my butt. Jurin's head had rolled directly in front of me only a few feet away. His eyes were open, as if he were staring. I shuddered, ripping my gaze away, and looking up, toward the sky.

Falin had stayed close by, concern written across his face. Now that I was breathing right, he sat back as well. He was shoulder to shoulder with me, his hands behind him, bracing some of his weight.

I leaned into him, and he wrapped an arm around me without a word. We stared up at the stars for a moment, ignoring the dead bodies on the hill around us. Then a laugh escaped me. It wasn't an amused laugh, and even I could hear the edge of hysteria in it. But I laughed, because otherwise it was going to come out as a scream. I laughed because our best lead was dead. I laughed because I'd fled from a devouring mist with two heads dangling from my hands. Because the horrible wasting disease that killed my mother was now killing me. Because I might be able to survive it if I was willing to kill other living things. And apparently I was willing, because I already had. I laughed until tears ran down my face. And then I wasn't laughing alone; Falin's deep chuckle vibrated up out of his chest, into me.

"Well, that was certainly a first for me," he said when his laughter faded.

"Fleeing from a devouring mist? I sure hope it wasn't

just normal fog, or I'm going to feel really stupid," I said, wiping the tears from my eyes.

We both laughed one more time as Dugan stared at us like we'd lost our minds. I didn't care.

I was home. We were safe. I had a moment to breathe. Literally.

The wind blew my hair and carried the scent of flowers across the hill. I drank it down, enjoying the warmth of the air. It was always warm here because this place was mine. I hadn't wanted it originally. Hadn't meant to inherit an entire Faerie castle. It had been self-defense that had forced me to kill the body thief. But as well as the blood on my hands, Faerie had given me the castle. And when I became independent, Faerie had moved it from Faerie proper to this folded space that was a mix of Faerie and mortal reality.

And now, Faerie had apparently tied a door to it.

That is unlikely to be good.

I dismissed that thought to somewhere I could deal with later. Right now I just wanted to have my moment of peace. I hadn't noticed while hyperventilating, but Falin had glamoured me a tank top to replace the corset, so I wasn't sitting on the hill half naked. The skirt of my gown was the same, and considering how much banging about the heads had done on my dash, I made a point of not looking at the bloodstained material.

Instead I sat staring up at the stars, on a grassy hillside filled with moonflowers, Falin's arm warm and strong around me.

With a couple dead bodies around us. Nothing is perfect.

I almost laughed at the thought, but I was afraid I

wouldn't be able to stop again. I sighed. That moment was over. We needed to get back to what had to be done—like deal with Jurin and Lunabella. Now that we were in the mortal realm, I could feel the grave essence reaching out from them. That also meant decay would start catching up to them. They definitely weren't going to get any easier to deal with, and there was a lot to do before we returned them to their courts.

"Time to deal with the dead," I whispered.

Falin nodded and stood. Then he turned and offered me a hand. I accepted, letting him pull me to my feet.

"We need to change. As you've so elegantly put it in the past, we look like we've just left the set of a horror movie," he said, gesturing to both of our clothes.

Yeah. Ew.

"I think we're still on that horror set. What do we do with the bodies?" I didn't want them in the castle. I'd already let him take bodies to my office. I wasn't allowing bodies in my home as well, case or no case. But, I didn't know if my roommates had made it back from the revelry yet. They had to drive home from the Bloom, not take the unexpectedly expedited route we had. I wouldn't want them to walk through the door to the folded space and trip over a dead body.

I sighed and answered my own question before Falin had a chance. "Maybe I should just do the ritual right here and then we can take them back to Faerie."

"No," Falin said at the same Dugan said, "You can't."

I frowned. "Why?"

"Look at them, Alex." Falin said it gently.

I frowned at him. I didn't want to. Hadn't it been enough that I carried the damn heads? I didn't want to look at them. But I would. I let my gaze run over the grass until I spotted one of the heads. It was Lunabella.

It was dark on the hillside. The moon was only half full, and while the glowing moonflowers supplied some light, it was still night. Also, mortal reality touched here, so my eyes suffered more than in pure Faerie. I walked over to the head and knelt next to it.

She had landed facedown in the grass. I didn't want to touch her, but I couldn't just leave her head where it had rolled after I'd dropped it. The dead deserved better treatment than that, even if they were suspected of murder.

Cringing, I lifted the head with both hands. My skin crawled at the contact, my stomach twisting. It hadn't exactly been easy to touch her head at the revelry, but the threat of the devouring fog had been a pretty big distraction. Now I was very aware of the cold blood and cooling skin under my fingers. I just needed to carry it five feet to her body, and then I was calling us even for my dropping her head in the first place. I would have rather closed my eyes and not thought about what was in my hands, but Falin had told me to *look* at the bodies, so I turned her face upward as I moved.

Lunabella's eyes were closed, at least, but her mouth hung open, and her hair had tangled badly during either the first roll after her beheading, my rough run through the woods, or her second roll when I'd dropped her. It was matted to her face with drying blood. Around it her skin . . . I gasped, nearly dropping the head again.

Dark purple lines webbed through her face; black lesions bubbled above her skin in places. I stared, trying to convince myself that what I was seeing was just more drying blood. But no, the black and purple lines were under the flesh. Basmoarte. As if in recognition, I felt the tips of my own infected fingers burn with the poison that would slowly kill me. I set her head down above the shoulders of her body where it lay on the hilltop. Then I scuttled back several feet from the corpse. She did *not* look like she was just sleeping.

I wiped my hands on my skirt, rubbing my skin hard against the material, but the feeling of Lunabella's blood on my fingers didn't brush off. Nor did the burn of the infection in my magic as I turned and searched for Jurin's head. I'd seen it earlier, near where I'd been sitting, but I hadn't really looked at it. Now I forced myself to look, and I found similar markings of infection. I should have placed his head with his body as well. But I couldn't. I just couldn't. One of the guys would have to collect it before he was returned to the winter court. I was done.

"They both have basmoarte." I said the words very carefully, fighting back the panic bubbling in my throat. Of course that forced it to my stomach and I went still, unsure if I was going to be sick.

"Yes. With extremely fast onset. Just like what hit you," Falin said, looking from body to head. "We saw Lunabella less than twelve hours ago and she displayed no symptoms. At the time of her death, the infection was advanced. Her beheading might have been a mercy."

"Then that is an undeniable tie to the crime scene," I said, still scrubbing at my hands. "Perhaps she was accidentally exposed. Or perhaps she was double-crossed. Either way, we need to question her and find out what she knows."

"Alexis, she has basmoarte," Dugan said, and his tone implied we shouldn't need to discuss it further.

"So do I." I yelled it. I couldn't help it. But I'd already

been exposed. What did it matter if I raised a few more shades with it?

"Yes, but remember it is an infection from a wound, not a disease." Dugan sounded like he was schooling a child, which irritated me. "Kordon was infected near or after death and showed no symptoms. You described feeling 'a prick' when your magic was injured. Imagine what would happen if you reached inside a body this badly infected. It would shred your magic, causing dozens of wounds. How fast would it spread through you then?"

Oh.

So raising the shades was out. "How do we confirm they were involved in Stiofan's murder and not just easy scapegoats? If they were meant to simply disappear after it was known we were searching for Lunabella, it would have been simple to assume she'd run into hiding because she was guilty."

"Well, it won't be definitive, but . . ." Falin walked to Jurin's body and lifted one of his hands. He carefully removed the dress glove he wore and examined the man's skin. Then he held the hand up, twisting it so moonlight trailed over the fae's palm.

His *bloody* palm.

Jurin was winter court. Falin was the only courtier in winter with sanctioned bloody hands. He hadn't necessarily taken part in killing Stiofan, but he'd killed someone, and recently. So Stiofan was a damn good possibility. Falin approached Lunabella next, gently stripping off one of her bright yellow gloves. Blood stained her palm as well.

I shivered, tearing my gaze away.

Dugan frowned at me. "You really don't like dead bodies, do you?"

"No. I don't. Does anyone?"

He considered that, opened his mouth, likely to mention any number of disturbed conditions people might have, but at my glare he smiled. "It just seems quite detrimental to have such a strong aversion considering your profession."

I shrugged. "I work through it. And up until about six months ago, it wasn't an issue. I never dealt with murder scenes, or weird unexplainable conditions with corpses, or having to carry bodies. I met with clients and the bodies were already nicely buried, or in coffins, or occasionally in body bags at the morgue." I turned to Falin. "You know, it was the day I met you that things all went FUBAR."

"I hope you're not blaming me," he said, but he smiled. Yeah, he was flirting over a dead body. Because this was my life now.

"I blame him," a masculine voice said behind me, and I jumped.

Whirling around, I found myself face-to-face with Death.

My mouth went dry. It had been over a month since I'd last seen him. Our last good-bye had been mutual but painful. He was a soul collector and I was mortal and it just wasn't a maintainable relationship. We both knew that. While the logical part of my brain had known it was for the best, my heart didn't believe me. Also, he'd been my best friend long before he'd been my lover, and losing both in one stroke was the worst part. If I was honest with myself, I was angry with him for not being there to help me heal from the heart he'd broken.

"What are you doing here?" I asked, and then cringed because even I could hear the edge of hurt in my voice.

"Alexis?" Dugan asked behind me, concern tinting his voice.

"She does this," Falin told him as a way of explaining my habit of talking to beings no one else could see. Then he turned toward me. "Ghost or collector?" He studied my face in the moonlight and scowled before answering his own question. "Collector."

Yeah, Falin and Death didn't like each other.

"You've been . . . busy," Death said, looking around. I was standing on a hill with a prince, a knight, and two dead bodies. Yeah, I'd been a little busy. He frowned. "I've been looking for you for the better part of the last two days."

I lifted my shoulders in an awkward shrug as I fidgeted with the skirt of my gown, wishing it had pockets. "I had Faerie stuff."

"You say this is normal? Who is she talking to? No one is there," Dugan said behind me.

I twisted around and shot him a glare. "Hey, you talk to shadows. I talk to ghosts and soul collectors. Just because you can't see them, doesn't mean they aren't there."

"You're hurt," Death said. "And the old wounds in your soul are inflamed."

He took a step forward, but I took a step back. It would be way too easy to fall into old habits, but we'd already had this dance and come to the inevitable end. Contrary to popular belief, I didn't go out looking to get hurt.

Death and I stared at each other for a long moment. He was the one to look away.

"Don't die in Faerie, Al."

"Not high on my to-do list." Obviously.

He didn't seem to know what to say after that. This

kind of awkward had never been part of our relationship in the past. But things were different now. I needed something to do with my hands, but there was nothing. No pockets. Nothing to fidget with.

Death clearly felt the same way. He at least had something he could do.

He walked over to Lunabella's body and bent down. Thrusting his hand into her chest, he pulled her soul free. It glowed a brilliant silver.

"Wait." I needed to talk to her ghost. I hadn't been able to get to it myself because of the basmoarte, but now that she was outside the body . . .

I knew Death wouldn't let me talk to her. He couldn't. Asking just underscored some of the reasons our relationship hadn't worked. But I would try anyway, which was another reason things hadn't worked.

Death hesitated, his shoulders tensing.

"Just one question?" I pleaded.

He didn't look at me as he said, "One."

That was better than I'd assumed I'd get.

"Did—" I started, letting my mouth get ahead of my brain in my hurry to get the question. I snapped my teeth shut. I'd been about to ask if she'd participated in Stiofan's murder. But whether she did or not didn't truly matter and wouldn't help us find the rest of the murderers.

"Who killed you?" I asked, hoping my hesitation wasn't too long.

With Death still grasping her soul, Lunabella hadn't transitioned over to the land of the dead and become a ghost. She was a soul, in its brilliantly raw form. There was no true shape, no features, in the radiant silver glow that made up her soul, so I couldn't read her expression.

Her voice, when she answered, was high and distant, and very unlike a ghost's.

"The scarred prince."

"Who is—?" I started, but I'd gotten my one question. Death flicked his hand and the soul vanished.

Lunabella was out of my reach now, unless I wanted to risk lacerating my magic to raise her shade. Death moved to Jurin next, sending his soul on in one smooth motion before I could ask him to wait.

I turned toward Falin and Dugan, opening my mouth to ask who the "scarred prince" might be, but then hesitated. I'd seen every noble in Faerie—aside from the high king—at the revelry. There had been only one prince present. Dugan.

I stared at him. Only his face and hands were visible, and they certainly weren't scarred. The rest of him was covered in armor. He didn't look like anyone who would be described as scarred, but who else was there? I thought about everything he'd said over the last two days, searching for loopholes in his words. Could he be involved? Why would he be here now if he were? And how could he have killed Lunabella when he and Falin had been together when they reached the clearing? Of course, it was only his shadow cat's odd actions that we were basing time of death on. Could he have orchestrated the discovery after having followed and killed them sometime while I'd been unconscious?

I didn't know. My gut said he wasn't involved, but I'd talk to Falin alone first. Find out if there were any other princes I didn't know about. I turned back to Death.

"There might be a broken ghost in my office," I said, because he hadn't had to let me ask Lunabella any questions, so I was showing my thanks in a peace offering. Besides, if Stiofan was still there, he needed help. There were no therapists for ghosts, and the land of the dead wasn't exactly a bright and happy place full of healing. Hopefully wherever souls went next would be better.

"I found him already," Death said as he straightened.

That's right, he'd mentioned that he'd been looking for me. But he hadn't said why yet. I waited. He would tell me why he was searching for me, or he wouldn't. That had been another major stumbling block. Too many secrets.

Death turned to me and brushed his dark hair out of his face. He looked around and scowled at Falin and Dugan, who were watching me, no doubt searching for hints about the conversation they could only hear my half of.

"You might want to go somewhere with less of an audience. *He* wants to talk to you about the debt you owe him."

I frowned, confused, and then the blood drained from my face as comprehension hit. There was only one *he* that Death would use that much emphasis about.

The Mender.

I grimaced and twisted my hands in the skirt of my dress. I didn't want to deal with a visit from the Mender. Not tonight. I'd had a long couple days, and a meeting with the very powerful—very scary—leader of the collectors was not something I wanted to contemplate. Unfortunately, I didn't have a choice. I'd made a bargain with him, and now I owed him an enormous debt. If he'd come to collect, I was bound by magic to grant him what he requested. The Mender's interest certainly explained why Death had sought me out despite his intent to stay away—I'd made the bargain and taken the debt to ensure Death's freedom.

"When?"

"Soon, now that you're back in a plane where we can find you."

Crap. I nodded. I didn't thank him—I didn't need any more debt floating around—but I think he understood that I appreciated the heads-up.

"Be safe, Al," he said, and I could see in his hazel eyes there was a lot more he wanted to say. But it was better for both of us if he didn't. He gave me a small smile. Then he vanished.

"I try," I whispered after he was already gone. Then I turned, looking first at the two fae who were watching me skeptically, and then down at the bodies laid out on the hill. I couldn't raise the shades, and the souls were gone, so I couldn't question the ghosts. There was absolutely nothing I could contribute further besides offering extra hands to help move them—which was hardly unique or irreplaceable.

"I hate to do this, but . . . can I leave these bodies for you two to take care of?" Now that was a sentence I never thought I'd utter. I lifted my skirt, starting down the hill even as I spoke. "You can get them back to Faerie, right? Don't leave them on the hill for my roommates to find." Another sentence that I shouldn't have ever had to use. "I have to go. Something's come up."

Then I turned and ran toward the castle, hoping I could change out of my gore-streaked dress before my meeting with the single most powerful being I'd ever met.

Chapter 17

❈⟶ ◉ ◉ ⟵❈

The Mender hadn't appeared by the time I made my way through the castle to my rooms, so I snatched a pair of clean clothes from my dresser and hurried to the bathroom. I only planned to change, but a glance in the mirror convinced me a shower was essential. My hair was a tangle of curls and pine needles, I had mud and things I didn't want to think about on my arms from my fall in the woods, my skin was sticky from dried sweat, and I had an overall feeling of ick after over a day without a shower. I peeked back at my room—it was dark and empty. I turned the shower on, jumping in before it had a chance to warm up.

I'm normally one to relish my showers. Not tonight. While I wanted to scrub myself pink, I didn't have time for more than a quick wash. It probably was one of my top five fastest showers of all time. Then I was out and pulling my clothes on over my still-damp body. Getting caught naked by the Mender was not something I wanted to happen.

I stepped out of the bathroom, towel-drying my hair, and stopped in my tracks. The door to my sitting room stood open. I'd definitely closed it when I'd walked through. I tossed the towel back in the bathroom and walked from my bedroom to the sitting room attached to my suite. The room had been empty when I passed through earlier. It wasn't anymore.

The Mender sat in one of the overstuffed lounge chairs in the center of the room. For a being of incredible power, he wasn't an imposing figure. Not currently, at least. His rounded shoulders dipped as he leaned forward, thin arms on knobby knees, and his balding head tipped to examine the books scattered across my coffee table—the one surface in the entire castle where I'd convinced Ms. B to let me enjoy my clutter. He picked up a book, examining the spine and nodding silently to himself, as if agreeing with some conversation only he could hear. His face had deep wrinkles and well-etched smile lines, and the impression was that of a kind old grandpa who would regale me with tales of his great-grandchildren.

I wasn't fooled.

By the time he looked up, he appeared younger, hale and strong. The wrinkles had faded to lines of definition. The change happened so subtly that I didn't realize his features had changed until it occurred to me that he looked different. And they kept changing as I entered the room.

How long had he been waiting?

"I didn't mind. It wasn't a long wait. I knew you were hurrying." He said this as if we were already in midconversation.

Yeah, one of the more disconcerting things about the Mender was that he was a telepath. And probably psychic. He definitely saw possible paths of the future, even if he didn't know which would come to fruition.

"He said you wanted to talk to me about the debt." I didn't need to clarify who "he" was. The Mender knew, either because Death was the only collector I was likely to talk about or because of that whole telepath thing.

"I've come to collect your debt."

I nodded, sliding into the seat across from him. He hadn't stated his demands yet, but I could already feel the magic binding me. I'd foolishly failed to set any terms on the favor he could ask of me. He could request anything, and I would have to comply—the magic in the debt would ensure I did.

The Mender's features settled on something I'd classify as refined middle age; I wasn't sure if he was in control of the shift, or if it was a natural condition of his existence, but this face made me think of a shrewd businessman. It didn't reassure me.

The Mender held out his hand. A small polished wood box sat on his palm.

"Take it," he said, nodding to me.

I reached out tentatively. I didn't need to use my ability to sense magic or peer across planes to know the box was more than it appeared—that was a given considering who was offering it to me. Still, I was unprepared for actually touching it.

The box itself had no physical weight, but the moment my fingers touched the polished surface, my magic rose unbidden. I jerked back, nearly dropping the box as I squeezed my mental shields closed tighter. The Mender clapped his hands around mine, keeping the box pressed against my palm.

I gasped, using everything I had to reinforce my

mental shields and keep my magic from spilling down into the box.

"What is this?"

"Just a little ball of reality," the Mender said. He looked like a kindly grandfather again when he smiled at me. "Stop fighting yourself. You cannot win a battle against yourself, and I'm not giving you something meant to harm you."

I didn't know if I believed him. I didn't understand enough about what the Mender was to trust him, but he was right about one thing—I couldn't win against my own magic. Even as part of my magic battered against the mental shields I'd erected to hold it in, another part oozed through those shields, exploiting pores in my walls. The more magic that slipped through the shields, the larger the small holes became. It would wear down the shields in a matter of minutes at this rate and all I'd have to show for my efforts would be the exhaustion I'd earned fighting a losing battle.

I let go of my shields, and my magic *moved*.

There was no other way to describe it. Usually I directed my magic like a pair of hands. A tool to reach out, to pull, to push. Sometimes, if I let too much of my grave magic build, it hemorrhaged out of me, rushing for anything it could reach. But this wasn't grave magic, it was my planeweaving ability. And it didn't react like any magic I'd felt before.

I stopped trying to block the magic, and it moved like a wave engulfing the box. At the same time, the magic never actually left me. It stretched, folding around the ball of reality in my palm, connecting me to it and mixing it with the main pool of my magic. And then it settled. Seemingly content.

I mentally poked at the box in my hand. Physically it still felt like it wasn't there, but my senses could feel the compacted strands of reality. I examined them. I could feel the land of the dead and the crystalline plane the collectors existed on. Other planes were there too, ones I'd felt before but had no name for. The ball of reality didn't feel that different from many of the strands of reality all around us right now, it was just far more compressed. Now that my magic had encompassed the ball of reality, it seemed perfectly content to let it be.

"What is this?"

The Mender leaned forward, his face that of an inquisitive youth. "It is exactly as you suspect. A compact ball of select realities."

"And what happens when I open the box?" I had a sudden vision of Pandora's box, which loosed horrible things into the world when she opened it.

The Mender chuckled. "Nothing so dramatic. Go ahead, you can try it now."

Saying I was unsure would have been an understatement, but if this tied into the debt I owed him, I'd have to do it eventually anyway. Might as well get it over with.

There was no lock on the box, but when I tried to flip open the lid, it didn't move. I tried to pull the lid. Nothing. I flipped the box over, looking for a latch or release. Nothing.

I looked up, frowning at the Mender. He smiled back at me, content to watch me fumble with the box.

"It doesn't open?" I asked, feeling like an idiot.

"It's not really a box, is it?"

My frown deepened. "Next you'll hand me a spoon, I suppose."

He didn't get the joke. I wasn't going to explain.

"Okay, so then what do I do with the box that isn't a box and can't be opened?"

"Take it to Faerie. Let the reality in it naturally unfurl and spread."

My jaw dropped, and I shook my head. I couldn't take death and decay into Faerie. The land of the dead didn't belong there.

The Mender's face shifted to the businessman again. "This is the debt you owe me. I'm calling it in. What I want you to do is take it to Faerie. The souls of the dead are stuck in Faerie. I want to collect them."

I shook my head again, clenching my jaw. He was right, I couldn't refuse. But there had to be another way. "There is more than just the collectors' plane here. This ball of reality contains the land of the dead. If I take it to Faerie, well, I don't know *exactly* what would happen, but it would definitely introduce decay."

"Much as the courts of Faerie balance each other, certain planes of reality balance each other. One cannot exist without the other, so you must release both."

"The very nature of Faerie might change. This could destroy it."

The Mender's lips pressed out as he gave a nodding shrug. "That's true."

"Don't make me do this." I couldn't do this. My own life wasn't worth destroying an entire plane and the people on it.

"Well then, I suggest you learn to open and close that box." The smile the Mender flashed me suggested that he'd played me. He'd offered me the worst option, to make what he really wanted sound better. I couldn't refuse either way, but if there was another way, I'd jump on it. And he knew it. He continued by saying, "You don't have to leave the reality to spread unattended if you can control it. Open the box, release reality, collect the souls, and then trap the realities foreign to Faerie back away again."

I glared at him. *Oh, that is all, is it?* And how did he expect me to do that? "The box doesn't open."

"You can feel the reality contained there?" he asked, and at my nod he said, "Unravel it, just a little."

I cocked a skeptical eyebrow, but dutifully focused on the box on my palm and widened my shields so that I could gaze across the planes. The room changed. Decay encroached on the furniture and rugs in the room, the material fraying and the wood rotting. Bright wisps of raw magic danced in the air. The Mender didn't change, and he didn't glow like a soul, but a rosy pink light surrounded him. I wasn't sure from which plane the light originated or what it meant, but I was guessing knowing wouldn't help me with the task at hand. I focused on the ball of reality.

The box in my hand changed and didn't at the same time. I could see it, and yet I could see through it. Considering it had no apparent weight, that wasn't surprising. My magical sense of it didn't change—the space above my palm still held a tightly compact ball of reality—but my perception of it did. I can't actually see the planes, instead seeing what is on those planes. So I couldn't *see* the ball of reality, but staring, I could catch a flash of iridescent color or splash of gray, like seeing something from the corner of one's eye. But the planes contained in the ball were already present all around me, so there wasn't much to differentiate them from the reality already surrounding me.

"Unravel it," the Mender urged again.

I reached out, fumbling for the tightly wound strands of reality. I caught several and managed to pull them a few inches. The illusionary box lid cracked, not opening, but a seam at least. Small wounds sprouted on my fingertips, the strands cutting deep into my flesh. I winced, pulling back my stinging, bleeding fingers.

The Mender tsked under his breath. "You're going to seriously injure yourself doing it that way."

"How would you suggest I unravel them?"

"You intuitively touch all the planes. You have consistently had no issue extending those planes to other beings. Extend these planes in much the same way. Push them out among the planes that already exist here. But weave them into the planes, not into a thing or a being."

"I . . . What?" Extending planes to beings? "You mean when I pull ghosts close to mortal reality?"

The Mender's youthful face took on a put-upon expression, as if he were annoyed that I was missing something that should be obvious.

"You don't pull ghosts or my collectors across to mortal reality—they never leave their plane as they can't exist outside it. You weave the two planes together, making the fibers of both realities touch, and you wrap those joined planes around them. You visualize it wrong, but you do it instinctively."

My mouth formed a small O but I furled my brow, thinking about what I did when I dragged ghosts across the planes. Or, I guess, thrust the planes together, if the Mender was correct. I'd assumed it was an evolution of my grave magic, admittedly supported with my plane-weaving. I'd only been able to do it by touch initially, extending my magic through me and into the ghost or Death. But in the last few months I'd become rather adept at making ghosts manifest at a distance.

I considered what it felt like to reach with my magic and pull across—or weave—the planes, and I reached for the ball of reality on my palm in the same way. Nothing happened. My magic had encompassed the ball as soon as I'd touched it. It was already *mine*, for lack of a better word. I glared at it.

"So jump to the next logical conclusion," the Mender said, his voice sharp and impatient.

If he was going to sit there, read my thoughts, and snap at me, why didn't he just give me the damn answer?

He lifted his eyebrow, obviously having caught that thought as well. Oh well. He was the one snooping. Not my fault if he didn't like what he heard. But as to what he'd said, what would the next logical conclusion be with the ball of reality?

Well, if my magic had made it "mine" and poking it with more magic did nothing, then maybe I needed to *reach* with it. I could feel the ball of reality, so I focused on it, and then tried to reach out the way I would to a ghost. Except there was nowhere to reach to. The ball of reality wriggled, but it didn't unfurl.

I considered how my magic had felt when it had enveloped the ball. Like a wave lifting from the ocean and pushing outward. Focusing on the ball of reality, I tried to simulate that feeling of magic flowing out, forward, and filling space without ever leaving the greater collection of magic.

The lid of the box flipped open. The threads of reality rolled out, spreading with the wave of magic.

"Very good," the Mender said, and he gave me a

grandfatherly nod, as if I'd made him proud. "That ocean analogy you visualized was a good one. It will limit you eventually, but for now it is helping you."

I looked around. I still couldn't see the actual threads of reality, but I could feel them. I was far more aware of all the planes I was touching—and that they were touching everything around me. Including the chair I was sitting in and the rug below my feet, both of which were rotting from their contact with the land of the dead. *Damn it.*

"Now pull it back."

I frowned at the Mender. "You make it sound easy."

"I never said it was easy. Though this you should probably be able to do as automatically as breathing."

Wouldn't that be the definition of simple?

I tried to focus on the magic. To concentrate on the strands of reality that needed to be pulled back apart. The Mender made a sharp clicking noise under his breath.

"You're trying too hard again. Go back to your ocean visual."

I didn't grind my teeth. Not much at least. Taking a deep breath, I exhaled the annoyance creeping through me. Then I pictured my magic like a wave again. I could feel it around me. I'd extended a full circle of magic around myself. Now I imagined it all flowing back to me, like the tide rolling in.

The magic moved, a little sluggish, but it returned. The extra web of reality wound itself back into a compressed ball. The box lid slammed shut.

I looked around. Not one tear or pocket of merged space remained. I'd never used my planeweaving without damaging reality before. I looked down at the rug. It still looked rotted, but with the land of the dead at a normal density, it didn't look as rotted as it had. I closed my shields. The frayed fabric and molded holes vanished, the rug still whole in mortal reality. The chair was too.

I stared at the chair. Shocked.

"You didn't weave the realities flat. You just wove them together," the Mender said, and my head shot up.

"What?"

His youthful face looked horribly put-upon. "The planes brush against each other naturally and constantly. You unrolled the layers of reality I gave you. You didn't push anything from one to another, just spread out the reality in this space."

That sounded accurate, but this was a lot of new information. Still, I'd definitely done something that I'd never known how to do before. And it hadn't magically slapped me down, so a point for using my ability without harming myself.

"Yes, yes. Good. Now do it again."

I blinked in surprise. "What?"

"Practice makes perfect, as they say. Do it again."

I looked down at the ball of reality in my hand, still shaped like a box. Then I looked past it, at my fingers. Three of my fingertips were deep blue, the veins of polluted magic running down the full length of the fingers and into the pad of my palm. I was using an enormous amount of magic to unfurl the ball of reality.

"Oh, that is a problem," the Mender said, his features turning to the middle-aged businessman, and he drummed his fingers on his leg. "Oh yes, that could definitely be deadly."

The blood drained from my face. "Is that the possible future you see? When? Do you see a way to prevent it?"

The Mender glared at me. "Even if I were inclined to give you those answers, I wouldn't. Now practice. You'll probably pollute most of your hand, but it is important that you can do this."

Because he wanted the souls in Faerie, one way or another. Though if he could teach me not to kill myself, maybe the changeling planeweavers being gone was not quite as devastating a blow as I initially thought. But how did the Mender know so much about my powers? "Are you a planeweaver?"

"Of course not," he snapped. "But obviously I can manipulate planes. Who do you think made that ball you're holding? Now concentrate. You have a lot to learn. I want the souls trapped in Faerie released. We both agree that fundamentally changing Faerie is a bad plan. So you must learn to weave reality neatly, instead of walking around ripping holes and fusing spots." His features turned younger than I'd ever seen, a teenager at most, and he crossed his arms over his chest. "And if you start thinking of me as a teacher, I'm going to charge you a second favor for this lesson."

Right. I definitely didn't want that.

He gave me a look that said I better get to the practicing. Taking a breath, I focused on the ball of reality again, letting my magic roll out of me like a wave. The ball unfurled, reality weaving in a small circle around me.

"Push out further," the Mender instructed.

I did.

"Further," he said, and though I complied, he circled his hand in a "keep going" motion.

I hadn't moved, but I was breathing heavy. The merged patch of reality spread all around me in a circle that was about eight feet wide. My magic felt stretched to the limit. If I pushed waves of magic out further, I'd start draining my reservoir.

"Enough," the Mender said, nodding. "You can draw it back in now."

I did, gratefully. It was easier this time, as if the magic had already started carving its own paths through my psyche.

"Good." The Mender's satisfied smile seemed to be more for himself than for me. "Now do it again."

The Mender had me practice the magic half a dozen more times before he was finally satisfied. While I managed to push my circle of merged planes out as far as nine feet a few times, on my last attempt I barely got the circle over six. I was panting and sweaty, and my whole body ached even though I'd been sitting the entire time. All of my fingers on my infected hand had deep purple spots in the tips, and the veins of fouled magic ran through the whole hand, all the way to the crease of my wrist. It burned, and hurt worse than any other part of me. I'd have to watch the spread carefully. I couldn't let it reach my shoulder and the weak spot in my soul again.

"I think you're ready," the Mender said, pushing out of his chair.

To sleep? I was definitely ready for that.

He chuckled under his breath, shaking his head. "You are ready to take that reality to Faerie."

Nope. Sleep was definitely the correct answer. I stifled a yawn. Now that my shields were closed, the ball of reality looked like a solid box again. I could hold it, move it from hand to hand, and yet it still had no weight. It was disconcerting.

"So exactly what is it you want me to do? Go find bodies in Faerie, unfurl the ball with the land of the dead and the collectors' plane, and then just stand there until someone shows up to collect the souls?"

"Of course not. My people can't sit around waiting in the wings hoping you open the box. When you find a trapped soul, you will have to be the one to eject it from the body. When you pull back the layers of reality, the soul will fold and compress as well since it cannot exist outside those planes. My collectors will check that space occasionally and collect any souls you've gathered."

I shuddered at the idea of walking around carrying ghosts in a box. Of course, first I had to find the souls he wanted. Deaths were rare in Faerie. Most of the bodies I'd seen there, I'd then brought across into the mortal realm. Then there were cases like Maeve, who'd been dead but were up and walking around again. If a collector were to spot her, he would probably take her soul. I did not see myself doing that. Oh, don't get me wrong, I'd popped free souls that were navigating dead bodies before, but those souls had been destroying themselves. I didn't think that was the case with the fae healed from death.

The Mender watched me, clearly following along with my unspoken thoughts. He frowned, his face shifting faster through the different ages as if unsure where to stop.

"How many souls will it take to clear my debt?" I asked, because how long was I supposed to carry around a box searching Faerie for dead bodies?

"What if I said all of them?"

My mouth fell open, and I gave a quick shake of my head. "That isn't possible. There are places in Faerie I can't go. Hell, there are places I probably could never even find. I mean, when is it you expect this to be completed?"

The Mender smiled. "I admit, all is not realistic, but your debt to me is very large. You have a lot of work ahead of you. But you have time. You must become considerably better at unraveling reality and stretching it. The ultimate goal is for you to eventually free the battlefields full of the dead."

"Eventually?" So was he giving me this task without a timeline?

"When you make it to a battlefield, I have a spell that will allow you to call my people so that you are not collecting hundreds of souls alone. When it is time, the spell will be available to you."

I blinked. I hadn't really thought out the implications of what he'd tasked me with, clearly. I tried to imagine myself walking among the dead in a battlefield, only nine feet of blended planes around me. It would be the most horrifically dead too. Those whose deaths were able to be reversed would have been healed. So these bodies would be in bad shape, and because nothing decayed in Faerie, these ancient battlefields would look as fresh as the day of the battle. A cold drop of sweat ran down my spine.

"Obviously such a small circle of reality would be insufficient," the Mender said, agreeing with my unspoken thoughts. "You need practice. More than you can acquire in a single evening." He leaned forward. "And I do expect you to practice. I want to see consistent growth in your abilities." As he said the words, I felt the debt tighten around me, binding his instructions to my very soul. It was not a comfortable feeling. The Mender continued, not noticing or not caring about my distress over the debt he held against me. "In the meantime, carry the box with you whenever you enter Faerie. You will likely find opportunities to free trapped souls, even if you cannot complete the full task yet. Each soul you release will whittle away your debt."

I nodded reluctantly and looked down at the box that wasn't really a box, unsure of the best way to carry it. It wasn't like it would fit in my back pocket. I rose to my feet, planning to put it in my purse, and the Mender shook his head.

"The shape of it is unimportant, only the function. And that you keep it with you always." He waved his hand, and the box faded. It reappeared a moment later as a locket on a long necklace. "Is this a more convenient shape?"

"That works," I said, and when the Mender tilted his head, one eyebrow lifting, I unclasped the chain and hooked it around my neck. I was afraid it would be unnerving having a compacted ball of the land of the dead hanging over my sternum, but I barely noticed it. If I reached for it, I could feel the ball of reality, but it wasn't distracting.

The Mender nodded as if satisfied, and his face shifted to that of an old man again. "Then I should be on my way. You've felt the weight of the debt you owe me. I am giving you no timeline, but if you do not collect enough souls to repay that debt during life, you will still owe me a debt in death. You do not want that."

I gulped. That last sentence was the understatement of the century. Usually death negated a debt. Apparently not for the leader of the soul collectors. I stared down at my purple-streaked hand. *Unless I die in Faerie.*

"I have thought of that," he said. "That is one of *his* greatest fears. That you will disappear into Faerie, never emerge, and he won't know if you are alive or dead and trapped for eternity."

I looked away. I knew he was talking about Death again. And I knew it was something Death worried about. He'd told me as much more than once.

"Keep that locket close, and you will always be tied into our lands," he said, and my hand flew to the locket. He smiled. "I know you think me some powerful tyrant for my strict rules, but I do care. Now, I must go."

With that, his form faded from the room. After he was gone, I turned, intending to have a conversation with Falin and then collapse into my bed and sleep at least twelve hours. Then his voice said, "And find the cure for your magic. Sooner rather than later would be best."

I whirled around. "So it's possible to cure basmoarte?"

No one was there and he didn't answer. I waited, hoping he'd come back or say more. He didn't. Eventually I shuffled back to my bedroom, but though I was exhausted, I felt lighter. A little more hopeful.

Chapter 18

‹⊱══⊙ ⊙══⊰›

I woke to the sound of loud pounding on my door. I rolled to my back and squinted at the window above my bed. The sky was still dark. Way too early to be awake.

The knocking sounded again, and I pulled the pillow over my head. It was probably Falin. I'd gone to talk to him after the Mender left, but he'd still been at the winter court. I'd texted him letting him know I needed to talk to him before we started working on the case again. I hadn't meant before dawn.

The knocking stopped.

Nothing that can't wait until morning. I rolled back over.

The door opened.

PC jumped off the bed, barking and growling. He charged the intruder with all the ferocity contained in his six-pound body.

I sat up, fumbling for my knife as I moved. PC knew and liked everyone who lived in the castle. He wouldn't bark at them. Which meant someone who didn't live here had just walked into my room.

I blinked, trying to see in the near darkness as I scrambled to my feet. My eyes didn't cooperate fast enough, and I opened my shields, knowing the glow from my eyes would give me away but wanting to see more than I wanted caution.

"Peace, dog," Dugan said from the doorway to my bedroom.

I lowered my dagger. "What are you doing here? And maybe a better question, how did you get here?" I glanced at my dresser, where the small globe attached to the wards sat. It glowed a cheery green, meaning all was well and no one uninvited had tried to pass the wards. *Caleb is going to have to recalibrate those.* Last I'd seen of Dugan had been on the hill hours ago. Surely he hadn't been hanging around this whole time?

"That's not important. I nee—" he started, but I cut him off.

"Yeah, it kind of is." I'd thought the castle was pretty secure.

"I—"

A knock came from the door on the other side of my sitting room, followed by a soft, "Alex? Everything okay?"

Falin. Apparently it was middle-of-the-night party time in my room.

"Come on in," I yelled.

The door opened and Falin walked in wearing only a pair of gray sleep pants, which almost distracted me from the fact that his gun was in his hands.

"What set off PC?" he asked, his eyes scanning the sitting room as he stalked through it. He reached the bedroom doorway, and the gun twitched, but he didn't *actually* aim it at Dugan. "How did you get here?"

"Exactly what I just asked," I said, as I knelt to scoop up PC. He was still growling at Dugan. He really didn't like the Shadow Prince. As I considered my dog to have excellent taste, I noted that fact against Dugan.

"We do not have time for this. Alexis, I need your help."

My first instinct was to tell him to contact me during normal business hours, but Dugan sounded frantic. He hadn't sounded desperate when he'd shown up in my office because his friend was presumed dead. Nor when we discovered our best lead had been murdered after the revelry, but now there was panic in his voice.

"We can negotiate whatever payment you wish, but we must hurry," he said, stepping closer to me. He looked like he was going to grasp my elbows, but PC was still growling in my arms.

I glanced to Falin. He studied the Shadow Prince with narrowed eyes.

"Go where? To do what?" I asked.

"The shadow court," Dugan said. He turned and stalked from me to my dresser. He glanced at the items arranged on the top, though I didn't think he actually saw them. The movement was what was important, like pacing could somehow work out his thoughts and words. Considering the sharp twitches of his hands and the heavy steps of his feet, I didn't think it was alleviating his agitated nervousness. He turned back to me. "The king is ill."

Now I was even more confused. "I'm not a healer."

"He has basmoarte."

I frowned, no less confused.

"Do you know how he contracted it?" Falin asked.

Dugan shook his head. "Serri said he was fine when they went to bed. She woke in the middle of the night and found him . . . like he is. The fouled magic is covering most of him already, and he is unconscious. He doesn't have much time."

I didn't know what to say. Basmoarte was a death sentence; we all knew it. *"I'm sorry"* would have been the human response, but none of us were human.

"What is it you want from me?" I finally asked, uncertain where this was going.

"You're the only person I've ever heard of who has reversed the spread of basmoarte."

"Only temporarily." I held up my hand. The fouled magic hadn't spread much further while I slept, but the entirety of my hand was covered in deep purple lines under the ever-present illusory blood.

Dugan stalked up to me again. "Even a temporary reversal would bring him back from the brink of death."

"Alex, no," Falin said, taking up a position beside me. "You would have to come in contact with the Shadow King's magic to remove the infection. You were able to remove your own without further injuring yourself, but basmoarte is spread through infected magic. You could do an unknown amount of damage to yourself and your own basmoarte would spread that much faster."

"I'm aware of the tremendous risk I am asking you to take." Dugan took a deep breath. Then he bowed. "I am willing to take the debt. Please, use the magic you used on yourself to cleanse the king."

With his words, the possibility of debt rose between us. If I accepted, it was a huge amount, at least as big a debt as I had promised the Mender. But that was because of the huge amount of risk. Cleansing the king wouldn't kill me outright, but if I developed more wounds that spread the infection, the basmoarte would kill me faster. *Though the Mender did indicate there is a cure.*

"No," Falin said again, crossing his arms over his chest. "She can't cash in a debt if she is dead."

"I am capable of making up my own mind," I said, frowning at him. Then I turned to Dugan and studied him. If the king was as close to death as he said, time was of the essence, but I wasn't following him into the shadow court without a couple answers first.

"Are you scarred?" I asked, and when his eyes widened to incredulous shock, I added, "Under your armor. I know you aren't hiding any facial scars with glamour."

"You are my betrothed. If you wish to examine my body, I will capitulate. But now is not the time." He ground out the words through a tense jaw, clearly upset by the question.

I shook my head. "That's not what I'm getting at. Do you have any scars prominent enough that you could be called, or have been called, the scarred prince?"

Dugan stared at me, confusion warring with his impatience. "No."

Falin watched me, and I could feel his curiosity at my questions, but he didn't intervene. I would have rather have had time to discuss this with him first, but time was not on our side.

I studied Dugan. "Are there any princes of Faerie known as 'the scarred prince'?"

"I am the only prince in Faerie currently," Dugan said, his brow furrowing but his fingers flexing, betraying his need to move. He all but buzzed with his anxious agitation. *Because of the questions? Or because of the king?* My gut said the latter.

I stared at him, aware that every moment I wavered could be the king's last. Dugan had been with us from the time the sun set and the truce ended until the bodies were discovered. He hadn't had time or opportunity to behead Lunabella or Jurin—at least not when we assumed their murders had occurred. He wasn't the scarred prince and I didn't think he was secretly working against us in this investigation.

I nodded, the gesture more toward myself than anyone in the room, and then I said, "I managed to ask one question of Lunabella's ghost. She said she was killed by 'the scarred prince,' but if you are the only Faerie prince . . ."

"I'm not the scarred prince."

We'd pretty much established that. But he was the only prince in Faerie, so who could she have meant? We didn't have time to puzzle it out now. We would revisit the conversation soon. For now, though, I could still feel the potential debt hanging in the air as Dugan waited for me to decide if I would go to the shadow court and help the king.

I nodded again, this time in answer to his request. "I'm not promising I'll be able to help the king, but I'll see what I can do. If he is as bad as you say, you might need to prepare yourself to become the new king."

Dugan's shoulders slumped. "Our court is already weakened. If he dies, there may not be a shadow throne left for me to rule."

Falin left to dress, and I sent Dugan to wait in my sitting room. Though I dressed in under two minutes, the prince was pacing by the time I opened my bedroom door. The sitting room wasn't huge, but it wasn't exactly small. Regardless, his agitated steps made the space feel cramped.

I sighed in relief when Falin opened the front door to my suite a moment after I left my own room. It said something about Dugan's desperation that he hadn't wasted time arguing when Falin insisted on coming with us.

"So how do we get to the shadow court?" I asked.

Dugan lifted his hands and the shadows hugging the wall beside the fireplace scattered. Once they were gone, the space that should have been a stone wall instead looked into a cavernous room with a hooded figure standing in the center. He was short, no taller than a child. I recognized him. I'd never seen his face, but I'd seen the color of his soul before. Yellow, human.

"The planebender?"

Dugan nodded. "Your castle has enough of Faerie that the planebender can reach it."

Well, that was an unintended side effect. I'd have to find out if his magics could be warded against. I didn't want the shadow court members showing up whenever they pleased.

Dugan stalked forward and stepped through the hole to the shadow court where my wall should have been. I followed close behind, opening my senses to examine the door—which was really more like a tear in space from one place to another—as I stepped through it. I could feel the change in layers of reality as I moved from my castle to Faerie proper, but I couldn't begin to guess how the planebender moved Faerie to touch in places it normally didn't. Of course, he was a planebender and I was a planeweaver, so while our skills might have been of the same family, they were quite different.

Once Falin stepped through the doorway, the planebender grabbed the tear in space with both hands and tugged it back together. With my shields open, I could almost see the strands of reality repairing themselves. Then the seam was gone, as if the door had never existed. *And now I have no easy way out of the shadow court.* I didn't like it, but I'd agreed to come and see the king, so I would.

The room we'd stepped into appeared to be a long hallway. The shadows seethed and writhed along the walls, and I made a point of staying squarely in the center of the hall as we walked. We didn't have to go far. Dugan turned to a patch of shadows and they moved aside to reveal a dark gold doorframe.

Dugan stepped through it, and I moved to follow but something caught my sleeve, holding me back. I glanced down to see the planebender, his hand tentatively wrapped in the knit of my sweater.

"You can help him, right?" His voice was young and worried, but something about it was incredibly familiar, as if I'd heard it before, long ago.

I had the urge to kneel down and reassure him that everything would be okay, but he wasn't actually that short, so it would come off wrong. Also, while he sounded prepubescent, he was almost certainly a changeling, so he could be far older than me. I didn't want to insult him.

"I'll see what I can do," was all I ended up saying. Which felt like not nearly enough, but I wasn't going to bind myself with a promise I couldn't keep.

With that, I walked through the door and into what could only be the king's bedchambers. A female fae sat on the large four-poster bed, her body cradled protectively forward, her large leathery wings stretched so that most of the bed was shielded from sight. She looked up as we entered. Her face was other, but beautiful, and her red eyes were glassy, her long eyelashes clumped from tears.

"Serri, this is Alexis," Dugan said as he approached the side of the bed. "I brought her to look at Nandin."

She stared at me, assessing. Ever so slowly, her wings retracted, the leathery membranes lifting to reveal the Shadow King tucked neatly in the bed, his head and shoulders on her lap. He appeared to be sleeping, but not peacefully. His face was pale around the dark purple lines of fouled magic, sweat beaded on his skin, his brows were furrowed, and his eyes darted behind his lids as if he was caught in a dream he couldn't escape.

"You are a healer?" Her voice was high and harsh, the worry in it almost a tangible thing.

"Not exactly."

Her red eyes shot to Dugan, the look questioning and slightly hostile.

"She's purged basmoarte before."

I frowned at Dugan. I hadn't agreed to more than look at the king yet. Serri wore no circlet and she hadn't been presented at the king's side at the solstice, so she wasn't an official consort, but she clearly cared about him. I didn't want to offer her false hope.

"If I can do this, do you have a receptacle?" I asked, looking around. While the space in the room felt large, most of it was lost in shadow, as if the bed were adrift in a sea of living darkness.

"Trees are not exactly plentiful here," Dugan said, frowning. He clearly hadn't thought about where I would *put* the basmoarte, but if I was able to purge the king, the fouled magic would need to go somewhere.

"Alex," Falin said, concern and censure in his voice. He stepped up behind me, into my space. I thought he'd put his hands on my shoulders, but he just remained behind me, close enough that I could feel his heat, a reminder that

I wasn't alone in the darkness surrounding us, but leaving me the space I needed to make my own choice.

I considered the king. He was distantly related to me—a great-granduncle several times removed—but I didn't actually know him and certainly had no pressing familial feelings for him. And yet anyone suffering so horribly when there was something I could do was awful. And then there was the conversation I'd had with my father to consider. Faerie required balance. If Dugan was correct and the already dwindling shadow court would fall with its king, the balance would fail. My father believed if the balance tilted too much more the wheel would break, and Faerie as we knew it would fracture once again. Faerie was beautiful and terrible, but did I want to see it shatter?

Change? Yes. Faerie could use some change. But I didn't want it to break.

I stepped closer to the bed and opened my senses. While the king looked like he was on his deathbed in my normal vision, when I peered at him through the planes, it was so much worse. The fouled magic covered his entire body, the tendrils digging in deep.

"How did it spread this fast?" I whispered, talking more to myself than anyone present.

"The basmoarte of ages ago never spread like this." Dugan hovered close to the side of the bed as if unsure where he should be. "It took weeks to consume a fae. Not a night."

"So maybe this isn't basmoarte." At least not the same strain that had infected Faerie in the past. I considered what the Mender had said on his parting. I'd thought about it quite a bit before sleep had finally consumed my exhausted body earlier. He'd said *the* cure.

Not *a* cure. Which made me think there was, in fact, a cure. Which meant that all the king—and I—needed was to stall. To survive until the cure was located.

"Bring me a receptacle for the fouled magic," I said, looking at Dugan.

"I will take it," Serri said, bowing her head to kiss the king on his sweat-slicked forehead.

I shook my head. "No. It would kill you."

"It would be my honor to die for my king," she whispered, tears welling in her eyes.

"One, this is not a cure, it's a stopgap, so you'd be throwing your life away. The infection will spread again." Though mine hadn't spread as fast as it had during the initial outbreak in my system. Hopefully it would be the same for the king. "Two, I'm not being the instrument of your death." I turned to Dugan. "Bring me something nonsentient."

Dugan stared into the space beyond me for a moment, and then he turned and vanished into the shadows. I stepped back from the bed as I waited. Falin moved to my side.

"You're sure about this?" he asked, his voice a harsh whisper. He sounded angry, and maybe he was, but I knew it sprang from concern. And he didn't try to stop me, or talk me out of it, so two points for him.

"There is a cure." I tried to keep my voice low. I was certain there was a cure, or I wouldn't have been able to state it as fact, but that didn't mean we'd find it in time. For the king or for me.

Falin's lips compressed in a thin line, and he studied me. Then his gaze dipped lower and focused on the small silver locket hanging in the open V of my sweater. "Did he tell you where to look?"

I blinked in surprise at the raw hurt in his voice. My hand moved to the locket that wasn't really a locket. Of course, no one else knew that it was actually a ball of reality. It just looked like a pretty piece of jewelry I'd never worn before. A bit of jewelry I'd acquired after meeting with Death on the hillside and then running off without explanation. Falin hadn't been able to hear Death's side of the conversation, so he didn't know I'd gone to meet the Mender. Everyone in the castle had figured out Death and I had broken things off a month ago—my moping around and copious consumption of chocolate ice cream for a few days had been a good hint. Yesterday Falin and I had spent the longest night at the festival together, and there was that kiss . . . Then I abandoned him with some bodies on a hill after talking to Death.

Yeah, that looked bad.

"It was the Mender who told me," I said, trying to keep my voice blank because part of me wanted to wrap my arms around him and reassure him nothing had happened with Death. The other part of me was irritated that he'd made the assumption and wanted to remind him that he and I weren't together, so it didn't matter if I had rekindled things with Death. Which I hadn't. Neutral was better. I pressed my hand flat against the locket, feeling not the expected metal but the cold layers of the land of the dead. "And this isn't a gift. It is part of the favor I owe the Mender."

I turned away, leaving it at that.

Thankfully Dugan reemerged a moment later, saving us from further conversation on the topic. Unfortunately, he brought with him something that moved.

Dugan carried a small black goat in his arms as he

stalked back into the room. It bleated pitifully, and my stomach tightened into a knot.

"That's not—" I started.

"There are no trees here, Alexis." Dugan set the goat beside the bed, holding it by one horn to keep it from running. "Unless you think mushrooms or moss will do as a receptacle, this is the best I can do on short notice." He produced a shiny red apple from nowhere and held it out to the goat, who calmed and rolled its lips back to munch on the proffered fruit.

I stared at the goat. I wasn't aware I was shaking my head until Dugan glared at me. "You eat meat, don't you? In the mortal realm, this goat would be food."

That made sense. I didn't think twice about buying a steak at the grocery store—well, okay, maybe for a moment because of the price, but not because it had been alive. There was something completely different about an animal that was literally still walking around and bleating.

In the bed, the king wheezed, his breath knocking in his chest. He didn't have long. If I was going to do this, I needed to do it now.

"It is just a goat?" I finally asked. "Not a human enchanted into a goat or some higher-thinking being that is more than a simple animal?"

"He is a Faerie goat. They used to be quite common, but like in the mortal realm, most Fae don't raise them anymore. But he is only a goat."

I didn't like this, but he was right about one thing: I didn't think the fouled magic would take to a mushroom or a bit of moss. Taking a deep breath, I approached the bed again, crawling on it to kneel beside the king. I rolled up the sleeves of my sweater, not because I thought the work would be particularly messy, at least I hoped not, but because I needed to watch the spread of my own fouled magic as I worked.

Opening my senses, I reached out and touched the magic I could see on the king's face. Serri tensed behind him, her wings spreading, revealing a sharp claw at the top joint. Dugan glared at her and she stilled, not preventing me from touching her king.

"You'll need to move," I told her, and her red eyes narrowed, the protest on her lips clear. "The magic will likely try to spread to you. So you can't be touching him while I work."

She looked to her prince—because even if I was the one they trusted to heal the king, I obviously had no authority. He nodded his agreement, and Serri ever so carefully slid out from under the king, arranging his head tenderly on a pillow before vacating the bed. She didn't go far, but hovered a few feet away, pensive and watching.

I plucked at a dark string of magic running through the king's temple. It tingled where it touched my fingertips, but it didn't actually hurt. *That's a good sign, right?* Probably not. I pulled it, ripping it up and free to leave the skin below spotless. I unraveled it only a few inches before meeting the first point where it had originated in a larger string of poisoned magic that fanned out into several tributaries. I moved to the next small strand, pulling it back to that point as well. Then the next, and the next, until the larger strand was no longer anchored and I could pull it back to where it had forked off an even bigger strand.

I kept working that way, moving quickly and as efficiently as I could as I untangled the mass of fouled magic. I freed the king's head and his eyes stopped darting quite so drastically behind his closed lids. It was his chest that really worried me, each strained breath loud but shallow. If the magic got into his lungs and heart, that would be bad. Unfortunately I had to get his arms before I could get his chest. His breaths continued to wheeze, and I tried to work faster, pull harder. Twice someone brought me water to drink and I realized I was drenched in my own sweat. Once I had to stop and pull my own fouled magic down where it had crept up my biceps toward my shoulder. Touching the king's basmoarte-fouled magic had opened new wounds in my fingers, and now the darkness was spreading up from both my hands. If I could find the cure, it wouldn't matter.

The goat died by the time I reached the king's navel, and Dugan had to retrieve a second one. No one mentioned my tears as I continued pulling the fouled magic free. The king woke as I freed his hips.

His eyes fluttered open only halfway before he was in motion. I didn't even have time to form a word before his shadow blade appeared, aimed at my throat. I tried to throw myself backward, but I knew I wasn't fast enough. An arm snaked around my waist, jerking me back as a shield of shadows materialized in front of me, stopping the blade a moment before it would have taken off my head.

I gasped as Falin pulled me farther back, off the bed. Dugan stepped in front of me, his shadow shield still in place, but he didn't lift his sword against his king's attack. Nandin blinked, first in confusion, and then recognition ran through his eyes and his forehead furrowed as he looked around at the crowd in his bedchamber. The sword dissolved into shadows, and the king collapsed backward, clearly exhausted from the brief excitement.

Serri launched herself at the bed, her arms sliding over his now-basmoarte-free shoulders. My adrenaline was pumping too hard in my ears to follow the conversation, but from what I caught, she was explaining what had happened. I leaned my head back against Falin's chest. I was exhausted. Not just tired from lack of sleep, but bone-weary. I'd been using a lot of magic. It was taking its toll.

Falin's arm around me tightened, holding me close. With his other hand, he passed me a glass of water. I accepted it gratefully, draining half the liquid in one series of gulps.

When I lowered the glass, I found all eyes locked on me.

"You can cure basmoarte?" the king asked from where he lay half propped by Serri.

I straightened and reluctantly stepped out of Falin's embrace. "I can move the poisoned magic. The infected wound is still there."

"So it will return?"

I nodded. My own creeping infection proved that fact. "It doesn't appear to spread as aggressively after the first wave, but yes, it will return. I have not finished cleansing your legs. Would you like me to continue?"

The king levered himself up onto his elbows and looked at the dark lines of fouled magic spiderwebbing his thighs and shins. Even that little bit of exertion seemed to tax him. He nodded, collapsing back into Serri's arms. She ran her taloned fingers through his hair gently before she glanced at me. That one look from her ruby-colored eyes was enough to know that she had no intention of leaving his side again. I didn't waste my breath asking. As long as she stayed at the head of the bed, she was far enough away from where I was working to not be at risk.

I crawled back onto the bed, and then hesitated. When the king had been unconscious, I'd barely noticed what part of his body I was working on. I'd simply been trying to unravel the basmoarte as efficiently as possible before it killed him. Now that he was awake and watching me, I was very aware that I was working very high up on his thigh and he wore very little to bed.

"Do you know how you were infected?" I asked to distract myself as I pulled inky strands free.

The king frowned, his gaze going distant. "It had to have been at the revelry. Nothing stands out except . . . I did have one odd encounter." He paused, clearly trying to recall details. "A Sleagh Maith approached me and propositioned me for the title of consort. She said she was skilled in pleasurable magics and my court clearly needed some new blood." Behind him, Serri went very still. The king reached up and placed a hand on the arm draped over his chest, the gesture affectionate and automatic, not even causing him to pause his narrative. "She attempted to demonstrate these magics, and I remember wondering what she assumed I found pleasurable, because her magic stung. I rebuked her for her presumptuousness and sent her away."

I looked up from where I was pulling free a strand of fouled magic over the king's knee, and searched for the wound where the infection had started. I'd done a thorough job pulling the poisoned magic out of his upper half, but there was a darker patch on his arm, just below his shoulder.

"Did she touch you here?" I motioned to the spot on my own arm.

He frowned, considering the question. Then he nodded. "I believe so, yes."

"What did she look like? Did she say her name?" Falin asked.

"I'm sure she did." The king's frown deepened and he shook his head, as if that could jar the memory loose. "She was brown-haired, brown-eyed. Looked to be a fae from one of the warmer courts."

Dugan reached into the shadows and pulled a handful out as if it were clay. With his magic, he formed it into a small but dark replica of Lunabella.

The king's eyes widened. "Yes, that was her."

I hissed out a disappointed breath, and Dugan and Falin deflated slightly as well.

"She is deceased," Dugan said, and the sculpted shadow dissolved.

"You . . . ?" the king began, but Dugan shook his head.

"We believe she was killed because we were getting too close," I said, pressing the basmoarte into the small goat. It bleated pitifully and I cringed, hating this, hating myself, but more than anything, hating whoever had masterminded this whole thing.

I was almost finished with the king's right leg, with his left still remaining, and I fell into silence as I worked. By the time I finished, I was starving, exhausted, and very much feeling the fact that I hadn't had a proper amount of sleep in days. I stripped my own fouled magic, which had spread like decorative gloves up both of my arms, and then pushed it into the goat. The poisoned magic wasn't quite enough to kill it outright, so the poor beast lay on its side, breathing heavy as its slitted eye rolled in its head. Dugan put it out of its misery.

I wanted to go home and sleep for a month, but that

wasn't an option. My own basmoarte was going to spread faster now. I needed to find who was responsible for the deaths and the spread of basmoarte. And I needed to locate the cure. I just hoped it all came back to one source.

"My court and I, myself, owe you an enormous debt," the king said. He'd extracted himself from Serri—though she remained by his side—and he now sat propped with pillows. He was still pale, but his breathing was normal. He would be okay until the fouled magic began to take over again.

I only nodded. I could feel the debt, and I would cash it in eventually, but I wasn't going to commit to a price for my help. Not yet.

"His Majesty should rest," Serri said, fussing over the blankets around him. He batted her hands away, gently but resolutely.

"Someone has made an attempt on my life. I don't have time to rest." He swung his feet over the side of the bed and stood. Then he swayed.

Dugan approached the edge of the bed and bowed. "Sire, we are looking into the matter. You are still afflicted. Rest would be better. Let me investigate this matter for you. That is why you have a prince, isn't it?"

The king looked unconvinced, but he also looked like a strong wind would knock him over. At its peak, my own basmoarte had covered maybe a quarter of my body, and I'd barely been able to remain conscious. The king had been much more afflicted. I doubted he'd be back on his feet anytime soon. *Or possibly ever, if we don't find the cure.* I glanced at my hands. Even though I'd just purged them, the tips of my fingers were already showing signs of discoloration.

"Rest, Sire. We will get to the bottom of this," Dugan said, bowing deeply to his king.

Nandin frowned, but after a moment, he collapsed back onto the bed. We made a hasty exit before he could change his mind, though I wobbled unsteadily as I scurried for the door.

"You need to rest, as well," Falin said as soon as we reached the hall.

"I'm . . ." I couldn't say "fine." That was a blatant lie. I swayed, throwing out an arm to steady myself. Falin caught it, concern heavy in his features. Probably because the arm he'd caught was the one that hadn't been infected before. But the tips of all ten fingers were a bruised purple now, magical wounds from where I'd contacted the king's poisoned magic.

"Sitting down would be good. And some food," I admitted. But I didn't have time to rest for long. I was going to get worse, and the more magic I used to cleanse the poison, the faster it would spread.

"This way," Dugan said, leading us through a nearby doorway.

It led to a sitting room. There was a small table with meals already laid out, so apparently we were expected. Falin deposited me in a seat before taking one himself.

The meal was a simple one for Faerie: a half wheel of cheese on one plate, another loaded with salted fingerling potatoes, a basket of rolls, and a plate with some sort of roast on it. After the incident with the goats, I didn't even want to look at the meat. I knew that most likely it had never been a living animal—in my experience food in Faerie was mostly magic—but I couldn't eat it. I helped myself to a large serving of the rest.

"I think this proves there is a cure," I said between large mouthfuls.

Both men looked at me quizzically and I realized I'd started a conversation in the middle of my own thoughts, which I hadn't been sharing. I drained a glass of water before speaking again.

"Lunabella must have willingly allowed herself to be infected for the purpose of infecting the Shadow King. Assuming she wasn't a martyr, she wouldn't have done that without assurances there was a cure."

"But she wasn't cured," Falin said. "It was rampant in her body at the time of her death."

True. So had the mastermind tricked her? Or had he changed the plan after learning we'd been looking for her? And who was the scarred prince? Was the fae in the gold cloak Lunabella's scarred prince? Who was he?

"Is there anyone in Faerie who is close to being named a prince?" I asked.

Dugan ran a hand over his chin as he thought. Falin leaned back in his chair, looking contemplative. After a few moments, they looked at each other, as if silently confirming their thoughts. Then they both shook their heads.

"There is a potential princess in spring," Falin said. Which we all knew wasn't helpful.

"The only fae there were even rumors of potentially being named prince was the Winter Queen's nephew. It was assumed he was already practically a prince except the icy old bitch will never relinquish any power," Dugan said, and I blinked at his description of the Winter Queen. Clearly there was no love lost between cousins. Not that I disagreed with the description, it just surprised me from him. "But he hasn't been heard of since he was banished."

And he isn't scarred.

I paused, a buttered roll halfway to my lips.

"Iron poisoning leaves scars, doesn't it?" I asked. I had a small scar on my back where I'd been grazed with an iron dart. It was hardly noticeable, but I'd been raised in the mortal realm and had a higher-than-average tolerance to iron—which wasn't to say the small wound hadn't been dangerous, but the fae healers who'd cared for me had been surprised by how well it had healed.

Falin lifted an eyebrow. "It leaves the worst kind of scars. And glamour won't hide them."

I nodded. "Scars you might wear a cloak to hide?"

"The gold-cloaked figure from the revelry?" Falin said slowly, clearly picking up where I was going with this. "You think it could have been Ryese?"

"Would the banishment on him keep him from the revelry?"

Both men shook their heads.

"Then I think it's a distinct possibility. I saw only a flash of a hand under the cloak, but the skin was gray, sickly."

No one said anything for several seconds. Then Dugan said, "He—whoever he was—did not meet with Lunabella again while I was watching her. He trailed her at times, but sporadically. I wasn't following him, so I'm not sure where he went or to whom he spoke when he wasn't trailing Lunabella. I have no clue where he went after you fainted."

"But I saw him right before I passed out. Him and that stone that flashed light no one else saw . . ." I paused. "Ryese was—is—an alchemist. If he was able to resurrect and weaponize basmoarte, could that flash of light have triggered it to activate?" I held up a hand when Dugan began to disagree and continued by saying, "I know I didn't contract the basmoarte from that magic, but you keep saying this strain is much more aggressive than in previous outbreaks. I walked around with it for far longer than the king before mine began spreading. What if it lies dormant until triggered?"

Both men looked contemplative. It was a guess, but it felt right. Of course, I had no way to prove it. Not until we found Ryese—if the gold-cloaked figure was in fact the Winter Queen's nephew.

"When I returned the bodies to the winter court, I sought out the healer who examined Kordon," Falin said after a long moment. "She recalled feeling some discomfort when she used her magic to examine him, but she appears mostly fine. There is a small discoloration on her palm—unnoticeable unless one is looking for it—that is likely the basmoarte wound she received from Kordon. I quarantined her, obviously. But her disease hasn't spread at all, even though she was exposed before you, Alex."

"That is consistent with historical cases. You questioned her extensively, didn't you? Ensured she has had no magical contact with anyone since her exposure?" Dugan asked, the alarm on his face enough for me to raise an inquisitive eyebrow. He noticed and turned to me. "The last outbreak of basmoarte became an epidemic largely due to healers. They would contract it without realizing it because the symptoms appear slowly. So they spread it to other fae before anyone realized basmoarte had returned."

Falin nodded. "I believe we contained the situation before an epidemic could occur in the winter halls. But her lack of symptoms does seem to confirm that Alex and the Shadow King were targeted specifically, and that this strain can be aggressively triggered."

Well, no epidemic was definitely a good thing, but if the basmoarte was weaponized, could mine be triggered a second time? I doubted I'd survive a second aggressive wave of the disease. We had to find that cure, fast.

"Has anyone heard anything about Ryese since his banishment? I mean, is he even alive? We could be barking up the wrong tree."

"Tree?" Dugan asked, looking confused.

"It's an expression. 'Looking in the wrong place,' is that clearer?"

He nodded, then frowned. "I can ask some of the listeners specifically, but I have not heard what befell him."

Now it was my turn to be confused. "Listeners? Like fae who sit around listening to the rumors the shadows carry?"

"More or less."

Good to know.

I looked to Falin. He'd been the one to order Ryese removed from winter's lands, right after he'd driven the iron dart Ryese had intended to assassinate the queen with into the other fae's hand.

"I've heard nothing," he said, mouth pinched. "Though it is rare to be accepted into another court after an attempt to kill your previous monarch. The queen banished him because she didn't want to watch him die, but she was sentencing him to almost certain death."

"Almost" being the key word?

"If it was Ryese, I wouldn't be surprised that he laid that trap with me in mind. He knew what my abilities were and has seen me raise a shade before. Also, he hates me. Pretty sure he blames me for him not having the winter throne."

Falin nodded, but his jaw clenched, anger thinning his

lips. "You would definitely be a target. And if your guess is correct and he is behind this, he might have been targeting the entire winter court to punish the court for his banishment. But I think that was unintentional. Stiofan would have been the one infected if the target was the court."

That was true. Lunabella could have infected both bodies as easily as she'd infected one. But why shadow? Was the goblin just an unfortunate but random victim? Or had Ryese found allies and they were enemies of shadow?

"Did the gold-cloaked fae enter with the light court?" I hadn't noticed him for the first time until he'd spoken to Lunabella.

Dugan frowned, shaking his head but not in disagreement, more like in uncertainty. Falin, on the other hand, pursed his lips, the movement slow, as if he was still arranging his thoughts.

"I believe he was already in the clearing, with the independents." Falin paused. "I didn't note him until he joined the end of the light court procession as they entered. Which doesn't mean he didn't enter with a different court and I didn't notice, but at the time I remember assuming he was with the independents."

"Does that happen often? Fae jumping into the back of a procession?" I asked.

Dugan shrugged. "The doors being what they are, occasionally someone gets separated and shows up at the revelry out of the proper order. It isn't common, but it happens. I had to do it once, a long time ago."

"But it is also possible the Queen of Light did not allow him to enter with her procession," Falin said, a growing sureness filling his voice. "If the golden-cloaked figure truly is Ryese, she might not have wanted the Winter

Queen to know he had returned to her court. He might be an embarrassment to her."

Or she might be complicit in everything and didn't want to be seen conspiring with an ambitious fae still attempting to usurp a throne. I didn't add that out loud. As Dugan had reminded us frequently, the shadows had ears. And there were a lot of shadows here.

Dugan turned to Falin. "Was Lunabella's body returned to the court of light yet?"

Falin shook his head. "The queen had retired already when I took the bodies back to winter. I decided not to wake her with such news, so they are under guard awaiting morning."

"Which even on the second-longest night of the year is soon," Dugan said, and stood. I had no idea how he could tell dawn might be approaching. There were no clocks here, and the shadows hadn't changed in any discernible way since we'd been here. "These rooms are mine. I invite you both to rest here. An hour of slumber is not nearly enough, I know, but it would be better than nothing."

Without another word, he turned and walked through a door in the back wall of the room. I glanced around the small sitting room. At least we weren't locked in the shadow court this visit, but it wasn't like I wanted to wander the halls. The furniture in the room was functional but looked comfortable enough.

I smiled at Falin. "I call the couch."

Chapter 19

━━━◦ ◦━━━

The hour of sleep I snagged seemed to make me more tired, but my fingers were completely purple with fouled magic, so I dragged myself up and ate a small breakfast. My sweater was wrinkled and stiff and I grimaced, hoping I didn't smell as bad as I looked. I'd only been in Faerie a few hours, but I could have used a shower and a fresh change of clothes after untangling the king's basmoarte. As if in answer to my thoughts—or maybe I really did just look that bad—Dugan dropped a neatly folded pile of clothing in front of me.

I lifted an eyebrow. "What is this?"

"A clean outfit; yours looks rather . . . slept in."

That was a nice way to put it. I excused myself to change without thanking him. Fresh clothes were hardly a reason to indebt myself, or forgive any of the debt he owed me.

The clothes were of exquisite quality, and fit perfectly, which was slightly disconcerting. Why did Dugan have clothes of my size just sitting around? Of course, they were probably glamoured and possibly enchanted to fit . . . but still. The black leather pants were supple and silent as I moved. The sweater was soft, though also black. The small pile even included gloves. Black. I was sensing a theme. Still, the new clothes were better than wearing my gross ones, so I dressed quickly, aware I was now more or less sporting shadow's colors in my all-black getup. I frowned at my pile of discarded clothes. Dugan had assured me they would make it back to my castle. I hoped they did. Faerie was claiming a lot of my wardrobe. Then I headed back out to the guys. We had fae to see, murderers to uncover, and a cure to find.

"So do you think the Queen of Light knows?" I asked Falin as we crossed the clearing that joined the courts.

"Knows what?" he asked. "That her son plotted to overthrow his aunt? That he could now be pitting shadow against winter?"

"Both. Either. I never thought Ryese was clever enough to engineer the drug he used on the Winter Queen."

Falin turned and frowned at me. "I don't suggest you share that theory with the queen. She adores her sister."

"I noticed." And I had. There had been true affection when she'd greeted the Queen of Light at the revelry. But was that affection returned?

The guards that greeted us on the winter side of the door made no attempt to stop us. They nodded respectfully to Falin and watched Dugan, but they must have been growing accustomed to the Shadow Prince following us around, because no one even fingered their weapons today.

"Can the guards see through glamour?" I asked as we walked down the long ice halls.

"Their hoods allow them to see through most glamours that could be used as disguise," Falin said.

"Only most?"

He nodded without expanding on an explanation.

It was Dugan who said, "Faerie is run by the strongest and most clever. If someone can slip past the queen's guards, then they are probably strong enough to challenge her rule. There is no penalty for using any means available unless they fail."

But it also meant someone very strong in glamour—or working for someone masterful at glamour—could walk into the winter court and there would be no one who noticed. Jurin was probably the inside person who got Lunabella and whoever else helped her kill Stiofan inside, but they'd somehow managed to transport Kordon's body through the winter halls without anyone noticing.

"How good was Ryese's glamour?" I asked.

Falin cut his gaze toward me, a warning in his eyes. Now that we were inside winter, there was a chance we could be overheard, and the queen had forbidden anyone from mentioning her nephew.

"Masterful. Now we are here."

Which meant it was time to be silent. I nodded and followed Falin through the archway.

The queen lounged in a chaise, a breakfast tray set up beside her. Her frost-covered robe was nearly see-through and she wore only a thin gown underneath it. She had clearly only recently started her day and I had the distinct impression we should have at least knocked before entering. She looked up as we entered, her pretty features cold as she studied us.

"Knight, while I have no qualms receiving you this early, I do not appreciate the extra company."

Falin bowed deep. I mimicked him. Hey, it had worked out for me last time and I didn't get stuck in a never-ending curtsy. Dugan inclined his head only marginally.

"My queen, we have an issue to bring to your attention that could wait no longer," Falin said without looking up.

The queen plucked a strawberry from her breakfast tray. "I'm listening."

"We located two fae we believe were involved in Stio-fan's murder."

"Good news with breakfast." The queen took a bite of the strawberry and lifted her shoulders slightly, as if this news were trivial.

"Unfortunately, both were murdered directly after the revelry and we did not get a chance to question them thoroughly. One belonged to the court of light. We would like to return her body to her queen."

She dropped the strawberry and swung her legs around until she was sitting up straight. "What?"

"May we return the body?"

The queen chewed at her bottom lip. "Where did this happen? How? Has an attempt been made to revive the fae?"

"There will be no reviving her. She had basmoarte." He left off the part where we'd taken the body to the mortal realm and her soul had been collected, but I wasn't going to be the one to tell her that.

The queen's brows knitted together and she shook her head. "How did she get basmoarte?"

"She was acting as a mule attempting to pass it to the Shadow King," Dugan said, his voice low and challenging.

"Did she succeed?"

"The king rebuked her advances. He is well." He

smiled as he said it, the expression dark and somehow far more threatening than a smile should be. But I did understand that twist of truth. If the Winter Queen realized how weak the shadow court actually was, she might strike at them whether she thought they were responsible for the attack on her court or not.

The queen paced in front of her chair. She seemed to be silently arguing with herself, ignoring us as she moved. After a moment, she turned, some decision met.

"Take the body to the mortal realm and destroy it. My sister does not need to know that one of her people was killed following my revelry."

My jaw fell open, and I snapped it closed quick, hoping she didn't notice. From the corner of my vision I saw the skin around Falin's eyes tighten. It was a direct command, so he had to obey. We couldn't just happen to lose our way and accidentally take Lunabella to the light court and check if Ryese was hiding there. No, she'd said destroy the body.

"Cousin, do you think that the kindest move?" Dugan asked, his voice smooth and sweet. "What if she worries over the welfare of her courtier? You could be the one to alleviate her concern and give her closure."

I managed not to snort a laugh. If the Queen of Light was anything like her sister, she would never notice one missing courtier, especially since Lunabella had been part of a new influx into her court. Still, the Winter Queen paused, pondering this, so I had to give Dugan credit.

"What are your thoughts, Knight?"

"She deserves to know if a potential threat exists."

The queen considered this as well. I stayed quiet and left manipulating the queen to them. I was more likely to stick my foot in it and get us barred from ever speaking to the Queen of Light for fear we'd someday mention this conversation.

"I will ask her if she would like the body returned," she said after several minutes. "Dealing with death can be so . . . distasteful."

Right. That was the word she was going with. No mention of sad or hard.

The queen walked over to a full-length mirror in the corner of the room. She placed a single finger on it, and frost crept over the glass. A moment later the frost vanished as a brilliant light filled the glass.

I squinted, looking away. When I looked back, the reflection was that of a different room. It was arranged almost identical to the Winter Queen's, right down to a breakfast tray beside a chaise. But whereas the room we stood in was clean, cold ice with hints of silver and blue, the room of the Queen of Light was soft and warm. Layers of gauzy fabric draped the walls in the soft shades of sunset, all orange, pink, and red. The chaise was similarly fashioned, with the Queen of Light lounging on it in a burnt-red gauze robe, her position almost identical to how we'd found the Winter Queen.

"Darling sister, I'm barely awake this early," the Queen of Light said, leaning her head back dramatically on her cushion, but her tone was playful, friendly.

"Greetings, dear sister," the queen said, walking back to her own chaise. I almost expected her to collapse dramatically, but she sat primly, the picture of poise. "I fear I call with unpleasant news."

The Light Queen's head snapped up. "Oh?" She narrowed her eyes, waiting.

"My knight informs me that the body of one of your courtiers was discovered last night."

One of the Light Queen's perfectly styled golden eyebrows lifted. "Where?"

Not *who*, only *where*. And no sign of sorrow.

The Winter Queen looked to Falin. That was his cue. "At the revelry site, just before it emptied. Would you like us to return the body to you?"

The Light Queen studied us. "Is that your planeweaver, little sister? And the . . . Shadow Prince? My, what strange company you are keeping this morning."

"It is as you say," the queen replied. "And strange indeed. But of your courtier . . . ?"

The Queen of Light sighed, a wistful sound that made the heart ache. I frowned. Her glamour was getting to me.

"Send her home. Will this lot escort her?" She waved a hand to encompass Falin, Dugan, and me.

"My knight can deliver—"

The Queen of Light leaned forward, her long golden braid falling over her shoulder. "Oh, do send them all. You can't be the only one to have such strange company."

The Winter Queen smiled, but it was tight and small, the kind of smile someone offers because they are trying to prevent themselves from frowning. "Only if you promise to give them back." It was said teasingly, but with an edge. She really was afraid her sister might keep us if she let us go.

"You may not promise my attendance, Cousin," Dugan said, and the queen shot a glare at him so cold, it could have frozen a summer day.

"Ah, then let me cordially invite you," the Queen of Light said. Then she turned toward the queen again. "I will make arrangements for my departed courtier. Do send her promptly." And with that the light in the mirror winked out, leaving only frosted glass behind.

The queen collapsed back into her chaise. "Well, hurry along," she said, "and when you figure out who killed her, let me know. I should be the one to tell my sister."

I almost asked her what about Stiofan, her courtier whom Lunabella had helped kill, but I knew better than to draw that kind of attention to myself when we'd already been dismissed.

"Anybody notice that the Queen of Light knew that the courtier we'd found was female?" I asked as soon as we reached the hall.

"Yes." Falin didn't sound happy about that fact. "And I also noticed she insisted we come and didn't offer any form of safe passage."

An hour later we were back in the clearing that held all the doors to the courts. We'd picked up two extra winter guards, who carried a stretcher with Lunabella's body laid out prettily. The guards' body language was stiff, unhappy. Because of where we were going? Because they were accompanying the Winter Knight and Shadow Prince? Or because Lunabella's body was covered in dark basmoarte lines? I wasn't sure which.

"So I guess we can take any of the light paths?" I asked, glancing around. There seemed to be even more light and less shadow now than two days ago when we'd visited the summer court. If the balance continued to shift, how long would it take for Faerie to break under the weight?

"Stay together and stay alert," Falin said, holding out a hand toward me.

I took it, then offered Dugan my other. My gloves covered the spreading evidence of my own fouled magic, but he glanced at my offered hand, the hesitation clear. He hadn't been reluctant to take my hand when we'd visited the summer court. Basmoarte wasn't contagious through touch, but I realized he'd been keeping his distance since it had appeared. *Fine by me.*

We walked into one of the paths of light, and the soft glow enveloped us, surrounding us in a warm ambiance. We emerged on the other side in a colorful hallway. I wasn't sure of the color of the walls because every inch seemed to be covered in paintings, tapestries, and murals. Intricate mosaics covered the floor, and sculptures of all sorts were scattered along the hall. At first I thought the sculptures were guards, like winter's ice golems, but these pieces were all so different, some figurative, but more were abstract. It would be a chaotic army.

"Welcome to the court of light," a dreamy-sounding voice said, its owner stepping out from behind one of the statues. A second fae followed him, smiling at us.

Both fae were blue-skinned and radiated a soft iridescent light. One was male, the other clearly female, but otherwise they looked identical, with fine features and silver hair that floated in the air around them as if they were underwater.

"We will take you to the queen," the female of the pair said. They turned in sync and padded along the mosaic floor barefoot.

I glanced at Falin. Were these guards? They carried

no weapons that I could see, and they wore no armor, just gauzy, togalike clothing. Was the Light Queen so powerful that she saw no reason to guard her door? Or did these two have such formidable magic that they had no need for plebeian armor and weapons?

Falin's features were cold and closed, betraying nothing of his thoughts. It was what I thought of as his knight face. I tried to remain as neutrally aloof, but I couldn't help ogling our surroundings as we followed the two blue fae. Walking the halls of the court of light was like visiting a chaotic art museum.

We walked down corridor after corridor, each filled with paintings, drawings, sculptures, and many other types of art, and each more magnificent than the last. Music played all around us, and not the ever-present harmonious sounds that seemed to permeate Faerie just outside hearing range, or at least, not only that music. No, this was identifiable. In one hall a violin played a mournful, but exquisitely beautiful, solo. In another a piano. In the next I could hear an entire unseen orchestra.

"Here," the female blue fae said, stopping before a door inlaid with stained glass. It depicted the Queen of Light surrounded by mortals busily creating art of all different forms. The light court was also known as the court of muses, so I assumed this depiction was of her inspiring them, though all the art the rendered mortals were creating seemed to be of the queen herself.

One of our guides pushed open the door and escorted us inside. There was the familiar swirl of uncertainty as the doorway took us where we were going, and then I stepped into an enormous throne room.

Fae thronged the sides of the room, leaving the path between door and throne unobstructed. The Queen of

Light sat on a throne of gold, the metal glowing with the light emanating from her so that trying to stare at her was like gazing at the sun. I looked away, studying the room instead. There was less art here than in the halls, though the walls still sported several towering tapestries, most of which depicted the queen. The crowd murmured when we entered, but a hush fell around us at the appearance of the two winter guards carrying the stretcher with Lunabella's body.

Falin and Dugan kept their heads lifted, their steps seemingly carefree and purposeful as they strode toward the golden throne. I tried to mimic them, rolling my shoulders back to prevent myself from cringing under the scrutiny as I walked.

The queen became easier to look upon as we approached, her radiant glow less blinding, which made no sense from a scientific standpoint but was perfectly logical for Faerie. She wanted her presence to cause awe, but she also wanted to be adored. We had to see her to marvel at her beauty.

And she was beautiful. Her golden hair cascaded over one shoulder in an intricate braid hanging all the way to the floor. Her gown was the color of sunset accented with gold. She smiled, and my breath caught in my throat. The urge to fall to the ground before her struck me so hard my knees buckled. I wanted to prostrate myself and beg to be allowed to remain in her presence and bask in her radiance.

Glamour.

I knew it was glamour, but that didn't temper the urge. I forced my shields open, just a crack. Enough that I could pierce glamour, but hopefully not let more of it into my mind.

Her glow diminished significantly. She was still beautiful, still radiated power, but the urge to throw myself at her feet lifted. I let out the breath that I'd been holding; it tasted old and a little too nervous for my liking.

The queen gazed down at us benevolently, and yet, maybe it was only because she looked so much like her younger sister, I thought I caught a hint of cruelty in the curve of her smile, malice in her bright blue eyes. Falin bowed at the waist, not going down on one knee like he did for the Winter Queen, and then he straightened immediately, not waiting to be released. I wasn't sure if that was because he didn't owe the same level of respect to another monarch, or to show he wasn't being cowed by her glamour that whispered that we should worship her. I followed his lead, dipping into a respectful, but short, curtsy.

A golden eyebrow arched at our actions, but the queen didn't say anything until her gaze moved past us to the two winter guards with the body. Then her lips twisted as if she'd bitten something sour.

"Take that elsewhere," she said, waving a dismissive hand. Then she seemed to remember she was supposed to be sad about her courtier's death. "How very tragic for . . ." She searched for Lunabella's name, but when it didn't come to her, she finished with a simple, if delayed, ". . . her. I'm sure she will be missed."

Not by the queen, obviously.

"Your Majesty, we were wondering if we could speak to some of her friends," Falin said, keeping his words bland but his tone respectful.

"And why would you want to do that, knight of my sister?"

"Her death was of a most unnatural cause," Falin

said, and I gave him a look out of the corner of my eye because that was an understatement if I ever heard one.

"That seems like it would be my and my court's concern. Why would you look into it?"

"Because she was involved in a murder in the winter court," I said.

The queen's golden eyebrow rose a little, and her mouth quirked in a maliciously pleased way that made me think I shouldn't have said that.

"That sounds like an accusation, little planeweaver. Surely my sister did not send you here to challenge my court?" Her tone was mocking as she asked the question, and I fought the urge to cringe back. "Or perhaps it was you who put such ideas in her head, dark prince?"

"Oh, Lexi. Always dragging everyone around you into trouble," an eerily familiar voice said behind me.

I whirled around. A yard behind me stood a gold-cloaked figure. The hood was low, obscuring the face hidden beneath it, but I knew that voice. Only two people called me "Lexi." The Winter Queen, and her nephew, Ryese.

I knew it. Not that I could take any joy in being correct.

I opened my mouth, but Falin put a cautioning hand on my arm. Right. If the Queen of Light took an accusation against a fae whose name she couldn't even remember as a slight against her court, she was unlikely to think too favorably of me accusing her son of masterminding all our recent troubles. I bit back what I wanted to say and instead gave Ryese a sickly sweet smile.

"You're alive," I said in a syrupy tone to match my smile.

The malice radiating off him made the air between us prickle. Then he gave a low laugh that cut at my skin.

"In a manner of speaking." A hand emerged from the cloak, the skin grayer than any Sleagh Maith I'd ever seen. He pushed the cloak over his shoulders, leaving the hood, but exposing his other hand. At first I thought he wore a black glove, but then I realized that the skin was shriveled and dark. The flesh was black like char, not the purple black of a bruise like my own basmoarte-fouled hands. The arm attached to that hand was skeletally thin, atrophied.

Iron poisoning.

Ryese had smuggled an iron dart into Faerie with the intent of assassinating the Winter Queen. We'd barely thwarted that plan, I'd been injured, and the queen all but driven mad. When Ryese had been revealed, Falin had driven that iron dart into Ryese's palm. And it had destroyed Ryese's entire arm. It didn't look like he had any movement in the dark, twisted fingers, and the arm certainly had no strength.

As if he'd been waiting for us to take in the condition of his arm first, he then lowered the hood of his cloak. The black veins of iron poison had reached all the way to his face. He'd always been a particularly vain man. I'd found him more pretty than handsome, and one side of his face still was. The other was a twisting mass of dark scars.

One dark scar reached the side of his lips, and they drooped on that side, giving him a perpetually lopsided frown. His eyes had always been pale, but now the one on the damaged side of his face had clouded over, the pupil lost in what was certainly enough damage to cause blindness in that eye. Even his hair, which used to glitter like cut crystal, was now dull and limp and had been sheared short.

I glanced at Falin and saw he was thinking the same thing I was: There was no way Ryese could have decapitated Lunabella and Jurin. Even if the two nobles had been incapacitated already because of the fouled magic in their system, their heads had been cleanly severed. Ryese's dominant hand was mangled. He wore a dagger at his waist, but even if it was a magical blade that could cut through anything, I doubted it could have done the work in the clearing. Not in the amount of time between the shadow cat startling and Falin and Dugan reaching the bodies.

"Ryese!" The Light Queen hissed his name like an admonishment.

He ducked his head and pulled up his cloak, covering his face and ruined arm.

"My deformity disturbs the golden throne," he whispered, the words hard but meant for me, not the light court.

I might have felt bad for him, except he'd poisoned me and made a damn good attempt to kill me. Twice. I held a grudge.

Also, he was still the best candidate for Lunabella's scarred prince. Just because he couldn't have been the one who held the blade didn't mean he wasn't the one who commanded it. But we were missing another conspirator in this party. I was guessing someone with a tie to the shadow court, as we'd already found our leak in winter. Someone had helped get murderers in and out of the shadow court with Kordon's body and Dugan's dagger. And then there was the shadow spy that had been watching my ritual. We were definitely still missing someone.

Of course, we still didn't have proof that Ryese was involved with any of it. Him being alive wasn't exactly condemning evidence. Though it did strike me that the poison he'd chosen this time mirrored his own scars. There were differences, and I bet he would have tried iron itself if he could find a way to control it, but the dark veining of basmoarte disfigured his victims in a similar way to his own scarring. That couldn't be a coincidence.

"You fainted on the shortest day," Ryese said, and the words held menace, not concern. The unasked question of *How did you survive?* hung in the air.

I smiled at him and rolled up my sleeves, leaving my untainted arms mostly bare. The fouled magic was completely concealed by my black gloves, so I looked unmarked. I could all but feel him scowl under his hood.

"Yes, planeweaver, I did hear that you collapsed during the revelry," the queen said, drawing my attention back to her. "I sent my best healer, but she said you were dying of a wasting disease and there was nothing that could be done." She made a face that came off as a pout, though I think it was meant to be sympathetic. "You seem much improved now."

"I had to purge the poison in my magic," I said, very aware of Ryese at my back. "I am much better now."

It wasn't a lie. I was far better. I just wasn't cured.

"How very fortunate for you," she said, flashing that beautiful smile with its cuttingly cruel edge. "And how unique your abilities."

I bowed my head in acknowledgment, because what was I supposed to say to that?

"You are familiar with my son?" She asked the question pleasantly, but there was more under the current of her words, and I wasn't sure what.

"We've met," I said flatly. "He is an . . . accomplished alchemist."

The queen frowned. "He dabbles. Now tell me why you really came to the court of light." There was compulsion in her words, I could feel it. We had been invited to her court, so she couldn't outright harm us without it being seen as an attack, but in the might-makes-right way of Faerie, she could use any magics against us that didn't directly harm us.

No one answered. Dugan was old and a prince, Falin carried all the blood of the winter court and the magic from the knights who had come before him, and my own magic offered me a degree of protection. She was going to have to try a hell of a lot harder if she wanted to compel us.

She apparently realized that as well.

The compulsion flowing off her thickened, wrapping around us.

"You insisted," Dugan said, and that was true enough; she had. But he wasn't falling under the compulsion or he would have said more. We'd intended to visit the court of light, one way or another.

The compulsion grew stronger again, the queen clearly unsatisfied. If I squinted, I could almost see the golden threads.

What I could see, I could touch.

Reaching up, I exerted a small amount of magic and batted the tendril of compulsion away. The queen's brows bunched for just a moment as I contacted the tendril, her small nostrils flaring in a microexpression of pain. The compulsion glamour drew back, but a small purple stain covered the place where I'd touched the tendril of magic.

I glanced at my hands where my basmoarte infection still raged under my gloves. An infection I'd just spread to the queen.

She'd asked about my health before she'd used magic on me. I'd indicated that I'd managed to cure myself. Had she known about the basmoarte? Had she been part of her son's schemes?

Or had I just accidentally started the slow assassination of an uninvolved Faerie monarch?

Crap.

Chapter 20

If the queen realized she'd been infected, she gave no indication. She looked mildly annoyed, but that seemed to have more to do with the fact that we wouldn't fall for her compulsions than anything else.

"Yes, I did insist," she finally said, responding to Dugan's earlier answer. "It was alarming to see you in my sister's morning room. I was caught quite off guard."

So she invited us all here?

I glanced at my companions. Both wore carefully blank faces. I tried to mimic them but knew mine still held a hint of my confused disbelief. Even if she wasn't colluding with her son, she was definitely scheming. Of course, she was a Faerie queen. That was kind of like saying she was breathing.

She hadn't asked any questions, so we didn't answer. We'd gained about as much out of this trip as we were likely to get. She'd made it clear we couldn't question her people—or even suggest it without giving offense—but we knew Ryese was alive and in the light court, making him our prime suspect. Anything else was gravy. We just needed to be dismissed and take our leave until we could put together enough evidence to force the queen to hand over her son for crimes against the winter and shadow courts.

The queen pouted prettily at our silence. "If you are looking for a new, stronger court, dark prince, I would gladly accept you here." She gave him her best benevolent smile again. "And there is a place for your betrothed, as well. I could always use a planeweaver."

"You are very well informed," Dugan said, but I blanched at the words.

Very few people knew about my supposed betrothal. How had she learned of it?

To cover my reaction I said, "Your sister would be most displeased if I left her court." Not that I had any particular loyalty to winter, but still.

The queen laughed, a soft tinkling sound that made Faerie itself laugh with her. "She is my *younger* sister. Younger siblings are used to their older siblings taking their things. It makes them good at sharing."

Yeah. No. *"Good at sharing"* wasn't something I'd ever use to describe the Winter Queen.

"So what say you, Cousin? Are you ready to come into the light? I could even offer you a council position," the queen said, and the fae closest to her throne, who I guessed were her current council, looked among themselves nervously.

"I must humbly refuse your generous offer," he said, bowing stiffly.

Her eyes narrowed. "I thought you were smarter than

that. Your king's plan to restore his court is doomed to fail. I will not make such a gracious offer twice."

Again, he bowed. "The rumors of your generous offers are whispered throughout shadow. Many of my courtiers have left to take a place in your light, and yet I see so few of them here." He looked around the assembled fae.

I looked around as well. I hadn't really paid attention to the gathered fae individually, but only noted them as a group. Now that I looked, though, I noticed that the gathered fae were the least diverse I'd seen. All were what humans would call beautiful. None were of the monstrous or less humanoid variety.

There were a few wings, but all were feathered like what one might find in a Renaissance painting of angels; a very few were bright like giant butterfly wings. None were leathery, tattered, or membranous, though I spotted some fae that I could tell by height and facial structure should have had such wings. Instead they wore ornate cloaks, keeping them out of sight. Several fae wore elaborate wraps or headdresses that hid horns or hair that contained leaves or feathers. Fauns wore pants and skirts with their hooves shoved in shoes. There were no trolls or giants towering over their neighbors, or small goblins or noseless brownies. No one had extra limbs, or bodies twisted in unexpected ways. While there were fae with skin tones of every shade of the rainbow, there were few who sported unusual textures to that skin. I did spot one fae who appeared to be made of living stone, but I could only tell by the pebbles surrounding her eyes—the rest of her face was obscured by a heavy veil. There were certainly none of the far more grotesque fae I'd encountered in the shadow court.

"Anyone or thing of beauty is welcomed in my halls," the queen said magnanimously.

Dugan kept searching the crowd, his frown growing. I could almost see him counting how many faces he expected to find that were missing. *Where are his former courtiers?*

"You're sure they were coming here?" I whispered the question as quietly as possible, and he gave me the smallest nod.

The queen didn't seem to notice. She turned to me.

"And you, planeweaver? Will you join my court?"

"I am under contract to winter until my year and a day as an independent has expired." It was an easy out that let me not answer the question.

"And I suppose you'll go to the shadow court after that?"

I didn't know what I'd do after, but I had nine more months to figure it out. I doubted I'd go to shadow, though. I liked my life in the mortal realm, and I needed to be tied to a seasonal court to remain outside Faerie. I didn't say as much only because Dugan was at my side.

"I'm undecided."

The queen pressed her full lips into a line. "I see. You'll understand if I'm reluctant to allow you that choice."

I frowned at her. It wasn't her decision.

"Oh, don't get me wrong, I have nothing in particular against shadow. But their loss is my gain, so you repairing the nightmare realm would impact me most severely. I would take it as a personal attack."

"I—wait—what?" Repair the nightmare realm?

The queen cocked her head to the side. Then she laughed. "You didn't know?" Then she turned to Dugan. "You didn't tell her?"

She continued laughing, as if it was all too funny.

moved my frown from her to Dugan, lifting an eyebrow in question. At my side, I could feel Falin staring at Dugan as well.

Dugan didn't turn, didn't meet either of our eyes. He just stood there, expressionless, watching the queen. It was as good as an admission.

"You, and possibly whatever offspring you create with this one"—she waved a hand to Dugan—"are intended to fix the damage to shadow and reweave the nightmare realm to the court. I'm *shocked* no one has told you of shadow's desires." She didn't sound shocked. She sounded smug.

I thought about what my father had said about the high king having the realm of dreams severed before the Magical Awakening. The shadow court expected *me* to fix it? "To restore the balance . . ." I said, thinking out loud more than to anyone.

The queen sat forward, slamming her palms down on the arms of her throne. "I don't care about the balance. Shadow cannot exist without light, but light needs no shadows." The glow around her blazed as she spoke, and I winced, looking away.

Right. I glanced at Falin. It was time for us to go. The look he gave me seemed to agree.

"My queen sends her regards, as well as her regrets over the body we had to deliver to your court," Falin said, bowing to the Light Queen. "We should return to her now."

"You may leave, knight of my sister." She made a dismissive gesture and we all turned. "I said the knight. Planeweaver, I still have business with you."

The glance I shot Falin was no doubt all deer-in-the-headlights, but I managed to get my face under control before I turned back toward the Queen of Light.

"Your Majesty?"

She glanced over the top of my head and nodded to someone behind me. Ryese stalked up to the throne, his golden cloak rustling as he swept past me.

My pulse quickened with each of his limping steps. This was not going to be good. I knew it wasn't.

"My son says you are responsible for his current condition," she said, gesturing from me to Ryese.

"I—What?" Was that the second or third time I'd responded to the queen exactly that way? At this rate she was going to think I was incapable of full sentences. But I didn't have any other response. In what way could it be construed that I was responsible for Ryese's condition? I'd revealed him, and physically pushed the Winter Queen out of the way of the iron dart, but nothing else.

Falin stepped in front of me. "I am the one who introduced the iron to his flesh. I acted in my capacity of knight in protecting my queen."

The queen dismissed his words, her gaze fixing on me. "Only due to the machinations of this one."

My head was still spinning from her abrupt change from inviting me into her court to accusing me of mangling her son.

"Machinations? He poisoned me and then tried to kill the queen," I said, and then snapped my teeth shut as a beautifully cruel smile spread over the queen's face. *Why do I feel like I just stumbled headfirst into a trap?*

"Outrageous," Ryese roared from under his hood. "She now intends to cripple me again with an unbearable defilement of my character." He pressed his gray hand against the front of his cloak, as if physically wounded by my words.

I glared at him. He hadn't accused me of lying—he

couldn't because everything I'd said was true. If mention of his past crimes tarnished his reputation, tough shit.

The queen clearly didn't agree.

"Yes, that is a rather reprehensible thing to say about a member of my court, let alone blood of my blood."

Crap. I cringed. This was *not* good.

I fell into a deep curtsy. "I meant no offense."

"But you gave great offense. I cannot let such a slight pass, unless, dear son, you can?" She turned to Ryese.

He stood very still, as if considering whether to forgive me. I glanced at Falin; he studied Ryese, his eyes tight with worry. Dugan had stepped to the side, watching.

Ryesé cleared his throat. "It is a challenge to my name I cannot let stand. I accept your challenge, planeweaver."

"I didn't—" I started, but the queen wasn't listening.

She spoke over me. "Then as the one challenged, you set the terms."

His golden hood bobbed in a nod. "The duel will be to the death."

Chapter 21

The gathered fae all began chattering at once. Some voices were obviously excited to see a deadly duel. Others spoke in low worried whispers.

I moved closer to Falin. "How do I get out of this? I did not challenge him to a duel."

He shook his head. "It does not matter. She's twisted it until you have no choice but to engage. If you try to run, it will be judged as a loss. As it is to the death, you'll be executed."

Great. Well, on the plus side of a duel to the death, Ryese was not exactly in his top form.

"I name a champion," Ryese called from his spot before the throne. "Teaghan will fight to remove this blemish from my name."

A woman with dark hair in two braids that ran down her back strolled forward. She wore silks in burnt orange and golden yellow, but they didn't suit her nor the variety of blades strapped to her body. Blood stained her hands, so the blades were not only for show but were deadly accessories she'd used before. She didn't have the glow common to the court, and shadows slipped around her as she walked, so I assumed she was a recent addition to the court of light. The stunned look on Dugan's face as he watched her approach the throne seemed to confirm that theory.

"It would be my honor to fight for you," she said, bowing to Ryese in a movement that spoke of both strength and grace.

The blood drained from my face. "He gets to name a champion?"

"And you do not because they twisted it to where he was the one challenged," Falin said, staring at Teaghan with obvious concern in his face. He might not want to say it, but we both knew I didn't stand a chance in this duel.

"You do get to name what you are fighting for. He cannot deny you a prize if you win." He glanced at my hands, and I took his meaning.

Standing up straighter, I raised my voice and announced, "I did not intend to initiate this challenge, but if I must fight, I'm fighting for the cure for basmoarte. Multiple doses."

I slipped my gloves off as I spoke, letting them drop to the ground. Then I held up my hands, revealing my purple-stained fingers. I couldn't see Ryese's reaction under the hood, so I watched the queen instead. For a moment she looked confused, and then her eyes grew wide in shock. Her eyes tore from my hands to look down at her own arms. A purplish bruise the size of a thumb had sprouted on her arm, corresponding to where I'd touched her magic to slap away her compulsion.

Her pretty features twisted in alarm, disgust twisting her lips as she lifted one delicate hand to cover the blemish of poisoned magic. Then the moment passed, the panic washing from her face, her features softening as if the fear had never been there. Her gaze cut toward the hooded figure at her side before returning to the scene in front of her, unconcerned.

Not worried about a deadly infection?

Yeah, there was a cure. And she knew her son had it. She probably knew about the rest too. Maybe not all of it. Maybe just enough to claim plausible deniability. But she was involved.

"Then the terms are set," the queen said, smiling benevolently at her people. "Duelers, prepare yourselves."

I swallowed, the movement feeling tight as if my fear had gotten lodged in my throat. I looked at Falin, my eyes surely giving away my panic. I didn't know anything about duels. I wasn't a fighter. "Do we fight at dawn? Are we going to stand back to back and take twenty paces?" No, that was for a Wild West showdown. Not a Faerie duel. "What are the rules?"

"Deep breath, Alex," Falin whispered. "You can use any weapon or magic that is yours to use. No one may help you or lend you anything. This fight is to the death, so . . ."

"I have to kill her to win," I finished for him, a cold sweat breaking out over my entire body.

"Mind your shadow," Dugan said, stepping up beside me.

I glanced up at him. "What?"

"She is recently of my court, so her magic will still be that of shadow."

Right.

"Any other tips?"

He seemed to hesitate, his eyes moving to where Teaghan still conversed with Ryese. Then he said, "She is a formidable fighter, skilled in both magic and blades. Many of her weapons are enchanted, so be wary." His frown deepened. "The blade found with Kordon's body? It was a courtship present from her many centuries ago."

I blinked in surprise, more pieces of this puzzle falling into place. We'd known Dugan's dagger had been planted at the scene, and I'd assumed it had been done to further implicate shadow. But if Teaghan was our shadow connection—and she almost certainly was—the choice of stealing her own courtship gift, one Dugan still kept in his private rooms, seemed very personal.

Also, I was about to duel to the death one of my ally's former lovers. This wouldn't end well. Even if I somehow survived.

"Clear the space," the queen yelled, and Dugan stepped back.

Falin hesitated a moment longer. Then he leaned down and kissed me. Magic fluttered from his lips into mine. I jerked back in surprise, both by the kiss and the magic, but he held me close, pressing the spell into me. "It's a truth spell," he whispered directly into my lips. "It won't last long, and you have to be touching her to make it work, but she will be compelled to answer any question you ask. If you can, try to get her to confess. But be careful, you will be compelled to answer any question asked as well." Then he kissed me again, and this time there was no transfer of spells, just concern, affection, and desire. "Survive this," he said as he pulled back.

Then hands locked on his upper arms, drawing him back, away from the makeshift dueling ring, and I was left alone in the opening void of space. Well, almost alone. My deadly-looking opponent studied me, her hands hovering over weapons strapped to her sides.

I licked my lips, still feeling the heat of the kiss, but also the small tingle of the spell. I was familiar with this particular magic—Falin had used it on me when we'd first met, and it definitely cut both ways. I'd have to be careful. I stared at the arsenal of blades strapped to Teaghan. *Oh yeah, get close enough to touch her and ask questions—no problem.* This sucked. But I'd try. If I won, she'd be dead and I doubted the queen would allow me to question her shade. If I was going to find answers, it would have to be during the fight.

"Prepare yourselves." The queen sounded far too cheery considering two fae were about to try to kill each other in front of her.

I wiped my damp palms on my pants and pulled my dagger from my boot holster. My sweat immediately slicked the hilt. This was ridiculous. Barbaric.

"Go!"

Teaghan sprang forward, rushing across the throne room toward me, her sword arm crossed over her chest, elbow out, ready to slash. The dagger I held jerked upward, guiding my hand. I let it. The bloodthirsty enchanted blade knew more about fighting than I did.

My dagger caught the longer sword by the blade before it could slash through me. The enchanted blade sank into the sword as if the other metal was made of nothing more substantial than warmed butter. I reached up with my other hand and grabbed Teaghan's bare wrist, letting the spell Falin had given me flow into her.

"Were you involved with the deaths of Kordon of shadow and Stiofan of winter?"

Teaghan's eyes flew wide. "Yes," she barked out, unable to help but answer. A gasp sounded around the throne room at her confession.

"What are you doing?" she hissed.

"Investigating." The answer sprang from my lips before I could stop it, the spell compelling me as well.

Her lips curled in rage and she ripped her arm from my grasp. "Well, you should probably focus on fighting instead." She jumped back as the top half of her sword clattered on the floor.

I half expected the queen to stop the duel at her courtier's confession. Wishful thinking. It might have been a surprise to her court, but it was no surprise to the queen.

Teaghan studied me from a distance. "Enchanted dagger, huh?" She glanced at the broken sword in her hand. She tossed the hilt to the side and pulled two daggers, one in each hand. "I have some of those as well."

She didn't mention the spell, or the confession. Her goal was to kill me. Nothing else.

She circled me. I turned, keeping her in sight. She lunged forward, and I jumped to the side. She missed by over a foot, but pain seared across my upper arm.

Blood soaked my sweater. My blood.

What the hell?

She lunged again. Missed. But a cut opened on the back of my dagger hand, and another on my forearm.

Fuck. What was the enchantment on her daggers? What was a safe distance?

In a distant part of my brain, I noticed the buzz of cheering from the audience. Not all, but I didn't have time to see who was rooting for her despite her confession, and who was just hoping to watch some bloodshed.

She lunged again, driving me back. From the corner

of my eye I saw the shadow of her dagger nick my shadow. A deep gash opened on my shoulder.

Mind your shadow. That was what Dugan had told me. Now I knew why. She didn't have to hit me. Just my shadow. I'd slowly bleed to death.

And I'd never get close enough to use the truth spell again.

I scrambled away from her, searching for an angle where my shadow wouldn't hang out in front of me. But the light in the court came from everywhere. Faint shadows stretched out from me in all directions.

How could I change my shadow? By changing the light. If I could summon a little ball of glowing glamour directly above me it would chase away the shadows. But that was outside my ability. I couldn't control glamour. Hell, I needed a charm just to stop from glowing all the time—

Oh.

I reached up and pulled the chameleon charm from my neck. Its concealing effect shattered and my natural Sleagh Maith glow broke free. I became my own light source.

My shadow vanished.

"Aw, you're no fun," the other fae said, giving me a mock pout as she straightened. Then she switched the grip of her dagger and hurled it at me.

I jumped aside. The blade sliced off a curl beside my ear. Teaghan held up her hand, and the damn dagger stopped. Turned. Then it shot back toward me again.

Fuck.

I hit the ground, panting. The blade whizzed over me.

She threw it again. I dodged the first pass, but the second one caught my shoulder. The cut was only a grazing blow, but I was now bleeding from at least four spots.

This was not going to work.

My own dagger jerked in my hand. I followed it. My blade caught the guard of her dagger just as her blade sliced through my biceps. This wound was deeper. But as my dagger impacted hers, slicing into the hilt, the flying dagger made a sizzling sound. Then it dropped like a lead weight, its enchantment fried.

Teaghan snarled again. I'd ruined two of her weapons, but while I was bleeding from numerous wounds, I hadn't even scratched her yet.

"I'm getting bored now," Teaghan said. "Let's finish this." She pulled a short sword from a sheath on her back and stalked toward me.

From the corner of my eye, I saw Ryese produce something from beneath his cloak. A yellow stone the size of his fist glittered in his hand.

No.

It was the stone from the revelry. The one that had almost certainly triggered my basmoarte to spread at an unprecedented rate. If he triggered it now, and I passed out, I was dead.

He was cheating, interfering with the duel—not that I expected anything else from him.

I opened my mouth to call him on it, but the queen's hand closed over his wrist. I thought, for a heartbeat, that she was stopping him from cheating. Then her wide eyes darted from the stone to her own purple wound.

She didn't want him to trigger my basmoarte and possibly be caught herself. He had the cure, but I bet it wouldn't reverse the damage. No way would she want her perfect flesh tainted.

I smiled to myself, but the momentary distraction cost me. Teaghan closed in fast, and I had to throw myself back to avoid her blade. I rolled as I hit the ground.

I had no offensive magics. No real defensive ones either. So I did the only thing I could. I opened my shields and released my magic. It had only been a dozen hours since the Mender's lessons, and my magic followed the new routes he'd drilled into me when he'd insisted I merge the planes over and over again. The locket burst open as I rolled out the planes locked inside. I hoped to stun Teaghan with the touch of death, maybe buy me a moment.

Faerie shivered as the land of the dead unfurled in a circle around me. Faerie didn't like the planes I'd forced into it, but it didn't fight me. I gasped. I could feel the magic in the air. Feel the glamour. Feel the layers of reality like I never had before.

"Nice light show," Teaghan said as she stepped into the radius of my merged planes. I could feel the magic in her weapons. Feel her magic. Feel . . . her.

"You've died before," I said, my voice sounding hollow, distant in the sudden wind whipping around me. I could feel the death clinging to her. She'd been revived, and while she wasn't exactly a corpse, the land of the dead was drawn to her, as if it knew it had been denied its prize. My grave magic lifted unbidden.

She cocked her head to the side, sending her black braids trembling around her like a pair of snakes. "That was a long time ago. I learned from my mistake. You won't have that luxury."

She lifted her arm, sword preparing to strike.

I didn't try to block this time. Didn't dodge or run. I just lifted my arm, hand extended, and I sent my grave magic spiraling into her. A small push, and the death-weakened tethers binding her soul to her body snapped. Her soul popped free.

Her sword clattered to the ground. Her body followed a moment later. Her soul stood above it, looking confused.

I grabbed her ghostly wrist. I wasn't sure the spell Falin had given me still held—I could already feel it failing—or if it would affect a ghost, but I was willing to try.

"Who conspired with you on the murders?"

The ghost had looked confused when her body hit the ground, but since I could touch her, so could the spell. She couldn't help but answer. Her translucent eyes snapped into focus, anger filling them as the spell dragged her words from her.

"Lunabella and I killed the goblin. He was a prick who never helped when I desired to learn shadow weaving. Jurin helped when we killed the winter noble."

More gasps around the room at her confession. The queen pushed herself to standing. "The duel is complete," she yelled.

As if that could distract me from this line of questioning. The spell compelled Teaghan to answer, but even dead, her forced answers were careful. I'd have to word my question a different way.

"Who ordered you to commit these murders?"

Her mouth opened. Closed. Opened again. No words emerged. *Damn it. She's oath-bound.* She couldn't name her master, likely why she was still alive. Well, had been alive, while Jurin and Lunabella had been killed.

Teaghan's gaze cut toward the throne and one—or both—of the figures at it. Then she lunged at me, determined to tear me apart with her own ghostly hands.

I pulled my magic back, rolling in realities with it. Like

a tide pulling a sand castle from the shore, Teaghan's ghost followed the retreating reality. She shrank down, compressing, and then vanished into my locket. The door of the locket swung closed, the clasp sealing.

Silence fell over the throne room. I leaned down and sheathed my dagger in my boot. A slow clap started, and I looked at where Dugan stood, clapping. I searched his features for anger that I'd killed his former lover, sadness over her death. Neither appeared to be present. Falin stood beside him, relief clear on his face as he smiled at me. I returned the smile. Then I turned back to the throne.

I could have gone around Teaghan's body, but I chose to step over it for the statement it made. I kept my face neutral as I did so, my gaze locked on the queen and Ryese. The gold cloak trembled in such a way that I assumed Ryese was near to exploding in rage. Or perhaps he feared I'd rip his soul out next.

For her part, the queen said nothing. She stared at me, her normal golden glow tinged with red.

I didn't smile as I approached. Or offer any banter. I marched up to Ryese and held out my hand, palm up.

"The cure for basmoarte," I said. "Now."

"It's not—" he started, spluttering.

"Give it to her, curse of my loins," the queen commanded.

Ryese grumbled and the cloak rustled as he dug in his pockets. Finally a gray hand emerged. He hesitated, his hand stalling only half raised to mine. I could guess why. Most of the damage I'd taken had been to my arms. My dark sweater hid most of the blood staining the fabric, but it offered nothing but a contrast where the fabric had been cut and my glowing skin made my own blood glitter like liquid rubies. Dark veins of fouled magic trailed up my arms, and my dark purple hands appeared damp with blood. He gave a disgusted sneer and then dropped five small vials onto my palm without ever touching my skin. Which was a shame. I couldn't feel any trace of the spell anymore, but I would have liked to use the truth spell on the little weasel.

Of course, doing so likely would have gotten me into another duel. One was enough for the day.

"How is the cure administered?" I asked, looking over the small vials.

"It's a potion. You drink it." His curt words made it sound like he questioned my intelligence, but I wasn't leaving until I knew exactly how the cure worked.

"How many and how often for a full cure?"

He hissed, and the queen turned her glare on him. He'd promised me a cure. He would deliver it. He was magically bound to do so.

"One vial. It has to be administered before the infection spreads too far. It can't heal the fouled magic, but it will close the wounds that cause it."

I nodded. That was exactly what I needed to know.

"You have your cure, now get out of my realm, plane-weaver," the queen commanded.

With pleasure.

Chapter 22

❖══○ ⟩═══❖

Neither Falin, Dugan, nor I spoke until we had safely left the light court behind.

Once we emerged in the clearing of doors and the odd golden light was far behind us, Falin stopped, then laughed. It was a deep, full-belly laugh, all bottled stress mixed with pure joy. When I turned to look at him, he pulled me to him, wrapping his arms tight around me.

"You were amazing," he whispered, pressing his mouth against my hair so that his words were only for me. "I was so scared I'd lose you and could do nothing to stop it."

He released me a moment later, the laughter now just a memory at the sides of his lips. "Alex, I do think you established yourself as a formidable dueling partner, and someone not to be entered into a challenge with lightly."

I shrugged off the praise. I didn't deserve it. If Teaghan hadn't been healed from death in the past, I'd be dead now.

"I got lucky. I—" I started, but Dugan held up a hand.

"Do not downplay your win nor share the secrets of how you did it," he said. "You are far safer if all Faerie hears of it and thinks you can repeat such a feat at will."

Falin nodded his agreement.

Right.

I bit my bottom lip. "Your courtier . . ." I wasn't going to apologize for being the one to survive the duel, but I needed to know if he was going to hold a grudge for her death.

Dugan seemed to realize where my thoughts had traveled. He gave me a small smile. It was sad, but kind and probably one of the most genuine expressions I'd seen on him.

"Betrayed me and my court. Affections between Teaghan and I soured long ago, but even if they had not, she murdered my friend, conspired against my betrothed, and attempted to implicate me and my court in crimes which could lead to war. You secured both confession and vengeance. My court is appeased."

I nodded, though I noticed he mentioned only his court, and not himself. Time to change the subject. I fished one of the vials out of my pocket.

"The cure for your king," I said, holding it up.

Dugan bowed his head. "My court is in your debt."

He reached for it, but I didn't hand it over. Not yet.

"The court is already in my debt for purging the initial round of infection. The cure I will trade for something else."

Dugan's face turned guarded, but he said nothing while he waited for me to lay out the bargain.

"Don't look so glum. What I want is simple. In exchange for the cure, I want out of our betrothal."

His shoulders fell. "That is not as simple as you may

think. The agreement was between your father and my king."

I shrugged. "Then agree to refuse with me. That's good enough for one small cure to save a king."

He looked away. "You don't know what you're asking."

Seriously? Was this such a hard choice to make? I sighed.

"We've been through a lot the last few days. You're not a bad guy, but at this point, I wouldn't even classify you as a friend yet. A friendly ally is probably a more accurate description of our relationship. There's no affection between us, so you aren't following through with the betrothal because of me the person—just because of me the planeweaver. Trying to force me into a contract isn't going to win the shadow court any goodwill. And breaking the betrothal doesn't mean I won't look into reconnecting the shadow court and the realm of dreams." Though I wasn't about to make promises on doing it— especially since severing it had killed two planeweavers. But if I figured out how to do it safely, I wasn't opposed to fixing the balance of Faerie. Particularly if it curtailed the Queen of Light.

Dugan bowed again. "I will refuse the betrothal."

"Then the cure is yours, with my blessing."

Dugan took the vial and held it between two fingers, examining it. He chuckled low, the sound soft and quiet. "Something so small that will cost me a Faerie throne two times."

Falin and I both gave him questioning looks and he shook his head. "Now, because the throne would pass to me if the king died. And later, because the condition on the king stepping down was the successful birth of our first child." He nodded to me.

Anger made my cheeks flush hot. He'd agreed to that deal? A child planned simply for political gain? My father and his damn planeweaver breeding program! When I saw him next I was going to . . . I didn't even know what. Something, though.

Dugan slid the small vial into a pouch on his belt. "I do believe I chose the high road in both cases. I hope time proves they were the wiser choices." He smiled at me. It was a kind smile, real. "You may no longer be my betrothed, but I think that, one day, I should like to be elevated from friendly ally to friend. You seem like a good friend to have."

"Friends are not for personal gain, and friendship is not one-sided."

He bowed his head to me, ever so slightly. "A hard distinction for a very old Faerie prince. Friendship is a weakness strong rulers often regret. But for you, I think it might be worth the effort and risk. Fare ye well, Knight and planeweaver."

He gave me one last bow, and then he turned and walked into one of the shadowed paths, disappearing. I watched him go, then fished a second vial out of my pocket.

"I suppose I should purge this first," I said, pushing up the sleeves of my sweater to study my arms. The fouled magic had crept up over my elbows.

Falin nodded. "You might reinfect yourself otherwise."

He helped me find a small sapling outside the main clearing that was not on any path. I stripped the poisoned magic quickly, apologizing to the dying plant once I was done.

"Well, bottoms up," I said, lifting the small vial in mock salute before tipping the contents into my mouth. The liquid inside was bitter, and my tongue curled as I gagged down the single swallow of liquid.

"Any change?" Falin asked, reaching out and taking one of my hands in both of his.

I waited. My mouth pooled with saliva, as if trying to wash away any remaining hint of the potion. Otherwise, there was maybe a small tingling feeling? I examined my fingers. They looked normal, but I'd just purged the fouled magic, so they would. After a few moments passed, I shrugged.

"I guess we'll have to wait and see." I pulled out two more vials and handed them to Falin, but I pocketed the final one in case I needed it later. "One for the quarantined healer," I said before nodding to the second vial. "Are there any alchemists in the winter court who can synthesize this serum, in case we need more?"

"Maybe. You were correct when you said Ryese was an expert alchemist. The queen has a few others in her court, but he was the best."

Great.

"What are we going to do about him?" I asked as we walked across the clearing toward the door to winter.

"Not much we can do while he is hiding in the light court."

"But he was behind the murders."

Falin shrugged. "Didn't you notice? His hands were clean."

Weren't they always? He'd also managed to keep the blood off his own hands when he'd been draining fae to create a drug that had killed several mortals and poisoned the Winter Queen. Teaghan, Lunabella, and Jurin had committed the actual murders, but he was behind them. I was certain. Teaghan's glance at him was confirmation. Though it wouldn't be considered damning proof to any ruler—especially if the Queen of Light was involved.

Under Ryese's direction, Teaghan had no doubt killed her two co-conspirators after the revelry. No proof of that one, but it fit. I had a sinking suspicion most of Dugan's missing courtiers arrived in the light court only to find themselves as experiments when Ryese was searching for a way to harness, weaponize, and cure basmoarte. Unfortunately that would be impossible to prove without access to the light court. And that wasn't going to happen.

"The queen was complicit at best. She knew about the basmoarte, the cure, and that Ryese had a way to trigger it. She is a threat," I said, and Falin jerked his hand back from where he was about to open the door to winter.

"I know it, and you know it, but you must not say such things. Not here in Faerie, or back in the mortal realm. But particularly not once we are back in court. You have seen how the queen views her sister."

I nodded. Ryese and the Queen of Light were out of our reach. We'd found the direct killers in the case, and stopped this particular attempt to overturn the balance of Faerie. For now, that would have to be enough.

Chapter 23

A platoon of guards met us inside the door to the winter court.

"The queen wants to speak with you, immediately," the foremost guard said.

Falin frowned at him, his eyes narrowing. "I'll escort Alex to the door to Nekros, and then I will meet with the queen."

That hadn't been the plan, and Falin suddenly trying to hurry me out of the court made me even more nervous than the way several ice-gauntleted hands wrapped around their sword hilts. Something was wrong. Of course, our meeting with the Queen of Light hadn't exactly gone well. The Winter Queen was going to be pissed, and she hadn't been what one would call stable in a while. Falin was trying to get me out of here and take the brunt of her anger himself.

The guard in front shifted on his heel, the slight movement making him draw back from Falin a few centimeters, but he shook his head. "She has ordered us to bring you and the planeweaver. Now."

Well, damn. Looked like I was going to see the queen. An angry queen, no doubt. Another one.

The guards took up position around us. Were they afraid I'd turn and run back through the doors and to a different court? Actually, that didn't sound like a horrible idea. Shadow owed me several favors, and the planebender could deposit me back into my own bedroom. Not that I had that option unless I wanted to fight my way through the winter guards.

I glanced at Falin. His face was blank, maybe even haughty. I recognized the expression; it was his emotional armor and it hid his thoughts perfectly. He didn't meet my gaze at all, which meant he probably wasn't about to turn on his own men and make a break for it. I might have just won my first duel, but I had no illusions that I could take on a dozen winter guards. I had no choice but to see the queen.

Tension churned in the hall as we passed down the endless icy corridor. The guards said nothing, but their hands remained near their weapons. They didn't like being at odds with their knight. For my part, I was tired, hungry, and just plan sick of Faerie. I hadn't gotten any measurable amount of rest in days, I'd used way too much magic, I hadn't tended the dagger wounds I'd gotten in the duel, and I really just wanted to go home. I was *done*.

The guards deposited us at a large door without a word, and then fanned out, blocking any path except through the archway. Falin glanced at me, and for a moment the ice in his eyes thawed enough for me to see his concern. For me. Not himself. I reached out and squeezed his hand.

He looked like he wanted to say something, but there were too many eyes around us, watching. He didn't need to say anything. While my mouth sometimes got ahead of me, I was determined to keep it in check and get this over with as fast as possible. I wouldn't mention my suspicions of the queen's beloved sister, and we could honestly report that those directly involved in the murders were dead. We stepped through the large archway.

I recognized the space as soon as we stepped into the Winter Queen's throne room. Unlike when we'd visited the court of light, this throne room was empty aside from the queen sitting alone on her huge throne. Her head snapped up as soon as we entered, her cold glare bearing down on us like an iceberg.

"What have you done?" she asked, pushing out of her chair.

"My queen?" Falin asked, falling to his customary kneeling bow.

I curtsied this time. With the way she was glaring at me, I didn't want to risk irritating her more with what she considered unladylike behavior.

"I sent you to deliver a body to foster goodwill. Instead you accused my sister's people of crimes, challenged my nephew to a duel that cost my sister one of her courtiers, and then made demands on her."

I cringed. It sounded a lot worse when said that way. Of course, the truth was a lot more complicated, but somehow I didn't think it would help to interject that the Queen of Light was an egomaniac who was more than happy to step over her younger sister to gain more power.

"We found who murdered your noble," Falin said, still kneeling. "All three who committed the crime are dead."

All who *committed* it. Not all who were *involved*. A very fine line of truth to walk.

"At what cost, Knight?" Her words were glacial, her gaze filled with a mad storm waiting to break free. "She is my one ally in all of Faerie. And *you*"—she lifted a hand tipped with sharpened nails and pointed it at me— "have soured her opinion of me."

She wasn't her ally. The Queen of Light was no friend to winter, sister or not, but I wasn't foolish enough to say as much.

"Now I have to find a way to make amends. To soothe this wound you've caused," she hissed. "I offered her you, and she said you were more trouble than you're worth."

I said nothing, simply held my curtsy and my tongue. I could feel Falin's tension building beside me despite the fact that he also hadn't moved a muscle.

"My sister's was the only court in Faerie that did not send challengers to my throne during my . . . illness. Did you know that? She proved her loyalty and her love. And now I've repaid her poorly."

The queen was deluding herself. The only reason the Queen of Light hadn't sent any challengers for the winter throne had been because she already had her ringer inside the court, orchestrating the whole fiasco and ready to step into the throne. Her son.

"Ryese—" I started, but the queen took a step toward me, off the dais and her throne. Her icy blade materialized in her hand. She pointed it at me, and I swallowed any further words despite the fact that she was still several feet away.

"Don't you say his name. Your lips are not worthy of uttering his name." The storm in her eyes had raged into a full-blown blizzard. There was madness in those icy depths, the sanity she usually tried to maintain washed away by her fury. "On top of everything else, I am told you are betrothed to the Prince of Shadows." The queen gritted her teeth in a scowl. "I should have known. Look at you, covered in blood and wearing all black. Has this whole investigation been a sham? Are you a spy for shadow?"

"No, Your Majesty. And I am no longer be—"

She didn't let me finish.

"Here is what you didn't consider, dear *Lexi*." She ground out the nickname she'd given me as if it were a curse. "I'd rather see you dead than in the hands of an enemy court. And regardless of what you claim, or what you've convinced my knight, shadow is clearly my enemy. And so are you. Knight, execute the planeweaver."

Falin's head snapped up. "My queen—"

"I said kill her."

I jumped free of my curtsy, stumbling away from Falin. He rose slowly, moving as if he was fighting against every inch he gained. His eyes were wide with horror, but his daggers appeared in his hands.

I didn't wait to see if he could stall—even if he could, it wouldn't last long. He was the Winter Knight. The queen's will was his command. I had to get out of Faerie. And if the queen wanted me dead, out of any territory held by winter.

I ran toward the doorway. I was only a few feet away from the threshold when the queen made a grand sweep of her arm and two ice golems woke from their recessed nooks by the door. They looked like they should have been lumbering and dull. They weren't.

The golems raced forward, intercepting me before I could switch direction. They grabbed me, each catching an arm. I struggled, twisting and pulling, but they were

solid blocks of moving ice. The golems could have killed
me then and there as I sagged between them, but instead
they dragged me forward, toward Falin, who was making no effort to kill me with any efficiency. Maybe the
blood would have been on the queen's hands if her golems killed me. Or maybe the sadistic bitch just wanted
Falin to have to do it.

The golems dragged me in front of Falin, and then it
didn't matter that he wasn't hurrying to chase me because we were both right there. They shoved me at him,
and one of his daggers vanished as he grabbed my wrist.

I screamed. Fury washed through me, chased hard by
fear. I writhed. Twisted. *He'll let me go . . .* I could slip
past the golems before the queen realized . . .

Falin couldn't disobey the queen.

His grip was as viselike as the golems' had been. He
jerked my wrist upward, so that I had to stand on my tip-
toes. Then he grabbed and pinned my other wrist, both
gripped in one strong hand. His lips parted like he was
going to tell me something, but the queen spoke first.

"I want her heart, Knight. No one will bring her back
to use against me."

Falin growled in anger, frustration, anguish. It was all
of it wrapped into one sound. I shook my head. I wasn't
going to beg—it wouldn't help—but damn it, there had
to be a way out of this.

Falin lifted the dagger, and it hung in the air, hesitating before the deadly descent.

"Your affection makes you soft," the queen called
from behind him. "Think of this as excising weakness."

Bitch.

Falin's eyes met mine, and I saw the sorrow there. He
had to do what she commanded. There was no other

choice. But there was something else in his eyes. Something I didn't expect.

Resignation.

That didn't ring true. And I realized a second before he changed his grip what he planned to do.

The only way he didn't have to obey her, was if he was dead.

His dagger turned inward, heading toward his own heart.

"No!" That wasn't any more acceptable than him killing me.

I dropped my shields. All of them.

The planes slid into focus around me. My locket burst open, and realities not meant to touch Faerie flowed outward. Falin was touching me where he still held my hands aloft. My magic washed over him like a wave, tying all the planes together around him as well.

The shock of it was enough to make him hesitate. His grip loosened, just slightly, and I jerked one arm free.

I turned my focus to the dagger, planning to push it into the land of the dead. But my eyes caught something else.

With my shields wide open and Falin enveloped in my magic, I could see the bonds tying him to the queen. They pulsed like thick icy cords wrapped tight around his throat.

What I could see, I could break.

"Kill her now, Knight," the queen yelled.

Horror spread over Falin's face. The *now* limited his options.

I didn't try to pull away this time. I flung myself forward, pressing myself into him, and grabbed at the bond at his throat. My fingers sank into the magical bond and

I pulled with every ounce of will, magic, and strength I possessed.

Fire exploded in my back as Falin's blade pierced my flesh.

I yanked the magical bond. It peeled free, dissolving in my fingers as soon as it lost contact with his skin.

The dagger stopped, not yet piercing anything vital. Then the dagger clattered to the ground. Falin stared at me, his eyes wide. Unbelieving.

I was alive. He was alive.

"What? Knight, I said kill her." The queen stepped forward, her icy gaze narrowed.

Falin wrapped his arms around me, pulling me close and locking his mouth on mine. His lips tasted of amazement and joy. With my shields open, I could almost see the emotions in the air around him. But as he clutched me tight, pain blossomed across my back. My shirt was hot and wet with blood. I could feel it soaking into my pants. I must have winced because Falin pulled back, concern written in his face.

"You need a healer."

I did, but . . . "I think we have bigger things to worry about."

"Obey me, Knight," the queen screeched.

Falin twisted around to face her, deftly moving me behind him as he did.

"Never again." His words were cold. Unmovable.

Her mouth opened and closed twice, her shock making her look like a broken doll.

"Then you will both die," she yelled. She threw out her hands.

I saw the glamour forming. I'd never seen glamour taking shape before. But now, with my blood spilling onto the floor in this patch of reality I'd made mine, I saw it. A dozen ice spears that would spring up from the ground to impale us both.

And I denied them.

This was my reality. I didn't let her glamour change it.

Her eyes widened in shock. Falin scooped up his dagger in one smooth movement as the queen formed an ice spear in her hands. She hurled it at us. Two yards in front of us, it hit the edge of my magic and dissolved into nothing, unable to cross into the reality that was mine.

Falin threw his dagger. It flashed through the air, hurtling straight at the queen.

She formed an ice shield, but after the last two failed glamours, she must have doubted herself because she also threw herself to the side. The shield was too far away for me to do anything about it. Falin's dagger embedded itself deep in the glamoured ice. The queen hit the ground, unharmed, but her panic had made her sloppy. It cost her time.

Time Falin used.

He dashed across the room, sword in one hand, his second dagger in the other. The queen scrambled back to her feet a breath before Falin reached her, getting her sword up at the last moment. She blocked his swing. Blocked a second. Attacked. He blocked with his sword and swung out to score a glancing blow with his dagger.

She hissed in pain, jumping back as red blood spilled down her silver gown. Then she charged forward.

They both moved in a blur of attacks and blocks. A gash opened on Falin's cheek. Blood trickled from two wounds on the queen's arm.

"You are the Winter Knight," she said amid attacks. "Your oaths belong to me."

"You own nothing of me, and never will again," he said between gritted teeth as he dodged her attack.

"Is that a challenge?"

"Yes," he said, swinging hard.

She dodged and laughed, though it was a thin, slightly panicked sound. "You will always belong to me. I hold your oaths, Knight."

Blue wisps of magic stirred between them, as if the bond woke at her words, looking to attach itself.

No.

I rushed forward, but what could I do? If I tried to get close enough to grab the forming bond, I'd distract him and she'd cut him down. If I did nothing, she'd ensnare him and he'd be unable to move against her.

Falin faltered.

I'm too late.

The queen struck outward, her sword arcing for a death blow. "You will always be mi—"

She froze. In slow motion, she looked down. A dagger protruded from her middle.

Her sword clattered to the ice floor. Falin had taken part of her strike to his shoulder, and the wound bled freely, but it had allowed him to get under her defense.

She stumbled back. "No," she whispered. "You are mine. Winter is mine."

"You have been doomed to lose winter for a long time," Falin said.

She fell to her knees, her head shaking in disbelief. Blood soaked the front of her dress, trailing down to the icy floor.

"You loved me once. You were such an awestruck youth who looked at me with such adoration. Can you find that loving youth inside you still?" Her voice was barely a whisper, all the rage and fury suddenly gone. She sounded scared, delicate, and she gazed up at him, her beautiful features pleading.

But I could feel the glamour she was weaving. Something dark. Deadly.

She was within my merged realities, but I didn't feel as connected as I had when I'd denied her glamour earlier. A moment of doubt that I could do it again flashed through me, and as glamour was belief magic, my own doubt was enough to make me powerless against it. I opened my mouth to yell a warning to Falin, but he was already moving.

He swung outward. His sword slid through her neck so smoothly that her head didn't move. She blinked, her blue eyes wide in shock. The glamour dissolved.

"You are the one who made that youth ruthless," he said.

Then her body fell.

Her head rolled, lips moving in words that would never be heard. Through my contact with the planes, I felt the moment the land of the dead recognized her death.

And Faerie shook.

The floor jumped, the walls rumbled. Falin and I both fell to our knees.

Faerie shook again. A great rumbling quake. I fell to all fours.

The ground continued to shake. Discordant notes originating nowhere and everywhere pierced the air.

"What's happening?"

Falin drove his sword into the ground to help lever himself up despite the disconcerting way the floor lurched. "The queen is dead."

"Well, obviously, but I wasn't expecting the winter court to implode!"

The ground continued to shake. My shields were still wide open, and now that the queen was dead, the grave essence in her body called to me. Without shields, I couldn't stop my grave magic from rising. It had already started slipping out of me. Too late to call it back. The best I could do was direct it. *Well, the Mender wanted souls.* Here was another one for him.

I sent my grave magic spiraling into the headless corpse. The queen's soul popped free of her body in a brilliant silver flash. I didn't give the ghost time to adjust. Imagining my magic rolling back in like the tide returning to the ocean, I pulled back the planes. The realities separated effortlessly, Faerie happily releasing the points where I'd forced it to brush against other planes. The land of the dead and the collectors' reality curled, compressing. The queen's ghost was swept up with it before she even realized she was out of her corpse. As my magic withdrew, it restored all the planes to where they should be, leaving no holes or patches.

The locket closed.

I threw my shields up, erecting them quickly. Then I huddled low, waiting out Faerie's wrath.

Eventually the court stopped shaking. The air turned sweet. The melody of Faerie began again, similar but different from before.

Then Falin screamed.

He released the sword and doubled over, holding his head, the heels of his hands pressed to his eyes. I scrambled to my feet as the door to the room burst open. Maeve and Lyell ran inside. They screamed something when they saw the queen's body, but I wasn't listening. I ran to Falin.

He'd stopped screaming, but he was still clutching his head. His shoulder was in bad shape, the blood running thickly down his arm and torso. He had other less severe wounds here and there, but whatever was wrong with his face, I couldn't see for his hands.

I knelt in front of him. More fae spilled into the room. Droves of them, likely coming to find out what had shaken Faerie. I didn't know what would happen. We'd killed the queen. That was probably not good. If we needed to fight our way out of here . . . Well, that wouldn't be easy. Especially if Falin was badly injured. Would Faerie blind him for his crimes? What was wrong with his eyes?

I reached out, putting a hand on his good shoulder and the other on one of his wrists. I made small soothing sounds, trying to get him to let me see what was wrong. Falin dropped his hands. His eyes blazed a brilliant blue, brighter than I'd ever seen them before. And ringing his forehead, made of intricately woven ice, sat a crown.

Lyell's voice cut through the roar of whispers in the room. "All hail the Winter King."

Chapter 24

I sat in my favorite of the castle's gardens, PC asleep in my lap and a book open in my hands, but I wasn't reading it. It had been three weeks since I'd fled from Faerie, the ground still trembling, and Falin's urgings that it wasn't safe for me in my ears. All the doors to the winter court had closed after I stumbled into the Bloom. No fae could cross in or out of the independent winter territories either. Faerie had completely sealed off winter while the court adjusted to its new king.

Things had been pretty quiet since. No visits from Shadow Princes in the middle of the night. No more lessons from the Mender—though I had been practicing what he'd taught me. I wouldn't want to be accused of reneging on our bargain. There had also been no reemergence of my basmoarte, so Ryese's cure had worked.

These were good things. I wasn't dying anymore. The Winter Queen was no longer trying to ensnare me. And while I hadn't located any other planeweavers, I had found an unlikely mentor in the Mender, so I could now access at least some of my planeweaving abilities without maiming myself.

But I was anxious. I checked on the door in the Bloom every day. I'd tried to get the door to the folded space holding my castle to take me to the winter court, but it refused. I'd even tried summoning Dugan by whispering into shadows, hoping I could bargain with him and his planebender for a door into winter. No luck.

Who would have guessed that after spending all this time avoiding Faerie, I'd put so much effort into trying to get back inside?

I sighed and set the book down on the grass beside me—I wasn't even sure of the name of the main character and I'd been on the same page for at least twenty minutes.

"Not a recommended read?" a voice asked behind me.

I jumped to my feet, startling poor PC as he dropped from my lap, and then I whirled around. Falin stood by the garden wall, his thumbs hooked into the pockets of his jeans and his white button-up shirt loose at the collar. His long hair was down, blowing lightly in the wind, but that didn't hide the thin ice circlet on his brow.

"Nice headband," I said, forcing myself to walk—not run—toward him.

He gave me a lopsided smile. "Yeah, I can make it bigger." He lifted his hand and the circlet grew to an elaborate crown with shimmering ice jewels. "Or smaller." It shrank back down to the thin circlet again. "But I can't take the damn thing off."

"Guess Faerie wants everyone to know a king when they see one." I shrugged. Why was this weird and awkward? He was free of the Winter Queen; shouldn't that have made things easier?

Yeah, except now he's king.

"Faerie has a lot of opinions on what everyone should know," he said. "You've been added to the official history of the winter court. Not my doing, by the way. But you now appear carved in ice for all to see on the pillar leading to the court. Actually, you're in several sections, most notably at my side, blazing with power, as I behead the former queen. I've heard rumor that you are in the shadow court's mural as well, depicted in moving shadows and pulling sickness from Nandin. I haven't seen it myself. The fae are calling you a kingmaker."

I winced. That didn't seem like a particularly good thing. I would rather be less noticed by Faerie, not more. Faerie clearly had a different agenda, and I was definitely on more royals' radar than ever before.

Not that every Faerie ruler was my enemy.

"So . . . Winter King, huh? That's quite the promotion. I guess you came to clean out your old rooms here?"

"You kicking me out?"

"What? No. I—" I was spluttering.

Falin leaned down and kissed me. It started gentle, questioning. But when I stepped toward him, he wrapped me in his arms and pulled me close, deepening the kiss. He tasted of snowflakes and new beginnings, and I met the passion in his lips with my own. By the time we broke away we were both breathing a little too heavily and grinning like children.

"You are amazing," he said, staring into my eyes, and I got that feeling again, like that he saw me. Really saw me.

"Don't you forget it."

He laughed, the sound thick and joyful, and I wished that moment could last forever.

Then he ruined it.

"I'll need to appoint a new head of the FIB."

I blinked, confused by the sudden topic switch. "You said Nori was your second in command. She seems the obvious choice?" The woman was a thorn in my side and I hated the idea of her being the one in charge of the policing force on the mortal side of the door, but it was what it was.

Falin's nod was slow, his blue eyes fixed on me. "She would be my second choice. Alex, I'd like you to step in as agent in charge."

"Me?" The single word was somewhere between a shocked laugh and a squeaked exhale. "I don't think so. One, I have no training. Two, I don't do blood. And three, I have Tongues for the Dead to run."

Falin looked around for a moment, then sat down in the grass. He straightened his legs, crossing them at the ankle. When I didn't follow, he glanced up at me and patted the ground beside him.

I had a Faerie king lounging on the ground in my garden. It was absurd, but then I looked at him and I didn't see a king. I just saw Falin. The friend who had been there for me in whatever way he could, even when it cost him dearly. I sat down next to him.

"It's true," he said. "You need some training on how to deal with the bureaucratic side of law enforcement, but your investigative instincts have been well proven since we met. And while you might not like blood, you deal with it. I've seen you wade through crime scenes when needed, destroy decaying zombies with your bare hands, and let's not forget the little jaunt through the woods carrying a pair of heads. When push comes to shove, you do what has to be done." The smile he gave me was both encouraging and admiring, and I felt a flush of warmth rise to my cheeks. "As for Tongues for the Dead, you wouldn't have to abandon it completely. You might not be able to work at it full time, but you do have Rianna, and it isn't keeping you that busy currently."

He had me there.

I tried to consider the offer, but head of the FIB? I shook my head. "Would that make me your knight?"

The softness bled out of Falin's face, leaving him looking severe and cold. "No. The winter court will not have another knight. Not as long as I am king." He glanced at his gloved hands and a jagged smile crooked the edge of his lips, but there was no humor in it. "Besides, I could never hold the throne if I gave up the power in the blood I carry. I'm the youngest Faerie ruler in history."

"That doesn't sound like a safe position."

He turned that wry smile on me. "No. I suppose, in the end, if Ryese's goal was to destabilize the winter court, he succeeded completely."

Though I doubted he'd intended to put Falin on the throne. Ryese had previously been in the position to gain the winter throne, but he no longer was. It was possible he'd been targeting the winter court purely out of spite, but I doubted it. His recent machinations would have deeper ramifications. Ryese and the Queen of Light were unlikely to be kind to Faerie's newest king.

My worry must have shown on my face because Falin reached out and cupped my cheek, his smile softening. "It's going to be interesting for a while. Which is why I'd like to have you watching my back as head of the FIB. We would not run the organization as it was run under the queen's rule. We could modernize it and make sure the independents receive fairer treatment."

That did sound good, but I wasn't sure I was the one who should be tasked with doing it. "I'll consider it," I said, not committing to anything. "I'm guessing such ideas aren't making you very popular?"

He laughed. "When have I ever worried about being popular? But in truth, fae who wouldn't have spit on me had I been on fire a month ago are now all fawning and flattery. Each vying for a higher position in the new court. It is all horribly fake and exhausting. I haven't disbanded the old council yet, but I need to at least fill the empty seats, so every ambitious fae is falling all over themselves to try to claim one. Add to that the fact that Maeve and Lyell have been very vocal with the opinion that I need to take a consort or queen to shore up my power base, and the courtiers are intolerable."

The bottom dropped out of my stomach and I looked away, trying to keep my face neutral as I asked, "And did you pick one? A consort?"

"I have an idea of one I might consider, but she has commitment issues. I'm thinking she would be more comfortable starting with dinner and a movie and seeing where things go." He paused. "So, any restaurant preferences?"